Summer of the Dead

Also by Julia Keller and available from Headline

A Killing in the Hills
Bitter River

Digital Short Stories
The Devil's Stepdaughter

Julia Keller

Summer of the Dead

headline

First published in Great Britain in 2014 by
HEADLINE PUBLISHING GROUP

1

Cataloguing in Publication Data is available from the British Library

Hardback ISBN 978 1 4722 1561 1
Trade paperback ISBN 978 1 4722 1562 8

Typeset in Sabon LT Std by Palimpsest Book Production Limited,
Falkirk, Stirlingshire

Printed and bound in Great Britain by
Clays Ltd, St Ives plc

Headline's policy is to use papers that are natural, renewable and
recyclable products and made from wood grown in sustainable forests.
The logging and manufacturing processes are expected to conform to the
environmental regulations of the country of origin.

HEADLINE PUBLISHING GROUP
A division of Hachette UK Ltd
338 Euston Road
London NW1 3BH

www.headline.co.uk
www.hachette.co.uk

To my father, James Richard Keller
(1931–1984), a son of Appalachia

For, what other dungeon is so dark as one's own heart!
What jailer so inexorable as one's self!
—Nathaniel Hawthorne,
The House of the Seven Gables

Part One

1

The flat-roofed shack was situated along a country road sunk deep in summer darkness, the kind of darkness that comes after a day of brash sunlight and thus seems more intense and deliberate than ordinary nightfall. The lights in the small tavern made it look, by odd contrast with that shadow-blackened road, like a living thing, shimmying and caterwauling and ready to leap up and lurch away, leaving behind a shallow hole and the sullen stink of piss.

Bell Elkins knew it was an illusion. She knew the only real motion came from the quivering lights in four porthole windows across the building's front and from the ugly thuds of the live band's bass beat, a percussion that hit like a fist on the heart. Yet she hesitated anyway, remaining for a few more minutes in her vehicle at the edge of the dirt-ridged parking lot. Other cars were stuck at crazy random angles, abandoned by their drivers with don't-give-a-damn nonchalance.

It was 3:42 A.M. on a sticky-hot Saturday night – no, Sunday morning – in the middle of June, and Bell was angry. The anger moved across her mind like a wire being threaded slowly through her veins, millimeter by millimeter. It didn't flare, the way her anger usually behaved; this time, it was gradual. A steady, ominous rise. As she reminded herself of each galling fact, the anger ticked up a notch, and then a notch past that.

Fact: Her sister Shirley hadn't been home in three days. Shirley was a grown woman, and the house rules were loose – but still. Three days. And no call, no text.

Fact: The cell on Bell's bedside table had played its perversely chipper tune just before 3 A.M. On the other end of the line was Amanda Sturm, a deputy sheriff in Collier County. 'Got a call 'bout a ruckus over at Tommy's,' Sturm said after identifying herself. She didn't have to identify Tommy's. It was a bar – this bar – out along Burnt Ridge Road, a place notorious for fights and drugs and trouble. 'Looked in on things,' the deputy went on, 'and got the lay of the land and then figured I oughta give you a call. Sorry 'bout the time.'

She hadn't awakened her; Bell hardly slept these days, and spent many of her nights sitting up in the battered old easy chair in her living room, reading or trying to. Tonight, she'd actually made it upstairs to bed, but sleep was a nonstarter. Still, though, the call had startled her. 'What do you mean?' Bell had asked. Her cell was as light and sleek as a Hershey Bar, yet she used both hands to wrangle it, one to secure it against her ear, the other to keep the bottom half tilted against her chin.

There was a pause, and then the deputy said, 'Well, ma'am, one of 'em says her sister is the Raythune County prosecutor and I better lay off. Checked her wallet and sure nuff – you're listed as contact person. Shirley Dolan's her name.'

Fact: Commingling with the clientele in a place like Tommy's could put Shirley in real danger of violating her parole.

4

Fact: Shirley was well aware of that. She also knew Bell was grappling with a terrible case, the brutal and apparently unprovoked murder of a retired coal miner two nights ago, right in the man's own driveway on the west side of Acker's Gap. The town was still reeling from the shock of it, from a crime that had injected a paralyzing chill into the warm, loose-limbed languor of summer in the mountains.

Fact: Shirley didn't give a rat's ass. She didn't care what sort of extra hassle she caused for Bell, what kind of shame or embarrassment or inconvenience.

Fact: Shirley was not only selfish; she was reckless, too. Dropping Bell's name to a deputy sheriff to garner special treatment was bad enough, but when you added the risk this posed to Shirley's fledgling status as a free woman – well, the whole thing made Bell so incensed that she wrapped her hands even tighter around the steering wheel of her Ford Explorer, glad to have a way to channel her rage, a place to direct it temporarily.

She'd done everything she could do for Shirley. In the three months since her sister's return, Bell had given her a place to stay, bought her clothes, tolerated her smoking. And she'd stayed out of her hair, letting Shirley make her own decisions – and by 'decisions,' Bell meant 'mistakes.' The two words had become synonymous in her mind, when it came to Shirley.

There'd been trouble from the start. One night, Shirley fell asleep in a kitchen chair with a burning cigarette notched between two fingers, jerking awake just in time to avert disaster, and another, she came home drunk and surly, and when Bell tried to guide the weaving woman to a bed, Shirley shook off the helping hand, and the foul word that fell out of her mouth made

Bell shudder in shock, as if Shirley had coughed up a toad or a spider.

Such behavior confirmed her sister's lack of judgment, of manners, of respect, of – well, maybe Sheriff Fogelsong had nailed it. 'Lack of gratitude,' he'd said to Bell when she confided her frustration about Shirley. 'That's what's really eating at you. You expect her to be grateful. Even humble. For sticking by her, for waiting, for taking her in. Plus – ever held a cork underwater? And then let it go? Shoots up like a geyser. Way the hell up in the air.'

The sheriff, Bell quickly decided, had a point. 'Ever get tired,' she had countered, 'of being right all the damned time?'

His reply: 'Oh, I'm wrong on purpose every now and again, just to keep things interesting.'

The recollection of that encounter reminded Bell of how much she missed him – and not just because she was staring straight in the face of an unsolved homicide that had left the town edgy and restive. Fogelsong had taken a month's leave of absence. He was scheduled to return in the coming week, at which point Pam Harrison would hand back over the top spot and resume her job as chief deputy – but still. Even a short spell without him was too long for Bell. Nick Fogelsong knew her better than anyone else; he understood her right down to the ground, and she appreciated his perspective. Needed it, more to the point.

Shirley, he'd gently remind Bell when her irritation got in the way of sound thinking, was a forty-six-year-old woman who'd never had a chance to be young. She'd been in prison for three decades, and in that bleak and tightly regulated place, every step was monitored, every spontaneous impulse blocked.

So Bell had cut her some slack. Backed off. Held her tongue.

But tonight an entirely new threshold had been crossed. This was the first time Shirley had stayed away for several days running. Or used Bell's name in a scrape with the law. This was disturbingly fresh territory. And it came at a time when Bell ought to be focusing on public safety in general, not a misbehaving sister in particular. If Shirley was caught up in a sweep at Tommy's – the bar's proprietor, Tommy LeSeur, was himself a convicted felon, having served four and a half years on a narcotics charge – her parole could be revoked.

'Hey, pretty lady.'

At the same moment Bell heard the words, she smelled the hot oniony stink of the man who had suddenly thrust his face in the Explorer's open window. He'd taken her by surprise, so intent was she on her thoughts as she stared at the run-down bar. But she wasn't frightened. She was pissed off. The man had a fat face, swollen to the point of resembling an allergic reaction. Bristles of beard stuck out from his round cheeks and from the undulating rolls of blubber that propped up his tiny chin. Booze, sweat, and the heavy fug of a recent bout of vomiting invaded her space.

Before Bell could react, he was talking again. He'd hooked his hands across the bottom of the window and hung on as if it were an upper-story sill.

'Lookin' for somethun?' he slurred. 'Or some*body*? Wanna party?' A wicked leer seized his mouth, making both ends of it pointy. A pearl of sweat – or maybe another liquid, although who'd really want a positive ID? – was poised on the bottom rim of a nostril. His eyes were bleary. 'How 'bout it, baby?'

First Bell wanted to laugh – *Oh, yeah, here I come, you're freakin' irresistible, mister* – and then the anger roared back, this time mixed with revulsion.

'Get the hell away from me,' she said. Low voice. Words measured and calm, but laced with threat. Only a fool would miss her meaning.

'C'mon, baby. Don't be doin' me like that,' the intruder said. His oily wheedle – delivered on the back of a gust of smelly breath – was enough to make Bell's stomach turn.

With a gesture so quick that it caught him in the middle of a wink, she flung open the car door. Knocked back, he teetered for a tenth of a second and then landed flat on his ample butt.

Behind him, starkly visible in the glare of the crude spotlight rigged to a corner of the building, was a stumpy ring of three men – his buddies, Bell assumed, because these types always traveled in packs. The men pointed at Fat Ass and stomped their work boots and laughed, a hard-edged, mirthless laughter that sounded like another variety of assault. They wore baseball caps and long-sleeved plaid flannel shirts with the cuffs buttoned and the shirttails flapping out behind them, even though this was the middle of summer; such, Bell knew, was the year-round uniform of the good ole boys, the kind you could find lining the back roads around here like lint on a comb.

'Bitch!' Fat Ass yelled at her. He'd yet to rise from his seat on the ground, thwarted by, in equal measures, obesity and drunkenness. 'Goddamned bitch.'

That only made his friends laugh harder. 'Looks like she up and tole you what she thinksa you,' one of them opined, nudging Fat Ass with the toe of his boot, as if his buddy were a clump of dirt that needed relocating. The others re-upped their laughter, hooting like fools, slapping at their knees when they weren't using their fingers to point at Fat Ass. A gray scab of moon regarded the scene indifferently from above.

Bell pondered her next move. Her mission was simple: Go in the bar, find Shirley, and somehow persuade her to come home. She wasn't looking for a fight. If these creeps kept it up, though, and interfered with her, she would handle it. Fat Ass didn't know what trouble was until he'd tangled with the likes of her. Her seventeen-year-old daughter, Carla – currently living with Bell's ex-husband, Sam, but due back in Acker's Gap for summer vacation in a week – had put it best: 'Mom,' Carla said, 'when you get mad, I think I'd sorta rather deal with the guy in the *Texas Chain Saw Massacre* movies, you know?'

The bar's double doors flapped open. During the few seconds that the interior of the establishment was exposed – the hot wild noise, the undulating red lights framed by the solid black night – it looked, to Bell's eye, like a peephole into hell.

A female deputy sheriff – short, hatless, and heavyset – came striding out of Tommy's, turning this way and that to cut a path between the parked cars. Her long gray hair was funneled into a twisty braid that perched on her shoulder like a pet. Black boots chopped at the gravel with each forceful step. Her gun was holstered on her wide hip, but she kept her big right hand in contact with the grip, a *Don't make me use this* set to her meaty jaw.

The three men scattered like scrap paper swept off a desktop by a sudden draft. Fat Ass, also highly motivated, flopped over on his hands and knees and crawled a short distance and then hoisted himself up, courtesy of the rusty back bumper of a Dodge Ram 1500.

As he and his buddies hustled away, the deputy nodded in approval. 'Evening, ma'am,' she said to Bell. 'Deputy Sturm. Thought you might be arriving right about now.'

'Met the welcoming committee.' Bell stepped out of the Explorer and gestured toward the severe darkness that bordered the lot, a bottomless pit into which the four men had disappeared. The darkness seemed all the more menacing because of its adjacency to the garishly lit space. There was no middle ground. If you left the illuminated area, it was as if you'd fallen off the edge of the world. *No dark like summer dark,* Bell thought. *No end to it. Goes on forever.*

She shuddered. She'd had a sudden unwanted memory of the crime-scene photo still on her desk back at the courthouse: Freddie Arnett's lanky body facedown on the oil-stained concrete of his driveway, blood and brain matter shining wetly in the velvety glow of the front porch light.

'Those boys tried to get friendly with me, too.' Sturm chuckled. With two fingers, she tapped the badge pinned to the left breast pocket of her gray polyester shirt. 'Then they saw this.'

Bell nodded. Enough with the small talk. 'Where's Shirley Dolan?'

'Right where I left her – rounded up in the back of the bar with a bunch of troublemakers, waiting to see if I'm going to give 'em even more of a hassle than I already have. Maybe haul 'em in for drunk and disorderly. They've been calling me every name in the book and then some.'

'What started it?'

'Don't know. I mean, Bobo Bolland's here with his band, and it seems like he brings trouble wherever he goes. Somebody calls somebody else a low-down sumbitch or a man-stealing whore or something similar, and before you know it, the whole place goes crazy.' Two more cars fishtailed into the lot, one right behind the other. The drivers must have caught the glint of the badge on Deputy Sturm's broad chest – or, the more likely scenario, simply sniffed out the presence of the law after long experience with dodging same – because their hasty U-turns back onto the road were executed with a panic-fed zeal.

Sturm barely noticed. She and Bell had begun walking toward the door of Tommy's, and something else was on her mind. 'Listen,' Sturm said. 'Before we go in, I wanted to say – well, I heard about that poor old man. Hell of a thing. Bet folks in Acker's Gap are plenty shook up.'

Bell nodded. Freddie Arnett had suffered multiple blows to his head from a sledgehammer – that was the coroner's preliminary analysis, given the shape of the wounds and the fact that the probable murder weapon was lying in the grass next to the driveway – in an astonishingly vicious assault. No prints, no motive, no suspects, no leads; it was, Bell had reflected, almost as if the summer night itself had reared up and come after Arnett, as if the darkness had taken shape just long enough to grab a handy weapon and use it to crush an old man's skull, then spread itself out again in a soft black ooze.

'Makes you wonder,' Sturm said.

'Yeah.'

They had reached the entrance to Tommy's. Bell heard muffled thuds from the other side of the wall, along with wicked guitar licks and fuzzy throbs from a cheap amplifier and the ominous insect hum of packed bodies rubbing up against one another.

Sturm's big right hand reached for the dirty wooden handle. The upper half of one of the doors was smothered by a thumbtacked white poster that showed off the wobbly work of a black Sharpie:

TONITE! BOBO BOLLAND AND HIS ROCKIN'
BAND!!! 11 pm to ????

Bell followed her into the bar – and into the kind of frantic, sweaty bedlam that Bell had spent a good portion of her adult life trying to avoid, because it reminded her too much of her childhood, when the world was big and bad and loud and out of control, and she was the weakest, frailest thing in it. The prey.

There she was.

Shirley Dolan stood at the far end of the bar, her back to the nicked brown counter that featured what looked to be at least a century's worth of interlocking rings from wet-bottomed glasses of beer. Long gray hair frizzled down her narrow back. Bell had anticipated that it might take a few minutes to locate her sister in the raucous crowd; she'd thought her eyes might have to rove over at least a dozen or so sweat-shined faces with sloppy grins and pinprick eyeballs – but no. She picked her out right away, even though Shirley was dressed in an echo of what everybody else wore: cowboy boots, tight jeans, T-shirt, untucked flannel shirt.

Shot glass pressed to her lip, Shirley took a long soulful slug. Then she shook herself with gusto, like a dog after a deluge, as the fiery liquid pitchforked its way through her insides. She twisted her torso to thump the glass back down on the bar. It was then – with Shirley in a half turn, licking her bottom lip – that her eyes met up with Bell's. The three-man band in the opposite corner had just commenced another number, and the blistering bass beats seemed to make the small building shimmy and throb.

Before Bell had a chance to speak, another commotion erupted. Several chairs tipped and crashed, the top rails of their wooden backs clattering against the red concrete floor as people jumped and scattered. Three round tables were upended; glasses slid off and shattered. First one woman screamed, then two more. The band stopped playing – not gradually but abruptly, as if someone had kicked out a power cord.

Jesus, somebody muttered. *What the hell*, came from somebody else, followed by yet another opinion: *Drunk as a goddamned skunk, just like always. Leave him be, why doncha.* There was a sudden batch of ear-ripping static from the electric guitar, until the skinny, big-nosed guitar player – having brushed the strings with his sleeve – silenced it again with a hand clamped over the fret.

The crowd parted clumsily, opening up a Z-shaped lane to the source of the tumult. Sprawled facedown on the greasy floor was a wiry, black-haired man in a pale yellow flannel shirt and dirty white carpenter's pants. Sturm and Bell moved simultaneously to the spot. The deputy, reaching it first, called out sharply, 'Hey, mister – you okay?' and then lowered herself to his side with the velocity of a dropped rock. Sturm's movements, Bell saw, were surprisingly nimble and efficient for a woman her size. She groped under his chin for a pulse. Nothing. With two hands, she turned him over.

An orange-handled screwdriver had been punched into the man's chest, after which the force of his fall pushed it sideways, ripping the wound wider. A dark stain fled rapidly across the front of his shirt, as ominous as a storm system filling out a digital weather map. His acne-chipped face was white, his jaw slack. Eyes open. Pupils fixed and dilated.

Sturm's big head swung up to look at Bell. There was a stunned, uncertain quality to the deputy's stare. *When you do this for a living,* Bell reminded herself, *you always think you're prepared, but you're never prepared. Never.* Bell felt a swell of nausea cresting in her belly. She fought it, clenching her jaw. And she was aware as well of a cold sense of dread throwing a shadow over her thoughts like a cloud crossing an open field. *First the old man back in Acker's Gap. Now this. Jesus.*

The deputy quickly recovered her composure. Still on one knee, she unclipped the radio from her belt and thumbed it on. The bar had grown eerily quiet – no one so much as coughed or shuffled a foot or bumped a table – and that fact gave the few simple words of Sturm's summons for an ambulance the chiseled mien of a haiku.

Call completed, she barked at the stunned on-lookers: 'Anybody know this guy? Anybody see what happened? Anybody?'

More silence.

The deputy reached in the dead man's pocket, hunting for ID. Bell was just about to tell her to back away to preserve the integrity of the crime scene when Sturm pulled out a small white business card. She scanned it, then passed it up to Bell. *Can't matter much at this point,* Bell thought, accepting it. There had already been enough contamination of the scene to piss off the state forensic folks, the ones who would be showing up in their fancy van just as soon as the techs back in Charleston finished their argument about whose turn it was to make the drive over crummy roads in the tricky dark. Communities as small as this one didn't have their own crime-scene units. They had to wait their turn, just as Bell and the deputies had had to wait two nights ago, when they stood, helpless and appalled, alongside Freddie Arnett's shattered body. And they would have to wait now.

Bell scanned the black embossed letters on the card:

SAMPSON J. VOORHEES. ATTORNEY-AT-LAW. NYC.

No phone number, no fax, no e-mail address. *Strange way of doing business for a law firm,* Bell mused. *Usually they're throwing their contact info at you so fast, you have to duck.* Her ex-husband worked for that kind of firm. *Hell,* she'd often thought, *given half a chance, he'd probably slap the company logo on the toilet seats in the men's room.* She turned over the card. Along the bottom edge, another name had been hand-scrawled with a blue pen:

Odell Crabtree

Sturm was reaching up now to retrieve the card, because it was evidence. Part of the official record. Bell wanted a longer look, but complied; this was Deputy Sturm's turf, Deputy Sturm's investigation. Collier County would be calling the shots. Which was good news: Raythune County had all it could handle right now.

Still, Bell was curious. She wondered what link there could possibly be between a publicity-shy New York City lawyer and a body on the floor of Tommy's bar in the middle of West Virginia on a sweat-oiled summer night, the life in that body having recently seeped away amid a sour backwash of sloshed beer, bad jokes, loud cackles, high-hanging gray webs of cigarette smoke, and the foot-stompin', good-time tunes of Bobo Bolland and His Rockin' Band.

2

He was moving around again. She could hear him bumping into things, and with each thump, Lindy winced; she imagined the pain of a knee hitting a box or a cheek scraping a rough wall. But she was reluctant to check on him. She didn't want to open the basement door and call down into the darkness, 'You okay, Daddy?' Not anymore. She had done that at first – in the early days, she had reacted to every noise – and like as not, he'd come roaring up at her, swinging his fists over his head and yelling: 'Leave me be! *Told you to leave me be!*'

So now Lindy just listened. Listened hard. In ten minutes, she would have to leave for her overnight shift at the Lester gas station, and she couldn't be late. Summer Saturdays were a zoo. A twenty-four-hour place in these parts was a magnet for every drunk, every weirdo, and every druggie in a thirty-mile radius; Saturday nights seemed to bring out the crazy even in normal people. But before she left, she had to make sure he was okay.

There were three or four bumps in a row. Then a spell of quiet. That meant, most likely, that he'd gotten his bearings again; his internal radar had mysteriously kicked back in. She pictured him as he moved amid the loose branches and the jumbo rocks. Three years ago, she had dragged in those loads from outside, inch by inch, scavenging them from the ravine out beyond the big hill. She also tracked down, from yard sales and thrift stores, a mess of old wooden tables, chipped and rickety. Some were round, some square, some rectangular; some were as small as TV trays, while others were long enough to host a dozen family members at Sunday supper.

She had made a place for him that was like the place he knew best, the place he loved: a coal mine. The coal mine that had closed down five years ago, leaving him and thirty-two other miners stunned and bereft, not knowing where to go or how to be.

He didn't walk upright; he crouched. He had to, because long years spent working underground had left his back as curved as a question mark. His habit was to reach ahead in the darkness, swaying from side to side, picking and scrabbling at the hard surfaces that surrounded him, surfaces he sensed rather than saw. He tried to restrict himself to the space under the tables because he liked to stay bent and the tables enabled him to do just that. It was the one position that didn't hurt. He dozed often, curled in a clenched circle like a barrel stave, and when he first woke, there was always a period of disorientation. Always a span of time during which he'd forget and rise too quickly and – with a furious yelp, because a scalding-hot starburst of pain was born over and over again in that torqued, ruined back of his – ram into the things with which she'd filled the cellar, the tables and the crates and the rocks and the mounds of dirt. He was still a big man, big and solid and strong. When he hit something, you heard it.

Lindy went back to her reading. If she had only ten minutes to go before leaving for her shift, she'd spend it reading. She'd propped up her book against the stack of still more books on the kitchen table. This was her domain now; her father rarely came up to the first floor these days. She had filled his space with what he liked, and so she felt entitled to fill her space with what she liked. And what she liked were books.

The Fabric of the Cosmos. That's what she was reading. He didn't like to see her reading. If he were still a regular part of her daylight life, the way he'd been until a few years ago, he might have come up behind her and grabbed the book right out of her hands, holding it up too high for her to snatch back – he wasn't a tall man to begin with, and forty-seven years in the mines had shortened him even further, but he was still taller than she was. And then he would sidearm the book into the trash can next to the sink. She never said a word. She would cross the small kitchen and pick the book out of the trash, sweeping away the coffee grounds and wiping off the gelatinous white-yellow globs of skillet grease and try not to react. She didn't want him to see how hurt she was.

He'd always had a temper. A terrible waiting rage that could spring to life the way a flame leaps up when you click on a lighter – just that suddenly, just that easily. From the time she was a little girl, Lindy had learned how to cope, how to deal with his temper, how to walk carefully around it the way you'd sidestep an injured animal along the road, never knowing when it might rally and come after you, all teeth and claws and survival instinct. He hadn't liked her very much back then. Lindy's mother loved her – there was no doubt about that – but her father had seemed to hold some obscure grudge against her. He'd accepted her presence, but he didn't have to be happy about it. Six years ago, the cancer had taken away his wife, Margaret, and now it was just the two of them. Just him and Lindy. And he changed, bit by bit. He softened. Part of it, she knew, was fear – fear of what was happening to him. He needed her. But she didn't care about the cause. Didn't mind the fact that it was panic and desperation that drove him into finally being a father. She loved him. And now, it seemed, he loved her, too.

'Something's happening to me, my girl,' he had said to her, back when it began. 'In my head. Clouds. It's like big black clouds moving in before a storm. Getting between me and what I want to say or do. Clouds. They come and they go. Makes me mad. I can't think no more. I can't—' He would stop. Shake his head. Lindy would reach up and lay her hand flat on his chest, and keep her hand right there. He'd close his eyes. The two of them would stay that way for a long while, and he'd be himself again. For a time.

Now he spent most of his days in the cellar. In the place she had built for him three years ago, to calm him down. She'd hauled in the big rocks. She'd stacked up the boxes, arranged the tables and the old barrels. She'd procured the sticks and the scrap lumber, and she'd scattered all of it around the cold dirt floor. Dumped coal here and there. Gravel, too. He wanted it dark, insisted on it, and so she had unscrewed the lightbulb from the overhead fixture. Then she had climbed the stairs back up to the first floor. Closed the door behind her.

He spent his time in a blackness that matched the blackness rising inside him. Except for the occasional thumps and groans, she didn't hear much from him. She knew he came up the stairs at night. She'd find the results in the morning: A box of Kellogg's Corn Flakes with the top flap torn off and three-quarters of the contents gone, courtesy of a frantic plunging hand that spilled half its load on the floor on its way to his mouth. Melon rinds, with an unevenly spaced row of shallow dents marking the spots where his remaining teeth had gnawed at the sweet meat. And a sick-making, dizziness-inducing smell from the sink, where he sometimes emptied his bucket, not bothering to run the spigot to rinse the feces and urine down the drain. She had to disinfect the sink daily with Clorox. The smell was like having fingers poked in your eyes.

Two and a half years ago, the last time he'd let her take him anywhere, the doctor at the Raythune County Medical Center – the only neurologist left in the area who would see Medicare patients – had been blunt with her: 'Your father has significant and chronic health issues in addition to the neurological deficits, including emphysema and congestive heart failure. There's no way to tell how long he might survive. The end could be fast, or it could be slow.' What the doctor didn't say, but allowed Lindy to extrapolate from the silence that descended on the beige-walled room after his pronouncement, was this: *Given his current mental state, fast might be better*. She had nodded, and then she helped her father get down from the examination table. She tried to help him put on his jacket – he kept ramming his fist in the wrong armhole – but he smacked at her hands and cursed her.

The only place her father was comfortable now was the past. The past, for him, meant the Acer Mine No. 40, twenty-seven miles out on Route 6 in rural

Raythune County, where he'd worked his shift well into his sixties, tilted like a tree pushed from behind by a permanent hurricane.

Lindy was just finishing up Part IV of *The Fabric of the Cosmos*. She loved the book – it was all about space and time and gravity, things you could measure, things that rewarded your deep thinking about them by proving to be solid and comprehensible, unlike things such as your feelings and your family – but now she had to stop. Time to get ready for work. She was the night manager at the station, a job she'd held since her graduation from Acker's Gap High School two years ago.

Another thump.

She waited. No more noise. No yelling. *Good*. He probably hadn't hurt himself, then. No reason for her to open the basement door and call down to him, asking if he was okay, a gesture that might very well be met with a yip and a snarl. Her father was in a nasty mood today, restless and surly, knocking things over and bellowing about it. He'd probably heard the mail truck earlier and was riled by the sound. He didn't like anybody coming by the house. But there wasn't a bookstore within a hundred miles of here. What she wanted, she had to buy online and have shipped. She'd ordered enough books to take her all the way through next fall. The white-haired, scraggly browed postman, Perry Crum, his sixty-two-year-old body scrunched up like a lumpy quarter-moon after so many decades of lugging heavy mail sacks back into the hollows of rural Raythune County, often teased her about it; if he had the time, Perry would drag the heavy carton of books inside for her, even though he wasn't required to, and as he lifted it onto the kitchen table, he'd say, 'Heavier'n a box of rocks! Sure wish you were collecting crocheted pot holders instead of books.'

He was teasing. He didn't really mind. In fact, Perry Crum talked to her about the books she read because he, too, was interested in science; he'd planned to be a biology major in college, but in the end he couldn't go, because he had to take care of his sister Ellie, who had Down syndrome. Their parents were long dead, and there was no one else to do it. He mentioned his family situation to Lindy just once, and only in passing. It was not the kind of thing that people in these parts talked about. Your burdens were your burdens. Everyone had them. It was a given.

Last month, Lindy's father had been in the kitchen on the day when Perry came in with a carton of books. Perry smiled and waved. Her father glared darkly, his lip raised in a snarl.

'Daddy, you know Perry Crum,' Lindy said. She patted the top of the square cardboard box, which Perry had dropped on the kitchen table. 'He brought my books. You remember Perry.'

Her father growled something indecipherable. Putting a twisted-up hand on the kitchen wall to steady himself, he groped and lurched to the basement door. He didn't look back at the postman or his daughter. His journey down was a heavy and solemn one, each step a separate chunk of thunder that made the staircase shimmy.

A wince of concern had redistributed the wrinkles on Perry's face. 'You okay here, Lindy?' he said.

'Fine. Really.'

And she was. She could take care of herself. She'd been doing it for a long time. Even before her father got to be the way he was, he had worked long hours at the mine. Came home practically comatose with exhaustion.

Lindy looked around for a bookmark. There was a stack of mail at her elbow, mail from the past week or so because she always put off going through it, envelopes thick and thin, mostly white but in a variety of sizes, plus slick flyers from the discount stores up on the interstate.

She grabbed the envelope on the top of the heap. Her father still received mail from time to time. Nothing of a personal nature. Junk mail mainly, along with Social Security and Medicare bulletins, although Lindy had long ago arranged to have his meager retirement income direct-deposited, and she used that to pay the mortgage. Otherwise, she never touched his money. She bought her books with her own salary.

The letter – she stuck it in the book to designate her place between pages 376 and 377, giving the envelope a glance as she did so – looked like another blind solicitation from some company wanting him to buy something he didn't need. New York City postmark. In the center, in the space for the recipient's information, was her father's name and address in typed black letters:

ODELL CRABTREE
COUNTY ROAD 76
ACKER'S GAP, WV

3

Long after this night was over, Bell would remember how thin her sister's arm felt in her grip. She had first grabbed Shirley's wrist, but Shirley jerked it out of Bell's hand. Somebody else in the bar – Bell didn't know if it was a man or a woman, and she couldn't tell by the sound and didn't care enough to check – laughed a loud two-note laugh, amused by Shirley's active disinclination to be dragged out of the place. The laugh infuriated Bell, and she clamped her hand around Shirley's upper arm. The arm felt like a kid's arm: wiry, hard, all bone. Bell marched her roughly out of Tommy's and into the soup-warm West Virginia night.

Neither spoke during the drive from Tommy's back to Acker's Gap. The silence continued – in fact, it seemed to spread out and calcify – as Bell reached her destination and made an abrupt right-angle turn into the driveway, punished the gearshift into Park, doused the headlights, shushed the engine, slid out. Squinting in the strong porch light, she worked the key, flinging open the front door. Only then did she turn around to address Shirley, who'd kept her distance during the climb up the porch steps.

Bell was fuming. Her jaw was set so tight that she'd

resigned herself to maybe grinding down a molar or two on account of it. She stepped to one side of the threshold.

'Get in,' she said. 'Now.'

Shirley had hesitated, looking down at the scuffed and discolored wood on the porch floor, working the toe of her boot into an especially large knothole.

'Go on,' Bell said. 'I'm in a hurry. Got to get back to the courthouse.'

Surprised, Shirley lifted her head. 'Not even daylight yet.'

'Yeah. But you know what?' Bell's voice was hard and sharp. 'I'm a prosecutor. You know what that means? It means that at any given time, I've got about a dozen or so open cases. Right now we're trying to find out who murdered an old man in his driveway. And you know what else? I'm an officer of the court. And because I was present during the commission of a felony tonight, I've got to file about ten million forms, give or take.'

'Didn't have nothin' to do with you,' Shirley said, but she'd mumbled and Bell couldn't make it out.

'What?' Bell was on high alert for defiance.

'Just sayin' that what happened at Tommy's tonight didn't have nothin' to do with you. Or me, neither. That fella comes in the bar all the time and starts trouble. Seen him lots. Somebody had to set him straight.'

'So that's where you've been keeping yourself? Tommy's? You sleeping there, too?'

Shirley didn't look at her. 'Staying with friends.'

'Friends.' Bell put a sneer in the word. 'Friends who hang out at places like Tommy's.'

'It's not so bad. Things just got outa hand.'

'Yeah,' Bell said. 'I'd say they got outa hand, all right. A man's dead.'

Shirley didn't answer. Bell shook her head, trying to clear away the last few seconds and get a fresh start on the conversation. She didn't much care about the dirtball who'd gotten himself killed in a seedy bar in Collier County – as long as the death was unrelated to her murder case here in Acker's Gap, which seemed likely. She cared about her sister, toward whom she felt an immense and solemn weight of obligation.

Bell peered at her. Shirley would be forty-seven years old next month. She could pass for sixty, what with the long, spindly gray hair that was rapidly thinning on top, just like an old man's hair. The bones in her face looked as if they were thrusting forward, pushing the flesh away, and soon would take over the space entirely. Her eyes had no shine; they were flat, and the papery skin around them was dry and crosshatched with brief lines.

Yet when Bell looked at Shirley as she was doing right now – looked at her intensely, letting the resentment and disappointment slide away – she felt an unruly rush of raw emotions: pity and love and guilt and abject tenderness. Shirley had given up so much for Bell that the debt was past all reckoning. Their father had molested Shirley for years, and when Donnie Dolan seemed to be turning his attention to ten-year-old Belfa, Shirley had protected her. She'd protected her the only way she knew how: Shirley had stabbed their father in the throat and then used gasoline and matches to destroy the trailer in which they lived. Destroyed the dread and the fear and the menace. Destroyed all the monsters, the living kind and the memory kind. Or tried to, anyway.

Thirty years had passed since that night. Yet even now, when Bell contemplated her sister's sacrifice, a sacrifice that had consumed so much of Shirley's life – the prison sentence had been extended again and again by Shirley's fighting and insubordination and by an escape attempt – Bell was overwhelmed. Shirley had made Bell's life possible. College, law school, motherhood, public office – none of it could have happened without Shirley. None of it.

Thus even when Bell's irritation with her sister rose to a high jagged peak, just as it had this evening, she would consider the slack-skinned, sad-eyed woman in front of her. And Bell would find herself wishing that she could simply forget the whole damned world for a moment and sink wearily to the porch floor, taking Shirley with her, whereupon the two of them could just stay there in a clumsy embrace, fused by sorrow and long regret, not crying, not talking, just breathing, swaying back and forth as if this spot were an island of light on the darkest and scariest of nights, and each little girl was rocking the other one back to sleep.

But Bell couldn't do that. She was a grown woman. She had things to do. Enormous and ongoing responsibilities. Along with her duties as prosecutor, and the gruesome reality of Freddie Arnett's unsolved murder, there was also the fact that her daughter would be arriving next week. Bell winced at the thought that Carla might see her aunt Shirley in this shape: furtive, simmering with rebelliousness, reeking of alcohol and cigarettes and self-pity.

The anger surged back into the picture. It never seemed to stay away for very long.

'I told you to go inside,' Bell declared. 'Get some sleep. I'll be back later. We'll talk then.' Shirley, head down, hands rammed in jeans pockets, started to shuffle past her into the house.

Bell abruptly clamped a hand on her sister's upper arm, the same way she'd shepherded her out of Tommy's. Bell's tone was firm but also earnest, searching. 'So what's going on, Shirley? For God's sake – what the hell do you want? I mean, I've done everything I can. Every damned thing I can think of. But you just keep screwing up. So what is it? What do you want? *What?*'

A bleak smile briefly lifted the skin on Shirley's face. 'I want the last thirty years back,' she said. 'Can you do that?'

4

'Got an ID on that stabbing victim at Tommy's.'

Deputy Mathers had to repeat it twice before Bell looked up. Even then, his sentence didn't fully register. Her elbows were balanced on twin stacks of file folders that appeared to have replicated themselves at will across the broad top of her desk. She'd been making notes on a yellow legal pad, compiling an urgent to-do list for Assistant Prosecutors Hickey Leonard and Rhonda Lovejoy. The investigation into the killing of Freddie Arnett hadn't progressed beyond what Bell called the OMG stage – characterized by shock, panic, and hand-wringing in virtually everyone she encountered, all of which was understandable, but none of which would do a damned thing toward actually tracking down the bastard who had bludgeoned the old man to death. Time to get creative. Time to do something – anything – that might lead them to the perpetrator of one of the most vicious crimes anyone around here could remember. And this was a place of long memories.

It was just after sunrise. Bell had left Shirley at home and then driven straight to the Raythune County Courthouse, a stolid, dome-topped, three-story limestone structure on Main Street that dated back to

1867 and had the plumbing to prove it. A soft lemony light filled the tall leaded windows in her office. Dust turned in the air. No matter how well or how often her office was cleaned, the dust rose up; the courthouse was so old that the dust, Bell believed, had more right to the place than the people did.

'What are you talking about?' she snapped back at him. She'd been startled, so totally was she focused on the details of the Arnett case, and that made her sound meaner than she'd intended to.

Charlie Mathers didn't mind. He understood. They were both under the same intense pressure. Both felt the weight of the faith and trust of the people of Acker's Gap – faith that they'd find Freddie Arnett's killer, trust that they'd see to it the case was airtight and error-free and culminated in a sentence stretching into the next millennium or so. West Virginia had eliminated the death penalty in 1965, and cases such as this one caused a lot of townspeople to openly regret it.

The deputy stood in front of her desk with his booted feet spread and his thumbs tucked in his belt, a belt creased and folded almost double beneath his overlapping gut. When Bell had called him fifteen minutes ago – he was on weekend jail duty – and asked him to check with his colleagues in Collier County about a homicide in a bar reported a few hours ago, she had added, almost as an afterthought, that she'd been present at the scene. He knew there had to be more to the story, but he'd have to scavenge the details later.

'No connection to Freddie Arnett,' Mathers said. 'Leastways, that's how it looks so far. Collier County gave me IDs on the victim and the perpetrator. Dead guy was a fella named Jed Stark. From over in Steppe County. Twenty-six years old. Been getting into trouble ever since he was old enough to say, "Hell no – weren't me that done it." But it always was.' Mathers tilted his head philosophically. 'He was married. Had a three-year-old girl named – Lord help me – Guinivere. Imagine having to live your life in Steppe County with a name like Guinivere. Might as well paste a "Kick Me" sign on the kid's backside right now and be done with it.'

'Alleged assailant?'

'Local dirtball named Larry McCoy. Seems Stark was messin' with his woman.'

Bell's interest level dropped to near zero. Two liquored-up rednecks fighting over the same over-perfumed jailbait: She heard that story, with only the names changed, a dozen times a month. *About as romantic a scenario,* Bell thought, *as a couple of pigs rooting around in the same trough.*

'Okay,' she said to Mathers. Waved her hand dismissively. 'Not our lookout.' Except for the contents of his pocket – the out-of-town lawyer's card – there was nothing remarkable about the fate of Jed Stark. She'd make some inquiries about the business card later. If she had a moment, which wasn't likely. 'There was a deputy present,' Bell added, 'and I gave a statement at the scene. Just finished faxing my report to Mason Dittmer's office.' Dittmer was the Collier County prosecutor. 'Can't think there's anything else they'll need.' She tapped the tip of her pencil on the legal pad. Thinking. 'Make sure you follow up with Deputy Sturm about McCoy. We need to verify his whereabouts on Thursday night – when Freddie Arnett was attacked. Just in case.' If there was any kind of link between the two homicides, they'd better find it fast.

'You got it,' Mathers said.

Had this been a typical weekend morning, he might have been surprised to see Bell Elkins in her office. It was true that the prosecutor and Sheriff Fogelsong rarely confined themselves to the parameters of a normal workweek. But on Saturdays and Sundays, they tended to be out on the road interviewing witnesses or going over case notes while they compromised their insides with endless cups of black coffee at a diner just down the block called JP's – short for Joyce's Place. They weren't office-sitters.

But here she was, stationed at her desk in the otherwise-deserted courthouse on a summer Sunday morning. And Mathers didn't have to ask why.

Sometime late Thursday night or early Friday morning, Freddie Arnett had been putting the final touches on the cream-colored 1967 Ford Thunderbird convertible with red leather upholstery that he'd intended to give to his grandson when the boy started community college in the fall. The car was unscathed. Nothing was stolen. Nobody'd had a beef with Arnett, at least not according to the reports from the initial canvas of friends and neighbors. Freddie Arnett was just a sweet old guy with a broken-toothed grin and a magical way with a carburetor, and he'd ended up dead in his own driveway, his skull cracked open and a goodly portion of his brain matter smeared across the concrete, while his wife, Annie, slept in their bedroom not twenty feet away. A neighbor leaving for work on Friday morning found him. The neighbor's screams – high-pitched, sharp-edged as broken glass – tailed off into one long shrieking howl, slaughtering the peace of a region across which the sun had just begun its gradual daily passage. That animal howl still echoed in the heads of many people who lived up and down the street. Mathers knew it to be true because he'd done the interviews. House by house. Person by person. Story by story.

Mathers also knew how such a crime affected Bell Elkins, tormenting her, living in her skin like a bad case of shingles. He was eager to help, but his work had turned up nothing. Yesterday he'd gone back and reinterviewed the people with whom he and Acting Sheriff Harrison had already spoken – plus a couple of hitchhikers spotted along the interstate that night and tracked down early Saturday morning in Beckley – and he had e-mailed his notes to Bell. But no one had seen or heard a thing. The killer apparently knew his way around Acker's Gap, at least well enough to sneak up on Arnett, smash him in the back of the head with the old man's own rust-ravaged sledgehammer, and then drift away again, leaving not so much as a whisper of evidence.

Bell's cell rang. She looked at Mathers and he nodded, meaning that he had more he needed to say to her, and so she held up an index finger, indicating that he should stick around. She checked the caller ID. 'Dammit,' she said, then answered the call. 'Elkins.' She paused. 'No comment. Okay? Just like I told you yesterday. We're not ready to—' Another pause. 'I understand. But any information I give you right now would be speculative and premature and could compromise the investigation.' Another pause. 'No. No connection. The homicide in Collier County last night appears unrelated to the murder of Freddie Arnett.' Pause. 'Yes. You can quote me.' Pause. 'No problem. It wasn't too early. Already at my desk.' Pause. 'No.' Pause. 'One more time. *No*.' She ended the call.

Mathers grinned. 'Lemme guess. Donnie Frazey.' Frazey was the managing editor of the *Acker's Gap Gazette,* a weekly newspaper that serviced Raythune, Collier, Steppe, and Atherton counties. His full title was longer – managing editor, sole reporter, advertising sales director, and circulation supervisor – but Frazey had a hard time fitting all that into his byline, so he didn't mind if people just referred to him as the editor. He was a gangling, sandy-haired fifty-four-year-old veteran of three marriages and father of six children spread evenly amongst those relationships, a recovering alcoholic whose occasional lapses were easily charted by subscribers – the paper's usually reliable publication day would be pushed back for at least twenty-four hours, a period of time referred to as the 'hangover delay' – and he operated out of a cramped storefront that served as the *Gazette*'s office.

'Just doing his job,' Bell said, frowning at her cell, 'but still a damned nuisance. Can't wait till Nick's back in town. He's got a lot more patience with Donnie Frazey than I do.'

A month ago, Sheriff Fogelsong had taken his wife to a psychiatric facility in Chicago, where doctors sought to find a combination of medications to stabilize her, to help her deal with the symptoms of her schizophrenia. Nick and Mary Sue would be returning to Acker's Gap on Tuesday.

Bell put a hand flat on the yellow legal pad and looked up at Mathers, hoping he would take her meaning: She had work to do. 'Anything else?'

The deputy moved his tongue around the inside of his mouth as if he were searching for a lost kernel of last night's popcorn. 'Well,' he said, 'I thought maybe you'd want a few more details about that stabbing at

Tommy's.' Mathers was a born storyteller, and Bell's lack of interest in his harvest of data had disappointed him.

'Okay,' she said. It came out as more of a sigh than a word. 'Sure, Charlie.' She sat back in her chair. She needed a break, anyway.

'So it happens like this.' The deputy untucked one of his thumbs from his belt and used the thumbnail to scratch the top of his left ear. 'Mandy Sturm questions this McCoy character in the bar for an hour or so this morning. Knows what she's doing, too. She's a damned good deputy. So McCoy confesses. Says he just got sick and tired of Jed Stark bothering his lady, and so he goes out to his pickup in the parking lot and he gets in the Craftsman toolbox that he keeps in the truck bed and he lightens the load by the weight of one Phillips-head screwdriver. Barges back in and sits right down beside Stark and strikes up a conversation. Bides his time. Right after the band plays the first chorus of 'Sweet Home Alabama,' seeing that Stark's relaxed and all, McCoy leans over and takes care of our little redneck Romeo, good and proper. Now, soon as he comes clean to Deputy Sturm about what he did, nine-tenths of the folks who've been sitting at the surrounding tables are suddenly able to verify it. When it first happened, nobody said a word. Not even the gal who'd started the whole fuss in the first place. Everybody just sat there, tapping their feet to the damned music while Jed Stark's life was dripping out of him like gas from a leaky fuel line.'

'Must be nice,' Bell muttered, 'to have friends like that.' She pushed her chair away from the desk and stood up.

Mathers gave a little snicker. 'Guys like Stark don't

have friends. Oh, they may *think* they do – they might run with some other bad boys from time to time, raising hell and sharing a bottle or a joint or both – but in the end, nobody cares about 'em. They're alone, really.' He shrugged. 'No telling how long Stark was propped up there in his seat, dead as a post, until he just tumbled out of that chair onto the floor – which musta happened shortly after you and Deputy Sturm got there.

'McCoy's being held in the Collier County Jail,' Mathers added, winding up his narrative with a *Don't that beat all* nod. 'This one'll be easy. No muss, no fuss.'

'Good. Enough on our plates around here as it is.' Bell wandered over to the window. The brown drapes were tied off on either side. She looked out through the clear glass but didn't see a thing; she was too preoccupied. How was it that you could look out a window and not see beyond your own thoughts?

'You got that right,' Mathers declared. 'But it's not all bad news, you know? Folks're already talking about Friday. Plenty excited. Might take our minds off our troubles.'

Bell, her back to the deputy, nodded. Friday was the day former West Virginia Governor Riley Jessup was scheduled to show up at the Raythune County Medical Center and – with substantial assistance close at hand, Bell hoped, given the fact that Jessup was eighty-nine years old and possessed not only a pacemaker but also two artificial hips and a catheter bag and at least a hundred more pounds than a man with his frame ought to be hauling around – climb on the back of a flatbed truck to speak at the dedication of a new MRI machine. Jessup had written the check to buy it. A great many people in town were thrilled about the visit because he was a local boy, born and raised in Raythune County. Jessup had left office decades ago and rarely returned to his homeplace, but he was still revered in these parts.

To Mathers and Bell, though, and to anyone with any connection to public safety, the governor's visit meant only one thing: extra hassle. He would have to be met, escorted, monitored, protected, catered to, fed, watered, waited on, hoisted up, helped down, ferried about, and generally fussed over. Sheriff Fogelsong would be back by then, and he'd coordinate everything, but still.

'Wouldn't it just figure,' Mathers went on, 'that we'd have the governor coming by for his little visit right in the middle of a homicide investigation? I mean – any other time, I'd be looking forward to shaking his hand, same as everybody else. But things being what they are right now – well, we're bound to be a little skittish.'

Neither Mathers nor Bell spoke for a moment; neither wanted to acknowledge out loud the bad luck that seemed like a permanent resident around here, instead of an occasional visitor. Unlike Collier County, where the civic fortunes were boosted by the presence of a metal fabrication plant just outside the county seat of Donnerton and a wholesale beauty supply shop in Swanville that shipped products to three states, Raythune County faced a bleak economic future. It had no manufacturing plants left, no industry. The men – and it was all men back then, Bell liked to remind people – who had ruled Raythune County throughout the twentieth century rarely spent any time wooing businesses; they'd been satisfied with the coal mines that kept the taxes rolling in and the trucks rolling out, staggering happily under their high-peaked loads.

Now most of those mines were shut down: Brassy-Waltham, Acer, Milltown Limited. West Virginia coal was not nearly so coveted as it once had been. The region had settled into serious decline, a decline made worse by the bad habits people developed to distract themselves from it: violence and alcohol and drugs. Bell and her two assistant prosecutors had more cases than they could comfortably handle.

'My grandpa knew Riley Jessup pretty well,' Mathers added. 'Knew him before he got so danged rich and famous, that is. Lots of folks around here remember Jessup. Look up to him, too. I've heard it said that politicians are the new celebrities. Hard to think of Riley Jessup in the same picture frame with Brad Pitt, but maybe so. Maybe so. What do you think, Mrs Elkins?'

Bell didn't answer. She reclaimed her seat at the desk. Her mind had been circling back to the events at Tommy's, and to the single nagging detail that made them interesting. 'The victim in the bar,' she said. 'Jed Stark. He had a business card on him. Deputy Sturm put anything about that in her report?'

Now Mathers pulled out his other thumb from the other side of his belt. He used the hand to which it was attached as a curved tool, answering a scratch on the back of his neck. 'Nope. Once she got the confession, she just moved on, I guess. I'll make sure I follow up, though.' He paused. 'Got a question.'

'Shoot.'

'Well.' Suddenly he felt like a daredevil, given the degree of risk. When it came to personal questions,

Bell's temper was infamous. 'None of my business, Mrs Elkins – but I gotta ask. What in the world were you doing at a place like Tommy's on a Saturday night? Don't strike me as your kinda hangout.'

'It's not.'

He waited for more. Most everyone knew about Shirley Dolan's return to Acker's Gap and the problems thereof. *Smart lawyer would've gotten her off,* a lot of people said, a lot of years later. *Right advice, she would've walked away, free as a bird,* they liked to add. *Plainly justifiable. Self-defense. Bastard had it coming. Good Lord, she shouldn't have served one damned hour, much less thirty years.* Fat lot of good those opinions did Shirley now, Bell always thought when she heard the murmurs.

Mathers had already guessed the reason for Bell's improbable presence at Tommy's, and that guess came down to one word: Shirley. Had to be. But he'd said as much as he could, daredevil or no. There was a boundary with Bell Elkins.

'Thanks for the information, Deputy,' she said. Her meaning was unmistakable: *Back off.* And so he did.

5

Between 3 and 5 A.M. on Sunday morning, the Lester station on Route 7 might as well have been the surface of Mars, for all the human activity it hosted. Two gas pumps, huddled under a yellow cone of flickering, bug-studded light, looked positively forlorn. Before three, the station could sometimes be a wild circus of action and noise, of stretched-out honking and cranked-up bass beats throbbing from open car windows; after three, there was a steep drop-off. Nobody came by.

Or almost nobody. At 3:12 A.M., a drunk woman in yellow short-shorts, red halter top, flip-flops, and a sparkly pink scarf knotted around her scrawny neck tried to walk headfirst into the glass double doors of the store that came with the station. She back-pedaled, then rammed the door again with her forehead. Confusion scrambled her features. Her hands remained at her sides; apparently she had forgotten that doors commonly had handles, and that handles required pulling.

From inside the store, standing behind the high green counter where the cash register was, backed by a towering metal rack of cigarette cartons sorted and stacked by brand, Lindy watched with dispassionate curiosity, as if the whole thing were a reality TV show. The woman's forehead bounced off the glass one more time. She raised both fists above her head and shook them in impotent fury, then mouthed two words through the glass. Lindy couldn't be sure what they were. Odds, of course, favored *Fuck you!* or *Screw you!* but the woman's lips were as loose and wobbly as the rest of her, so it was hard to say.

Jason Brinkerman, the assistant manager, was coming out of the employees-only bathroom in the back. He caught sight of the woman as she attacked the glass doors for a fourth time – she still hadn't recollected their method of operation – and he laughed.

'Don't laugh, okay?' Lindy said. 'It's not funny.'

'What a skank.' Jason grinned and waved at the woman, and stuck out his tongue, all of which infuriated their would-be visitor. She stomped her feet and glared. She looked as if she might be ready to bull her way right through the glass. Anything to get at him.

'She's drunk. Big deal,' Lindy said. They usually dealt with three or four drunks during the overnight shift. Weekends, that number could double or triple.

'Don't think she came in a car,' Jason said. The woman had wandered away now, to his disappointment. It was time to get back to work. 'Bet somebody dropped her off along the road to let her puke and then just drove away. Good riddance.'

'Get the coffee started, will you?' Lindy said. She was tired of talking about the silly woman. Her first month on the job, she'd dutifully called the sheriff's department when drunks showed up; she worried they might hurt themselves, wander out into the road, or – if they blundered into the woods – trip and roll down a ravine.

But the 911 dispatcher had set her straight: The

county couldn't send out a deputy every time a resident got herself shit-faced. *Forget it* was the advice Lindy received from the dispatcher. Not meanly, just firmly. *Have a nice evening, hon.*

Lindy and Jason got along fine. He was a year younger than she was, and he hid his admiration and affection for her behind a wall of cool. Toward the end of the shift, though, they both had a tendency to get testy and short with each other. The last hour or two seemed to last twice as long as the previous seven, Lindy often said, and Jason always agreed, shaking his head up and down so vigorously that his long brown hair flapped like a dish towel on a clothesline. Summer or winter, Jason favored an XXL flannel shirt, unbuttoned and untucked and worn over a T-shirt, plus baggy khaki shorts, and sneakers with no laces or socks. Sometimes he wore a backward Yankees cap, a blue one with the interlocking white letters *NY.*

It was Jason's job to keep the coffeepots filled. The station offered regular roast, dark roast, hazelnut, and decaf, and the four round-bottomed glass pots lived in a row of hot plates in a section set off from the rest of the store by an overhead sign: FILL 'ER UP. He also was responsible for keeping the cardboard cups in a tidy tower next to the pots. People were astonishingly sloppy with those cups, knocking over the whole stack when they tried to grab the top one and then just walking away and leaving the mess. And the lids? *Don't get me started on what those fuckers do with the lids,* Jason would say to Lindy. It was his standard lament. *Been picking them lids up off the floor for, like, my whole damned life, feels like.* Lindy knew what he meant. People were slobs. Most of them, anyway. They just didn't pay attention.

In another fifteen minutes or so, the guy who dropped off the Sunday papers would park his lopsided orange Dodge Dart in the fire lane directly in front of the building and hoist himself up and out. It was always the same guy, but Lindy didn't know his name. He'd turn his back to the glass double doors and push open one side with his butt, because he was lugging two twine-wrapped bundles, one in each hand, and then he'd turn around and fling the bundles at the front counter, not caring where they landed or what they knocked over. Just before the fling, he'd yell, 'Incoming!' and then add a spidery cackle of a laugh. Once, he knocked over a whole rack of smokeless tobacco tins and shiny foil packets. Lindy couldn't tell how old he was, but he was old. Lots older than her and Jason, for sure. No matter what the weather was like, he wore a long greasy raincoat. The acne scars on his face looked as if they'd been made with a hammer and chisel. He had the careless swagger of a teenager, the standard *You talkin' to ME?* smirk, but he also had wrinkles in his face and a sagging gut and – Lindy had spotted this right off – he walked as if his knees and his hips hurt. She knew that walk. You couldn't disguise it. It was one of the first things she'd noticed about her father, long before he retired; he walked like a man in pain – who was trying not to walk like a man in pain. Same for Newspaper Guy.

'Incoming!'

He was early. As the glass door closed behind him, Lindy moved away from the counter, in case his aim was off, as usual. The two stacks came sailing her way. He was supposed to cut the twine himself, and leave the papers in an enticing pile in front of the cash register so that when people were paying for their

44

unleaded or buying their cigarettes or their Jack Link's jerky, they'd maybe pick up a copy and drop it in front of her. *This, too.*

Typically, though, he didn't cut the twine. He'd fling and flee, barely looking at Lindy and Jason.

Which was why his behavior tonight – odd, unprecedented – put Lindy on alert. She used her Leatherman to saw through the twine, and then she put the stack of papers, headline on the top copy facing out so the customers could see it, on the counter, but she was well aware that Newspaper Guy still stood there, hands hanging at his sides. The sleeves of his raincoat, she saw, were unraveling; it was the kind of coat that even the Goodwill store over in Blythesburg would probably reject. He let his eyes take a little trip around the store. His nose was drawn to the direction of the coffeepots, where Jason was pouring the leftover regular into the decaf pot.

Like anybody'll notice the damned difference, Jason had snapped back at Lindy, the first time she caught him doing that. *All the same shit, anyway.*

Newspaper Guy twisted up his face as if he might be thinking hard about something – and it wasn't coffee. He pointed a short soiled finger at her. 'They got a way for you to contact the cops or the home office, right?' he said. 'Some kinda panic button? In case of trouble in the middle of the night? I mean, you ain't out here with no backup, right?'

'Yeah.' She didn't elaborate, because she didn't trust his sudden concern. Could be some kind of trick. She was used to fending off the clumsy advances of men like Newspaper Guy. She'd had to develop a strategy. Because – despite the fact that she thought about her looks only every six weeks or so, when

45

she got her reddish-blond hair cut over in Swanville and had to stare in the stupid mirror – Lindy was an attractive young woman. She'd had to come to terms with it. She was slender, with small hands and feet, but she had large, high-riding breasts. So unlike her mother's small bustline.

One of the last conversations she'd had with her mother embarrassed them both, but it had been necessary: 'Men'll be after you, my girl,' Margaret Crabtree said to Lindy on her fourteenth birthday. 'Don't mean to make you self-conscious, but you're growing up now, and you gotta face it. They'll stare at your chest. Some'll make rude comments. You'll have to reckon with that. Way of the world, sorry to say.' A few days later, her mother died from the ovarian cancer that had been diagnosed only two months before.

Lindy made a habit of wearing loose-fitting men's shirts and no makeup. She kept her hair cut short and she acted the part of a hard-ass, never speaking if a bored shrug or a quick noncommittal laugh would suffice. Mostly, it worked. The men who came into the station to pay for their gas or their six-packs rarely looked at her long enough to get an inkling of what might exist beneath that billowing flannel shirt. One rainy night, it was true, Jason had given her a sideways stare of peculiar intensity; she'd had to check on a pump and she came racing back inside, shirt sticking to her skin, revealing the full and perfect outline of her breasts. Jason had started to say something, and then didn't. Just looked at her. Lindy's return glare had been enough to enforce his silence. Still, she'd felt his attraction to her. She didn't want any part of it, but it was there. So far, it hadn't interfered with their working relationship.

'Okay, then,' Newspaper Guy said. He sneezed. It made Lindy want to laugh, but she didn't. He even sneezed like an old guy: His whole face wrinkled up like a used washrag, his nose scrunched to a button as he bent over at the waist, catching the residue in two scaly hands. *Gross,* Lindy thought. She wondered why he didn't just use the sleeve of his raincoat. Surely wouldn't have been the first time.

'Okay,' Newspaper Guy repeated. Looked over toward the coffee section. Jason hadn't even turned around to acknowledge his presence. 'Hey, kid. You there. I'm talking to you, too.'

Jason continued to fuss with the cups. Still didn't turn around. 'Yeah. What.'

'Just making sure you can protect this girl here,' Newspaper Guy said. 'It's important. You know what's going on, right? Out there in the dark?'

Jason made a sound, a combination of 'huh' and 'yeah' and a snickering noise in the back of his throat. Now he was playing with the little plastic tubs of nondairy creamer, building a pyramid on the coffee counter.

'I'm *talking* to you, fuckface,' Newspaper Guy went on. The agitation in his voice had ratcheted up several degrees. 'Least you can do is look me in the eye.'

Right before Lindy started to intervene – she didn't want any trouble – Jason turned. 'Okay,' he said. 'I'm looking.'

'Good.' Newspaper Guy settled down. 'Listen to me. Both of you kids. There's trouble out there. Bad trouble. Things're happening. You heard, right? Old man got attacked. His head was split wide open. Right in his own driveway. So you two better watch out.'

Jason grinned. 'Oh, yeah. We'll watch out, all right.'

47

Newspaper Guy's head whipped around. He glared at Jason. The glare was packed with such pure and earnest hate that Lindy was rattled by it, even though it wasn't directed at her.

The *ding-ding* sound startled Lindy. Someone had pulled up to the pumps outside.

Newspaper Guy took a few hectic shallow breaths. 'Okay, then,' he said. 'Long as you got a way to get help out here. You watch yourselves, hear me?'

He pushed at the glass door and departed. As soon as his decrepit orange car had coughed and swayed and grumbled away, Jason laughed. 'Crazy bastard. Yeah, we'll keep a lookout – we'll be looking out for assholes like *you*.' He laughed again.

Lindy didn't comment. From her outpost behind the counter she rose up on tiptoes, in order to see over the cardboard ramparts of Diet Pepsi and Mountain Dew twelve-packs that were stacked on both sides of the doorway. She needed to keep an eye on the customer out at the pumps. This building, though, featured glass walls, so that when she looked out into the darkness from the lighted spot, the thing she always saw first was her own reflection.

6

Deputy Mathers finally left her office. Bell looked at her watch. It was still far too early to disturb anyone for whom you had the slightest shred of affection or respect – which made it the ideal moment to call her ex-husband.

She had tried to reach him twice yesterday and once the day before. Her calls went straight to voice mail. No return call. Which wasn't a surprise: Sam Elkins believed that only losers made themselves accessible. Winners should be perennially hard to reach.

This time, he answered after three rings. 'I was getting ready to call you back, Belfa,' he said.

'Sure you were. How's Carla?'

'Not packed yet, if that's what you mean.' Sam sounded touchy and defensive, as always. 'She'll be ready by Saturday, though.'

'Are you driving her over?'

'No. Can't get away. I got her a flight into Charleston, then booked a limo from there over to Acker's Gap.'

'A *limo*? Jesus, Sam, I could've picked her up.'

'She'll enjoy it. Make her feel like a celebrity. Like Miley Cyrus.'

'Great. Just the role model I was hoping for.' Bell didn't want to argue with him about the limo. It was a ridiculous, extravagant gesture, but it was also his decision. And he could afford it, so what the hell.

When Sam spoke again, his voice was different; it had shed a bit of its edge. 'Heard about Freddie Arnett. My great-aunt Thelma called and told me. Good God. Totally unbelievable. And no suspects, right?'

'Not yet.' She didn't want to discuss it with him. There was a time when she'd looked forward to talking over her cases with Sam Elkins – but not anymore. He didn't deserve it. He'd demonstrated to her, too many times, his contempt for Acker's Gap, even though it was his hometown as well as hers.

'I'm just counting the hours,' Bell added, 'until Nick gets back.'

'Won't matter, Belfa. You know that. Nobody can stop it. The violence – it's everywhere now. People are scared as hell.'

Her ex-husband had a knack for stating the obvious as if it were an original insight. Bell waited, giving her anger a chance to dissipate. Yes, the crime rate in Acker's Gap and the surrounding vicinity was far worse than it ought to be, given the population; that was due in large part to the thriving trade in illegal prescription drugs. Sam knew the cause as well as she did. He also knew that a great many small towns in Appalachia suffered from a similar blight. But he still hinted that Acker's Gap was worse somehow, a sad, sick, pitiful little place, filled with danger and mayhem and despair. He seemed to believe that Acker's Gap was uniquely cursed. It was special, and not in the way that anybody or anything wanted to be special.

What bothered Bell most of all, of course, was the fact that these days, she was half-inclined to agree with him.

'Gotta go.' She ended the call before he did, which would, she knew, infuriate him. Sam liked to run things, liked to decide when a conversation was over, liked to be seen as the busy one forced to go because he had another call coming in or somebody waiting in his office or an appointment on tap – something, anything, that would prove his superiority. Bell knew she'd annoyed him by turning the tables; his annoyance, in turn, pleased her unduly. It was petty, sure. Pettiness, she'd discovered, was an occupational hazard when dealing with an ex-spouse. She didn't fight it anymore.

She and Sam had grown up together here, but always dreamed of leaving. And they had done just that, moving to the D.C. area after Sam's graduation from West Virginia University College of Law. Then Bell, going slowly out of her mind with boredom as a stay-at-home mom, had enrolled in law school herself, at Georgetown; shortly before graduation, she began to feel the urgent tug of home. After the divorce, she'd returned here, bought a house, made a successful run for prosecutor. Bell still didn't know – and frankly had no idea if it was ever something you *could* know with any certainty, any finality – if coming back to Acker's Gap had been the right decision. Right for her, right for Carla.

Right for Shirley.

Shirley. Bell reached down and retrieved the briefcase at her feet. She had delayed as long as possible, but now she had to go home. Home to deal with her sister. Home to try, one more time, to get Shirley to open up to her, to admit what she was feeling. To talk about all those years in prison. Or to go back even further: to talk about the night three decades ago in the ragtag trailer by Comer Creek, when everything changed. Each time Bell tried to persuade Shirley to confide in her, to have a real conversation about real things, her sister had put her off. *Later,* Shirley would say. *Real tired right now. Gonna take myself a little nap. That okay with you?* Which meant that Bell still didn't know – she could guess, of course, but guessing wasn't the same as knowing, and she needed to hear Shirley say the words – why her sister had broken off contact with her all those years ago, why she had sent back Bell's letters without opening them, why she had refused Bell's visits and phone calls.

Why. Why. Why. Sometimes it still could drive Bell crazy, her sister's boarded-up face and silent stare when the conversation turned to the past. But Bell would keep trying. She had to. The past, she'd decided, was like one of those stumbling, dead-eyed creatures in a zombie movie, the kind that Carla and her friends loved and dreaded in equal measure: You could pretend to ignore it, you could try to bury it, but it wouldn't stay in the grave. It always came back – stronger each time, and in a meaner mood. Aware of its power.

Bell locked her office door. The courthouse was closed to the public on Sundays; hence, the corridor was empty. Her steps sounded like a series of crisp earnest smacks. Back when Carla still lived in Acker's Gap, back when she was twelve and thirteen years old, she'd accompany her mother here on weekends, and while Bell worked at her desk, Carla would race up and down the long empty halls, arms outstretched, swooping and turning and relishing the clacking cascade of echoes.

Bell pushed open one side of the heavy courthouse

doors. She paused on the threshold. By now the sun's face had popped beyond the top of the mountain, a familiar but still spectacular sight.

Darkness gathered at her back, forming the cool shadows in the long main corridor of the courthouse, but in front of her, the light spread itself evenly across sidewalks and storefronts, across bricks and picture windows and lampposts and rooftops. The same elements that she had been seeing – save for her years away at college and her brief time in D.C. – for her entire life. Forty years. Sometimes that sameness exasperated her, because nothing ever changed around here; other times, it gave her solace. And no matter how it seemed, Acker's Gap did indeed change. Too much. A terrible explosion in the spring, a drug-related triple homicide the year before, a murder two nights ago and another one just down the road from it: Acker's Gap had joined the world, and all portions of the world were connected now, the moving parts of a volatile whole. The town Bell saw from the courthouse doorway this morning was sun-glazed, shadow-striped, a cupped hand that offered up an unknown share of future trouble, but right now, it looked calm and drowsy and benign. Heat rapidly stacked up in the deserted blocks.

Not entirely deserted: Her gaze was caught by a small black dog of indeterminate breed, trotting along on the other side of the street. His graying face wore the wise contemplative expression in which old dogs specialized, that look of universal tolerance and patience. Seeing the rich oily sheen on the dog's lean flank made Bell feel even hotter.

She had many things on her mind, but the murder of Freddie Arnett was foremost in the mix. The crime seemed incongruous, coming as it did in summer. Winter seemed by far the more likely season for evil. Winter with its early-onset darkness, its stranglehold grip of cold, its icy malice. Summer was too bright, too amiable, too easy-going for anything mendacious to have dominion. Everything was right out here in the open, simple and guileless.

But she knew that wasn't really true. There was nothing innocent about summer. Nothing soft or simple. The notion that summer held no peril had been exposed, two nights ago, as a cruel and dangerous illusion.

Abruptly, Bell changed her mind. She wouldn't go home to Shirley just yet. She had one more stop to make first.

7

The small living room had a buttoned-up, desert-dry, closed-in feel. The drapes, delicate and diaphanous as pink tissue paper and faintly printed with the repeating shapes of roses, were shut, yet they only marginally impeded the sunlight and its attendant heat. From the clock on the weathered white mantel came a regular series of ticks that sounded less like time passing and more like the work of a small pickax as it tunneled through an impossibly large slab of some impossibly hard material; there was an endlessness embedded in the rhythm, and a hopelessness, too.

The old woman sat in the straight-backed wooden chair. She wore a gray linen dress that might once have fit, but now swallowed her up. Her vacant eyes were an almost translucent shade of blue; her cheeks were markedly hollow, falling back into her face. Her long white hair was parted in the middle. It broke across her bony shoulders like water split by a rock.

'Yes?' she said in a shaky voice. She seemed more befuddled than distraught. After she spoke, her eyes returned to a resting position on the frayed brown carpet. In multiple spots, the carpet had worn almost all the way through to the hardwood beneath.

Bell introduced herself for the second time. She was

sitting on the blue plaid couch across from Annie
Arnett, notebook on her lap. Even though it was still
early in the morning, Bell could feel the sweat starting
up in the crooks of her elbows and behind her knees.
Few of the older homes in Acker's Gap were air-
conditioned. They relied on screen doors and open
windows and the casual mercy of a cross breeze.

'I see.' Annie Arnett nodded. She folded and then
refolded her hands. The plump blue veins on the tops
of them looked like centipedes inserted under the skin.
'Well.'

Bell wondered if the old woman had forgotten the
question, the one Bell had asked right after identifying
herself when Annie opened the front door: 'How much
money did you and your husband routinely keep in
the house?' If the answer was anything over ten dollars,
Bell's next question would be: *And how many people
knew about it?*

But Annie was still stuck. She continued to gaze at
Bell. 'Who did you say you were, dearie?'

It had to come down to money. Most crimes eventually did – at least if they didn't come down to sex or
jealousy, which seemed unlikely in the case of Freddie
and Annie Arnett, both of whom had passed eighty a
good while back. And in Acker's Gap, 'money' didn't
have to mean millions. It didn't even have to mean
hundreds. For the desperate people in these parts,
twenty dollars was incentive enough to kill.

There were serious problems with Bell's theory. For
one thing, Rhonda Lovejoy had already come by and
asked the old woman the same question. Moreover,
the perpetrator hadn't taken Freddie Arnett's wallet
or tried to enter the house after murdering him, so
the robbery motive was implausible. Still, Bell had

felt an irresistible impulse – an itch that packed the same kind of fierce drawing power, she speculated, as the promise of a couple of bucks did to an addict – to visit Annie Arnett and ask again. To make sure they weren't missing something. Or someone.

'Your grandson,' Bell said. 'The one Freddie was fixing the car for. Maybe you told him that you keep money in the house. Just mentioned it in passing a few times. Or maybe just one time. And maybe he told a friend.'

Annie blinked. 'No, I don't think so, dearie,' she said. 'We don't talk much to Tommy anymore. Not since they all left town. We don't like to bother him. And we know he's too busy to call.'

Bell remembered that from Rhonda's notes. The rest of the family – Annie's and Freddie's son, Luke, and Luke's sons, Tommy and Mike – had moved away. Better jobs, bigger cities. Different skies. It was just Annie and Freddie, still here in Acker's Gap.

Now, it was just Annie.

'Is your son staying with you?' Bell said. 'Luke's his name, right?'

Surely someone was helping Annie Arnett get through this. The old woman shouldn't be alone. Her husband had been savagely attacked just a few days ago, and grisly reminders of his death were everywhere: The crime-scene techs from Charleston had finished their work but the driveway still was cordoned off with plastic yellow tape. An evocative dark stain remained on the concrete, baked into the gray by the fierce unrelenting sunlight. That sun, Bell recalled from Rhonda's report, was the reason Freddie Arnett had been working on the Thunderbird so late at night; it was too hot during the day. The chrome on a car could raise a blister if you touched it at the wrong time.

'Oh, Luke was here Friday,' Annie said. 'All day, or thereabouts. But he had to go back to Louisville. Couldn't take any more time off work. He'll be back next week, he said. To pick up the car for Tommy.'

Bell looked around. 'But somebody's staying with you, right?'

'Oh, my, yes.' Before Bell could ask, Annie added, 'Rhonda Lovejoy. I've known her family for ages. She's been spending the night. Ain't that sweet? She came by here to ask me some questions the other day, same as you are now, and when I told her how scared I get at night, with Freddie gone, she said she'd be pleased to keep me company. I'm so happy to have her. Till Freddie gets back.'

Bell thought about her assistant, whose roots in Raythune County ran deep and true, and who had an everlasting compassion for the people who walked these roads. As an employee, Rhonda could be infuriatingly scatterbrained, and her flamboyant wardrobe carried more than a hint of the bordello with its frills and its flounces, but Bell had come to have a significant appreciation for Rhonda Lovejoy, sequins and all.

She wouldn't tell Rhonda that she knew. That wasn't how things were done around here. A kind gesture wasn't undertaken to get a pat on the back. Charity that brought you compliments wasn't charity; it was public relations.

A thought occurred to Bell. 'Excuse me, Mrs Arnett. Did you say, "Till Freddie gets back"?'

Annie nodded. 'Don't know what's keeping him. Never been gone this long before.' She sighed, but it was a sigh of affection. 'Keeps me guessing, that man of mine. He's a handful. Gonna give him a good talking-to when he walks through that door, tell you that for sure.'

Bell paused at the end of the driveway. A ribbon of tape had worked itself loose from one of the green metal stakes and fallen across the concrete. Now it lay there, looking as flat and sad and useless as the tail of a grounded kite. There was no breeze to rouse it. There was only heat, the kind of dense, hard-packed heat that presses on the skin everywhere all at once.

The neighborhood was quiet. Strange for a blue-skied summer Sunday, Bell thought. Where were the kids, the dogs, the bikes, the shouts and the clatter? Maybe it was still too early in the day. Or maybe – and this was a thought that pained her – a lot of people were staying indoors, pinned there by the shock of their neighbor's fate. Up and down the tattered little street her gaze made its fitful way, seeing closed doors and silent yards and windows across which the curtains had been yanked shut. It was temporary, Bell told herself. Had to be. The street would come to life again.

She looked back at the driveway. This was where Freddie Arnett had died – here on a strip of concrete next to his small brown stick-frame house. This was the house in which Freddie and Annie Arnett had lived for sixty-two years. Freddie had left here every morning, long before the sun came up, for his shift at the Milltown Mine No. 12. He would return long after that sun had gone down. And he worked underground, so as far as Freddie was concerned, there might as well not have been a sun at all. Until he retired, the single prevailing truth of his world was darkness.

Freddie's long white Silverado truck was still parked in front of the house. He always parked it there, leaving the driveway free as a workspace for his loving labors on the Thunderbird, which he kept at the upper end of the concrete slab, next to the house. The high polish on the Thunderbird's tubular flanks gave it a sleek, missile-like look. You could tell how much Freddie Arnett loved this car, how much he'd fussed over it, gushed over it, pampered it; it had been unconditionally adored. Same was true for his grandson, Bell guessed. She knew how tempting it was to give everything to a beloved child, to make any sacrifice. It wasn't always the right thing to do – it was almost never the right thing to do – but you did it, anyway. Couldn't help yourself.

'Okay, old man,' Bell murmured. Even if someone had been standing right next to her, they couldn't have made out the words; her voice was soft and filled with grim wonder. 'What happened here? Who the hell did this to you – and why?'

It took her a moment to realize that she was talking to the dead. And another moment to realize that it didn't bother her one bit.

8

Shirley shuffled into the living room. She parked her backside on the couch, the bony knees of her faded Wranglers jutting out in front of her. She'd been up in her room when Bell called her name. Quickly, she lit a cigarette and took a series of vicious nips at it, as if she'd been warned that somebody might grab it away from her at any minute and so she had to get what she could, while she could.

'You been gone a long time,' Shirley said.

Bell shrugged. 'Work to do.' She felt an unpleasant twinge of remembrance; Carla had said the very same thing to her, back when her daughter still lived here. On more than a few occasions. Pointed out that, no matter what was going on with her family, Bell's job came first. And it was usually true.

She was certain that her sister hadn't slept since she dropped her off. Shirley was wearing the same clothes she'd been wearing when she left the house three days before: same jeans, same flannel shirt. She hadn't opened the curtains or raised the blinds. In the dim half-light of the dark-walled room, the skin on Shirley's face and neck and hands was a gray-yellow shade; it was coarse, too, stretched taut in some places, loose-hanging in others.

'Did you get something to eat?' Bell said. The anger that she'd felt at Tommy's six hours ago when she first spotted Shirley – anger that consumed her, like fire racing across paper, turning it to ash in an instant – had faded. It happened over and over again, just like that: Time passed, and her fury at her sister's behavior surged, crested, and then retreated again into a quiet lake of sadness. Bell was slammed back and forth between rage and forgiveness a thousand times a day.

A thousand and one.

She sat down across from Shirley in the battered old chair. It was her favorite piece of furniture; its comfort was uncomplicated, utterly reliable. She'd be needing that comfort for this conversation. She could tell from Shirley's sour face that her sister was still brooding. *Like she has any right to be mad at* me, Bell thought. *Like* she's *the injured party here. Go figure.*

'Yeah,' Shirley said. 'I'm good.'

She was lying, and Bell knew it. Her sister ate very little these days. And when she did eat, the meals generally came from McDonald's, Pizza Hut, KFC. Or consisted of shiny-packaged snacks from convenience stores: Doritos, mini-doughnuts, Little Debbies. Bell was a reluctant cook, but she tried to bring Shirley decent dinners from JP's: chicken, fish, green beans, steamed broccoli. The next morning, Bell would find the white Styrofoam shell wedged in the kitchen trash, the food inside looking just the way it looked when Jackie LeFevre, owner and operator of JP's, had put it there with a spatula and two fingers. Shirley had tossed the meal without tasting it. Hell, she probably hadn't even opened the container.

'How do you feel?' Bell asked. Trying to get along. Setting a cordial tone so that they might have a decent conversation. For once. 'If you want to rest a little, we can talk later.'

'Don't matter.'

Bell let some silence build up in the room. She hoped her sister might say something – anything – that would give Bell a clue about what she was feeling these days. And why she seemed determined to sabotage any attempts to make smooth her reentry into life outside of prison.

'He confessed,' Bell finally said. 'The guy from last night. He's in jail. It was a fight over a woman. Just like you said.'

'Figures.' Shirley's hand twitched. She looked around suspiciously, having noticed that the objects on top of the coffee table had been rearranged. 'Where's the ashtray? Forget it. I'll just go outside.'

'No, hold on.' Bell didn't want her sister to get up. Didn't want another conversation between them to end prematurely, cut off by some dumb excuse. So she rose, retrieved it from the kitchen, returned. 'Just put it in the dishwasher yesterday. Tidying up.' She set down the square glass ashtray, reuniting it with the pack of Pall Malls and the green plastic Bic lighter that seemed to have taken up permanent residence here, at least when they weren't shoved in the breast pocket of Shirley's flannel shirt.

'So,' Bell said. 'We need to get a few things straight, okay? I mean, I've tried to be patient. Tried to give you your space. But after last night – well, there've got to be some changes. Some give and take.'

No response, so Bell went on. 'I'm not asking for a lot here, Shirley. Just some regular hours. And a better attitude. Carla's coming, okay? And like it or not, you'll be setting an example. I need to know where you are at night. And the job search – how's it going?'

Shirley scowled. 'How do you think it's going? World's just dying to hire somebody with a record.'

'You're getting help, though, right? From your parole officer? With résumé writing, job-placement assistance, things like that?'

'Yeah. Things like that.' Shirley, restless, shifted her feet. 'You know what, Belfa? After they found that old fart in his driveway, I got a call from my PO. Asking where I was. Asking if I could account for my where-abouts that night. Asking if I had witnesses. Thank God I did.'

'It wasn't personal.' Bell had known that call was coming. She hadn't interfered, realizing that it was better for Shirley in the long run if she didn't. 'Standard procedure. With your felony conviction, he's required to—'

'Yeah. Standard procedure to make me feel like a friggin' criminal.'

'I know it's hard.'

The scowl intensified. Shirley triple-tapped her cigar-ette in the vicinity of the ashtray. 'Anyway,' she said, 'I got a job.'

'You did?'

'Yeah. You're surprised, right? Nice. Real nice. Appreciate that.'

Bell ignored the sarcasm. Kept moving forward. 'When do you start?'

'Already started.'

'Then where—?'

'It's not some lame-ass thing at a fast food place, okay? It's not flipping burgers.' A cold, knowing stare.

'Which is what you were thinking, right? 'Cause that's about all you expect from me. That's, like, the upper limit of my abilities, right?'

'I'm happy for you, Shirley. I just want to—'

'It's not a regular kind of job. It's special.' Shirley scratched at the faded denim fabric that covered her right knee, picking at it, the way you'd bother a scab. She didn't look at Bell when she spoke. 'I'm managing a band, okay? Getting some gigs lined up. Putting together a YouTube video. You heard 'em the other night. Bobo Bolland. Been around awhile, but this is a fresh start. He writes these great songs. The kind you remember. The kind that get under your skin, you know? I think he's got a shot. This could be big. Really, really big.'

Bell struggled to keep the disappointment out of her voice. 'You don't know anything about managing a band,' she said quietly. 'Do you?'

Shirley abruptly bolted forward in her seat, as if a few thousand volts had just been delivered to her extremities. Her head bobbed up and down. 'See? You see? I *knew* it,' she said, looking around the room, mumbling her umbrage to invisible witnesses. 'I knew you'd try to piss all over it. That's why I didn't tell you.'

'I'm just asking—'

'You're trying to take care of me. Like I'm a baby or something. And you know what, Belfa? *I don't want your fucking help anymore.* Okay? Got it? Got that straight? I have to be in this house right now – my PO says so – but the second I don't, the second I'm back on my feet, I'm outta here. Got it?'

Shirley lit another cigarette and flopped back against the couch cushion. She'd had a hard time holding the lighter still enough for it to meet up with the end of the cigarette.

Bell waited. Whatever she said right now would be misconstrued. Whatever she did would be wrong.

It was her sister who broke the raggedy-edged silence.

'You know what?' Shirley said.

'What?' Bell replied. She said it cautiously, warily, expecting another jab.

But Shirley was smiling now. A real smile, not a bitter, ironic one. Her mood suddenly shifted; her voice was back to normal. It was as if the last few minutes hadn't happened. Just that fast, Shirley was a different person. Ever since she'd come back into Bell's life, she had exhibited these out-of-the-blue turnarounds. Bell found them a little unnerving – they were too much like her own quicksilver switches from rage to sympathy – but she'd learned not to look surprised. Hell. Maybe it was genetic.

'When you were a little kid,' Shirley said, voice warming, 'you'd cry up a storm sometimes. Not for any reason. You'd just cry to be crying, I guess. Daddy'd go crazy. Tell me to shut you up or else. So I'd take you outside, night or day, and try to distract you. Daytime, it worked okay – you'd see a bird or a flower, some shit like that, and you'd start pointing and get all excited and stop the blubbering. But nighttime, it was harder. Nothing to see. And you'd just be screaming and throwing yourself around. Daddy said that if you didn't shut your mouth pretty damn quick, he was going to shut it for you.' Shirley winced. 'And he'd do it, too. You bet your ass he would.'

'I don't remember.'

'Course you don't. You were two, three years old. Just a baby.'

'So what did you do?'

Shirley took a minute to lift the cigarette off her lip. Her hand trembled. She aimed a jet of exhaled smoke at the ceiling. Even after the smoke had dissipated, she kept her chin tilted up; her eyes stayed on the ceiling, as if crucial parts of her story had fled there a long time ago for safekeeping, and she was reading sentences – crafted in a private language knowable only by her – right off the uniform swirls of faded white paint.

She lowered her face. Looked at Bell, still smiling. 'There was this time once in the summer,' she said. 'I took you down by the creek. Being summer and all, it was real hot at night, just like now. Thought it might settle you down. Oh, you were *real* upset that night – screaming and crying. Man, you were something. Worse'n a siren. Daddy was more pissed than ever. Royally, royally pissed. He was back in the trailer but he could still hear you – hell yeah, he could still hear you! – so he came charging out and then he went right down to the creek after us and he hollered, "I told you to shut her up! Give her whatever the hell she wants – just get her to shut her fucking mouth!" I said, "I can't." And he said, "What the hell? I told you to give her whatever she damned well wants!" And I said, "I *can't*." Now, at this point he's ready to haul off and hit me. So I explain it to him.'

'Explain what?'

Shirley took her time before speaking, enjoying the memory before she shared it, letting it wash all over her like a cat's tongue, both rough and smooth.

'I told him,' Shirley said, 'how you'd seen the moon in the creek – the reflection of the moon on the top of the water – and that's what you wanted. The moon. You kept on reaching for it, reaching and reaching, trying to touch it, and when you couldn't, you were so mad that all you could do was scream.'

'The moon.'

'Yeah.'

'Guess I was a real dumb-ass, right?' Bell said. A rueful wince. 'Even at three.'

'You knew what you wanted. And just because you couldn't have it – well, that didn't mean you didn't still want it with all your heart, you know? I carried you back inside, but if I hadn't, I swear you'd still be down there today, trying to get at that damn moon.' Bemused smile. 'Lord, you were stubborn.'

For a moment, neither spoke. There was so much Bell wanted to explain to her sister, so many important points she needed to make, so many questions she still had to ask. Things were going to have to change in this house, and change fast, because Carla was coming, and Bell couldn't allow Shirley to go on this way – wild, reckless, unreliable. She had to make her see. There was a violent criminal in the area, someone who hadn't hesitated to take a sledgehammer to an old man's head, and she knew that her sister and her daughter were at risk, just as everyone was at risk, always.

Those were the things that Bell needed to say to Shirley, and to say urgently: *Be alert. Stay on the main roads. Don't take chances.* And more. There was always more to say.

But right now, here in this dim room early on a summer morning, Bell was silent for a little while longer, feeling the ponderous yet somehow not burdensome presence of the past as it weighed down her thoughts, blocking everything coming in or going out, the stopper in the bottle, the stone at the mouth of the cave.

9

When her shift ended at 7 A.M., Lindy didn't much like to drive home. She liked being finished with work, of course. But she dreaded the moment each morning when she had to turn off the highway and bump down the county road and then make a right-hand turn at the rock-dinged red mailbox marked CRABTREE and see, once again, the ugly house set back in a snarl of old trees, reachable only by this dirt lane that kept visitors away more reliably than a NO TRESPASSING sign. Perry Crum often gave her grief about the decrepit road that ran back here, telling her she deserved better. 'One of these days,' he'd add, 'this here mail truck's just gonna disappear in one of them big ruts, taking a couple of big boxes of these books of yours along with it.' She knew he wasn't serious, so she'd just smile and shrug her narrow shoulders. Besides, there wasn't much she could do about it. Not about the road, and not about the house, either.

The gray paint on its wood sides was peeling so badly that it resembled a skin disease. The roof leaked, and one look could tell you why: At least a third of the shingles were split or rotting and needed to be replaced. Shingles worked themselves loose at regular intervals, exposing the wavy black swaths of warped

tar paper beneath. Lindy knew she'd eventually have
to hire somebody to come by and put on a new roof,
but delayed for two reasons: money and company.
She didn't have the first, and she didn't want the
second.

She parked on the left side of the house, on a
concrete pad that she had installed herself. She'd
done it last summer. First she had cleared out a
rectangular space that was roughly the size of her
car, digging down about two inches, and then she
leveled the dirt foundation. She bought thirty-seven
bags of Quikrete. Found her father's old red wheelbarrow, its sides so badly rusted that in some spots
you could poke your finger clear through, and she
mixed batch after batch after batch, stirring the thick
gray clotted stuff with the wood-handled shovel she'd
seen her father use so many times on tasks around
the house – projects he'd done a long time ago, before
everything changed. The wheelbarrow held itself
together just long enough for her to finish the job.
Not a minute longer. Just as she was winding it up,
just as she was using the shovel tip to poke and
scrape the last gooey bits of the last bag of watered-
down Quikrete out of a corner of the wheelbarrow,
the whole thing kind of disintegrated, the fragile
filigree of its rusty sides collapsing in on themselves,
red flakes showering the ground. It was almost as if
the wheelbarrow knew it was the right time to go,
like an old, sick animal that wanders off into the
woods to die.

The pad worked fine. It wasn't perfect, because she
hadn't leveled it out right, and so it slanted significantly
toward the house, not to mention the neuron-like
sprawl of cracks that inched a little farther across the

surface each time she checked. But it did the job. She had an easier time getting her car out in the winter, when the snow piled up and then froze into solid, thigh-high walls, impossible to knock down or burrow through. With the parking pad, she had a fighting chance; she could clear the snow as it fell, and then get traction – a clean running start – when she tackled the path that led out to the county road. Winter before last, she'd been trapped at home for three days before the big thaw came. She liked the quiet it brought – no cars went by until the county cleared the roads, and Lindy had lots to read, and the district manager for the Lester chain called and told her not to worry about getting to work until it was safe to do so – but she still decided, then and there, to build the pad as soon as rising temperatures made it possible. Not for that winter, but for the next one. *Think ahead:* That was her father's motto. Or had been. When Perry Crum first saw the pad, he bowed low and said, 'On behalf of my van and its axles, I salute you.' They both laughed.

Two days after she'd finished the pad, her father had one of his good days. Part of one, anyway. The clouds cleared out of his brain. He stood on the porch and he nodded. 'Nice job, my girl,' he said. 'You're good with your hands, and that'll do well for you. Long as you can use your hands, you'll never lack for work to do or a place to live.' Just a few hours later, the clouds came back, and when Lindy tried to talk to him about undertaking another project around the house, he roared at her, waving his arms and telling her to go to hell. There was no recognition of her in his eyes. No light.

It was an ugly house, but once she was inside,

Lindy didn't notice that anymore. She closed the front door behind her and immediately felt a simple, familiar wash of relief. Of satisfaction. And, on a still more fundamental level, of peace. This was her space, filled with her books. She knew what she'd find around every corner. There was a meager living room, a skimpy kitchen, a ratty bathroom dominated by a cast-iron tub with rust stains that flared dramatically around the drain, and two minuscule bedrooms, which Lindy had combined into one. Her father didn't need a bedroom on the first floor anymore. Besides, the two bedrooms had originally been one room, anyway.

Her father had put up the wall when Lindy was eight years old. She remembered that day, remembered him setting the studs and then screwing in the Sheetrock and applying drywall tape to the seams, talking to her the whole time, narrating his actions, and even though she hadn't been able to comprehend much of what he was saying, she loved listening to him anyway, absorbing a wisdom that was beyond her years, because wisdom was wisdom, whether you understood it or not. It got into your bones, howsoever it could. Found its own way in, her daddy liked to say. And then one day, when you were old enough to use what you knew, you realized all the knowledge that was already there inside you, waiting.

Her father was a good teacher, except when he lost his temper, which he did one afternoon when they were almost finished with the wall. She was watching him countersink a nail. 'How come,' she asked, 'you didn't have any more kids? Why'd you just have me?' He was facing the wall. He stopped what he was doing, but didn't turn around. 'Don't you worry 'bout that,' he said, and it came out hard, as did his next sentence: 'You mind your own damned business, girlie.' He grunted. A few minutes later, he turned around and rubbed the top of her head. His way of apologizing, without having to say the words. Words were difficult for him, then and now.

Lindy kicked off her shoes and dropped down on the couch, sinking into the flaccid cushions. She had two days off, and she knew precisely how she'd spend the time: reading. She wasn't sleepy, even though she'd been up all night.

Just before she'd driven away from the station that morning, Jason Brinkerman sidled up to her car, right next to the driver's-side window that she'd rolled down to let out the accumulated hot air. Jason didn't have a car. His brother Eddie usually picked him up after his shift.

'You want to, like, go get some breakfast, maybe?' Jason said. Acting casual. But Lindy knew better than that. 'Eddie can drop me off,' Jason went on. 'I mean – like, he don't have to come along or nothing.' He used the long tail of his flannel shirt to rub at a spot on the door of her car. Killing time. Cool. Like it didn't matter to him, one way or another, if she accepted or not.

'Nope. Got things to do.' She, too, kept her voice casual, so that it didn't reflect what she really felt: *No freakin' way*. It wasn't that she disliked Jason; she had no strong opinion of him at all, pro or con. He was a coworker. That was all. She'd barely spoken to him back in Acker's Gap High School.

Hell. She'd barely spoken to anybody.

'Okay,' he said. 'Later.'

'Yeah. Later.'

And then she backed up and drove away, lifting her eyes to the rearview mirror only once, and then only for an instant, because she knew he'd be watching to see if she did just that: looked back at him. Even a glance might encourage him. Give him hope. She'd met his brother, knew a little bit about his family – you couldn't live your whole danged life around here and *not* know somebody's family – and so she knew that Jason came from a rough bunch of people. Emotionally, he was fed on scraps, and then told he ought to be full.

Things had been a little easier between her and Jason, more relaxed, before the stunt he pulled last fall. Out of the blue, he showed up at her house one afternoon. No notice. No warning. She was in the kitchen, stirring a can of Campbell's tomato soup and a cup of water in a pan on the one gas burner that still worked, and she heard the knock.

'Hey,' he'd said.

He stood on the wooden porch, grinning a nervous grin. Holding, rather than wearing, his Yankees baseball cap. Thumbs on the visor, flapping the cap up and down, as if he were fanning his knees.

Lindy had stared at him. Her hand was gripping the doorknob so hard that her wrist hurt.

'What is it?' she said, thinking that maybe something had gone wrong at the station, but also wondering why the hell he hadn't just called or texted her. *Jesus.* She was really, really pissed, but she didn't want to show too much emotion. That would mean she cared.

'Got my brother's car today,' Jason had said. 'Thought you might wanna go for a ride or something.'

Anger moved through her in a long shuddering ripple, so intense that she worried it might show on the outside. 'No,' she said. 'I don't.' She had refashioned her grip on the doorknob. 'Kinda busy now, okay?'

What she'd wanted to say was: *Don't you ever,* ever *do this again. Don't you ever come by like this. Never.* But she didn't. Anything other than a preoccupied dismissal was a bad idea; a passionate reaction was just what he was after.

'Okay,' he'd said. Still pinching the visor with his fingers, he flapped the cap up and down a few more times. The goofy grin continued. Then it slipped off his face, as if he'd suddenly become aware of it. He had one more thing to say: 'Listen. I got a question.'

He was stalling. Buying time, so she wouldn't shut the door. He was trying to think of something to ask her, to keep the moment going.

'Make it fast, Jason,' she said. 'I gotta go. Like I said.'

He nodded. Moved his jaw around a few times, in a circle. He had a wad of gum in his mouth, she saw, or maybe it was smokeless tobacco. Probably the latter. Almost every guy in her senior class had the telltale circle imprinted on the right rear pocket of his Wranglers. The exact circumference of the Skoal tin that he stored there.

'Okay,' Jason said. 'It's about your name. Been meaning to ask. It's short for Linda, right? Or Lindsay? Something like that.'

'No. Short for Lindbergh.'

'Like Charles Lindbergh? The pilot guy?'

'Like Anne Morrow Lindbergh. The writer.'

Jason shrugged. 'Never heard of her.'

'Big surprise.' That was mean, which was something Lindy didn't like to be. 'You're close, though,' she added. Her tone was milder, more amiable, to make up for the sarcasm. 'She was his wife. My mother's favorite writer.' Lindy jiggled the doorknob. 'See you at work, okay?'

She could still remember watching him as he trudged back to his brother's car, shirttail hanging way past his butt. He whacked the cap against his right thigh in rhythm with his steps. He'd probably had to pay his brother to borrow the car. Probably cost him at least a week's salary. Eddie Brinkerman was a big jerk. Everybody knew that.

Lindy sat on the couch now and thought about Jason's face, the way it had looked that day at her front door: big round chin, skin energetically colonized by red pimples, small eyes, black wispy loops and dabs of hair where sideburns ought to be, and a strained look overall, a kind of yearning, which all the false bravado in the world couldn't cover up.

She heard the sound. She stood up from the couch.

It came from the basement. Right? That's what it seemed like, anyway.

Usually she checked on her father first thing, immediately after her arrival home, in case something had happened to him while she was gone overnight. But not today. Today, she'd been distracted by her encounter back at the station with Jason Brinkerman – and, granted, she'd been a little bit lazy, dumping her butt on the damned couch before looking in on her father, wandering in a mental thicket of the past. *My bad,* Lindy scolded herself. *Better make sure.*

She opened the basement door.

Darkness stared back at her. The mustiness came

up in a rush, the same stale smell of earth and dirt and dead insects that kindled in every ancient cellar, but this one was spiced with something else, too. Something extra. Something *other:* a clammy cold, a closed-in, folded-over, cutoff cold, a nowhere kind of cold, a cold that no amount of summer heat could ever dispel. She hated opening this door. She didn't mind it when he came upstairs, but she hated opening this door.

'Daddy?'

There was a rattling sound, a sound like dry branches being dragged rapidly across hard-packed dirt. Like a series of tense whispers or hopeless sighs. Plaintive and shadowy, half-real, half-imagined. Her father sometimes liked to cramble around the space with a dirty blanket flung over his shoulders; when he bumped the basement walls, the fabric rubbed against the rugged surface, making a scratchy sound, a sound that clawed at Lindy's conscience even when she wasn't hearing it for real.

'Daddy?' she repeated.

'Shut the goddamned door.' His voice was hoarse and ugly, a blunt bitter jab. It was filled with haste and anger.

'I'm home now. Just wanted to see if—'

'*I said shut that goddamned door or I'll come up there and rip your goddamned face off.*' He almost screamed it. The thrust and rush of his voice made her flinch, even though this was nothing new, even though his was an impersonal rage. He'd been like this before. Many times. The cursing had accompanied his decline; in the time before, she'd rarely heard him utter a profanity. Never, in front of her mother. But now his language was foul, clotted with obscenities, as if he'd reached into a muddy hole and pulled out the dark wet roots of the nice regular words, discovered their dirty hidden origin. As if he'd tunneled to the secret end of language, blindly fingering its rotten, burnt-out, dead-smelling, joyless core, and now insisted on bringing the rancid bounty to her attention as often as he could, shaking the dangling, dirt-caked clumps in her face: *Here. Get a load of* this, *girlie.*

She closed the basement door.

She looked around the kitchen. The summer Sunday morning was still here, still intact, no matter what was going on in the basement. Sunshine skittered in through the red-and-white-checked curtains that trimmed the window over the sink. Her mother had made these curtains by hand many years ago, and they were threadbare by now, thinned by time and by repeated washings, so insubstantial that they blocked little of the light. But Lindy would never replace them. Never.

He's okay, she told herself. *He made it through the night. It's all fine.* She turned. Her books were stacked on the table, right where she'd left them, next to the pile of mail. The sight of them steadied her.

Her eyes fell to the floor just inside the back door. She didn't go in and out of the house that way, because the backyard was a mess; it was too slanted, too cluttered with rocks, too shaded by a gnarled congress of old bent trees. Grass never had a chance to take hold. In the summer, it turned into a dust-choked desert, except on rainy days, and then it became a swamp. So when she saw the filthy outline of a footprint on the floor – she knew the print of his boot, knew the size and the shape, knew the distance between the ridges – the realization knocked her back, filling her with surprise and dread:

Her father had gone out last night. He was at it again.

10

Sunrise was still a ways away, but Charlie Frank didn't mind. He wasn't afraid of darkness. He liked it. His habit was to walk along the road every morning before the sun came up, hands in his trouser pockets, humming a hymn – the selections varied, but he was decidedly partial to 'In the Garden' – and relishing the fact that he didn't need any lights to guide him. He knew his way in the world – this world, at least – without the constant interruption of light. Light was a crutch. A sure sign of weakness. There were too many damned lights in the world, anyway, too many spotlights illuminating too many things that weren't worth seeing: stupid billboards out on the interstate or signs telling you route names and numbers. If you didn't already know where you were and where you were going, then you had no business being out in these parts in the first place. And you didn't want to get him started on vehicle headlights, the bright kind, the kind that splashed up in your eyes like acid. When cars and trucks came along this road, Charlie had to wince and throw up an arm to keep from being blinded. *Damned lights,* he'd mutter. *Lord have mercy.*

His mother liked him to keep all the lights on in the house, all night long. And he complied, because it was important to her. But if he'd had his way, he would have unscrewed every durned lightbulb in the whole durned place; come sundown, he'd settle into his chair in the precious dark and put his head back and breathe easy. Maybe, if he lived alone, he'd go off the grid entirely. Just get himself a generator for heat and cooking.

But his mother wanted light, lots of light, and so for now, that was that. He'd never go against her. No telling how long she had left; one doctor said one thing, another doctor said another. And a third one said a third thing. All Charlie knew for sure was that Martha Frank was growing weaker by the day, and eating was getting harder and harder for her, and you didn't have to be a doctor with a fancy degree to know what happened when somebody couldn't eat anymore.

He found his solace in walking. Walking in the dark. For Charlie Frank, walking and thinking went together, just as one step follows another. This was when and where he did his best thinking: along Godown Road in Raythune County, in the time before the sun came up over the top of the mountain – at which point everything changed, and not for the better. All that light! It was as if somebody had suddenly started banging the bottom of a saucepan with an old metal spoon, banging and yelling, demanding that attention be paid. The sun's arrival was showy and brassy, disturbing the peace of the great dark world. Charlie much preferred the world as it was right now: drizzled with darkness, edges dissolved, no shape more important than any other shape.

He had lived here for his entire life. Never thought of living anywhere else. But after his mother died, he would be free. That was what some people – including his brother, Wally – had already pointed out to him when they visited, speaking in low tones, shaking their heads gravely, keeping an eye on his mother across the room, his twisted-up, long-suffering mother. They meant well. They truly did. They just wanted what was best for him. No matter how often he cleaned her, changed her diapers, there was still a smell that rode around with her. The smell had become part of her now. He smelled it when he picked her up; the top of her mostly bald head rubbed against the bottom of his chin, and he could smell everything. It would not – it could not – be long now. Could it?

He knew what they said about him: Forty-seven years old. Lived with his mother. Always had. Surely still a virgin (not true, but it was none of their goddamned business). He ought to be thinking about himself for a change. Once his mother died, it would be time. Time to kick up his heels. Move on. Well, to hell with them: He *was* thinking about himself. Anywhere else he went, there would be lights. Towering racks of them. Lights blazing from every porch and pole and rooftop. He was happy here. Happy to walk along a blacktopped road edged by a thin strip of dirt and then woods, dense and high, woods that absorbed the darkness the way a thick wool coat draws in old smells and holds them.

Charlie's humming had gradually changed into a faint singing, a melodic murmur, and the shift into words was a natural progression, like a leaf turning over in the warm breeze to show its tender veined underside: *And He walks with me and He talks with me, and he tells me I am His own, and the—*

Charlie stopped. He'd heard a noise in the woods off to his right. A steady rustling. It was too loud and

83

it went on too long to have been produced by a squirrel's hectic scamper. It was too robust. Charlie knew night noises as well as he knew his own name. And that was no squirrel.

'Hey,' he said.

The rustling stopped.

'Hey,' Charlie repeated. 'Who the hell—?'

He heard a flapping sound, like the long tail of a coat. Then the big shape rose up out of the woods. It came roaring at him, pile-driving Charlie down into the dirt, flat on his back. He was stunned but still conscious. Charlie's eyes had long ago adjusted to the darkness and so through a haze of pain and confusion he saw the knife, raised up high.

'NoNo— Oh, NoNoNo,' Charlie cried out, his breath coming in frantic bits and whispers, which was all he could manage. He felt a blow to his shoulder. It dazed him and he stopped fighting, just for a second, and so did his attacker. *What the*—? Charlie roused himself one more time, punching and gouging, and then the attacker started up again, too. 'No!' Charlie yelled. 'Don't— Why—' He raised his hands and he fought, scratching and reaching and clawing, but the knife thrusts came in a flurry now, too strong and too fast, and there were too many of them. After a final series of twitches and a shuddering groan, Charlie Frank was quiet, a part now of the longest darkness of all.

11

Nick Fogelsong stood at the threshold of Bell's office on Tuesday morning. He'd shed his hat as he passed Lee Ann Frickie, Bell's secretary, whose desk in the outer office served as the last line of defense between the prosecuting attorney and the general public.

Lee Ann, sixty-seven years old and still spry of limb and mind, had looked up at him and nodded. The sheriff was the only visitor she didn't have to announce.

Now it was Bell's turn to look up. Fogelsong's generously sized body occupied a good portion of the doorway. For a few seconds, Bell didn't say a word. She wanted to savor her quiet joy at seeing him again, after what had felt like one of the longest months of her life. Part of what made it seem so long, of course, was the unsolved homicide of Freddie Arnett right at the end of it, and her hunger for Nick's expertise, but there was another reason, too. Fogelsong was the closest thing to a father she'd ever had – a real father – and his absence was an acute reminder of what her life had been like before they met.

He looked different when he wasn't wearing his hat. Incomplete. Older, too. Or maybe it wasn't the hat. Maybe it was something else.

'Can't believe it,' she said, a soft tease in her voice. She stood up. 'Nick Fogelsong. As I live and breathe.'

'Told you we'd be back today.'

'You did. But things happen.'

'They do.' He paused. 'This a good time to talk?'

'Absolutely.'

He took four steps into the room and dropped himself into the middle of the small couch across from her desk. Used both hands to gently set down the hat next to himself on the couch, as careful as a debutante dealing with a corsage she's marked in her mind as a keepsake.

Bell wanted to ask him about his trip, but she knew that would have to wait. This wasn't a social call.

'I'm sure,' she said, 'you're pretty much up to speed on the Arnett murder. We're planning to canvass the neighborhood again today, and I've been going over the autopsy report. Looks to me like—'

Fogelsong held up a hand to stop her. 'Need to tell you something. Sorry to say, it's not good news,' he declared. 'Deputy Harrison called me ten minutes ago. She was going to call you next, but I told her to hold off, since I was headed here myself.' He took in a deep breath and then he let it go. 'There's been another homicide. Happened either late last night or early this morning. Victim was found dead by the side of Godown Road.'

'Jesus.' Bell grimaced. 'ID?'

'Charlie Frank. I know his brother, Wally.' Fogelsong looked at a spot on the wall just to the left of Bell's head. 'Charlie was cut up real bad. Knife wounds in his chest and abdomen – and on his hands. Put up a pretty damned good fight.'

'Robbery?'

'Unlikely. Only thing missing was his boot. Might've

86

come off in the struggle and the killer nabbed it. Or somebody else happened along and picked it up. Maybe an animal. No telling.' The sheriff rubbed his chin. 'Wally has five kids and a wife who's dying of melanoma. So Charlie was the one who took care of their mother. Lived with her. Martha Frank's had MS for the last fifteen years, maybe twenty. There's no money for a nursing home. Charlie carried her from room to room, Belfa. From her bedroom to the front room to the kitchen. To the bathroom when she needed it. With Charlie gone, who's gonna do that now?'

It wasn't really a question, at least not a question that anyone could be expected to answer. Bell waited a decent interval and then said: 'Forensics?'

'Techs're just getting started, but it's not promising. Harrison had already faxed me the preliminary report on the Arnett murder while I was in Chicago. This is similar – that is, a cleaned-up crime scene.'

'You think we're looking at the same perpetrator?'

'Sure as hell hope not.'

She didn't want to say it – she hated to give the idea life by speaking it out loud – but she had to. 'You know as well as I do, Nick, what folks will be thinking. We're bound to get the question. Two homicides, right in a row. We'll be asked if there's a serial killer running around.'

He looked as if he'd been punched in the face. 'God, Bell. Just what we need. A bunch of panicked people hoarding ammo and buying pit bulls from their cousins. You know what I think? I think people ought to give us at least a few goddamned days to sort it all out. And if we come to a dead end, then – *then* – they can start yelling about a serial killer.'

But on the other hand, Bell knew, he fully understood the town's apprehension, and the sense of abject helplessness that was almost worse than the fear. Nothing seemed too outlandish anymore for a small town. No amount of trouble and tragedy. There were no more safe places, no more spots beyond the reach of violence. Truth was, Bell believed, such places had never existed in the first place. Violence was everywhere. But people liked to tell themselves that small towns were exempt. Small towns were sweet and tranquil and quaint. Small towns were tucked away in the hills like peppermints in a grandmother's handbag; they were special treats, hidden from the nasty old world.

Screw that, Bell thought, picturing the crime-scene photos from Freddie Arnett's driveway. The shattered skull. The wet bits of brain matter. Freddie's stringy, old-man's body, facedown, arms and legs askew. His trousers had hiked up in his sudden awkward fall, and a strip of bare skin showed just above his thin white socks; the strip on each leg was pale and hairless. Somehow that bothered Bell almost as much as did the sight of the smashed brain: that inch of skin above his socks. It was so tender, so intimate. Men like Freddie Arnett never wore shorts. So this was a part of him that only his wife, more than likely, had seen for a long, long time, maybe since he was a little boy, when he took baths on Saturday nights with his brothers, and now here it was for strangers to gawk at. Law enforcement personnel, crime-scene techs – anybody on official business could look at him without his permission. Murder was the ultimate violation, yes, but there were other violations, too, that came in its wake. Smaller, heartbreaking indignities. Such as a strip of skin between a rucked-up trouser cuff and the folded-over top of a ribbed white sock.

Fogelsong was talking again. 'I'm meeting with Deputy Harrison in half an hour to coordinate the investigations. See where we stand. I'll keep you posted.'

Bell nodded.

'By the way,' he said, shifting his position on the couch, signaling a shift in topic, 'I heard about your own little adventure. That stabbing you stumbled across in Collier County on Saturday night. Shirley's okay, I take it.'

'Yeah. But she's out of control, Nick. Won't listen to me. Goes her own way.'

'She'll settle down.'

'You think so?'

'I do.'

'Anyway,' Bell said, 'the homicide in Tommy's appears to be unrelated to Freddie Arnett's murder. Killer confessed to Deputy Sturm at the scene. We're checking on his whereabouts Thursday night – but this one seems tied up nice and neat. No loose ends. Not about who did it, that is. There are a few questions about the victim and a business card he had in his pocket, and I might be looking into that just as soon as I—'

'Sturm?' Nick asked, interrupting her. 'Mandy Sturm?'

'Yeah. Do you know her?'

'Not her,' he said. 'Not well, anyway. It's her husband I know. Virgil Sturm. Good man. Works for the CSX railroad. Or did, before all the layoffs.' Fogelsong dusted off his knee, as if he could somehow get rid of bad news the same quick way. 'He's related to Mary Sue's family.'

Bell let a short but decisive length of time go by. 'Speaking of Mary Sue – how'd things go in Chicago?'

The sheriff discovered the cuff button on his right sleeve. He pressed it with his thumb, then twisted it, as if checking to make sure it wouldn't fall off at an inopportune moment.

'Fine,' he said. Voice flat, neutral.

Bell was disappointed but didn't show it. His business.

'One thing.' Nick was speaking again, which surprised her. Usually she was the one forced to break the occasional silences. 'I went by to see Clayton Meckling,' he said. 'The hospital he's at – the Rehabilitation Institute of Chicago – is right downtown. Real close to the hotel where Mary Sue and I stayed. Spent a couple of afternoons with him.'

Now Bell was the one who looked around for a bit of busywork in which to indulge. She picked up a yellow pencil, one of several she kept at the ready alongside a short stack of paper on her desktop, and nervously worked the pointy end against the sheet on top. In a few seconds, the paper wasn't blank anymore.

'How's he doing?' Bell asked. She kept her voice casual.

'Pretty well. He's a fighter. Not a surprise, but still good to see. They're working him hard and he's eating it up. Just about ready to come back, he told me.' Fogelsong rolled his shoulders, then leaned forward so that he could arch his back. Couch-sitting was not a natural condition for him. 'I don't know how you two left things, Belfa. Don't know if you're in regular contact anymore. But he's not the man he was four months ago. No more self-pity. None of that left in him. He's got plans again.'

She was glad to hear it – thrilled, actually – but hesitated to show any portion of her joy to the sheriff.

She was closer to Nick Fogelsong than to anyone else on the planet, but there were still areas of Bell's life that she didn't discuss with anyone – including Nick. Bell and Clay Meckling had been romantically involved until Clay was maimed in an accident in the spring. He withdrew from her, from everyone, and she and Clay hadn't spoken in over two and a half months. It was Rhonda Lovejoy who'd told her about Clay's trip to the Chicago rehab hospital, one of the best in the world.

'Appreciate it,' Bell said. For all the emotion in her voice, she might have been thanking him for opening the courthouse door for her.

The sheriff waited, just in case she wanted to say something else, ask any more questions about Clay. She knew why he was waiting, and she also knew how impossible it was for her to reveal how deep her feelings ran for Clay Meckling – as impossible, come to that, as it was for Fogelsong to discuss his wife's illness. *Put Nick and me in a contest to see who's more stubborn,* Bell thought, *and it'd be a tie, no question. He won't talk about Mary Sue and I won't talk about Clay. Won't – or can't. Same thing. Both of us were taught to keep it all inside.* Sometimes it felt as if they'd both been sentenced to prison – not the kind that had held Shirley, but the kind whose invisible walls were even taller, even stronger – on account of how and where they were raised, the hard and constant lessons they'd learned.

'Well,' Nick said, 'better get back to it.' He stood up, having first leaned to his right so that he could use his palm to push off against the arm of the couch. It bothered the hell out of him, Bell knew, that he needed help these days, even inanimate help, to assist his rise.

91

Nick hated dependency in all its forms. But he was fifty-five years old. Gravity pushed back harder these days. 'After I meet with Deputy Harrison, I've got to get ready for tonight's meeting with the county commissioners,' he said. 'Soon as word gets around about Charlie Frank, they're going to have a lot of questions about the murders. And they're right to be asking.' Another complication occurred to him. 'I'm going to request funds to hire private security for the ceremony on Friday. It'll bust the budget wide open – but it's worth it. Everybody's jumpy as hell. And no wonder.' He put his hat on his head, leveled it up.

'Extra security sounds like a good idea.'

'Thing we really need,' he said, 'is another deputy. I'll make my pitch again, but it won't work. Can tell you that right now. Commissioners might go for a temporary fix, but a new hire? Forget it.'

'A couple of unsolved murders might change their minds.'

'Hell of a way to get their attention,' he shot back. 'Anyhow, way I hear it, there'll be a record crowd on Friday. Maybe close to a thousand people. Maybe more. Can you beat that? A thousand people – all in one place – in Raythune County. Riley Jessup spends his days in a big house over in Charleston now, but he's still a popular man in these parts.

'You know what?' Fogelsong went on. He was switching gears again. Bell could hear it in his voice. That voice had toughened up, the anger threading blackly through it. 'No way in hell I ever thought we'd have two homicides in a row like this. Not again. Not after last fall. You just don't expect it.' He ruminated for a quick run of seconds. 'Don't imagine Freddie Arnett or Charlie Frank were expecting it, either, until

92

events proved otherwise.' He started to go, then turned his head in her direction one more time. 'Deputy Harrison did a good job while I was away,' he said. It was both a question and a statement. 'Considering.'

'She did her best. Baptism of fire, I'd say.'

'Coffee later at JP's?'

'Sure.' Even in the midst of the slow-motion crisis of two murder investigations, they needed to keep their rituals. They'd agreed on that five years ago, when they first began working together. 'Bet you missed that bottomless cup at JP's,' she added. 'Coffee's kind of hit-and-miss in big cities, as I recall.'

Bell saw something come into Fogelsong's eyes before he answered. She and the sheriff had a fierce and steady mutual affection. They rarely alluded to it, even in passing. And that, she believed, was a large part of what had enabled its survival all these years: They didn't wear it out or distort it by analyzing it or even naming it.

'Yeah,' he said. 'That's the main thing I missed, all right. The coffee.'

12

Lindy could not bring herself to lock her father in the basement when she left at night for her shift at the station. She could have done just that; there was a dead bolt on the kitchen side of the basement door, and she kept the key. It would be easy. But if anything happened – a fire, say – she would be trapping him, dooming him, and she couldn't do that. The basement had no outside entrance. No windows, either.

So she took her chances. She repeatedly questioned herself about it, going back and forth with the pros and cons, over and over again, but she wouldn't lock him in. Nor could she afford to hire someone to watch him in her absence – even if she could have persuaded her father to put up with a stranger in the house. Which he didn't want. And neither, come to that, did she.

Sometimes her apprehension seemed misplaced, her worry unwarranted. There were mornings when she arrived here and it was clear that he hadn't come out of the basement at all, not once, much less left the house. But something was changing. He was getting angrier, more restless. Unpredictable. These days, when she got home and waited a minute or so in the kitchen, letting the house settle in around her, listening, then climbed down the rickety basement stairs, moving slowly, keeping a cautious hand on the rough-feeling rail, and called his name, doing it softly so as not to startle him – *Daddy, hey, Daddy, it's Lindy, it's just me* – she would hear him scuttling away from her like a frightened animal, thrashing, kicking, banging, tripping over boxes and tables, snarling at her. If she tried to approach him, he would lurch away to another corner, cringing at the doorway-sized punch of daylight at the top of the stairs, flinging up a meaty hand in front of his face to block it, then dipping his grizzled gray head. *Damned double shift,* he would sometimes mutter. *Gotta work a double shift. Ray, you got your end? Ray-boy. You hold on there, Ray. I'm coming on through.* Ray Purcell was her father's best friend. They'd started out in the mines together in the 1960s. Lindy had heard a lot of stories about Ray, although she never met him; he died of lung cancer in 1973.

Her father's agitation was definitely escalating. She didn't know why. She knew only that he was suffering even more these days, tormented by some frantic inner vision that chased him around the basement and – to her growing concern – sometimes out of the basement, too, and out of the house. These days, when Lindy came home in the morning after her shift and moved through the house into the kitchen, passing window after window, each window freshly anointed by the light of the rising sun, she would often find the back door ajar from where he'd come back home. Boot prints on the kitchen floor. And in her heart, a clutch of fear.

Like this morning.

Her knees felt wobbly, so she sat down at the kitchen table. She took several deep breaths, fighting off a wave of dizziness that emanated, she knew, from her apprehension. If she'd had anything in her stomach, she would've thrown it up; her guts felt kinked and clawed-at. At times Lindy was overwhelmed by everything, by the responsibility and the fear and the confusion. Was she doing right by her father, after all? Hiding him this way? Enabling him to stay where he was, the way he was? She thought she was protecting him, but was that what she was really doing?

There weren't many family members left. No one who lived nearby. And no one, certainly, whom Lindy trusted enough to confide in. She had some distant cousins on her mother's side in eastern Kentucky and another set on her father's side who lived up near Morgantown, but that was all; they never visited, and they picked up on partial truths and made their judgments from that. They knew Odell was big and mean and 'touched in the head' now, as her second cousin Jeannie Stump liked to put it, but they had no idea about the true extent of his rages, or his night prowls, or about the fact that he lived mostly in the basement, in a space tricked up and fitted out to look like an old coal mine.

A week after Lindy's high school graduation, Jeannie Stump had made an unannounced visit. For a graduation gift, she brought Lindy a flowered tote bag and a makeup kit. Jeannie was a tall, broad, slump-shouldered woman in her late fifties with wiry gray hair and gray eyes. She lived by herself and worked at a nursing home, where her job was to push the chest-high rolling cart up and down the corridor each morning and each evening, dispensing pills to the old folks in tiny room after tiny room, a task that required her to speak loud and slow and to maintain, at all times, a sunny

optimism blatantly at odds with the accelerating decay
she witnessed daily.

Jeannie had taken one look at the way Lindy and
Odell lived – the crumbling house, the isolation, the
mess in the cellar – and declared, 'Honey, listen to me
– we've got to get you some help with your poor
daddy. Gotta call somebody, okay? A government
agency, maybe.' Jeannie meant well. Lindy was sure
of it. But her failure to mind her own business caused
problems.

Two days after Jeannie had gone back to Morgantown,
there was another knock at the door – Jeannie's knock
had been enough of an irritating surprise, now here
was another – and Lindy found herself in the bustling,
meddlesome presence of someone who identified
herself as Gladys Davies, a caseworker with Raythune
County Family Services. It turned out that Jeannie,
suspecting Lindy might not make the call, had made
it herself.

'We have a real good adult day care program,' Davies
had informed Lindy. She blinked behind a large pair
of rectangular eyeglasses that dominated her face. 'I
can sign you up right here and now.'

'No thanks,' Lindy said.

Davies frowned. She had dull red hair, and her fleshy
body was corralled into a chocolate brown pantsuit.
Lindy hadn't invited her to come in and sit down, but
the woman had done so anyway, pulling a clipboard
out of her gigantic black vinyl purse and placing it
across her lap like a TV tray. There was a practiced
snap and prim efficiency to her movements, as if the
world were one big to-do list and she was on the lookout
for boxes she could tick.

'We're fine,' Lindy added. She'd remained standing.

Hand still on the inside doorknob, to facilitate – she hoped – a swift exit by this interloper.

'We've got lots of craft activities,' Davies said. 'And a county bus can pick him up here every day.'

'No thanks.'

Davies seemed perturbed as well as puzzled. Then she sensed the real issue – or so she thought – and offered Lindy a brightly commiserating smile. 'It's free, honey. Won't cost you nor your daddy one red cent.'

'Don't need it.'

A tiny sigh. So maybe that wasn't it, after all. The woman's voice was flat now, all the enthusiasm ironed out of it by Lindy's truculence: 'Well, I can't force you, Miss Crabtree, but I hope you'll give me a call soon to set something up. You can't take care of him forever. Not all by yourself.'

'Yeah. I can.'

'Don't you have things you want to do?'

Davies's tone had dropped lower, and the effect was to produce an instant, insinuating try at intimacy. She went on, 'Friends you want to hang out with? A boyfriend, maybe? Maybe check into courses at a community college? As long as you're looking after your daddy, your life is pretty restricted, honey. It doesn't have to be this way.'

'Yeah,' Lindy said. 'It does.'

She was still sitting at the kitchen table, where she'd slung herself when the dizziness commenced, her bowed forehead pushed into clasped hands. A head-ache smashed repeatedly behind her eyes, like waves striking a high black rock. The recollection of the people who had recently tried to help – Jeannie Stump, the lady from the county agency with the big glasses

– only made things worse. Made her feel even more alone.

They didn't get it. Nobody did. Lindy couldn't abandon her father. Couldn't let anybody see him this way. Couldn't let anybody know just how bad he was. She loved him, but it was more than that, too. More than love. It was something that didn't have a word to go along with it. *Not everything in the world has its own damned word,* Lindy told herself, the anger and the sorrow and the uncertainty building up inside her whenever she thought about her father, a shifting combination of emotions for which she had no vocabulary. *Some things just are what they are – and there's nothing to call them. No way to describe them. They just are what they are.* So she'd made him a place in the basement, in the darkness he craved. She wasn't trying to shut him away, out of her sight; she only wanted to make things the way he liked them. And she promised herself that as long as he lived, she'd take care of him. By herself.

Lindy lifted her face. The kitchen was bright now; another summer Sunday was under way. Each object in the small room – table, book, chair, floor, sink, counter, coffee cup, knife block – was clear and blunt and particular.

Knife block.

Black handles protruded from the wooden block, the heavy blades resting in their designated slots. She knew there were six slots – which meant there ought to be six knife handles.

Lindy counted the handles silently: *One. Two. Three. Four. Five.*

She counted them again. Faster this time, agitated, needing to know, afraid to know:

OneTwoThreeFourFive.

There was a knife missing. The last one in the line. The biggest one. The one that, when Lindy was a child, used to frighten her. Each time she would see her mother pulling it out of the block by its handle, Lindy – knowing full well that the knife was intended for ordinary household chores, for harmless things, for chopping and slicing food – would be fixated on that blade, because it was as gray and dangerous as a shark's fin, and she would feel the fear growing inside her, as if its ascending gradations were precisely synchronized with the rising of the knife as her mother drew it slowly from the wooden block.

The last knife wasn't there.

Lindy's gaze scoured the floor, the countertop, but she already knew. It wasn't there. And she hadn't used the knife. She wasn't the one who had removed it.

Her eyes dropped once more to the floor, to the boot print, a terrible and unambiguous stamp verifying that – at the bottom of it all – she had no control over anything, not her father, not her world, and that no matter how much she tried, no matter how much she pretended otherwise, now she knew the truth.

It was coming.

13

'Buster.'

'Hey there, darlin'.'

Bell winced, glad that the conversation was occurring on the phone and not in person. If Buster Crutchfield, Raythune County's infuriatingly misogynist coroner, had been standing in front of her, she might have been tempted to pop him a good one, right in the mouth. She had had to endure his inane iterations of 'darlin'' and 'sweetie pie' and – most egregious of all – 'cupcake' for many years now, but his mellifluous name-calling never seemed to get any easier for her. She made a fist with the hand that wasn't holding the phone and set that fist on top of the file folder in the middle of her desk. Then she closed her eyes, and kept going.

Back when she was new to the prosecutor's job, Sheriff Fogelsong had advised Bell to overlook Buster and his sexist lexicon, arguing that the coroner was an old man, set in his ways, and she'd be better served by outlasting him than by making a fuss. Well, the joke was on her: Five years later, Buster was still going strong. She'd missed her chance to demand that he address her as a fellow professional and not as a cocktail waitress.

It was Thursday, two days after Sheriff Fogelsong's return and one day before Governor Riley Jessup's visit to Raythune County, and Bell and the sheriff were still no closer to finding out who had murdered Freddie Arnett and Charlie Frank. The heat had continued to build – the heat from the summer sun, certainly, but another kind of heat, too, the kind that falls on sheriffs and prosecutors when the people who elect them are scared and angry. And have every right to be.

'I've been reading your notes on the Arnett and Frank autopsies,' Bell told him, 'and there are a few things I'd like to go over. Do you have a minute?'

Buster indulged in a robust, prolonged sigh. She could imagine his round red cheeks puffing up, like those cartoon versions of the west wind, and his rubbery lips vibrating. 'Oh, my, my, my,' he said. 'Sorry to say, sweetness, but I've got a visitor here right now from the WVU medical school. This afternoon suit you?'

No, this afternoon most definitely did *not* suit her, Bell fumed. But she appreciated – grudgingly – the fact that Buster consulted regularly with physicians from the medical school to keep his lab procedures up to date. Hard to argue with that kind of initiative.

'Okay, fine,' she said. 'Make it after four. I'll be in court till then.'

'Will do. Looking forward to it, hon.' Buster's concluding chuckle had a lascivious twist at the end, like a coiled dollop of soft-serve ice cream at the top of the cone.

Bell was disappointed. And yet it wasn't as if she lacked for diversions. An important trial was starting up that afternoon, one that Bell had decided to handle herself. If she were a mature person, a reasonable person, a levelheaded and rational person, she'd take a break now. Go for a walk. Get a cup of coffee, maybe.

Hell with that.

She popped open her laptop. She was still curious about the man killed in Tommy's last weekend. How did the business card of a New York City lawyer get itself in his pocket? She clearly remembered the names on the card: Sampson J. Voorhees and Odell Crabtree.

She did a quick Google search for the first. Even with the refinements 'attorney' and 'New York,' the results were disappointing. There was a property transfer record from the early 1990s for an 'SJ Voorhees & Associates' and little else. No news stories. No company Web site. Bell scrolled up and down the page, and the next several pages, just to make sure. Nothing.

The other name on the card, Crabtree, was a common moniker in Raythune County – which meant that getting to the bottom of it would require an altogether different search engine. For inquires of a local nature, she'd go to a woman whose knowledge base – and the speed of her retrieval of same – would leave Google gasping for breath while she thundered past, panting and sweaty but triumphant: Rhonda Lovejoy, lifelong resident of Acker's Gap and close relation to 98 percent of the residents of said county.

'Hey, boss.' Rhonda had answered after half a ring.

'Need to see if you recognize a name,' Bell said.

'Hit me.'

Bell could picture the assistant prosecutor leaning back in her creaky chair, clutching the heavy black rotary-dial phone, having hurriedly brushed the Doritos crumbs from the lap of her skirt when she realized it was Bell on the line.

Cells were useless in the courthouse basement, where Rhonda and Hickey Leonard had their office. The thick plaster walls were the guilty parties. A dank, low-ceilinged, markedly unpleasant space, the office spread out at the base of a crumbling stone staircase and was dominated by two rickety oak desks that Rhonda and Hickey had shoved together to make one larger surface. When the ancient furnace kicked on during the winter months with its shuddering, gas-pain groans and constant palsy, objects had been known to vibrate right off the edges of the desk. In the summer, moisture freckled the wooden baseboard. The assistant prosecutors' office had a seedy, beat-up, stripped-down feel to it that Rhonda and Hickey had come to appreciate. It rhymed with their view of their jobs: This was a place where justice was pursued, and justice was a thing not of glamour, but of grit and perseverance.

'Odell Crabtree,' Bell said.

Silence.

'Rhonda? Still there?'

'I'm here, boss.' Rhonda sighed. 'Yeah, I know Odell Crabtree.'

'Tell me.'

'Well, I've known the Crabtrees forever, seems like. Leroy Crabtree used to live right next door to my aunt Bridie over in Swanville.'

'And how is Leroy related to Odell?'

'Leroy is Odell's great-uncle. But he's been dead for twenty years.'

'You mean Odell?'

'No. I mean Leroy.'

Bell had been flicking a pencil tip against a sheet of paper on her desk. The pace of the flicking intensified. 'Okay. So who the hell is Odell Crabtree?'

'Retired coal miner.' Rhonda was a bit hurt by Bell's impatience, and her voice reflected it. As she went on, though, captivated by the story she was telling, the umbrage wore itself away, replaced by the simple awe that always accompanied Rhonda's contemplation of the infinite varieties of human destiny. 'Odell lost his wife about six years ago,' she said. 'Margaret Crabtree was a real good woman. Maiden name was Schoolcraft. A lot younger than Odell, but they were a good match. Margaret – oh, my, she was sweet. Heart of gold. Born and raised in Raythune County. Surely didn't deserve to die the way she did – in pain, pain like you wouldn't believe. At least it was quick. Merciful, you ask me.' Rhonda paused, pondering things, then returned to her narrative. 'She and Odell had a child. A little girl. Surprised people, really, what with Odell being so much older. And he'd always said he didn't want any children. Made that clear. But – oh, goodness, how Margaret loved her! Lindy must be – let's see, I guess maybe nineteen or twenty by now. Graduated high school a few years back. Little thing, no bigger'n a minute. Kind of a tomboy, but she's got these green eyes. Those eyes – well, one look and you know you're dealing with a smart girl. Quiet. Keeps to herself. Got some pride. The kind of pride that can get you in trouble sometimes. 'Cause you don't ask for help. You try to do everything all by yourself. You know what I mean?'

Bell knew better than to chastise Rhonda for her digressions. Might as well get mad at the river for its tributaries.

'So,' Rhonda quickly continued when Bell didn't answer, 'it's just been Odell and Lindy for some time now, living way out there. A while back, the mine shut down – and Odell just seemed to shut down with it. Started acting real peculiar. Well – he'd been acting peculiar before, I have to say, and the disappointment just made it worse. Way I hear it, Lindy takes care of things around the house. Sees that the bills are paid and keeps up with repairs and whatnot.'

'Peculiar how?'

'Oh, I don't know. He has a lot of pain from his years in the mine – back pain, mainly – and he has a funny way of walking. He's a real big man, still strong as an ox, and it's hard to see him brought low like this. Hunching along. Mostly, though, the problem's his mind. He'll be okay for a spell, and then he just goes off. He can be real nice and polite and then – *boom!* – it's like everybody's a stranger who means him harm. Took a swing a few years ago at a little boy in Lymon's Market. Kid was being a brat, making a racket, but still. So Lindy keeps him home. He's afflicted with – well, my grandma Lovejoy used to call it "hardening of the arteries." I don't think that's scientifically accurate, but you get the picture.'

'Alzheimer's?'

'Don't know. Does it matter, though? If they can't cure it, does it matter what they call it?'

Bell let a few seconds go by. 'One more thing,' she said. 'The guy who was stabbed at Tommy's last weekend. Jed Stark. Know anything about him?'

'Oh, yeah. He was a real shady character, that Jed. My neighbor's cousin April Lloyd used to go out with him – although it was years and years ago, and she came to her senses real quick, first time he raised a hand to her.' Rhonda paused, and Bell could visualize the shudder of repulsion that ran through her assistant's body. 'Had a bad, bad temper. Lived over in Steppe County, which is why you never had to deal with him in a courtroom. Count your lucky stars. He was lazy and stupid – and he would've shot his own granny if it put an extra nickel in his fist.'

'Any reason you can think of that Stark might be doing business with a New York City law firm?'

Rhonda made a snickering sound in her nose. 'Jed Stark's ambitions generally stayed a whole lot lower than that, but – stranger things have happened. Promise I'll think on it, boss.'

14

There were trials that bothered Bell more than others. She kept that knowledge to herself. It didn't do any good to show your feelings; it only made you look weak and foolish, not to mention selfish and unimaginative, as if you could measure a thing only against your own experiences, as if you couldn't fathom the bedrock evil of a particular behavior unless you had personally been injured by it, or by something similar. She was a prosecutor, which meant she was sworn to pursue all kinds and degrees of criminal offenses, and to hold the perpetrators accountable. She couldn't play favorites – not just favorites among individuals, which naturally was unacceptable, but among crimes, too. There were degrees of crimes, to be sure, but she was required to pursue every case with the same relentless but thoroughly neutral vigor.

Hell with that.

Children abused by their parents: Those were the cases that dug their hooks into her, and with every shift of the fortunes of the trial, every wrinkle in the proceedings, every slight twist and new development, those hooks were driven deeper. The reason such cases troubled her was obvious. But the fact that she'd had a violent father herself – a fact that a good portion of the county seemed to know as well – was not relevant to her work. She wouldn't allow her staff to discuss it. She was always alert to the possibility that some enterprising defense attorney might bring up her personal history and demand that she recuse herself from a child abuse case. Question her objectivity. Thus she was scrupulous about not crafting a prosecutorial strategy based on emotion or histrionics. Her visceral disgust and skin-prickling revulsion were carefully concealed beneath a steady, deadpan presentation of evidence. Bit by bit, fact by fact, Bell built her cases, never raising her voice or deviating from a logical progression of linked and irrefutable truths. Yet deep inside, she was demanding: *Kill this sick bastard, kill him right now.* The brutal character of her internal monologues often startled her. She had tried to talk about it once with Nick Fogelsong, asking him if it was normal to harbor such terrible visions of revenge, and at first he said, 'Lord, Belfa, don't ask me about "normal," nobody knows the answer to that,' and when she persisted, he said, 'I'm a damned sight more worried about the people who *don't* think those thoughts, the ones who don't get it out of their system that way – because they're likely to just bust loose in real life. Got no escape valve.' She wasn't sure she totally bought it, but his theory calmed her down nonetheless.

On Thursday afternoon, Bell stood in the hot box of a courtroom presided over by Judge Ezra Tripp. She was ready to continue the prosecution's case against Lanny Waller. The latter, who had opted for a trial before the judge instead of a jury, was an exceptionally loathsome individual who hailed from a section of Raythune County known as Briney

Hollow. Fifty-three years old and unemployed – unless you counted the oxycodone tablets he sold to the jangling, desperate people who met him in parking lots and behind trailers in and around Acker's Gap – Waller was as gray and skinny as a vent stack poking up from an old roof. The skin on his face hung in vertical yellow folds, like the nicotine-stained drapes in a halfway house. His teeth – the three or four still in residence – stuck up like broken-off branches driven into scorched ground, and they were tilted and jagged.

The criminal charges against Waller were even more repugnant than his physical appearance. He had spent the last four years regularly raping his girlfriend's three daughters, now aged five, twelve, and fourteen.

'Hold on,' Bell had said when Deputy Harrison first briefed her on the case, after Waller's arrest. 'The youngest is barely five now. You're telling me that Waller raped a twelve-month-old child?' And Harrison, who generally let her eyes do most of her talking, had simply looked at Bell, those eyes reflecting a vivid incomprehension and deep-set sorrow that no amount of law enforcement savvy could mitigate. Nothing much ever rattled Pam Harrison – but this, it seemed, did. Not for long, but it did.

Waller's explanation was the same one Bell heard over and over again, in sexual abuse case after sexual abuse case, year after year. He had offered it during their initial interrogation: 'You gotta understand. I didn't do nothin' to them girls, but that's only because I got a strong will. Them girls come on to me. Okay? They did. Don't you be fooled by that innocent shit they try to pull. All that crying and hollering and carrying on.

I'm telling you – they swing them hips and shake that thing at me. All the damned time. No normal man could see that and not want to get hisself some, you know what I'm saying? Good thing I got a conscience on me. Never touched them girls.'

Opening statements had concluded the day before, and the morning was taken up with various defense motions and rulings thereof. Bell, ready to leap into her case against Waller after the lunch recess, had just risen behind the square wooden table that served as the prosecution's outpost. The courtroom was sweltering today. The thick black drapes blocked the sun – but could not, to everyone's dismay, block the sun's pernicious effects. Portions of the old court-house were cooled by portable air-conditioning units, but the racket they made was prohibitive in court-rooms presided over by ancient judges with cut-rate hearing aids. Thus the hot, still air gathered in the room like additional spectators. Court Recorder Rosie Drake, a heavyset woman in a too-tight flow-ered blouse and tan slacks, paused regularly to lick at the fringe of sweat on her upper lip. It re-formed within minutes.

Looming above Drake was the wide, dark-paneled cabinet behind which sat Judge Tripp. Ezra Tripp was an old man, and summer afternoons were a particular challenge for him; he had a tendency to doze off after his habitually large lunch. Bell realized that she had a maximum of about twenty minutes to present her case before Tripp's head would start to wobble and his eyelids sag, and after that, a trickle of drool would start its familiar journey from the corner of his mouth to his chin and on down into the crinkled city of wrinkles on his neck. Bell had been present on several occasions when the judge's head had fallen irredeemably forward, chin on chest, the only movement thereafter coming from a sporadic shudder inspired by an elongated snore.

Hickey Leonard, the other assistant prosecutor, stood next to Bell. A big man, he looked pink from the heat, and pinched and uncomfortable in a blue suit, valiantly suppressing the urge to squirm and to yank off his tie. What hair he had left – Hickey was in his early sixties – was combed away from his forehead and kept there with the willing assistance of gel. It was hard to tell which entity – sweat or gel – was most responsible for giving his hair its drenched look. Hickey had spent the last ten minutes before the judge's return arranging the yellow legal pads upon which Bell had plotted out the county's case, making sure they were stacked in the proper order.

Sitting at the defense table, a veteran attorney named George Pyle – inevitably nicknamed Gomer – was engaged in a tense whispered conversation with the defendant. Waller listened, then shook his head violently; Pyle whispered something else, then Waller whispered something back, and finally the men nodded simultaneously. Bell had no idea what was going on. She didn't care. Waller was guilty as hell. And she was ready to prove it.

'Mrs Elkins,' Judge Tripp said, his voice a thin croak. He gestured with a scaly scrap of brown-speckled flesh that looked more like a claw than a hand. 'You ready to get us going again?'

'I am, Your Honor.' Bell signaled to Hick, who handed her the legal pad on the top of the pile. She knew what was written there, but glanced at it anyway. No mistakes. 'The prosecution would like to call—'

'Hold up, hold up.' Pyle was rising, buttoning his suit coat as he did so. He smiled, but the smile, Bell noticed, stopped well short of his eyes. 'Judge,' he said, 'we'd like to request a recess.'

'A recess? Lord in heaven,' Tripp declared. 'We ain't rightly started yet.'

'Well, sir,' Pyle replied, 'there's some extenuating circumstances.'

Judge Tripp tilted his head and peered down at Pyle through his thick-lensed black spectacles.

'That right? You got some new information?'

Pyle nodded.

'Son,' the judge said, 'the court recorder can't do nothing with a nod.'

'We have new information,' Pyle repeated, booming it this time.

'Well, then.' Judge Tripp raised a furry interrogative eyebrow in Bell's direction. 'You know anything about this?'

'No, Judge.' She was angry – Pyle was obviously trying to pull something – but she knew better than to show it. Tripp had an eccentric and unreliable temper; he'd overlook large things, but small ones – such as a sarcastic comment from a fed-up prosecutor about a defense attorney's shenanigans – sometimes elicited a testy lecture or a contempt citation. She had to remain serene, unruffled. Take it all in stride. At least until Pyle revealed his strategy.

'Well,' Tripp went on, 'what we got ourselves here is a dilemma. What's the nature of this new information, Gomer?' The judge corrected himself. 'I mean – Mr Pyle? And why wasn't the county prosecutor notified about it, before we resumed our proceedings this afternoon?'

'Your Honor,' Pyle said, 'this information only came to our attention about an hour ago, during the recess. It has a crucial bearing on these proceedings.'

'That right?'

Judge Tripp seemed intrigued rather than outraged. Bell struggled to maintain her composure. It was all she could do not to explode in anger, turning to the wily bastard across the aisle and letting loose with a fire-hose blast of expletives about his childish trickery and scathingly unprofessional conduct.

'That's right, Your Honor,' Pyle said. He looked, Bell thought, as earnest and endearing as a Boy Scout, with his simpering little half-moon smile and his glossy block of black hair – its color obviously enhanced by repeated applications of shoe polish – and his habit of raising his clasped doughy hands to his chest when he talked. The fact that it was all phony – she knew a thing or two about the particulars of Pyle's messy personal life, and she knew that his legal ethics, too, were a dirty jumble – did not appear to matter unduly to Judge Tripp.

'Well,' the judge said, 'just what is this new information you got yourself, Mr Pyle, and why in heaven's name can't it wait until the prosecutor's finished presenting her case? You'll get your turn, son.'

'Because, Your Honor, the county's case rests wholly upon the testimony of Missy Skylar Wills, fourteen years old, one of the alleged victims.'

Bell felt a sick feeling starting up in her gut. It was true: Waller's girlfriend, Regina, the mother of the abused girls, had refused to testify against him. And Missy's sisters were too young to take the stand; when Rhonda Lovejoy had tried to prep the middle sister for the trial, she wouldn't stop crying. Missy alone had agreed to speak against Waller. To describe what he'd done to them, and done to them over and over again. It was her story – a grotesque one, filled with descriptions of the nightly horror enacted by an unrepentant monster who'd been provided with laughably easy access to defenseless children – that was their only hope of convicting Lanny Waller. Missy wasn't in the courtroom yet; Bell had wanted to shorten the amount of time the young woman was forced to spend in Waller's company. At the moment Pyle interrupted her, Bell was ready to request that the bailiff fetch Missy Wills from the hall where – Bell had been assured – she waited.

'—And, Your Honor,' Pyle went on, 'we have new and conclusive evidence that the accusation against my client lodged by Missy Skylar Wills was coerced by a member of the prosecutor's staff. Furthermore, we've been told that Missy herself now wishes to thoroughly recant her earlier statement, which leaves the county with no credible evidence whatsoever against Mr Waller. Frankly, we're appalled at the actions of Mrs Elkins and her subordinates, who would seek to ruin the life of an innocent man by charging him with such heinous crimes – crimes allegedly perpetrated against the very family he has loved and supported for many years.'

Judge Tripp poked the tip of his tongue around the inside of his mouth. Bell watched its progress: Left side, right side, now digging at the trenches along the top and bottom gum lines. This was his thinking look. *At least we're keeping him awake,* Bell thought bleakly, fighting the anger that rose in her throat like bile. *He can't sit back and snooze on this one.*

The charge was absurd, of course. Pyle knew that

as well as Bell did. No one had attempted to coerce Missy Wills – no one, that is, except Missy's mother, who obviously had persuaded the girl to back down. To claim it was all a big misunderstanding. And thereby keep the family intact.

Bell recoiled from her own thought. Applying the word 'family' to the dancing circus of damaged souls over which Waller presided made the acid rise in her throat all over again.

But George Pyle was right about one thing: Without Missy's testimony, the county had no case. And the hell of it was, Bell had always known this might happen. She knew Missy was shaky, vulnerable. Bell had seen it before: a mother, afraid of losing the man in her life, offers up her children as bait. As the sweetener to keep Mr Wonderful around. And then Mom puts heavy pressure on whichever child is temporarily brave enough to rat out the abuser. *Keep this up,* the mother says, *and they'll tear us apart. Bust up the family. You'll never see me or your sisters again. That what you want?*

Another moment passed. All four of them were standing now: Bell, Hickey, Pyle and Waller. Waller, wiggling his narrow shoulders inside the oversized orange jumpsuit, started to rub his nose. He'd forgotten that his hands were shackled, however, which restricted the height to which he could raise his wrists. So after jerking his hands in frustration, he settled for twitching his nose, apparently in hopes that it might calm the itch.

'Your response, Mrs Elkins?' the judge said.

'My office did not coerce Miss Wills, Your Honor.' Bell forced herself to keep her words simple, cordial, on point. She wanted to throw back her head and howl at the outrage of it all, but she couldn't give way to umbrage; she had to be patient. Even-tempered. Professional. 'We believe her recitation of the offenses committed over the past four years in the trailer occupied by the defendant and by Regina Wills and her three children was true, relevant, and unimpeachable. We have no idea why – or even if – Miss Wills has changed her account of Mr Waller's ongoing criminal acts.'

'Mr Pyle?' the judge said. He turned back to the defense attorney. Tripp, like a spectator at a tennis match, was swiveling his head from one side of the courtroom to the other, taking in the serve and return.

'All I can say, Your Honor,' Pyle replied, 'is that I spoke with Missy a few minutes ago myself, and she's plenty upset. She realizes how she's hurt Mr Waller by her lies, and she feels just terrible about it. Wants to get back to her family and forget the whole thing. And she hopes that Mr Waller – the only real father she's ever known – will one day forgive her for all the trouble she's caused him.'

Judge Tripp pushed out his fleshy lower lip, another favored facial gyration when he was engaged in a bout of contemplation. The courtroom had grown exquisitely still. Only a few people occupied the wooden pews of the public section, and they had stopped fidgeting, stopped trying to find a cooler position in which to sit. Someone coughed. Someone else rattled a piece of paper. Bell looked over at the defense table and saw that the paper-rattler was Pyle; he had picked up a sheet from his notes and relocated it an inch away from its original spot. Busywork.

'Well,' Tripp said, 'if the young lady is, in fact,

withdrawing her accusation, that changes things. No doubt. No doubt.' He slid out and drew back his lower lip over and over, until it resembled a faulty drawer in a chiffonier that won't stay properly closed. 'Okay, then.' Despite the tension, Tripp yawned. He tried to disguise it, pretending that he'd just been revolving his jaw to keep it limber, but the yawn was unmistakable. 'We're finished here today, that's for sure. First off, we'll make sure that Missy Wills indeed is officially withdrawing her accusation against the defendant. If that's the case, I'll instruct the sheriff's department to initiate an immediate investigation into how the pros-ecutor's office dealt with Miss Wills from the get-go. Soon as I know what on God's green earth is going on here, I'll send the information to both of your offices. In the meantime, we're adjourned here, folks.'

Bell and Hick walked through the courthouse corridor side by side but silent. The yellow legal pads were crammed under Hick's arm. He hadn't taken the time to shove them back in his briefcase, so eager were they to get away from the courtroom before one of them – it would be Bell, of course, but Hick pretended that he, too, might be liable to react inappropriately – exploded in wrath and gave Judge Tripp, Gomer, Waller, and maybe even the court recorder a telling-off vicious enough to strip the finish from the crown molding that ran around the dusty uppermost edge of the plaster walls.

They were on their way back to Bell's office, without any clear idea of what they'd do when they got there. The realization that Lanny Waller would probably go free – and thereby return to his regular pillaging of three defenseless girls – had stunned them past the possibility of future planning. For the moment, at least.

Bell didn't greet Lee Ann Frickie. She went straight to her desk. Pulled out the chair and threw herself into it. She ignored a stack of square pink slips, the kind headed by the preprinted line WHILE YOU WERE OUT and featuring scribbled entreaties to return calls. Most of the messages, she knew, were from townsfolk who wanted to inquire precisely when she and the sheriff planned to get off their butts and solve the murders of Freddie Arnett and Charlie Frank. Lee Ann generally tried to clean up the callers' language when she wrote down the messages. 'Never even heard of some of the names they're calling you,' she had told Bell the day before. 'I guess I should be grateful for the education.'

Hick stood, waiting to hear Bell's instructions. They both knew what had happened back in that trailer this morning, just as surely as if they'd been present at the scene, appalled but – like now – essentially helpless, because families were what they were, did what they did. Regina Wills, fearful of being alone if Waller went to prison, had, in all likelihood, confronted her oldest daughter. Grabbing the girl by the arm, she'd surely pulled her down in a chair, leaned over, and shoved her face right up into Missy's face, so close that when she raged, her spittle flew into Missy's eyes, making the girl blink and cringe: *Take it back, you little bitch. You take it back, hear? You ain't dragging us all down. Got that? You tell 'em you was lying. You don't know why you said what you said to Rhonda Lovejoy – but it was a lie. Lanny never touched you – nor your sisters, neither. You hear me? Listen, girlie. You don't know nothing about the world. We need a man around to protect us – are you listening to me? We need him. If he goes, who's gonna take care of us? Who? You ever think of that, girlie, when they was telling you what to say? Telling you to lie about Lanny?*

Bell was certain that she knew what Regina had said, down to the last ragged syllable; as a prosecutor who'd dealt with a distressing number of child abuse cases, Bell had met a lot of Reginas. Her kind almost always picked the man over their own kids. Not because they loved him – that, Bell at least could've understood, because people did terribly misguided things out of love, or what they chose to call love – but because they thought they needed him. *Needed him.* Bell would let the phrase echo internally, disgusted and slightly in awe, too, of the breadth of the ludicrous illogic behind it. *Needed him. Jesus. Him and the bums just like him, the assholes who don't work, don't lift a finger, freeloading jerks who'd be lost without obliging females to take care of them. To cook their meals. Fetch their beer. Wipe their butts. So the women use their own kids as flypaper. To catch and to hold. Jesus Christ.*

She had warned Rhonda the day before: 'Make sure Missy Wills understands the pressure that'll come down on her, okay? Make sure she's ready.'

And Rhonda had done her best. Bell was sure of it. But after Missy had been prepared for her testimony, duly forewarned, bolstered with Cokes and with platitudes about the liberating power of truth, there was nowhere else for Missy to go – nowhere else except home to the trailer, where Regina waited. And as she waited, Bell knew, Regina had probably opened and closed her fist, opened and closed it, keeping loose, keeping limber, ready to grab Missy's arm the second she saw the girl, slinging her into a chair and telling her what's what. Lanny had taught her well.

Not a damned thing the prosecutor's office could do about it. There was no legal justification to relocate Missy or her sisters during the trial – and the vastly inadequate and chronically underfunded state apparatus charged with protecting them naturally required proof of imminent peril. During the proceedings, Waller would be in jail; Bell couldn't claim he posed a hazard at the moment to Missy and her sisters. The law assumed that a mother would protect her children.

The law was naïve.

Bell experienced a familiar surge of anger, an immense black wave that swept in front of her eyes and almost – almost – overwhelmed her better judgment. She felt a powerful urge to jump out of her chair and find Lanny Waller and break his fingers one by one with a twist and a jerk – reveling in each of the ten separate shrieks of pain – and smash his kneecaps with a hammer, assuming she could find one. If not, she'd settle for any heavy object likely to inflict maximum agony and lasting damage.

Then it all receded, just as suddenly as it had appeared: the anger, the outrage, the fantasy of seriously hurting the man. And Bell realized, once again, that this was why she'd chosen the law for her life's work: Because it offered something other than the closed loop of vengeance. It broke the black circle. It gave her a place to put those renegade emotions, the ones that spilled over the sides of her life, the ones that wouldn't fit anywhere else and that, if she hadn't found a way to control them, would certainly have destroyed her. The law wasn't always rational or fair, it didn't always work the way it ought to, it sometimes seemed to be only a half-step up from the chaos it was intended to bring to heel – but up was the right direction. Beat the hell out of down.

It saved her, again and again.

The law, she believed, wasn't there just to keep the bad guys in line. It was there to keep the good guys in line, too. The good guys who were tempted by adversity to think that ends ever justified means.

'Bell?' Hick said. Not out of impatience, just curiosity. 'What do you want me to do?'

'I want you to get hold of Rhonda right away.'

Rhonda was terrific in dealing with victims; she had a real knack for it. She wasn't mean, the way Sheriff Fogelsong could be when perturbed at their hesitations or their evasions, but she also wasn't too gooey-soft or instantly forgiving.

'She's taking a deposition,' Bell went on, 'over at the Monk County Courthouse. Tell her to get back here as soon as she can and make another run at Regina Wills. Regina's the key. Not much chance she'll back off and let the girl speak – but whatever small chance there is, we have to try.'

'Okay. Anything else?'

Before she could answer, the phone on her desk rang. Bell nodded to Hickey, releasing him to return to his own work. He waved back at her over his head as he departed.

'Elkins.'

'Howdy, Miss Belfa,' Buster said. 'Thought I'd take a chance and call you back early. Got finished sooner'n I expected with my afternoon business.'

'Yeah. Me, too.' Bell tried to keep the bitterness out of her voice.

'What'd you need, sunshine?'

She moved aside two piles of folders on her desk to find what she was looking for. 'Okay,' Bell said. 'I've got your notes from the Arnett and Frank autopsies right here.'

'Dreadful, dreadful. Tragic loss. Town's as shook up as I've ever seen it, and I'll tell you this – I've been around here a long time.'

'Yeah. Well, I wanted to ask you about Charlie Frank's injuries. The stab wounds. From the sketch you made, I can see that the wounds vary substantially in depth. The ones across the upper part of his torso – near his shoulders – are almost superficial. But in the middle and lower part of the torso, they're very deep. Deep enough to pierce vital organs.'

'Oh, yes. Yes, indeed.'

'Is that unusual? I mean, to have such a variety of force levels used in a knife attack like this?'

She could imagine Buster Crutchfield in full cogitation mode: the wrinkled sack of his face collapsing inward, rheumy eyes getting squinty. 'Well,' he said, 'not especially, darlin' heart. Lotsa things could account for that – the position of the assailant, which might've shifted during the attack. And Charlie himself surely moved around a lot, trying to defend himself. Man fighting for his life – he ain't likely to hold still.'

'Okay. Thanks.'

'Tell you this much, sweetie.'

Bell snapped back to attention, assuming he had suddenly remembered a crucial detail common to both victims. 'Like I said,' Buster went on, his drawl as soft as corn silk, 'I been around these parts a long, long time. But we've never had a summer quite as dark and sad as this one.'

'Stipulated.' She was disappointed, and grunted her good-bye accordingly.

15

Bell hadn't realized how hungry she was until, two hours later, she heard Lee Ann Frickie opening a package of peanut butter crackers in the outer office. The come-hither crackle of tearing cellophane was enough to lure Bell right out of her chair. She looked plaintively at her secretary. Lee Ann instantly capitulated and divvied up the contents.

'This,' said Lee Ann, stacking three round brown crackers in Bell's palm, 'does not constitute a proper lunch, Belfa.'

'Point taken.'

With a grin that combined sheepishness and gratitude, Bell returned to her desk. She had one more meeting and then she could call it a day. She had set it up the previous afternoon, making the call and getting Tommy LeSeur's voice mail – which was what she'd expected. She preferred it, in this case. She wanted to be clear. It was easier to state your business when you were leaving a message, when there was no chance of being inter-rupted by the other party.

'This is Belfa Elkins, Raythune County prosecutor,' she'd said. 'I'd like you to come by my office tomorrow at four thirty P.M. If you have a problem with that, I'll be happy to discuss it with your parole officer.'

That, she knew, would guarantee his attendance; an extra hassle with a parole officer was not the sort of thing that any ex-con relished.

At 4:37 P.M. – Bell glanced at her watch when Lee Ann called her extension from the outer office – Tommy LeSeur showed up. Bell looked through the half-open doorway. The owner of the bar bearing his name was a big man with a belly gone slack. He wore a long black leather duster and a black cowboy hat set far back on his head, giving him a look of aggressive nonchalance. His facial hair, mostly gray and white, was arranged in a sort of lazy goatee, more abstract scraggle than defined shape.

'Come on in,' Bell said.

LeSeur grunted and moved forward. Behind him, Lee Ann twisted to one side in her desk chair, catching Bell's eye. Did she want the door open or closed?

With a slight shake of her head, Bell gave the signal: *Keep it open.* It had nothing to do with her being afraid of Tommy LeSeur; the point was that he shouldn't get the idea he was that important. A closed-door meeting with a prosecutor was a privilege. He was a bum. Bell wanted him to know that. He wasn't worthy of a closed-door session. He was just another ex-felon with whom she had to deal. Didn't even rise to the level of requiring privacy.

'Yeah,' LeSeur said. That was his version of hello. After casing the place with a brief lick of a glance, he emptied himself into the metal chair that faced Bell's desk at an angle. Immediately he slouched even lower, scooting his butt forward and setting the scruff of his neck against the top of the chairback. He didn't bother removing his hat. Bell wondered why the hat didn't fall off, with his head tilted so severely, and she decided to chalk it up to the adhesive properties of sweat.

'You had some trouble out at your place on Saturday night,' she said. 'I was there, right at the end. Saw the guy on the floor. Helped out Deputy Sturm.'

He squinted at her, as if trying to recollect her face, then shrugged. No go. She wasn't the kind of woman he'd remember, anyway. She wasn't blond, she wasn't buxom, and she didn't giggle when he tongued a fingertip and then ran it slowly across the front brim of his hat with insinuating lasciviousness, which was what he did before replying.

'Yeah,' he said. 'So?'

'You're on parole, Mr LeSeur.'

'Tell me somethin' I don't know, lady.'

'Fine line.'

'Huh?'

'That's what you walk. A fine line. Your parole officer tells me that you're allowed to run your bar, because it's the only way you know how to make a living, but you're required to refrain from any association with other ex-felons or with anyone who has a history of engaging in criminal enterprises.'

'Yeah.' He stuck out his chin, making it easier to scratch. 'So.'

'So there was a murder at your place.'

'Yeah.'

'Not a good sign.'

'They caught the guy, lady, okay? Jed Stark just messed with the wrong piece of tail. Pissed off some jealous asshole. Case closed.' LeSeur smacked the handrests with his palms, ready to haul himself up and out of the chair. 'That it?'

'No.'

He waited. His hands stayed put.

'Your bar is in Collier County, Mr LeSeur, which puts it out of my jurisdiction.'

'Yeah.' A pleased gleam in his watery eyes. 'Yeah, I was getting ready to point that out. You got no call to be hassling me.'

'But when you were picked up several years ago for possession of narcotics with intent to distribute – that was well before my time here, Mr LeSeur, but you'd be amazed at how good record-keeping can be these days – the arrest took place in Raythune County. Not Collier. So it turns out that I *do* have a dog in this fight.'

The gleam faded. 'Okay, lady. What do you want from me?'

Bell drew a small photo from the middle of a stack of papers on her desk. She'd brought it in with her that morning. She slid it across the desktop. LeSeur had to sit up and lean forward to see it. One look, then he slouched back in his chair again, unimpressed.

'Who's that?' he said.

'My sister. Shirley Dolan.'

'You want me to give her a job at the bar or something? That it?'

'No.'

'Then what?'

With two fingers, Bell dragged the snapshot back across the desk and tucked it under a book. He hadn't touched it. Had he tried to, she would've slapped his hand away.

'Next time that woman shows up at your bar,' Bell said, 'you're not going to let her in.'

He looked amused. 'I'm not?'

'No.'

'Why's that?'

'Because I say so.'

LeSeur licked his bottom lip. Lip and tongue were an identical shade of gray.

'Lady,' he said, 'you ain't scaring me.'

'Not trying to scare you. Trying to educate you.'

He pondered this. 'Look, I wouldn't know her from Adam, okay? How am I supposed to keep an eye on everybody who goes in and out of my—?'

'No idea,' she said, interrupting him. 'That's your problem. But if I find out that she's been in your bar again, Mr LeSeur, I can make a lot of trouble for you. The kind of trouble you don't want.'

Once again, the pondering look came into his eyes. 'I ain't done nothing,' he said. There was an aggrieved quality to his voice, a practiced one. 'I could report you for harassment, calling me in like this. Threatening me.'

'You could.'

They regarded each other levelly across the cluttered expanse of desktop.

'She's your sister, huh?' LeSeur said.

Bell gave a single nod, dipping her head without breaking eye contact.

'And you think – wait, now, lemme guess,' he said. 'Hanging out in my place is gonna turn her bad or something.' The nasally snicker caused his head to jerk. 'Like it's measles and you can catch it.' Now he laughed outright. Thirty-five years of smoking cigarettes and anything else he could find to smoke had turned his laugh into a soupy, clotted bray. 'Got news for you, lady. Anybody who comes in my bar finds just what they're looking for. Nothing more, nothing less. And they go out the same way they come in.'

Except for Jed Stark, Bell wanted to say, but didn't. Not the time.

'Whatever,' she said. 'Just don't let Shirley Dolan in. Ever.'

He sat up even straighter and let his head swivel around the room: tall leaded window, brown drapes, glass-fronted bookcase. Across the shelves of that bookcase, the solemn march of lawbooks. Row after row of black leather binding. The leather looked as if it had sopped up centuries of serious thought. LeSeur squinted, silently reading the titles through the glass. *Or trying to,* Bell thought. *Pretending to.* The literacy rate in these parts was depressingly low.

He would capitulate – she knew it, and he knew it, too – but first he had to make her wait. His dignity required this brief delay. For all their macho bravado, for all their swagger, drug dealers – and Tommy LeSeur was a drug dealer first, last, and always, no matter what he called himself, no matter what fairy tale he told his parole officer – were a tender sort, Bell knew. Acutely sensitive to slights and insults. Like third-graders.

'Fine,' he declared. 'One question, though.' When Bell didn't speak, he went on. 'What's sis gonna say about all this? Next time I head her off at the door, I mean?'

'Don't know. Don't care.'

'She ain't gonna like it none.'

'Lots of things that I don't like, either,' Bell said. 'But I have to put up with them.' She tried to put some extra flint into her stare, hoping he would take her meaning, realize he'd been insulted. At no point in the conversation had she taken her eyes away from LeSeur's pitted gray face. Looking away was a sign of weakness, and she knew how important it was not to look weak in front of the Tommy LeSeurs of this world.

Hell. It was important not to look weak in front of anybody, period.

He lifted his shoulders and dropped them again. No telling if he'd caught her drift. 'That it? That's all I gotta do?'

'That's it.'

His capitulation came with a sneer. 'Don't matter none, anyways,' he said. 'I got plenty of business.'

And then it was over, the negotiation that wasn't a negotiation at all, because in this realm – the realm of daylight, of glass-fronted bookcases – she was in charge. There were other realms, Bell understood, where it would not have gone so smoothly, realms in which Tommy LeSeur would have had the whip hand.

He had a little trouble getting up, on account of how low he'd sunk in the chair while they talked, trying to look cool. She realized, with a smile she didn't bother to hide, that Tommy LeSeur was middle-aged. He might try to look young and cool, his body draped in long black leather – he took an abrupt step toward the door for the obvious purpose of causing the ridiculous garment to swing out behind him and then fall back dramatically into heavy, ponderous folds – but he was fast becoming an old man, dry and fat and used up, his joints stiffening and cramping if he sat too long. He was ordinary. He was a seedy, small-time hood who'd spent his life preying on other people's weaknesses, and now here he was, getting weaker himself by the day, his body spreading out, breaking down, right on schedule. His vanity was pathetic. Tommy LeSeur was a show-off. A loser. A joke. And yet – Bell knew this all too well, knew it just as surely as she knew that you must never turn your back on certain species of wild animals, even though they seem to be thoroughly tamed and domesticated – under no circumstances should he ever be underestimated.

Bell was almost home when her cell rang. The ringtone – it was Gloria Gaynor's 1978 anthem 'I Will Survive' – tipped her off that it was her ex-husband calling.

'Hi, Sam,' she said. Cordial, but just barely. His transgressions since their divorce ranged from mildly annoying to borderline unforgivable. Bell didn't waste her time or her emotional energy by hating him; instead, she felt a sort of general distaste at the prospect of a conversation with him. Bottom line: He was Carla's father, and that meant, like it or not, he would always be in Bell's life.

'Hey,' he said. 'How's it going?'

This was suspicious. Sam didn't make casual calls.

'Fine,' Bell said. She had paused at a four-way stop, waited her turn, then surged forward, punching the accelerator with more force than was strictly necessary.

'Okay. Well, I just thought I'd check. Heard from Aunt Thelma again. She knows the Frank family pretty well. Jesus, Belfa. What's going on back there? *Two* unsolved homicides, one right after the other? How are you holding up?'

'Did you need something, Sam?'

'Like I said. Just checking in.'

'Okay. You checked in. Has Carla made a start on her packing? Listen, if she doesn't want to haul a big suitcase on the plane, you can just ship her clothes and anything else she wants to have here. Might be easier.'

'Uh – sure.'

There it was again: something odd in his voice. Bell didn't care enough to figure out what it was. But a thought occurred to her: Sam was being cordial. God only knew why – but she could take advantage of it. He worked at the fancy end of the legal profession, the end filled with Audis and escargot. It was drastically different from her end – the world of Ford Explorers and peanut butter crackers.

Sam, she realized, might be able to satisfy her curiosity about the business card in Jed Stark's pocket.

'Hey,' she said. 'Ever heard of a New York City law firm called Voorhees? Guy named Sampson J. Voorhees?'

'Sure, I know him. By reputation, I mean. He's not really a lawyer, though. More like a slimy, bottom-feeding – wait, let's make that "ethically challenged" – fixer.'

'Fixer.'

'Yeah. There are a few outfits like that here in D.C., too. The "law firm" part is pretty much window dressing. They're muscle. Security. Plus some semi-legal private investigator work.'

'Such as?'

'Such as – well, let's say you're a Fortune 500 CEO and you think your wife is bumping uglies with the golf pro at your country club. You want pictures, you want transcripts of wiretaps, you want copies of e-mails – but discreetly. Under the radar. Because what you're really after is leverage. Blackmail bait. Voorhees and his ilk keep pretty busy, let me tell you.'

'So why isn't there any contact info on his business card? How does he do business?'

'He doesn't *want* your business,' Sam said, and he said the sentence slowly, spacing out the words to give it an exaggeratedly remedial feel, as if she'd asked him a simple math problem that even a kindergartener ought to be able to figure out. 'He works strictly on referrals. It's like the old story about the guy who applies for a job with a Chicago politician. The politician says, "Who sent you?" and the guy says, "Nobody." And then the politician says, "I don't want nobody that nobody sent." Voorhees doesn't want to be contacted – unless you already know how. If you're not part of the elite network of deals and favors that those guys live by, he's not interested. So naturally there's no information on his business card. But I can probably dig up a number somewhere.'

'Great,' Bell said. She was sitting in her driveway by now, engine off, listening intently. She'd arrived home a few minutes ago but didn't want to interrupt him.

'Why are you asking?'

'Too complicated to explain. Gotta go, Sam.'

16

By high noon on Friday the sun was a pale white blister in an even paler sky. That sun had turned the blacktopped parking lot of the Raythune County Medical Center into a sink of misery; today it was crowded with people, not cars, and in the shimmery heat-haze, the solid black rectangle with the bright yellow stripes seemed tentative, insubstantial, as if the edges might give way at any minute and make an instant river of scalding tarry goo. The hospital itself comprised two stories of topaz-tinted brick with, at one end, a perky, inviting-looking lobby entrance finished off with ornamental grasses, and at the other end, a grimmer, more serious-looking set of double doors with EMERGENCY stenciled in red block letters across the glass. It was ten years old, yet still was one of the newest buildings in the county.

The occupants of the lot looked both afflicted and exhilarated. They seemed to be engaged in a long, slow, inevitable melt, like crayons left on a radiator, but their eyes gleamed with anticipation. There were old women wedged into the plastic lawn chairs that they'd carried in and opened up and locked into position with a violent snap; old men in wraparound sunglasses and baseball caps sitting proudly athwart motorized scooters with American flag decals slapped across the shiny maroon flanks; small children sitting cross-legged in little red wagons, arguing over who was entitled to the last suck from the juice box; and at the outer rim of the crowd, skinny teenagers in cutoffs and tight T-shirts, pecking at their cells with alternating thumbs, even though the recipients of those texts were standing right beside them; plus an appreciable number of dogs whose pale pink tongues fell out of the sides of their mouths and stuck there, stiff as sticks. The aggressive PA system sent too-loud music thumping out of two tall black amplifiers, along with a constant garnish of static.

Bell had arrived here twenty minutes ago, having hitched a ride from the courthouse with Deputy Harrison in the black Chevy Blazer, one of two that the county owned. The other was assigned to Sheriff Fogelsong. Harrison was a petite woman, barely five feet two, as solid as a bridge abutment – and even less talkative. But she had compensatory skills: She could outrun just about any man in the county. Out-shoot him, too.

Moments after parking the Blazer, Harrison nodded to Bell and abruptly departed; she began her patrol along the crowd's outer edge, looking improbably cool even in her brown polyester uniform and flat-brimmed brown hat and black boots. She tucked her thumbs in her belt as she walked, but unlike her colleague Charlie Mathers, there was no belly fat to dig through in order to reach it. Harrison was lean and sleek. The lump of the black leather holster on her hip was the only rounded part of her.

Bell's eyes swept the sweltering lot. A few people recognized her and waved; dutifully, she waved back.

Faces looked as if they were being glimpsed underwater, the features blurry and distorted by smearing
curtains of sweat. Bell felt the heat rising from the
blacktop through the soles of her shoes, and she could
feel it coming from the other direction as well, pressing
on the top of her head. Even the applause was hijacked
by the heat; it sounded halfhearted, boxed in, a dry
rattle that crossed the packed space each time there was
a twitch of activity that might signal commencement
of the ceremony.

Two people – an old lady and a toddler – had
already succumbed to the temperature and, limp and
glassy-eyed, been hauled off by the paramedics. *At
least we're right here at the ER,* Bell thought. *Can't
get much handier.*

She tried to come up with a rough head count.
Were there a thousand people here today, as Sheriff
Fogelsong had predicted? Close to it, maybe. In any
case, it was one of the largest gatherings she'd ever
seen in Raythune County. Maybe the free hot dogs
and RC Cola served up on long tables at the back
were the principal lure – even though some visitors
had obviously smuggled in their own refreshments,
the kind classified under the 'adult beverages' rubric.
No wonder: This was a special day. And these people
were plenty excited to see Jessup, former governor of
West Virginia, on one of his rare trips back to his
homeplace.

So far they hadn't seen a thing, because the show
was running late. Jessup and his entourage had arrived
a while ago in a lumbering, big-hipped, white motor
home with a license plate that read wv gov and were
hustled forthwith into the building. All the crowd could
do now was wait and sweat.

Watching them, Bell did what she always did when in the presence of a large group, her eyes brushing quickly across each face like a feather duster moving down a row of balusters: *tick, tick, tick, tick.* She suspected that she probably kept up that careful vigilance in her sleep, too; behind the closed lids, her eyeballs were moving, shifting back and forth, because she was generally certain there was trouble brewing somewhere, and only her to stop it. Or only her and Nick and his deputies.

Which sins lurked in this heart or the other one, what guilty memories or bad intentions haunted which souls? That was what she wondered, peering at these people. She couldn't help herself. The cost of being a prosecutor, Bell had discovered only a few months into the job, was this ongoing appraisal: Statistics insisted that a certain number of people in any gathering had either committed a crime or were going to, in the near future; a certain number had gotten by with something or hoped to. A certain number hid terrible secrets.

Hell. Whoever was responsible for two violent homicides could be here right now. Whoever had smashed an old man's head and then stabbed another man – both of the victims were helpless, both of them were beloved to someone – might be within the shifting orbit of her gaze. He could be out there in the crowd at this very moment, mopping at the sweat on the back of his neck just like anybody else, muttering about the heat, grinning at somebody's joke, while in the locked basement of his mind, he dreamed of the darkness to come, of what he would do and how he would do it.

*　　*　　*

'Hot nuff fur ya?'

The crowd roared back various versions of 'Yeah!' and '*Hell*, yeah!' and 'Uh-huh!' followed by raucous spurts of hooting and whistling. Small children begged to be hoisted up on the hairy shoulders of fathers in tank tops, and the fathers obliged. Old people rose painfully from their lawn chairs and squinted toward the flag-festooned truck bed, flattening out one hand for use as an eyeshade, bunching up the other into a fist to place against a fleshy hip for stability.

Riley Jessup stood on the makeshift stage as if it were the most natural thing in the world for an eighty-nine-year-old man to be right here, clutching a cordless microphone as lovingly as an ice cream cone, blinking in the all-over sunshine. His head was a white hairless lump stuck on the wide plank of his shoulders. He was short and grievously overweight, but the seersucker suit had been tailored with such discreet and non-binding generosity that his true dimensions were obscured.

'Hot nuff fur ya?' he repeated. The echoes of his amplified voice bounced around the parking lot in tattered bits and scraggly patches. The crowd cheered and laughed and stomped and whooped and whistled, and Jessup, Bell saw, drank it all in, the voluminous love and the honest admiration. He inhaled it, he absorbed it, and she would have sworn that she could actually see the crowd's rowdy energy filling him up like an elixir, causing him to blossom and swell, restoring him, rejuvenating him, and as the magic stuff branched through his body, he seemed to shed a few brittle flakes of his old age and decrepitude; the crowd's energy straightened his spine by a tick or two and enabled him to lift his arms just that much higher as he gestured toward it, his sweaty red bulb of a chin raised up, his eyes aimed at a spot slightly above their heads, positively popelike in his all-encompassing, beatific gaze. He hadn't held elective office in almost three decades, but he still had the gift. He still knew how to handle a crowd, how to rile it up and smooth it out and rile it up again.

'My, oh my – it's *so-o-o-o-o* good to be back home!' Jessup hollered. 'Right here in Raythune County!'

More cheers, whistles. Then the crowd sank back down like a half-baked soufflé, rising and now cratering, the brief stir of activity having reminded everyone of just how wickedly enervating this heat really was.

'My friends,' Jessup said. Voice calm now. Softer. It caused the people to lean in, straining to hear. They were hungry for what he had to say. They needed him. Just as these people filled and energized Riley Jessup, he had the same effect on them. Bell had attended a few political rallies now and again, but never had she witnessed such raw and obvious synchronicity, such a mass symbiotic exchange. Jessup had moved beyond the confines of Raythune County in so many ways, but the place still energized him; it still moved in his blood and fed his dreams. It was still a part of him. And he of it.

'My friends,' he repeated, the public address system popping and crackling with every third word or so, 'when I was a little boy growing up in Briney Hollow, it was a terrible thing when somebody got sick. Nearest doctor was three counties away.' Jessup shook his head, initiating an answering ripple in the folds of flesh on his neck. 'If somebody *did* get sick – well, all you could do was pray. Pray and pray and pray. Sometimes the good Lord saw fit to bless your loved one with a little more time. And sometimes He didn't.'

Jessup paused. He frowned. He looked down at the pointy tips of his shoes. Every old person in the crowd, Bell guessed, was recollecting right along with him, remembering a parent or great uncle or favorite aunt who'd died a slow and misery-filled death a half a hundred years ago back in some inaccessible niche, a death impossible to contemplate in a modern era of painkillers and antibiotics. And paved roads.

'No more!' Jessup thundered. He'd raised his head abruptly, as if he'd suddenly heard his long-dead but eternally beloved mother calling his name from the back porch, fetching him home for supper. 'No more! 'Cause we got ourselves this *fine* medical center right here in Raythune County. And now it's even gonna have its very own MRI machine!'

Jessup sucked in a long, deep breath. He let it out with a wheeze, like a note held too long inside an accordion, so long that it managed to wander off-key. 'Now, as y'all might've heard,' he said, voice turning coy, 'I've done pretty well for myself.' A rolling tide of chuckles spread across the crowd. Everybody knew that Jessup was a millionaire who lived in sumptuous comfort and luxury, a universe removed from the poverty of his upbringing in Raythune County, and that fact seemed to enhance rather than detract from his credibility. 'Got my pick of hospitals. Wellsir, my grandson, Montgomery, is real, *real* sick. And next time the doctors want to have a crack at him, we're bringing him back. Back to the Raythune County Medical Center. 'Cause there ain't no better place nowheres!'

As the crowd stomped and hollered its communal

approval, Bell spotted Sheriff Fogelsong's brown hat across the crammed-full lot; he moved steadily along the perimeter, coordinating his actions with Deputy Harrison. Bell waved, but he didn't see her. He was too focused on his surveillance. He had a funny feeling about the event, he'd told her the day before. It wasn't a premonition, exactly, just an odd unsettledness in his belly. Too many bad things had happened already. He couldn't relax. No matter how much additional security was present, this was Nick Fogelsong's lookout. His county. His responsibility. And there were too many people, too much confusion, too many ways for things to go wrong.

The audience was at it again, interspersing the whoops and the cheers with two-fingered whistles. Jessup raised a hand to halt the hullabaloo; the people happily obeyed, their shrieks dying down and then winking out one by one like stars at sunrise. 'And so,' he went on, 'that's what I come to say to you today. That's it, plain and simple. But I dearly hope that some of you'll find a minute to come by and say hello before we head back to Charleston. I'll be in the lobby over there. And after that,' he said, a husky swagger in his old-man voice, 'I think you oughta find yourself a creek somewheres – so you can jump in and get outta this gol-durned heat, whadda say? Whaddaya say, folks, whaddaya say?' The crowd exploded as Jessup goaded them on: 'Huh? Huh? Can't hear ya! Louder, now – can't rightly hear ya!'

The speech had concluded an hour and a half ago, and still the people came, threading through the lobby and past the governor one by one, the very old and the very young and those in the vague indeterminate swath of ages in between, an earnest and anxious chain of well-wishers. The crowd was crushed and funneled through one side of the entrance doors and then the long line looped across the carpeted lobby, and after that it curved back out the other side of the double doors; from above, the squiggly line gyrating through the front section of the building surely looked like a toddler's clumsy scribble. There was a vast murmuring sound, the kind of anticipatory excitement that resists expression in mere words. No matter how long these people had to wait to see Riley Jessup, they would gladly have waited even longer.

It had required the best efforts of five security guards, two on each side and one at the rear, to help the old man totter down from the flatbed truck, courtesy of an overmatched stepstool, and then to guide him into the lobby and lower him into a custom-made chair, whereupon his body relaxed into its default pudding shape. Even though Jessup was now out of the sun and into the air conditioning, shiny buttons of sweat still popped spontaneously across the top of his head. His shirt collar was limp and sopping.

Bell watched from a corner of the lobby. These people seemed to crave physical contact with the man, even if just for a few precious seconds. A handshake. A fleeting brush of their fingertips against his. Certain politicians, she thought with bemusement, were wildly beloved in West Virginia, despite the record of corruption and incompetence and unabashed laziness that clung to them like pieces of toilet paper stuck to the bottom of their shiny shoes. Politics here was ruled by a curiously inverted ratio: The worse the people were treated by some scalawag of an elected representative, the more they seemed to revere him, especially in retrospect. Bell sometimes wondered if it came from the same impulse that made mothers defend their prodigal sons – the bad boys, the bums, the users, the troublemakers – and love them all the more for their rascally defects.

And there might be another reason, too, she surmised, why West Virginians rarely held a grudge against even the most grotesquely rapacious politician. They wanted to believe. Needed to. They were compelled to believe that, no matter how bad people – or conditions in general – had been in the past, they could be different tomorrow. It was a kind of shy, primitive optimism that sometimes irritated her, but she knew that it was also a survival technique. If you didn't have hope around here, what the hell else *did* you have?

'Hey, there.'

Bell turned. Rhonda Lovejoy was at her side, grinning despite a face so red that it resembled a freshly picked cherry tomato. Her sky blue dress with the big white bow at the neck was damp and bedraggled; overall, she looked as if she'd walked fully clothed into a shower and then changed her mind about it before soaping up.

'How're you doing in this heat?' Bell asked her.

'Tolerable. Ran into my cousin Evie outside. She's here with all six of her kids. Asked if I could use my influence to move 'em up a little bit.' Rhonda shook her head nobly. 'Don't worry, boss. I set her straight. No favors. Not how the prosecutor's office operates.'

The line was moving faster now as the security staff began to hustle people along. Jessup's handshakes were briefer, the small talk brusquer. His smile came and went like a DVD on fast-forward. Bell noticed a woman standing to the left of the governor's chair, hunched over a cell phone, ignoring the endless river of worshippers. She was middle-aged, excruciatingly thin, draped in a white linen pantsuit with dainty gold buttons, her small feet angled into lipstick-red heels. If you looked closely, you could see the faint imprint of Riley Jessup's heavy features on her much smaller face. She had a dimpled chin and tiny eyes and cinnamon-colored hair that cupped her cheeks like two hands. Bell recognized her from the picture that had accompanied Donnie Frazey's preview story in the *Acker's Gap Gazette*: She was Sharon Jessup Henner, the governor's daughter.

Bell couldn't hear what she was saying into the cell, but clearly it wasn't a cordial exchange. The woman's face was owned by a scowl. The skin on that face looked hard; it was thickened by age, and by the sneaky inroads carved by worry or debauchery or both. It told the story of her life. Skin always did.

'That's his daughter, right?' Bell asked Rhonda. The room was so noisy that she didn't need to whisper.

'You got it. Pretty notorious, back in the day.'

'How so?'

Rhonda licked her lips. She seemed to cool down all at once. Now she was in her element. She knew the backstory of a great many residents of Raythune County, along with their uncles and cousins and great-aunts and step-grandparents; she could even recite the lineage of the better-known hunting dogs in the region. And she enjoyed deploying the information, as long as she could do so at her own pace, letting the story unfurl bit by delicious bit, like a wide red ribbon coaxed slowly and dramatically off its spool.

But this time, there was a complication. Rhonda

knew the Jessups' saga only thirdhand, from listening to other people's stories. She hated to acknowledge that there were families in Raythune County about which she had little inside information; it was like finding a bad spot on a shiny apple. So she first had to justify herself.

'Well,' Rhonda said, tucking in gamely, 'you gotta remember, boss, that nobody ever heard of the Jessups until Riley went into politics. Before that, they were just another dirt-poor family from Briney Hollow. Now, you grew up around here, too, so I don't need to tell you about Briney Hollow,' she said, and then proceeded to do just that: 'Too many folks out there to keep track of. Too many kids running around with no shoes. No warm coats in the winter. No breakfast in their bellies when they head out to school. It's a shame, but it was true then and it's true now. Briney Hollow is one of those places you'd swear the good Lord forgot all about – and by the time He remembers, He'll be too embarrassed at His lapse to do much of anything about it. Anyhow, Riley Jessup was an ambitious fella, early on. Had a real knack with the crowds – guess you just got a look at that yourself – and kept on going. Up and up and up.'

Rhonda paused. She and Bell were both distracted by the sight of an elderly woman in a sweat-mauled blue blouse who had tottered up to Jessup's chair and offered her hand; when he took it and shook it and then tried to withdraw, she held on, as if his hand were the last rock sticking out of the cliff face and she was sliding down, down, down. Jessup's face quivered with the opening stages of panic. At last a security guard intervened, breaking the old woman's grip and leading her away, while she mumbled her outrage.

'Same time Jessup was rising up,' Rhonda went on, resuming her story with even more relish, 'Sharon over there was running wild. Gave Jessup and his wife, Tammy Lynn – Tammy Lynn, God rest her soul, died of breast cancer a few years back – no end of trouble, on account of her drinking and her sleeping around. Loved to embarrass her daddy, seems like. Ran away time after time when she was a teenager. Disappeared completely in her twenties and thirties. Straightened up, though, in the end. Came home to her folks after finding Jesus – or so she said, there being no way to independently verify that story with the other party.'

Rhonda paused once again. There was a kink in the line parading past Jessup's chair; like an ominous clog in a drain, the backed-up crowd was thickening into a confused lump. A chubby toddler with strawberry-blond pigtails – apparently mistaking the rotund governor for a shopping-mall Santa – had attempted to climb into his polyester prairie of a lap. A security guard snatched up the girl in a pincer-like grip and, with astonishing speed, deposited her back on the floor. She waited five seconds and then exploded into shriek-heavy sobs.

'Then Sharon married Whit Henner,' Rhonda said, now that the show was over and the line had begun to move again. 'Aide to the governor. Their son, Montgomery, was born sixteen years ago. Sickly child, right from the get-go, and he's only gotten worse. Bet you anything that Sharon's on the phone right now with one of his doctors back in Charleston.' Rhonda and Bell looked at Sharon; she had moved a few steps away from Jessup's chair and from the long motley string of his admirers, and was aiming another barrage of verbal abuse into her cell.

'Riley Jessup is just nuts about the kid,' Rhonda said. She had lowered her voice ever so slightly; this part of the story was sad rather than juicy. 'Do anything in the world for him. Now, mind you – Jessup was never much interested in family before, except when the cameras were rolling. But everybody says he's a changed man. The boy's health problems just bother him something awful. Tear him up inside.' Rhonda crossed her arms, a signal that she was winding things up. 'The governor tells anybody who'll listen that Montgomery is the only reason he's still on this earth – I mean, the old man's got a pacemaker and diabetes and enough arthritis to make every step a misery. But God granted him a few more years, he says, so's he can see Montgomery grow up.'

'Where's the kid?' Bell said, looking around.

'Oh, he's way too sick to travel. Some kind of heart thing. Real bad, I hear.' Rhonda scratched the side of her neck, a neck wet from copious sweating.

'How about Sharon's husband – Whit Henner?'

Rhonda shrugged. 'Been out of the picture for years. Comes around occasionally for photo shoots. Sharon and her son live with Riley Jessup. Ever seen that place? Believe me, he's got the room.' Her expression changed. She looked troubled; something else was on her mind. 'You know what?'

Bell waited.

'Don't get me wrong,' Rhonda said. 'I feel for the family's troubles. I do. But if you ask me, Riley Jessup's a first-class, ring-tailed hypocrite. Lives in a palace. He's got more money than God. When he was in office, though, and had the chance, he didn't do a damned thing about the falling-down schools. Or about the roads that're so bad, you can't even find 'em again after a hard rain. Lined his pockets with corporate money and then let those thieving bastards run the state as they saw fit, year after year, dumping poison in the rivers, taking shortcuts with safety regulations and cutting off mountaintops like a bored kid with a stick in a field of dandelions. You've seen that bumper sticker – "Almost level, West Virginia." Not even funny anymore, thanks to the Riley Jessups of this world.'

Bell was surprised. Rhonda didn't usually talk politics with such vehemence; her passion was generally restricted to new clothes and fresh gossip.

'Anyway,' Rhonda concluded, 'Jessup is trying to make amends, I suppose, with the MRI thingy. First we've ever had. Kind of amazing, really, that we even have an X-ray machine. Surprised they don't just rely on somebody poking you in the gut to see if you yell. And way over there,' she said, inclining her head toward the lobby entrance, and toward a tall, slender man in an artfully tailored gray suit, 'is the fella who persuaded Jessup to pay for the MRI – although I hate to have to give him the credit.'

Bell turned. It was Bradley Portis, a man to whom she had taken an instant dislike when she met him a few months ago. The CEO of the Raythune County Medical Center was the only person present who seemed unfazed by the heat. His thick chestnut hair had lost none of its luster. His eyes were unreadable, as glazed-over and generic as his smile. Hands clasped behind his back, he looked mildly bored as he surveyed the crooked trail of people inching feverishly toward Riley Jessup. In his posture, which Bell would've sworn had been perfected with the help of a laser level, and in the slight but perceptible lift of a black eyebrow, she sensed a massive distaste for these people and their second-rate clothes. Their second-rate lives.

'Yeah,' Bell said. 'I know Portis. Met him at a county commission meeting last fall.'

'Well, he's never actually moved here,' Rhonda muttered, lowering her voice, as if the accusation were too heinous to be discussed in polite company. 'Commutes two or three days a week from D.C. Bet he's never even stepped foot on county soil outside the premises of this place. And if you ask me—'

She was interrupted by another ruckus at the governor's chair. Three women screamed, one right after the other, as if they were handing a package down the row. In the midst of the handshakes and the nervous curtsies, the line had abruptly broken open; there was a mad scramble as people scattered like dropped marbles, grabbing their kids and tugging at elderly relatives by their belt loops.

A thin-faced, big-eared man with a wilted-looking Fu Manchu mustache, gray tank top, and baggy shorts had bolted from his spot well back in the line and – arms extended, legs churning, the words *Hey Gubner, Hey Gubner!* dropping from his mouth along with strings of saliva – was barreling toward Riley Jessup, bumping other people out of the way with a mean sashay of his bony shoulders. The governor was startled, the grin frozen on his face. Sharon gasped and staggered backwards.

A security guard leaped at Fu Manchu, knocking him flat on his back, flipping him over like a crispy-edged pancake and then linking his wrists with a zip tie while he bucked and he flailed. A third guard wedged a boot against the side of his neck. A fourth leaned over and jammed the chunky snout of a Glock behind his right ear.

Fu Manchu was drunk, a fact that became immediately apparent when he was hauled to his feet and promptly sent vomit rocketing onto the black shirtfront of the closest guard. 'Jush wanna,' Fu Manchu muttered, swaying back and forth, smacking his lips to get rid of the sticky yellow flecks of puke, 'say hi to Gubner Jezzup. Thazall. Thazall.'

In the heat, the smell of the regurgitated alcohol was irresistibly sick-making. Several people lurched and stumbled out of the lobby, heads bent, hands cupped over mouths.

'Jesus,' Bell murmured, as much to herself as to Rhonda, 'if that's how they react to some shit-faced fool, wonder what the hell they'd do with a *real* threat?'

17

Business was brisk at the station that night. Cars came in bunches, in twos and threes and even fives, and the little chimneys of exhaust fumes rising from the crooked line gave the hot air a dense, quilted texture, like something you could stroke or nuzzle.

Lindy, standing at her post behind the front counter, watched through the window. Across the road was a dark unremarkable scramble of woods, so there wasn't much else to see except the slow flotilla of dusty chrome. As one car departed, another would inch up to the pump. The moment the vehicle intersected with the dribble of light, everything was revealed: Dirty fender. Mud-colored tires. Dented-in door. Sunburned, grumpy occupants packed in behind the smeary windows. The driver – usually it was the driver – would wrench himself up and out to take care of the business at hand. Credit card punched in the slot, pulled out, repocketed. Gas cap twisted off, nozzle jammed in the black hole with the kind of modified violence that spoke of the heat of the day and the degree of accumulated frustration. Then he'd finish up and clear out and the next car would roll forward and the new driver would initiate the ritual all over again, the punch and the pull, the twist and jam. The scowl.

'Looks like the whole county's out for a drive tonight,' Lindy said.

The top of Jason's blue ball cap wobbled, which meant he was nodding. That was all she could see of him right now, because he was lost in the wilds of the chip aisle, restocking the slick crinkly bags after a recent assault on the supply of the barbecue-flavored kind.

'Yep,' he replied. 'Looks that way.'

The Lester station was one of only two filling stations left in the area. The other was Highway Haven, a truck stop out on the interstate. But if the hour was late and you needed gas and you didn't want to go thirty-eight miles out of your way, you either brought your car here or you got out and pushed it home.

Sometimes customers at the pumps required Lindy's assistance. They'd spot her through the big plate glass window and move their arm in a high arcing wave, rising onto tiptoes and mouthing whatever it was they wanted to say. Invariably they'd be startled by the sound of Lindy's voice when it crackled out of the perforated metal pad on the side of the pump: 'May I help you?' Most of the customers forgot about the two-way communication system until she talked, although it was alluded to on the sign above the pump, right next to the prices for Marlboros, a gallon of milk, Hershey Bars: PRESS BUTTON TO TALK TO ATTENDANT. Hearing her, they sometimes jumped as if bitten.

'Yeah,' they'd say, leaning toward the speaker. 'Pump don't work. Ain't giving me no gas.'

The pump did work. The pump worked just fine. The problem, Lindy knew, was not with the pump.

The problem was with their credit card. The problem was that they'd run out of money, run out of luck, run out of prospects. Running out of gas was just the latest item on the list of things they'd run out of. Children – they never seemed to run out of those – were jammed together into the backseat, pushing their lips against the window like curious fish in a dirty fishbowl.

'Try another card,' she'd say, wondering how her voice sounded when it came through the speaker system, wondering if she'd even recognize it herself after it was roughed up by all the static and distortion. At her end, the customer's too-loud voice always sounded blurry and mechanical, like the voice of a cartoon robot.

'Ain't got another card.'

She was required to stick to the script laid out in the Lester employee handbook, and so she said, 'Well, you'll have to come inside then and pay cash.' If she'd had her way, she would've said, *Listen, I'll override it. Just take the gas you need, okay? And then go. Just go, okay?*

Sometimes they came in. Sometimes they didn't. Sometimes the driver stared at her through the plate glass window for a good long minute – she was in a lighted space and the driver stood in a spotlight, too, courtesy of the bug-bedeviled bulb hanging over the pumps, and so they could see each other with penetrating clarity across the dark interval of asphalt – and at that point he might lean over and carefully articulate an obscenity directly into the speaker. He would say, 'Fuck *you*, bitch' – so that there would be no mistaking his mood or the extent to which his pride had been decimated. Then he'd fling himself back in the car and punch the accelerator as if it, too, had insulted him, bulling his way off the lot, swerving wildly around a car trying to enter from the other side and barely missing it, and all Lindy could think about were those kids in the backseat, unsecured by anything as emblematic of forethought or caution as seat belts, rattling around in that backseat like gravel in an empty pop can.

She remembered what her district manager had told her once. You can always tell when things are getting bad, you can tell when the already precarious economic situation in this part of West Virginia is worsening, by the numbers on the pump. Times like these, the numbers were low: $1.82 or $2 or $3.16. Never over five dollars. And never, God knows, a fill-up. People bought gas in dribs and drabs, waiting as long as they could between stops at the station. After a big event – Sunday church service, say, or a wedding or a funeral or a ceremony in a hospital parking lot – they'd be heading home and realize they couldn't risk it anymore and finally would have to spend the last little bit of what they had on gas.

At one point between 9 and 10 P.M., the line for the pumps was, Lindy noted to her astonishment, six cars long, with a hefty dump truck as the exclamation point. She called out that fact to Jason.

'Yeah,' he answered. 'Big thing out at the hospital. For a new MRI machine. Brought in some boring old fart to speak.' He'd finished with the chip aisle and was standing in front of the dairy case in the back, having repeatedly opened the door and leaned his head in for the clear purpose of cooling himself down, until Lindy told him to stop. 'Ginormous crowd, my brother said,' Jason went on. 'This's probably just folks who stayed around to visit family and whatnot. Getting gas before they start home. Don't want to run out – not with a murderin' sumbitch out there somewheres.'

Lindy nodded, as if she'd found his explanation helpful. But it was the sheer volume of customers, not the origin, that had perplexed her. She knew the origin. She read the papers. Hard not to, with the stack that lived right under her chin for a week at a time. She knew about the new MRI machine. She even knew what 'MRI' stood for – which was more, she thought, than Jason knew. That certainty made her feel lonely, not superior.

'Want me to get more coffee going?' he asked.

She shrugged. 'Guess so. Folks've been hitting it pretty good tonight.'

He answered her shrug with one of his own and headed over to that corner of the store. Along the way he passed the pastry case, giving it a quick obligatory frown. By this time of night, the contents arranged on the yellow slide-out trays looked battered and sagging and forlorn; the doughnuts and cinnamon rolls were delivered fresh every morning but steadily lost their confidence throughout the long humid day. Funny, Lindy always thought, how things could go from sparkly and inviting to rubbery and gross in the span of a few hours. Maybe it was the fact that they were trapped behind a little plastic door.

While Jason fussed with the coffeepots, she dealt with an abrupt influx of customers who wanted more than gas. Pop. Cigarettes. Doritos. Skoal Long Cut Mint. A Little Debbie Swiss Cake Roll. She was asked, by an older man with an outrageously bad toupee and liquor on his breath, if she'd like some company later on, when her shift was over. 'No, I wouldn't,' she said, handing him his change. She looked him right in the eye. She didn't look away, and she didn't get mad. She'd learned a few things, in the time she'd been doing this job; yes, she had. The man waited for more from her, waggling his eyebrows, hoping for a wise-crack, maybe, or a put-down, something he could counter with his cleverness, and when it didn't come, when she just looked at him, dead-eyed, he turned around and left. A little past midnight two teenage girls glided in on a moving cushion of giggles and asked if they could have the key to the bathroom. They hadn't made a purchase, so technically Lindy was supposed to say no, but the fact was, the toilets for customers were out back in a separate building, a dumpy tar paper shack that was cleaned about once a decade. Allegedly. If somebody wanted to use the space for whatever, it was fine by her. She knew they wouldn't linger.

By 2 A.M. the number of customers had thinned considerably. The blackness of the nicked-up two-lane road that ran in front of the station was broken only sporadically by a pair of bouncing headlights. Once per hour, tops. After that the darkness would return, swallowing the road whole, as if the world were a birdcage and somebody had flung a hand towel over it.

Jason was mopping up a spill on the floor by the coffeepots. The mess was the handiwork of a maybe-drunk-or-maybe-just-clumsy guy who'd stumbled in earlier that night, dumping an entire jumbo cup of Mountain Dew and crushed ice on his way to the counter to pay for it. Jason had put off the cleanup – with no customers around, it didn't matter – but

finally boredom, not necessity, pushed him to under-
take the task.

Lindy was busy as well. She finished sorting and
racking the cigarette cartons. She had to stretch to
reach the very top shelf, lining up the end flaps just
so, making sure that the brand names were visible.
Her father and mother had both smoked, once upon
a time; Lindy had vivid childhood memories of being
asked to find the open pack and bring it to the
kitchen or the living room or the front porch, wherever they'd seated themselves, and handing it to her
father or her mother and smiling, because they'd
compliment her on her detective skills and the praise
felt golden and wonderful, like sunshine on your
birthday. 'Never can remember where I leave 'em,'
her father would say, 'but this little girl, she's smart.
Sniffs 'em out, right quick. Don't know how she
turned out so smart. Nobody in my family's anywhere
near as smart as this one right here.' Lindy loved
pleasing them. 'She's a real good girl,' her mother
would add, sometimes touching Lindy's face with
her fingertips, the unlit cigarette poised between her
index finger and her middle finger. Her mother always
held off lighting the cigarette until she'd finished
with Lindy, worried she might burn her. Her mother
was careful that way.

These days, her father didn't smoke. Lindy wasn't
sure exactly when that had happened, there was no
announcement, no grand renunciation; he just stopped.
Sometimes she wondered if he'd just forgotten that he
was a smoker. Maybe that was it. Didn't matter,
though. The damage was done. His lungs were black-
scarred, tough as the hard bark on a long-dead tree.
Every breath he had was a gift, the doctors said,

because there weren't very many breaths left. Not in lungs that looked like that.

She turned back around to face the store, watching Jason work. The fluorescent lights that hummed overhead gave everything in this small space a crisp dimensional edge, outlined like the risen grain in a stained piece of wood: the narrow metal aisles, the dairy cases along the back wall, and, next to all four outside walls, blocking the bottom half of the tall glass, the stacks of plastic yellow containers of antifreeze and engine additives. Lindy had worked the day shift a couple of times, subbing for other employees, but she didn't like it; when the world outside was light, the store looked dingy and sad. It looked, frankly, like the piece of crap it was. At night, however, this place was its own little island of light. There was magic in it, although Lindy would never have said such a thing out loud. Not to Jason, not to anybody.

'Hey, Jace,' she said.

He stopped what he was doing. 'Yeah. What.'

'Nothing.'

He went back to work, eyeing the row of coffeepots. Most were down to the noxious nubbins. The smell of old, overcooked coffee lurked in the air, a smell that, both he and Lindy agreed, bore an uncomfortable similarity to dog shit.

'Want me to sweep up outside?' Jason called to her.

'Leave it for now.'

He shrugged and undertook his Cool Walk to the front counter. He leaned against it, standing in the same place where the customers waited for their change, his elbows angled, idly messing with the tins of Skoal and Copenhagen in the slanting wire rack.

'Don't get those all mixed up,' Lindy said. 'People don't like it.'

'Shit, girl, don't be gettin' on my case.' Cool Walk, Cool Talk.

She didn't respond, because there was something she needed to ask him about. Something serious.

'Hey,' she said.

'Yeah.'

'The bad stuff that's been happening around here,' she said, straining to sound casual. 'That old guy who got killed in his driveway. And that guy they found by the side of the road – all cut up.'

'Yeah.'

'Well, what do you think? Is it outsiders, maybe?'

'Don't know. Don't guess anybody knows.' He pressed a finger in the middle of a Skoal tin, as if he were ringing a doorbell. Pressed another one.

'But it's probably outsiders, right? Nobody around here would do anything like that. Right?'

'Sure they would. Them drugs – it's changing the whole state. Everybody says so.' Jason had another brother, too. Levi Brinkerman, three years older than Jason, was a tweaker. A meth head. His brain cells were fried, the way bacon curls up in a hot skillet, and now he sat on the front porch of the Brinkerman house and he itched and he shivered and he rocked back and forth and, when he could swipe enough change to swing it, he smoked the stuff that made him feel, he told Jason, and then Jason told Lindy, like that flame guy in The Fantastic Four – *What the hell's his name? Can't remember. But like that. That's what I feel like. Oughta try it, kid. You'll see.* Lindy and Jason rarely talked about Levi, just as they rarely talked about Lindy's father. But when they did, it was serious and important.

That, in fact, was why Lindy had brought it up tonight. Jason, she'd figured out, felt responsible for his brother. And he understood what it was like when someone you loved – someone in your own family – harbored a secret darkness, like a letter carried in an inside pocket. Jason knew what she knew, or at least what she might be on her way to finding out: that people could do things you never, ever thought they'd do. Terrible things. Unforgivable things. And yet you still had to take care of them. Right?

'So maybe it's the drugs,' Lindy said.

'Yeah. Maybe.'

'Yeah.'

But if it's him, if it's Daddy, Lindy asked herself, *then why don't I tell somebody? Warn them? Don't I have to do that? Don't I have to turn him in? Let them take him away? Don't I have to—?*

'Earth to Lindy,' Jason said. 'Kind of zoned out on me there.'

'Sorry.' She'd made a decision: She would search the house before she talked to anybody. Scour it. Take it apart, if need be. See if she could find any real proof of what her father did when he went out at night. Evidence. Anything – anything at all. She'd be thorough. She had to be. Had to know what was going on. Otherwise—

Jason was talking again. She struggled to pay attention.

'Anyway,' he said, 'you ask me, it's drugs – shit like that.' He nodded sagely, as if he were plugged into a vast and exclusive knowledge source labeled What's Really Going On In The World. 'The money's gotta come from somewhere, you know? Don't be growing on no trees.'

Lindy started to answer, but the perky little *ding-ding!* – the automatic signal that someone had pushed open the glass double doors from outside – startled them both. Focused on their conversation, they had turned away from the entrance. Usually they were more alert than that, especially after dark. More aware of who was coming and going, of what was happening outside the store, just beyond the scrap of light at the pumps.

The new customer looked vaguely familiar. Maybe, Lindy thought, she'd seen her picture in the *Gazette*. Definitely, this woman had patronized the station previously, although Lindy could pretty much swear she'd never come inside before. Just paid at the pump. Medium-length brown hair. Nice face. No makeup. White blouse. Light blue cotton skirt. The skirt had the rumpled, slightly wilted demeanor of a garment that had gamely done its duty throughout a ravishingly hot day and into an equally hot night. Lindy watched the woman's face. It was pale and stressed-looking; her nose was slightly red and her eyes were ringed with tiredness.

'Help you, ma'am?' Lindy said.

Jason had backed away a step or two, giving the stranger a clear lane to the counter to conduct her business, but he kept an eye on her. This late at night, he and Lindy had to look out for each other. Missing the woman's approach had rattled him.

'Yes, I—' The woman paused. Her face unwound into a smile. 'Looking for a cold pop. Hot as hell out there, you know? Never lets up, even when the sun goes down.'

'Cooler's in the back.' Lindy pointed.

The woman nodded, then left to go pick out the

chilled can of her choice. Neither Lindy nor Jason spoke until she returned. They were veterans of the night shift, old hands, but it always felt weird when the blackness was split wide open like this, at irregular intervals; there was no pattern, nothing that would make you expect a well-dressed, plainly sober woman to come walking into the station at 3:17 A.M.

'Thanks,' the woman said, taking her change from the five-dollar bill she'd given Lindy and sliding it into her skirt pocket.

'Anything else?' Lindy asked.

The woman held up the can of Diet Dr Pepper and waggled it. 'This'll do the trick.' The smile lingered longer this time, and Lindy had the feeling – it came as she looked directly into the woman's gray-blue eyes – that she liked her. She wasn't sure why, exactly, but she did.

Through the glass, Lindy watched her return to the Explorer parked next to the pumps. She had a purposeful, straight-line kind of walk. Very little wasted motion.

Lindy couldn't be absolutely certain, she wouldn't swear to it, but when she recalled the customer's eyes, and the smudged and rumpled look to the skin that surrounded them, it seemed to her that the woman had recently been crying.

Bell drove away from the little gas station and back out onto the country road. The Explorer's headlights worked like a pickax, chipping systematically at the dark tunnel but just a bit at a time; it revealed nothing except what lay a few feet ahead, after which the darkness collapsed again behind her, like a constant series of quiet cave-ins.

Her left hand was on the wheel. With her right, she held the unopened can next to her cheek, rolling it down onto her neck and back up again. She needed to cool off. The cold can, slick with condensation from the moment she'd stepped out of the little store and back into the night's mighty heat, left a wide wet trail on half her face. She didn't care.

She'd been driving for hours. At first she'd kept to the back roads, the ones that kinked and twisted as they rose and fell, the ones that passed slatternly trailers and crowded salvage yards and nameless creeks and long-abandoned coal tipples, but then she changed her mind and headed for the interstate. She could go faster on the freeway. The back roads enforced a lower speed limit. Enforced it, that is, if your desire was to remain on a solid surface and not conclude your evening upside down in a ditch with all four windows blown out, hanging by your seat belt while fluid leaked out of the radiator – and leaked out of you, too, if you'd had the bad luck to puncture something.

Bell drove through the darkness because that was what she always did when she was upset. It was a sweeping, ravening kind of darkness that arose out of heat and hopelessness and crimes and questions, a dark that seemed not the opposite of light but light's true master, as if it allowed the light to exist as a courtesy, nothing more, and when the time came, the dark would revoke the privilege. The dark was in charge.

So she drove. She drove until she ran out of problems or ran out of gas. The latter always came first.

And on this night, when she grew weary of the freeway, she had headed back to the county roads. They provided a different kind of solace. Not every kind of night driving was the same; on the interstate, you were never alone, while on the back roads, you almost always were. The high-up Lester sign – a white neon rectangle with LESTER spelled out in slanting blue block letters, rising over the small asphalt lot on a string-bean aluminum pole – had drawn her toward it. She didn't want to see or talk to anybody she knew. A safe bet in this place, she figured.

Still, Bell hoped that the young woman behind the counter wouldn't pick up on the fact that she'd been crying. If she did – well, to hell with her.

Bell had received the text at 6:47 P.M., just as she was getting ready to leave the hospital lot with Nick Fogelsong; he had offered her a ride back to the courthouse, where she'd left her Explorer. Deputy Harrison was busy dealing with the drunk who'd befouled the lobby. Riley Jessup was long gone, safely packed up in his motor home with his daughter and his private security staff – all of them plenty glad, no doubt, to have Raythune County in their rearview mirror.

The message was from Carla. It was so long that it had broken itself into two blocks of type that seemed to quiver with excitement:

> *Hi Mom. Know u will understand. Going to London!!! Dad got me a summer internship there. Total surprise!!! Some other girl got sick or something. Anyway, hate to miss summer in WV and getting 2 know Aunt Shirley and hanging out w/u, but – London!! London! Can u believe it????? ☺ Will call soon. Luv u lots n lots*

Bell hadn't said a word to Fogelsong. She didn't want his sympathy right then. She'd been stunned and hurt – and pissed off, too. Not at Carla, but at her ex-husband. He'd done it again. Performed a dirty little trick, deftly and cleverly undermining the spirit of their shared custody arrangement.

Could Bell insist that Carla spend the summer in Acker's Gap as originally planned? Yes, she could. She could do that. She could force her daughter to come to West Virginia and forgo London – thereby breaking Carla's heart. Not to mention making herself a villain in her child's eyes. A heartless, selfish, fun-spoiling bitch.

That was why Sam had called her the day before. He knew what he'd done, but didn't have the guts to tell her himself.

So Sam had won. He always did.

She had fired off a single-word text to her ex-husband:

Bastard

He didn't need any context. He'd know what she was referring to.

The sheriff had dropped her back at the courthouse and she retrieved her Explorer. All that was left to her now, her only recourse, was to drive. Drive fast. Drive hard. Drive long. Drive with all four windows rolled down. Drive – and try not to think about the rest of the summer and how much she would miss Carla.

She drove across a road that curled tightly around the mountain the way a cracked whip wraps around a fence post. Down an ancient lane pinched to a treacherous narrowness by high trees and massive rocks frowning over it. Past dusty mountain towns that closed up early, the junk-ringed houses now just gray humps lining the road, not a flicker of light in a front window or a shed.

And as she drove, she cried – not a lot, not for long, but enough. Enough to know she didn't want anyone to see her like this, weak and distraught and disheveled. She'd actually been glad when she remembered that Shirley wasn't home; she'd called there earlier, and nobody picked up the phone. Fine. *Fine*. Hell with her.

Hell with everybody.

She transferred the can to her left hand, using her right to maneuver the Explorer up the wicked incline of Fiddlers Run Road. She was on her way home. It wouldn't be long. She rolled the can against her cheek, again relishing its cool wet sides. She still didn't open it. Had no intention of opening it. Truth was, she hated Dr Pepper, diet or otherwise. Thought it tasted like cough syrup laced with shoe polish and served up in a rusty ladle. But it was Carla's favorite. And Bell desperately wanted to feel close to her daughter right now, even in small, silly, pointless ways.

That's why she had stopped at the Lester station. When she opened the cooler door and felt the sweet rush of the refrigerated air, she saw the cans – red cans, white cans, black cans, blue cans, yellow and green cans – lying on their sides, gleaming smartly in their designated rows. She reached for the Diet Dr Pepper. First thing when she arrived home, Bell planned to sink down in her favorite chair and silently toast her daughter's trip. *Have fun, sweetheart, and don't worry about me or Shirley or anybody else, just take care of yourself*. She would do it with a beverage that reminded her of Carla.

And she would do it the same way she seemed to do everything these days: alone.

18

'Lordy, look at that,' Rhonda said. She tilted her head and squinted out the car window, the better to take the measure of the luscious blue sky that started at the top of the mountain. 'Always looks bluer this time of year.'

'No,' Bell said.

'You don't think it looks bluer this time of year?'

'No, I mean I can't look.' Bell tapped the steering wheel. 'Better keep my eyes on the road.'

'Oh.' Rhonda emitted an embarrassed blurt of a giggle that could have doubled as a hiccup. 'Yep. Good point.' She settled back in the passenger seat of the Explorer, folding her hands on the roomy lap of her peach-colored skirt. 'Well, you'll have to take my word for it, then.'

It was Saturday morning, one day after the dedication ceremony at the hospital. Just after nine, Bell had picked up Rhonda at the courthouse in her Explorer. Twenty-five minutes later, they crossed the Raythune county line, and fifteen minutes after that, reached the trailer park listed in court records as the home address of Jed and Tiffany Stark and their daughter, Guinivere.

Bell would have preferred to work on the Arnett and Frank cases. Leads, though, were frustratingly few, and were being pursued by others. Deputy Harrison was reinterviewing one of the hitchhikers, who had called the sheriff's office to say that maybe he recalled something, after all, and that maybe he'd seen a man in the woods that night, wearing a long coat, close to the spot along Godown Road where Charlie Frank died of his wounds. He couldn't be sure – but maybe. Maybe he'd seen that. And Sheriff Fogelsong was meeting with a specialist from the state crime lab; he wanted help in consulting more extensive databases, checking for crimes with similar weapons and methodologies in surrounding counties. Digging deeper.

When Rhonda had proposed a trip to the Stark trailer, Bell was silently grateful. She wanted to be in motion today, just as she'd wanted to be in motion last night. She needed to keep one step ahead of her grief over Carla's absence. And if she and Rhonda weren't working on the homicides in their own jurisdiction, then they might as well be exploring the question that now needled Rhonda almost as much as it did Bell: Why would a man like Jed Stark be doing business with a New York lawyer?

Their conversation as they drove that morning had been mostly superficial, and mostly it emanated from Rhonda: The sky. The heat. The new youth minister at Rhonda's church. The goatee that Deputy Mathers was trying to grow, the one that made him look like he'd been two-fisting Oreos and ought to bother wiping his face every once in a while. The hip replacement surgery that Rhonda's mother would undergo next month.

Bell pulled into an unmarked lane. The Explorer bounced like a pogo stick across the pothole-pocked road until they reached a dead end. Clustered around the dirt-packed circle, radiating out from it like the spokes of a prone wheel, were some twenty house trailers. Each trailer had a rickety lawn chair on its stoop, a chair that took up most of the space; next to the chair on many of the stoops was an old metal coffee can, overflowing with cigarette butts. Sunlight glinted off the flimsy-looking trailer frames. Only a few had cars parked alongside them. Bell read the bumper stickers: KEEP HONKING. I'M RELOADING was one. PROUD WIFE OF A COAL MINER, another.

There had been no sign along the road to designate the trailer park. Bell's ability to locate it quickly and efficiently came from Rhonda's preliminary work. The assistant prosecutor had called her uncle Cam in Steppe County, told him the address, and gleaned the particulars: Dirt road, just after the turnoff for Muddy Hollow. If you get to the intersection that hooks up with Route 147, you've gone too far.

Rhonda shifted in her seat, peering around. 'Kinda odd that there's nobody outside. Nice morning like this.' She thought about it. 'Well – maybe not. This's not the kind of place that welcomes strangers, I guess. 'Specially not now.'

The Explorer had surely been spotted before they even made the turn off the main road, and the warning had spread via an informal network that couldn't be pinned down to a conduit as specific as a phone call or a text or even a yell, a network that moved as mysteriously as the wind. Unexpected visitors generally meant trouble. Might be somebody from the propane company, waving an unpaid bill. Or the bank or the sheriff's office. Could be a disgruntled ex-husband or a spurned girlfriend or a cousin who'd lent money against his better judgment and now wanted it back. Plus interest.

These days, it could be somebody with a sledge-hammer or a knife.

After a single glimpse of Bell's vehicle from a side window, doubtless the word had gone up and down this dirt road, flicking into each trailer like a snake's tongue: *Keep quiet. Stay low.*

'Over there,' Bell said.

The third trailer on the left-hand side was the one they were looking for. It was turd-shaped and dilapi-dated, brown with silver trim. Somebody had tried to make it look a little better by planting annuals in a half-moon track around the stoop. The heat had turned the tiny blooms into a damp wilted mess.

While Rhonda waited a few feet away, Bell went to the door. There wasn't room on the stoop for both of them. She knocked. Fatigue made her arm feel unusually heavy, as if she were moving in slow motion, fighting invisible pressure. She'd had, by her most optimistic estimate, about two hours of sleep between the moment she arrived home from her driving marathon to her departure for the courthouse. Shirley had stayed away all night; there was no word from her, either.

The door opened. A young woman peeked out. Dirty blond hair was teased up into a fragile swirl that topped her narrow face like cotton candy on a stick. Mid- to late twenties, Bell estimated.

'Yeah?'

'Morning.' Bell had her ID ready and held it up. 'I'm Belfa Elkins, prosecuting attorney of Raythune County. I'd like to talk to you for a moment or so about Jed. You're Tiffany, right?'

The woman blinked. 'Yeah. Okay.' She seemed hungry for company, a hunger that superseded any suspicions or hesitations. Opening the door wider, she spotted Rhonda in the yard. 'You can come on in, too, hon.'

The interior of the trailer smelled like cigarettes and soon-to-be-sour milk and socks that had gone too long without a washing, and, as a top note, a cheap air freshener, the plastic cone-shaped kind that you activated by sliding up the cover, a little at a time. Ocean Breeze – that was the name of the scent. Bell recognized it. It was a smell from her childhood. And the name was a joke, given the smells it was trying to cover. Impossible fight on its hands.

Ocean Breeze, my ass, she thought.

Bell and Rhonda had to move aside an impressive pile of toys to make room to sit on the red-plaid corduroy couch. The living room was small, so constricted that Bell felt slightly short of breath. The heat didn't help. There was no AC. No fan. Throw in the cloying fake-sweetness of Ocean Breeze, and Bell wasn't sure how long she'd be able to last in here.

While Rhonda and Bell methodically relocated a toy xylophone, the scattered accoutrements of a Barbie Country Camper, a seriously warped copy of *Goodnight Moon* that looked as if it had been dropped repeatedly in a wading pool and then left to dry in the yard, a colored-on Candy Land game board, a plastic pail and shovel, an upside-down carton of baby wipes, a sparkly tiara, and dozens of tiny sticks and sprockets from an Erector Set, Tiffany watched them. She lit a cigarette. She lifted her shoulders as she acquired a passionate lungful. Blew it out in a rich plume. Then she waved away the smoke with a spasm of impatience, as if somebody else had produced it.

'You all want sumpin' to drink?' she said. She sat

down across from them, on a wooden chair that didn't match any other furniture in the room. 'I got Mountain Dew and Pabst.' She was barefoot, and wore cutoff shorts and a sleeveless pink blouse. Her arms and legs were very thin and looked, Bell thought, a lot like the sticks in the Erector Set they'd just relocated.

'We're fine,' Bell answered. Rhonda nodded, backing her up.

'Okay, well. Guinivere'll be getting up after while. She sleeps pretty late. Still don't understand what happened to her daddy. Asks about him all the time. I just say, "He's with Jesus." Figure that'll cover it pretty good. Till she's older.' Tiffany shrugged and leaned forward, utilizing the orange plastic ashtray on the glass-topped coffee table. The glass was smudged with dozens of overlapping fingerprints and a long-ago spill of something brown and thick that had hardened into a kidney-shaped glaze.

'We're very sorry for your loss,' Bell said. 'How long had you and Jed been married?'

'Three years is all. We was together a long time before that, though. Years and years. Tied the knot when I knew I was having Guinivere.'

'Pretty name,' Rhonda said.

'It's from *Camelot*. She was the queen. The one married to King Arthur, till she ruint it all by falling in love with the wrong guy.' Tiffany grinned, an act that revealed the unfortunate fate of the majority of her teeth. 'Trouble is,' she went on, 'my mama keeps callin' her Gwen when we're out in public. Which makes people think I named her after Gwen Stefani. As *if*.' Energized by outrage, she took another long suck on her cigarette. She exhaled and then flailed again at the smoke, as if still mystified about its origins.

'Well,' Rhonda said, 'you can set them straight.'

Tiffany nodded. 'And so can Guinivere, once she's old enough. She'll speak up for herself. Gonna be a good strong girl. Go her own way. Just like her daddy. He never took no shit from nobody.'

Bell noticed how easily Tiffany had adopted the past tense. And she noticed, too, the total absence of anything resembling grief in the young woman's breezy demeanor. Yet Bell always cautioned her staff not to read too much into an individual's response to the loss of a loved one, and never to assume that it implied complicity in a homicide. Shock could make some people seem indifferent, even callous. Everyone grieved in her or his own way.

Still, Tiffany's response was a bit surprising. This woman had just lost her husband, the father of her child, and presumably the family's sole breadwinner – and lost him in a silly bar fight, to boot, inspired by his pursuit of another woman – and she seemed relaxed and casual. Not even especially perturbed. Was it significant? *Hell if I know,* Bell thought. *But maybe it's time I found out.*

'As I said, Mrs Stark, I'm the prosecutor over in Raythune County. I was sorry to hear about your husband's passing. Wanted to know more about him. How'd he make his living?'

'Little of this, little of that.'

'So he didn't have regular employment?'

'Not Jed.' Pride flashed in Tiffany's voice. 'He said he was too smart for that. Too smart to work for somebody else and break his back all day long so's they'd get the profit and he'd get nothing but the scraps. He wasn't no fool.'

Rhonda scooted forward on the couch. She'd sensed

where Bell was heading and wanted to help steer. 'So how'd he support you and Guinivere? I mean—' Rhonda leaned over and picked up a plush lime green tyrannosaurus from the floor in front of the couch and waved it in the air, smiling. '—how'd he pay for all these cute toys you got here for your little girl? If you don't mind my asking?'

'Errands.'

They waited. When Tiffany didn't go on, Rhonda said, 'Errands? Like, what kind of errands?'

'Well, you know. Somebody needed something taken somewhere. Or picked up. Or somebody needed to send a message to somebody else – like, "Back off" or "Gimme what's mine." Or whatever. See, Jed was real good at doing what needed to be done. No questions asked. I mean – sure, he'd get hisself in trouble sometimes. He couldn't pass a bar without stopping in for a cold one. But he took care of business. Believe you me.' With a forward bolt and a hard tap, Tiffany eliminated the lagging ash from her cigarette. She perched her cheek on the hand that held it, and the frowsy smoke headed into her hair.

'So what kind of errand was he doing for Sampson Voorhees?' Bell said.

'Who?'

'Voorhees. His business card was found in your husband's belongings. He's an attorney based in New York City.'

'Voorhees. Voorhees.' Tiffany, thinking hard, scrunched up her face. Shook her head. 'Nope. Never hearda that name. No, ma'am.'

'There was another name on the card, too,' Bell said. 'Looked like your husband had written it himself, maybe to remember it. Odell Crabtree.'

Tiffany, pulling her hand away from her cheek, studied the tip of the cigarette. She crossed her right leg over her left knee. Before that, she'd had her left leg crossed over her right knee. 'That one don't ring no bell, neither. Sorry, folks. Sorry you made your trip for nothin'.'

'So you have no idea what your husband's last job was about – or who it was for?' Bell said.

'Nope.'

'He didn't mention Voorhees? Or Crabtree? Say, before he left home that night?'

'Not a peep.'

'And you didn't—?'

Before Bell could finish her sentence, Tiffany was up on her feet again, leaning over and mashing what was left of her cigarette into the ashtray. 'Look, I got stuff to do, okay? I told you what I know – which ain't much – and now I gotta get some cleaning done before Guinivere gets up. If you all don't mind—'

'Mama.'

All three turned toward the sound, a kittenish mew as much as a word. Guinivere stood in the doorway of the trailer's sole bedroom, tiny face blurred with recent sleep, blond hair mussed and matted. She wore white shorts at least a size and a half too big – hand-me-downs from an older relative, Bell guessed – and a T-shirt with FUTURE HEARTBREAKER printed across a pair of plump red lips.

'Baby! You come on over here, honey, and let Mommy hold you.' Tiffany spread out her arms and waited for her daughter, still dazed with sleep, to stumble forward. Tiffany then scooped up the warm bundle of limbs and torso and hair and fell back into the chair, nuzzling the girl's nose with her own. 'How's my baby? How's mommy's little punkin?'

'What a sweetie,' Rhonda said, nodding and smiling. 'Just like an angel.' There was a note of gushing in her tone that irritated Bell – until she realized it was entirely strategic. 'Tell me something, Tiffany,' Rhonda went on. Her voice had dropped to a just-between-us hush. 'I don't mean to pry, but – aren't you just the teensiest little bit worried about keeping up payments on the trailer and making a nice home for that precious little child? Now that's Jed gone – well, I'm right concerned for the two of you. If you have to get a job, then who's going to watch her during the—?'

Tiffany's interruption came in a blaze. 'Don't you worry 'bout me. I'm *fine*. Okay? Gonna be just fine. Both of us. Got it all taken care of.'

'Really.' Rhonda looked mildly skeptical and gave Tiffany a chance to add to her explanation. Nothing was forthcoming.

'Yeah,' Tiffany finally said. 'Really. We're gonna be fine. Told you that. Got lots of help, matter of fact.'

The little girl squirmed in her lap, struggling to sit upright. 'Mama.'

'Hold on, honey,' Tiffany replied to her child. 'Mama's saying good-bye to these nice ladies. Then you can have some cereal, how 'bout it?'

'But, Mama—'

'I said *hold on*!' Tiffany snapped, giving her a hasty shake.

Bell nodded at Rhonda, and they rose from the couch. Time to go. At this point, they were only annoying Tiffany, riling her up. Bell didn't want to think about how that annoyance might manifest itself later, when it was just mother and child – with nobody around to witness the end results of Tiffany's temper.

'Mama,' Guinivere said, her soft voice still slurred with sleep, 'these ladies gonna visit? When we go to our new house?'

Bell and Rhonda looked at Tiffany.

'Mama?' the little girl persisted, wriggling and shifting. 'Them comin' to our new house?'

Tiffany patted her daughter's head. Short, nervous pats. 'Shhh, sweetness. Don't know. You be quiet now.' Her eyes flicked up to their faces. 'Was thinkin' about moving. That's all. Nothing's for sure yet.'

Silence ensued. It seemed to merge with the heat, consolidating into a single oppressive force that pressed down on the surroundings.

'New house,' Bell said. She glanced around the cramped trailer. 'That'll be nice. Glad you can afford it. I guess Jed had a good life insurance policy, huh?'

'Yeah.'

'What's the name of the company that issued the policy?'

'Don't remember.'

'How about the agent?'

'Don't remember that, neither.'

'You've got records, though, right?'

Tiffany shrugged.

Bell said, 'Could you check for us?'

'No.' Something else moved into Tiffany's voice, something darker. 'You gotta go now. Need to take care of my little girl. Get her some lunch, okay? That okay by you all? Case you missed it, I'm her mama. I'm responsible.' Tiffany didn't look at them. Instead she focused on the child in her lap, cuddling her, cooing at her, murmuring to her: 'There's a good girl. There's mama's sweet little girl.'

They let themselves out.

Before they even reached the hard road, Bell had split up the list. 'I'll pay a call on Odell Crabtree and see how he figures into all of this,' she said, 'and I'd like you to track down any recent payments into any bank accounts belonging to Tiffany Stark. From a life insurance company – or from any other source.' A source, Bell elaborated, such as someone who might want to buy Tiffany's silence about the precise nature of what had turned out to be Jed Stark's final assignment. 'Got to find an explanation for the fact that someone as poor as Tiffany Stark – with a child to raise – is so cavalier about future expenses,' Bell concluded. 'And ready to move into a brand-new house.'

'Gotcha.'

Bell didn't have a subpoena, of course, to compel a bank officer or anyone else to provide the information. But she didn't need a subpoena.

Not when she had Rhonda Lovejoy.

19

Bell's dreams could be frantic and unsettling. Often she had trouble falling asleep, and her dreams, when they finally came, had to do their work in a hurry. Thus they were as cold and abrupt as a drive-by shooting. Drive-by dreams – that was how she thought of them. They were black-hearted marauders who hardly paused long enough to do anything but spread panic, disorder, and dread. And then they were gone again.

This dream, though, was wonderful. It was languid and golden; it was a dream that made her feel warm and safe. She sensed Clay Meckling stretched out there beside her. They'd been lovers for only a few months, but she missed him – God, she missed him – and missing him was a dull ache that she never acknowledged during daylight hours, and the pain went away only during dreams like this one, beautiful dreams, dreams that wrapped her up and—

'God*damn* you to *fucking hell.*'

Bell, jolted awake by the words, felt herself being dragged toward the side of the bed. The room was dark and someone was pulling at the sheets, pulling hard and fast, and she was skidding over the edge. She tore at the fabric, trying to hang on, dangling for a second or so, but then she hit the floor with an ugly *whump*. Pain shot up her side. The words continued to pour down on her:

'You goddamned fucking bitch. You had *no right*. No right, do you hear me? It's *my* fucking life. *Mine*. Got that?'

Bell still couldn't see a thing, but there was no doubt about who loomed up there, flinging obscenities. When Shirley paused, needing a breath, Bell grabbed the chance to speak.

'What the hell?'

'You *bitch*. You *bitch*.' Now Shirley began to pace around the room, repeating the two words in a low-pitched snarl.

Bell's first instinct was to respond in violent kind – to grope for her sister's leg and pull her down, as if she were eight years old again, and she and Shirley were quarreling, wrestling, settling their differences with kicks and slaps and opportunistic yanks of hair.

She forced herself to calm down. The floor was hard, but it was also cool, cooler than her bed. She pushed the heels of her hands in her eye sockets. 'Jesus,' Bell said. 'What time is it?'

Shirley stopped pacing. 'I don't have a fucking *clue* what time it is. And I don't care. You know what, Belfa? You really screwed me over this time. Hope you're happy. Hope you're just tickled pink. Finally, *finally*, things were starting to go right for me. Matter of fact, they were going really great. And then you go behind my back and stick your big fat fucking nose in my business, and now—'

She stopped.

Silence. The sharp point of Shirley's anger had broken off like a pencil tip. Bell could sense it. This was another of her sister's sudden swerves. Another emotional U-turn from rage to blankness.

'Hey,' Bell said. She tried to sound lighthearted. 'Give me a hand here, so I can get off the damned floor. Unless I broke something in the fall.' She reached up. At first, there was no response. Then she felt Shirley's thin fingers wrapping themselves around her wrist.

'Easy,' Bell said. She groaned as she rose, staggering a bit before she found her feet. 'I'll say this. You sure know how to make an entrance.' She pulled down the front of her T-shirt, bunched and cockeyed from the dumping.

Shirley was breathing hard now. In this moment the two of them seemed to belong to different species: Bell, soothing and amiable, trying to dial down the tension in the room; Shirley, distraught, filled with anger and confusion, hoping to get through the next few seconds without doing something unforgivable.

'You know what, Belfa? It's all a big pile of shit.' Shirley's voice was ragged and lost-sounding, as if it had traveled a long way to get here and wore the marks of the road.

'Could be worse.' Bell was still striving for lightness. 'Startle me like that again, and I just might reach for the twelve-gauge I keep under the bed.'

No response.

'Come on, then,' Bell said. 'Let's go downstairs. Neither one of us is liable to get much more sleep tonight.'

Bell made the coffee. The clock on the stove told her that it was just past three on Saturday night. *No,* she corrected herself. *Sunday morning now.* Shirley sat at the kitchen table, head down.

After the trip to Steppe County, Bell had dropped

off Rhonda and then put in an afternoon of paperwork. Made a quick trip to Lymon's Market for some groceries. A quiet evening: First Patsy Cline, then Mozart, on the iPod dock. A cold Rolling Rock. Another. Still no word from Shirley. At 11 P.M. Carla had called, giddy with more details about the internship, which would start next week: She'd live with Sam's friends, Nigel and Natasha Hetherington, in their home in Central London. 'It's going to be awesome, Mom,' Carla said. Excitement danced in her voice. 'I'll text you every day. Twice a day! With lots of pictures. Swear. And we can Skype.'

A little past midnight, Bell had gone to bed. And then, a few hours later, she was awakened by an angry, flailing woman whose towering rage had now fallen back into an almost catatonic sadness.

Shirley stared at her hands. Her flannel shirt, sleeves rolled up to her elbows, was wet with sweat; it stuck to her back. Her gray hair was brittle and frayed-looking, and her eyes were pink and swollen. She started to light a cigarette but stopped before the lighter came to life, and then she swiped away the pack, the lighter, the ashtray, from the section of the kitchen table in front of her, all in one fed-up gesture.

'Okay,' Bell said, turning around. 'Ready in a jiff.' The coffee-maker was popping and wheezing and fussing, as was its custom. *Sounds like an old man blowing his nose,* Carla always said. And Bell always replied, *Gross.* And then they'd both laugh.

It really did sound like an old man blowing his nose. Bell shook her head. God, she missed Carla. Was there any end, she wondered, to missing people?

She sat down. She was surprised at herself, frankly, for not being more pissed off at Shirley. Waking her up like that, pulling her out of bed, was a shitty thing to do. The reason didn't matter. It was shitty, plain and simple.

Bell touched her sister's skinny forearm. Then she took her hand away again, because she knew Shirley well, as well as she knew herself, which meant she also knew this: a touch was okay as long as it didn't go on too long. Shirley's smell was not fresh, but nor was it definitely bad. She smelled like cigarettes and perspiration and earth. She smelled like some of the people who came into Bell's office in the course of a day, country people, the ones who didn't have an appointment; something bad had happened to them and they needed help. A husband or wife had run off, a neighbor had stolen something, a child might or might not be involved in drugs. *Can't you investigate? Can't you make it better? Can't you do that? Ain't that your job? Ain't you the law?* These were people who worked with their bodies all day, every day, and there was a certain kind of sweat that never came out of a garment or out of a life, no matter how often you tried to wash it. Just didn't. That was how Shirley smelled.

'Did I hurt you?' Shirley said, inclining her head toward the second floor to indicate the abrupt start she'd provided to Bell's day. 'Hope not.'

'I'll live.'

'Real sorry, Belfa.'

'Apology accepted. Okay, then. What's going on?'

'Got thrown out of Tommy's tonight.' Shirley picked at a spot on the tabletop. 'No, that ain't right. Not thrown out. I never got in. Tried to. I was with Bobo and the band. We're playing there. But they stopped me at the door. Just me. Everybody else, fine. But they said I wasn't welcome. I told them to go to hell. Then the boss come out. Tommy LeSeur. He said it was your doing. Said you'd told him not to let me in. What the hell are you—?'

'Shirley,' Bell said, interrupting her, but doing it gently. 'Listen to me. Not the kind of place you need to be hanging out.'

'I didn't have nothin' to do with that murder the other night. Told you that.'

'Yes, you did. That's not what I mean.'

'Then what the hell *do* you mean, Belfa? 'Cause the way it looks to me, it's just you interfering. Trying to control me.'

Trying to keep you out of trouble. Watching your back. That was what Bell wanted to reply, but didn't. Her aim was to settle Shirley down, not rile her up all over again.

'And you know what?' Shirley said, jumping ahead, taking advantage of Bell's delay in answering. 'Don't need you to take care of me, you got it?'

'Look,' Bell said. 'Tommy LeSeur is a bad guy. A really bad guy. Coming within ten miles of him or his kind is not a good idea. If you want a fresh start, then you ought to steer clear of that place.'

'I told you,' Shirley's voice was calm, but agitation lurked just behind it. 'I'm Bobo Bolland's manager. The band plays there a lot. How the hell can I manage 'em if I ain't allowed in the place they're playin' in? Don't make no sense.'

Bell picked up Shirley's lighter. With her thumb she rubbed its little plastic side, then set it back down on the table again. Buying time.

'Tell me,' Bell said, 'about this "manager" thing.'

'Nothing to tell. Just like it sounds. Bobo needs

somebody to book gigs for the band, make a YouTube video, pass out flyers, and such like. They're getting real close to a recording contract, Belfa. It's gonna happen.'

'Does he pay you?'

Shirley was beginning to get angry again. Bell could see it in her face: Her jaw was set tight, her chin tilted up. She raked the back of her hand across her red nose.

'Shit, yeah, he pays me. What do you think? It's a *job*, Belfa. For Christ's sake.'

'Can't be much.'

'No. Not yet. But that's how it works.' Shirley's voice was speeding up, bit by bit, as she made her points. 'I'm getting in on the ground floor. Later, once he makes it big, I'll get a percentage. I got it all in writing, Belfa. I ain't stupid, okay?'

'I know that.' Bell realized she had said it too quickly. It sounded phony. Falsely reassuring. The truth was, she didn't think Shirley was stupid. Just naive. Just rusty when it came to knowing how the world worked. 'How'd you meet him?'

'Mutual friend.'

Bell didn't have to say it out loud. Shirley, she knew, could translate her glance: *You don't have any friends.*

Hell, Bell automatically added to her thought. *I don't have many friends either, come to that.* Nick Fogelsong didn't count. He was family.

'I was in this bar, okay?' Shirley said. Belligerence seemed to drive tiny spikes into her words. 'While ago. Way before I came back to Acker's Gap. I was on the road. Traveling. Just going around. Not heading anyplace special. Ended up there. Bobo was playing that night. Fella I knew said to me, "You want to say hi to Bobo?" Well, I'd already told that fella how much I loved the music I was hearin'. So I said, "Hell yeah." Next thing I know, I'm shakin' hands with Mr Bobo Bolland hisself.' Shirley sighed. A smile shyly edged its way onto her face.

'Me and Bobo hit it off,' she went on. 'Got to talking. His real name's Harold. Bobo's a nickname. Had it since he was three years old. His mama tried to put a bow tie on him for church one day and he pulled it off and he threw it down and he said, "What? What that?" So his mama said, "It's a bow tie, honey," and he musta liked the sound of it 'cause after that, he went around the house going, "Bow tie. Bow tie." So naturally they started calling him Bobo.'

When Bell didn't comment on the story, Shirley doggedly continued. 'Heard they was playing at Tommy's – it's a regular gig – and I went out to hear 'em a couple weeks ago, and we made a deal. I'm the manager. So you'll tell LeSeur to let me in, right? You'll call him? I mean, like – this is my *job*.'

'It's not a job,' Bell said. She'd decided not to coddle her sister. She'd show her respect by telling her the truth, and telling it in a firm, deliberate way. 'It's nothing. And it'll lead nowhere. Bolland plays in bars, Shirley. Cheap bars. Filled with bums. I don't know him, but I don't have to know him to know this – he's a loser. And if you hang out with him, you'll be a loser, too.'

Shirley flinched as if she'd been smacked. She reached for a smoke. Her hand trembled. It trembled even more as she tried to light it. She gave up, taking the cigarette out of her mouth and holding it in the air in front of her face, like something she'd found on the street. A stick, maybe, or a broken-off piece of something unidentifiable. Something she could grasp at, cling to, while she spoke in a low, heartbroken mumble.

'You just gotta ruin everything for me, don't you, Belfa? Every last thing. Every time.'

20

It was the girl from the gas station.

Bell remembered her. She didn't know who the young woman was, but she'd seen her recently. *Oh, right.* That was it: behind the counter of the Lester station. In the middle of the night. After the ceremony at the hospital. She was the clerk.

'Yeah?' the young woman said.

She'd opened the door seconds before Bell gave up and walked away. Bell had knocked once, twice, and then, after a long interval, a third time. Waited. And then, just as Bell turned to go, wondering how long Odell Crabtree had lived in this shriveled-up house that looked as if it might be reclaimed any minute by the patchy, weed-thatched woods surrounding it, the front door edged open.

'Oh,' Bell said. She was startled. Slightly flustered. 'Hi. I'm Belfa Elkins. Raythune County prosecutor. I'm looking for Odell Crabtree.'

'What for?'

'I have some questions for him. And you are?'

'His daughter. Lindy Crabtree.' The young woman rose up on tiptoes, peering past Bell and out into the grass-challenged yard and the dusty driveway, vivid now in the headlong sunlight of midafternoon, checking to see if anyone else was there. 'He's not home.'

'When do you expect him back?'

'Look,' Lindy said. 'He's sick. Real sick. He doesn't come out of his room. He can't see anybody right now, okay?'

'I thought you said he wasn't home.'

The young woman's small face bunched up into a frown. 'Just go away, okay? Leave us alone.'

It didn't come out mean, Bell noted. It came out cautious. And weary.

Lindy started to close the door. Bell put up a hand to stop its progress.

'I'll talk to you, then,' Bell said. 'Don't want to bother your father. Won't take long.'

Lindy shrugged. She thought about it. Bell could sense her weighing her options, calculating the odds of getting rid of this stranger quickly and easily if she let her in for a brief conversation. Better to capitulate now, perhaps, than to say no and endure a return visit. A longer one, maybe.

'Okay.'

The interior of the house was similar to the exterior, like a dirty sock turned inside out despite the fact that both sides are equally filthy. It was ramshackle, compact, and claustrophobically cluttered. An ancient gray haze seemed to hover over the stuff, as if select portions had lain undisturbed for slow-turning centuries, like the spoons and combs and vases of Pompeii. Bell had been in a lot of houses in Raythune County that looked just like this, houses that were gradually sinking back down into the dirt they'd emerged from. At one point, someone must have cared for this place, must have kept up with the sweeping and the polishing, but that someone was long gone now, and the ongoing accretion of junk and dust was practically audible; Bell could swear she heard a steady hum, living just below the closely packed silence. She glanced at the thick closed drapes that fell in clotted folds, at the low ceiling printed with sickly yellow streaks from long decades of cigarette smoke. A bark-brown upright piano, mutely entombed in cobwebs, was pushed into a corner.

The one notable feature was the preponderance of books. They weren't corralled onto bookshelves – there were no bookshelves – but lived wherever they wanted to: spread out across the cushions on one side of the ragged gray couch and on both end tables; rising in sloppy piles that dotted the hardwood floor; shoved up along the walls like a second baseboard. Bell was able to make out a few titles on the top of the stacks: *Warped Passages* by Lisa Randall. *A Brief History of Time* by Stephen Hawking. *Time Reborn* by Lee Smolin. Lindy picked her way with ease amid the mini-towers of books on the floor. It wasn't as if she failed to notice them because they didn't matter to her, Bell thought; it was, rather, that they were old friends and Lindy was comfortable around them. She took their presence for granted.

'You work at the Lester station,' Bell said. She sat on the edge of an armchair. The maroon material on each arm was rubbed shiny.

'Yeah,' the young woman replied.

She reminded Bell of Carla, but only slightly. Actually, Lindy Crabtree reminded her even more insistently of someone else: herself. Belfa Elkins – then Belfa Dolan – at this age had been just as closed, just as stubborn, just as tightly sealed up with her troubles and secrets.

'I was there,' Bell said. 'The other night. You probably don't remember.'

'We get lots of customers.'

'I bet you do. How long have you worked out there?'

'A while.'

'Do you like it?'

'It's okay.' Lindy frowned. 'So is this about my job?'

'No. It's not.' Bell paused. She admired the young woman's directness and decided to emulate it. 'A man named Jed Stark was fatally stabbed in a bar the other night. We know who did it – that's not the reason I'm here – but the victim had a business card in his pocket. A business card for a lawyer named Sampson Voorhees.' She waited to see if any light of recognition flashed in Lindy's eyes. 'And on that business card,' Bell continued, 'was another name, too. Your father's. Odell Crabtree.'

Still no response.

'Any idea why,' Bell said, 'Jed Stark would be looking for your father?'

'Never heard of anybody named Jed Stark.'

'How about Sampson Voorhees?'

'Nope.'

The denial had come quickly, but Bell was fairly certain she had spotted a flicker of recognition. She pressed on.

'May I ask your father the same question? I mean, I understand if he's ill and doesn't want visitors – but if I can't see him, would you ask him for me?'

'Okay.' Lindy looked away. 'That it? I'm pretty busy.'

'Reading, I bet. Quite the library you've got here.'

'Yeah.'

'A lot of science books, I see.'

'Yeah.'

'You like science.'

Lindy shrugged.

'So it's just you and your father living here?' Bell asked.

'Yeah.'

'Must be hard for you,' Bell said, thinking: *No wonder the place is such a mess. Working full-time and taking care of a parent is a lot for a teenager to handle.* 'Doing everything yourself, I mean.'

'It's okay.'

The young woman's expression was as inhospitable as her answers. She let her gaze drop and drift, landing at random on one stack of books or another and then moving on – anywhere but back to her visitor's face.

Bell didn't push. She was accustomed to conversations like this one; awkward question-and-answer sessions were a prosecutor's lot. Most of the people she spoke to in the course of a workday were in some kind of trouble, and for many, she represented the outcome they most dreaded: an encounter with the court system. Bell never took it personally anymore, the way she'd done earlier in her career. She allowed silence to be her cointerrogator. People disliked silence. It made them uncomfortable and so they would often say something – something incriminating – just to get rid of it.

'Anything else?' Lindy said. She had let the silence go on longer than Bell expected; it might have been a new record.

'Here's my card.' Bell stood up. Lindy didn't. 'If your father can think of a reason why Jed Stark was looking for him – or if the name Voorhees rings a bell – I'd appreciate a call.'

Lindy looked at the card for a few seconds before

taking it. Tapped it into the breast pocket of her flannel shirt. Bell surmised that the card would ride around in Lindy's shirt for a few hours and then wind up as a bookmark. *Well,* Bell thought, *that's as honorable a fate as any other, and better than most.* She'd seen people tear it into pieces right in front of her, or spit on it, or use it as a toothpick – or mail the card back to her office, smeared with dog shit.

Bell was reaching for the front doorknob when she heard it: a heavy thump, followed by a muffled cry of pain. She couldn't tell from which direction the noise had come because it was over too fast and there was no echo, just a two-part crack of sound breaking against the banked quiet of the old house. Bell turned. Lindy rose quickly from the couch. Her indifference, the cool blank repose in which her face was set, had vanished, replaced by a ragged agitation.

'Just – just go, okay?' Lindy said. 'Go away.'

'What's going on? Did your father fall? If you need some help—'

'*We don't need your fucking help, lady.*' Lindy's interruption was swift and harsh. She moved across the room, toward what Bell assumed was the kitchen. 'Just go. Leave us alone.'

'But what if your father has—?'

'Please.' Lindy paused under the arch that separated the rooms – *Why is she going in that direction,* Bell thought, *and not toward the bedroom?* – and the look she gave Bell was so intense and pleading, so heartfelt in the raw urgency of her desire to be left alone, that Bell didn't argue.

'Please,' Lindy repeated. Her stare was stark with desperation. And then she was gone, rounding the corner.

Driving away from the Crabtree house, weaving carefully between the potholes until she reached the county road, Bell was bothered by a thought that quickly hardened into conviction: The noise had come from the basement, not the bedroom. And whatever it was, it had terrified Lindy Crabtree.

21

Two days after the visit from the prosecutor, Lindy found it.

She had made a mental grid of the house and then traveled from quadrant to quadrant, room to room, trying to be systematic about her search. Scientific. Or if not scientific – she knew what the word really meant, knew from her reading how true scientists worked, and thus scoffed at her own pretentions – at least thorough. Kitchen cupboards, dresser drawers, stacked-up shoe boxes, junk left on tables and chairs. She checked under the couch, under the bed, behind the piano. She pulled stuff out of the closets. She lifted the rugs. She patted the heavy drapes in the living room, shaking the hems, watching the dust bloom and dissipate in the dim sweltering air. She waited until her father was asleep and then she moved gingerly through the basement, too, stepping carefully amid the boxes and branches and old tables. Thank God he was a heavy sleeper. Always had been. His snores were loud, damp-sounding. He slept curled up in a ball, but sometimes he would flop over on his back, mouth open, and the snores would quicken and intensify, like something large and strong tangled up in barbed wire, trying to fight its way out.

She didn't know what she was looking for – or, more to the point, she didn't know what else she was looking for. She'd already discovered the things that worried her, that had made suspicions linger in her mind: Missing knife. Boot prints on the kitchen floor.

She wanted more. Before she did anything – before she could even contemplate telling anyone else about the outlandish idea that had so thoroughly infiltrated her thoughts – she needed more proof.

And now she had another worry: the visit from that prosecutor. Lindy had lied to her, of course, but the lie seemed justified. Yes, she'd heard the name Sampson Voorhees. And Jed Stark, too – but she wouldn't tell the prosecutor that. Not right away, anyway. Not until she knew what was going on. In the letter addressed to her father that had come a week or so ago, the one with the New York City postmark, the names had been right there:

Dear Mr Crabtree,
As you know, I have attempted to contact you several times. My letters have not been answered. Yet it is imperative that I speak with you soon about a matter of some urgency. This inquiry could result in a substantial financial opportunity for you. My authorized representative in your area, Mr Jedidiah Stark, will be contacting you shortly with details. I trust you will treat this correspondence confidentially.
Very sincerely yours,
S. J. Voorhees

After skimming it, Lindy had frowned and fumed. The words 'substantial financial opportunity' sounded like just another attempt to persuade senior citizens to invest in silver mines in Bolivia or some other scam. This 'Sampson J. Voorhees' had probably dumped a truckload of such letters on the older folks in Raythune County. *Swindling bastard,* Lindy had thought. *Freakin' con man.*

But now it seemed that too much was happening all at once. First her suspicions about her father, and now, a visit from the prosecuting attorney. Lindy was perplexed, apprehensive. And determined to ransack the house to see if there was anything here that might tie her father to the terrible rash of assaults. Anything more than what she'd already discovered. More than the knife and the boot print and the certainty that he'd been going out at night.

So that she could decide what to do.

She'd tried to ask him about it. Because if he admitted it, somehow that would be better. That would mean, at least, that he was aware of what he was doing, that he was still in charge of himself. 'Daddy, after dark – when you go out – what do you—?' And he'd roared back at her, eyes wild, unfocused, as if he were trying to figure out – and this part devastated her, even though she knew it was part of his illness – just who the hell she was, this young woman in the flannel shirt and jeans, this person who stood before him in the dingy kitchen, looking like somebody he used to know, or maybe not.

There were other times, too, of course. Times when he wasn't incensed, wasn't yelling. Times when he was the way he'd been before. Some mornings, the man who came rising out of the basement, his boots dropping heavily on step after step after step, enabling her to chart his progress, counting his steps while her anxiety ticked up in unison with each individual stair, was – out of the blue – the old Odell Crabtree. And those were the hardest moments by far, because they reminded her of how things might have been.

She could tell right away. Could tell that it was going to be a good day. The first thing he'd do when he reached the top step and opened the basement door and gazed at the person who sat at the small square table, her book propped up against another stack of books, her face rising from the page to meet his eyes, would be to smile at her. It was a thin smile, barely creasing his face, barely making a dent in the deep-set wrinkles. But it told her everything she needed to know. 'Mornin', my girl,' he would say, a greeting that served as further confirmation that, for an unknown interval – but never for more than a few hours, and never very often – he was back. He'd be flummoxed, of course, and sometimes grumpy, filled with questions, criticisms – he'd never been a saint, nobody would ever claim that – but he wasn't the angry, cursing stranger who paced back and forth in the basement. He was her dad again. The dad who had gradually come to love her.

At those times, he might walk around the house for an hour or so. Sometimes he asked for Margaret. 'Where'd she go?' he'd ask Lindy, and he'd ask it more in wonderment than in sadness, because he didn't remember. 'She off visiting somebody?' he'd say, adding, 'Back soon, I guess. Well.' He had to walk hunched over, and he kept one hand on the small of his back and another on the wall, steadying himself.

Lindy would reply, 'Yeah. Back soon.' Was that the right thing to do? She didn't know. Should she tell him the truth? Tell him that her mother was dead,

dead for six years now, and that it was just the two of them – just her and her father – left in the house? Or should she protect him, lie to him, let him live for these precious few hours in a kind of time-starved twilight, where the past was more real than the present? Hell, she'd rather live there herself. Who wouldn't?

So she'd say, 'Yeah,' and let him be. He'd nod and keep walking, making a slow satisfied circuit around the house. Waiting for his wife to come home. 'Back soon,' he'd murmur, and Lindy, if she was close enough to hear, would echo, 'Soon.' Sometimes he would add, 'Supposed to go fishing with Ray today, but I'm staying home. Need to be with your mama. Don't want to miss her when she gets home.' By the next morning, the anger would flood back in. He would spend his days in the basement again, and she could hear him down there, just as she'd heard him when the prosecutor was visiting, falling against the objects that Lindy had dragged and stacked, the dead branches and the rocks and the cinder blocks. Home.

And then, just when she was ready to give up, she found it.

At first, she didn't realize what it was. On her hands and knees, leaning over, she had pulled out the last flat box from under the massive oak dresser in what had once been her parents' bedroom. That box contained nothing unexpected; it was filled with old *National Geographic* and *Life* magazines. Her mother hadn't graduated from high school, but she'd been a passionate reader. Among Lindy's clearest memories was the sight of her mother at the kitchen table, marveling at something in *National Geographic,* flicking the pages restlessly, reading paragraphs out loud to eight-year-old

Lindy and then looking up from the magazine and addressing her daughter directly: 'Big world out there, my girl. You make sure you go see it.'

Lindy tried to shove the box back under the dresser. It wouldn't go. She pushed again, and realized that she was pushing it at the wrong angle. She tried again. Its progress was blocked by yet another object, small enough that she had missed it the previous times she looked. Something was jammed against the wall.

Lindy dropped onto her belly. She squinted into the dark area beneath the dresser, into the space created by the four fat wooden legs holding the dresser several inches off the floor. Reached under. She had to stretch out her arm. Her fingernail scratched metal and she scrabbled at whatever it was, finally getting her hand around the small tin box and pulling it toward her. She was certain she'd never seen it before in her life.

Sitting cross-legged on the floor, Lindy examined it. It was about the size of an old-fashioned cigar box, light blue with silver trim, badly discolored. On the top and sides was a swirling logo: SILVERMAN'S FAMOUS BISCUITS, with an etching of three sailboats poised on a tree-fringed lake. Lindy was so nervous that her hands trembled. She didn't know why the moment felt so fraught; over the years, she'd found dozens of little boxes squirreled around the house. Her mother had adored small, pretty boxes, along with elegant glass jars and pastel wrapping paper and curling ribbons, and she kept everything. When Lindy was a little girl, her mother had explained that it was a good idea to surround yourself with bits and slivers of beauty. With shiny scraps and dabs that reminded you of a radiant elsewhere, of something other than dirt roads and pinched-off horizons. Over the years

Lindy had found, tucked here and there around the house, the glass figurines and river rocks polished to a beguiling smoothness that her mother carefully, lovingly accumulated and then placed at strategic points throughout the small, worn-down house, perhaps as a sort of counterweight to the ordinary. As a way of telling herself – and telling the world, too, if it ever happened to notice – that she was more than a coal miner's wife in a shabby town that nobody'd ever heard of.

So it wasn't the mere fact of finding the box that made Lindy's fingers tremble when she touched it. This box felt . . . *different*, somehow. Charged with mysterious energy, like a magical object in a fairy tale. Or maybe something darker than a fairy tale.

She was almost sick with dread, afraid of what she might discover. What if it was something that implicated her father? That proved he was a violent criminal – and that the history of his rampages tunneled back a long way into the past? That they hadn't just started with his sickness? But Lindy was also aware of a kind of golden anticipation. This was something her mother had touched.

She opened the hinged lid.

22

The initials JP stood for Joyce's Place. The name was a tribute to the late Joyce LeFevre, owner of Ike's, the diner that formerly had occupied this spot at the intersection of Main and Thornapple in downtown Acker's Gap. For years Ike's had provided a consoling supply of greasy biscuits floating in fragrant lakes of sausage gravy, not to mention coffee as strong and ornery as a growl. JP's didn't do that. Jackie LeFevre, Joyce's thirty-five-year-old daughter, was adamant about it: JP's was not a substitute for Ike's. JP's had its own style. Its own rhythm. Its own rituals. The only sentimental touch allowed on the premises was the name.

Bell had admired Jackie's independence even as she wondered at the wisdom of it. The population of Acker's Gap skewed old, and older people, Bell observed, liked things to stay the same as they'd always been. *Hell,* she corrected herself. *Everybody's pretty much that way. Old folks just don't mind showing it.*

'Coffee for the both of you?'

Wanda Moore, one of two waitresses, barely slowed down to sideswipe them with the question as she barreled past. Bell and Sheriff Fogelsong had arrived here at roughly the same moment and grabbed the last available booth. Wanda and her colleague, Patty

Harshbarger, were swamped, thanks to the tumult of the lunch rush. The occupants of a large table in the corner had been yelling at Wanda for the past three minutes, as if they faced a desperate emergency – and indeed they did, if a lack of ketchup for crinkle-cut fries constituted a legitimate crisis.

Unlike Ike's, which had gotten along with a brief, splinter-ridden wooden bar and wobbly stools that looked as if they were seconds away from becoming kindling, JP's featured a gleaming stainless steel counter that followed a long wall, serviced by a series of sturdy, red-topped stools. Along another wall was – of all things – a salad bar. The stack of small white plates at one end of the salad bar looked perky and expectant, while a pair of shiny metal tongs waited dutifully next to each ceramic jar and its reservoir of shredded carrots or hard-boiled eggs or sliced-up cucumbers – none of which would have been even remotely conceivable in Ike's, where customers most likely would have used the tongs to hoist a cucumber coin into the air so that they could peer at it suspiciously, wondering if maybe a quick drag across a plate of gravy would render it edible.

Each time Bell came in here, she was momentarily assailed by the vivid contrast. JP's was compact and bright; Ike's had been large, dark, cavernous. JP's sported a vegan section on the menu. *The hell is that?* more than one patron had muttered, staring at the strange word and turning the menu upside down and then right-side up again, trying to trick it into revealing its meaning. At Ike's, menus had been largely beside the point: You knew what they had, and the daily special – chili mac or fried catfish or ham steak or spaghetti – had been indicated on a chalkboard propped up next to the cash register, along with the price. Bell could still picture Georgette Akers, Joyce's partner in business and in life, leaning over the blackboard first thing every morning, short stalk of chalk in her chubby hand, adding a smiley-face next to the words and the numbers, and then holding up the board and blowing off the excess chalk dust, admiring her handiwork.

Sometimes the ghosts could get to Bell. Old towns were thick with them. Sometimes she liked that; she liked the fact that she knew the history of these streets and these people. Among the living faces she saw every day, she knew the life stories of a good percentage of them, and she knew the faces of the dead forebears that stretched out behind them. Not so thoroughly as Rhonda Lovejoy did, of course, but enough to turn the town into a long hall of murmuring echoes.

In Acker's Gap the past never left you alone. At night, if your sleep was shallow and restless, the dead would show up in your dreams and say your name over and over again, in a rising tone, like someone calling for a lost dog, and in the daytime they walked around right next to you, pressing you, crowding you. You had to drive out beyond the city limits now and again just to get some distance from them, some peace.

She looked across the table at Sheriff Fogelsong. 'How's your morning going?'

'Lousy.' He lifted off his hat. Dashes of sweat flecked his forehead, which was bright pink from the heat. Fogelsong's tidy buzz cut should've kept him slightly cooler than average, but today not even that could provide any relief; his scalp looked as if it had spent some quality time rolling around on the grill that Jackie kept going behind the counter.

'Donnie Frazey's driving me crazy,' he added.

'Questions about the homicides?'

'You bet. But you know what? I gotta admit – he's justified. Got a deadline for next week's paper. And he wants to know what kind of progress we're making. Dammit, Belfa – I don't have any answers for him.' Fogelsong lifted a napkin and dabbed his brow. He looked down at the damp napkin, then over at her. 'Feeling about as useless these days as tits on a bull.' He wadded up the napkin and flipped it to the far side of the table. Any benefits he enjoyed from a month away, Bell noted, had fled already, judging from his face.

'How about the hitchhiker that Deputy Harrison interviewed?' she said. 'The one who saw somebody in the woods along Godown Road at the relevant hour?'

'Didn't pan out. Turns out our witness was pretty drunk.' Disgust burned in the sheriff's voice. 'Yeah, he claims he spotted somebody in a long coat out there. And the timing's right. But a witness back in Swanville reported that he'd had six PBRs that night and woulda barely been able to wobble in and out of the woods to take a piss. Won't help us a lick.'

She waited. She knew better than to offer false consolation.

'Okay,' she said. 'Let me know if you need any help with the investigation.'

'You've got your own job to deal with. Don't intend to saddle you with mine, too. Especially not with you being shorthanded and all.'

Bell's secretary, Lee Ann Frickie, had left for vacation the day before. Lee Ann took two weeks each summer to visit her son, Lance, in Clemson, South

Carolina. She had offered to cancel her trip this year
– she didn't feel right about leaving while two unsolved
homicides had the town on edge – but Bell insisted:
Go. Lee Ann needed a break. *Hell,* Bell had silently
amended that. *We all do.* Not much chance of getting
it, though, while the violent deaths of Freddie Arnett
and Charlie Frank were open cases.

Bell started to say something to Nick, but put it
aside for later. Perry Crum had ambled up to their
table. He was on his way to the front to pay his bill.
Big-faced, droopy-eyed, with hair the color of ginger
ale that had lost its fizz, Crum had delivered mail in
Raythune County for forty-two years, a fact to which
his posture gave painful-looking testimony. Sweat had
wrecked the crease in his government-issue pale blue
shirt and gray shorts.

'Hey, Sheriff,' Perry said. He knuckled the dirty-
white pith helmet farther back on his head. 'Ain't there
some kind of law against this heat?'

'Oughta be. You tell me how to enforce it, Perry,
and I'll be happy to do so.'

Perry pumped his eyebrows up and down a few
times, by way of agreement. He turned to Bell. 'How're
you, Mrs Elkins?'

'Doing fine, thanks.' She looked at Perry's stooped
shoulders, wondering what it felt like to hoist a heavy
mailbag in and out of his truck in this heat. Not
to mention the long, jarring drives into and out of
the hollows in his boxlike, butt-ugly government van.

That vision gave rise to another one: Perry out on the
country roads, all by himself. Vulnerable. An easy target.

'Listen,' she added, trying to keep her voice casual.
'You be careful, Perry. I know you've heard about the
assaults. Just keep your eyes open, okay?'

Perry tried to sop up some of the sweat on his neck with a handkerchief, first on one side, then the other. 'Appreciate the concern, Mrs Elkins.' He smiled.

She knew a bit about his personal life – Rhonda Lovejoy had filled her in on the situation a few years ago, and nothing ever changed for people like Perry – and so Bell felt compelled to add a coda: 'Your sister, Ellie. She doesn't go out by herself, does she? Especially not at night?'

'No, ma'am. Kind of you to ask, though. Ellie never leaves the house. She needs me to take care of her. Always will. Things've been that way since she was born. Promised my folks I'd look out for her and I do.' Perry stuffed the handkerchief in his back pocket. That was enough about that. 'Don't suppose you all are making any headway.' He read the answer right off their faces. 'Well,' Perry said, 'you'll get to the bottom of it. No doubt. Nice afternoon, you two.'

He moved along. Bell picked up her water glass and took a long reflective swallow. 'I've been thinking, Nick. Summer's a funny season. People relax too much. When it gets dark, it's still nice and warm out. So people forget. Let their guard down. They leave their windows wide open and their doors unlocked. I've done it myself. Stayed up till two, three, four in the morning sometimes, sitting on the front porch. Never give it a second thought. Truth is – a lot of bad things can happen once the sun goes down. Even in the summer.'

The sheriff's expression was grim. 'That's for damned sure.' He swiped at a runaway bead of sweat rolling down the right side of his face. 'I've been getting the serial killer question everywhere I go, just like you predicted. Really wish the folks around here watched a little less TV, you know? You sit yourself down in front of enough of those crime shows – and pretty soon, you think you're seeing a serial killer every time you push your cart through the produce section of Lymon's Market.' He wiped his wet finger on a pant leg. 'I guess I can understand their concern. I mean, both attacks happened at night. No obvious motive like robbery or revenge.'

'But there are some pretty significant differences, too.'

'Two different weapons,' he agreed. 'Sledgehammer and a knife.'

'Yes. But something seems – well, a little off.' Fogelsong looked at her, waiting for her to go on. 'The attack on Freddie Arnett was pretty straightforward,' Bell said. 'Three blows to the back of the head. All of generally equal – and equally deadly – force.'

'Okay.'

'But the stab wounds on Charlie Frank were different. I read Buster's report and then I called him to ask about it, to make sure I was interpreting his findings correctly. There were five wounds in the shoulder area – two on one side, three on the other – and those were fairly shallow. Didn't require much force. By themselves, they probably wouldn't have killed him. The lethal blows came after that. Eight very deep and very powerful thrusts into the chest and abdomen. One severed the aorta. He didn't have a chance.'

'What are you thinking?.'

'Maybe the initial blows weren't intended to be fatal. And if that's the case, then—'

Fogelsong cleared his throat. Bell stopped talking. He had spotted Wanda heading their way, order pad in one hand, pen in the other.

The waitress was a large-boned, middle-aged woman

with wavy brown hair that was gradually giving up its fight against gray. Her eyes had a tendency to squint, even when she wasn't straining to see something, and her left cheek still bore the broad, claw-like scars of a childhood car accident. Her father, Norbert Moore, had been taking Wanda and her younger brother, Cassius, for ice cream when Norbert crossed the center-line and smashed head-on into a coal truck. Norbert was drunk, and so the deaths of two people – the truck driver and three-year-old Cassius – meant that Norbert, only slightly injured, was sentenced to fifteen years in the state penitentiary in Fayette County. When he finally came back home, he met Wanda on the street and said, 'I'd know you anywheres, girlie, on account of that scar you got there. Better'n a name tag.'

Wanda looked at the pad, not at them, as she said, 'Whaddayall want?'

'Cheeseburger,' Fogelsong declared. 'No pickle, but everything else.'

'Fries?' Wanda said.

'You gotta ask?'

That made her smile. It also caused her to look up from the pad. 'Now, Nick Fogelsong, don't you be getting smart-alecky. I'm too busy today to keep you in line. Mrs Elkins?'

'Chicken salad sounds good.'

'You got it.'

They waited for the waitress to hurry away before resuming their conversation. 'Okay,' the sheriff said. 'What about the knife wounds?'

Bell didn't want to overplay her hand. 'Well, Buster said the variety in depths probably wasn't significant. Could be attributed to a lot of factors.'

'Then I suggest,' he said, 'that we talk about

something else until our food gets here. To make sure we're able to enjoy it. What do you say?'

'Agreed. Got to keep our strength up.'

So far Nick had avoided any substantive discussion of his leave of absence. Bell understood – he'd returned to a town that had suffered two grievous losses and looked to him to fix things – but she was curious. She was just about to break her rule about personal questions and ask him, when he beat her to it.

'Okay,' he said. Had he read her mind? Maybe. They'd known each other a very long time. 'Figure you'd like an update about Mary Sue. More of one, anyway, than I've given you so far.'

'No,' Bell replied. 'Not an "update." She's a person, not a weather report. And listen. I have my own relationship with Mary Sue. I can ask her myself how she's doing, and I will. What I'd like to deal with right now is you.'

'Me.'

'Yeah. You.' She shook her head in exasperation. 'Come on. You know what I mean. Before you left, you were questioning your whole life and what you've done with it. You weren't even sure you wanted to run for reelection next year, remember? Then you get back here and – Jesus Christ. Two dead bodies. And no leads.' Bell's voice was bleak. 'So – what now? What's your next move? And just this once, I'm not referring to open cases, okay?'

He didn't answer right away, so Bell went on. 'You can tell me to go to hell. It's really none of my damned business. I know that. I just—' She stopped. She didn't know how to phrase it without sounding weak and needy. Without sounding like the ten-year-old girl she'd been when she first met Nick Fogelsong. On a terrible night. A night that still spilled repeatedly out of her memory unless she kept the lid screwed down tight. A night whose horror had been alleviated, ever so slightly but crucially, by the kindness of a big man in a deputy sheriff's uniform.

The same man sat across from her now, three decades older and a great deal grayer and heavier, having ascended to the sheriff's job himself in that long interval, and having done it through dint of skill and diligence – instead of through politics, the usual route for such a rise.

'Forget it,' Bell muttered. They were in a public place. And what could she really say, anyway? He wasn't her father or her brother or her lover. She had no rights here. No claim on him. If she'd been able to speak the truth, if she could've somehow moved past the embarrassment and the fear of looking foolish, she would have said: *You don't owe me a thing. But I owe you my life.* Even the idea of saying those words, however, caused her to recoil inwardly, as if her thoughts themselves had touched a hot stove. She could no more say that to Nick Foeglsong than she could say it to her sister. And both Nick and Shirley had, in their own ways, rescued her.

'Belfa,' he said. The casual tone was gone. 'When I figure this out, I'll tell you, okay? Everything. Soon as I know myself. Won't keep it from you. My word on that.'

'Sure, Nick, but—'

Wanda suddenly was back in their field of vision, plates in hand. 'Anything else?' the waitress said dutifully, strain visible on her face, her meaning plain: *Please don't need anything else. I'm already getting run right off my damned feet here.*

'We're good,' Bell said. Nick nodded. The arrival of their food was fortuitous, and not just because they were hungry; it broke the spell, changing the emotional dynamic when things were getting intense, unsettling them both. Funny how they could talk about criminal cases with no hesitation, with boldness and candor, but a personal topic turned them into mute cowards.

Bell looked around the restaurant. It was more crowded now than when they'd first come in, having filled up quickly with townspeople and with strangers, too. Tourists, most likely, the brave ones willing to reject the Burger King out on the interstate to take a chance on a local eatery.

She looked over at the cash register, where Jackie LeFevre was running a customer's credit card. Jackie's black hair fell straight as a plank down her back; her black eyes were set in a flat, polished-looking face that hinted at Native American ancestry, and she displayed a calm and centered demeanor at all times. Jackie was still a bit of a mystery to people in Acker's Gap, a mystery they'd not had time yet to tackle. For now, it was enough that the new restaurant she ran featured reasonably priced and decent – if sometimes inexplicably exotic – food.

'Hey,' Fogelsong said. He knocked on the tabletop with two knuckles, to snatch back her attention. 'Did I lose you?'

Bell turned to him. Mild smile. 'Never,' she said.

They finished their lunch in twelve minutes. Not ideal for digestion – but necessary, Bell told herself, when a violent criminal or criminals still threatened the area. And plenty of other cases, too.

The sheriff walked to the door right behind her,

nodding to a number of his constituents on the way, barely slowing his gait as he replied to the repetition of inquiries if today was, indeed, hot enough for him.

'Sure is,' he'd say, as patient and amiable as if he'd never been asked that question before on a summer day.

Bell and Fogelsong stood beneath the red and white awning that shaded the entrance to JP's. He settled the big brown sheriff's hat back on his head.

'So when's Carla getting here?' he said. 'Thought I might be seeing her around town by this time.'

Bell hadn't told him – hell, she'd barely acknowledged the reality to herself – about Carla's whereabouts. Well, it was time. Past time.

'Yeah, well, Sam got her an internship in London. Last-minute thing. She's thrilled. Already on her way over there.' Bell looped her purse strap around her right shoulder.

She saw Nick's mouth open and close, as he started to speak and then didn't. He wasn't fooled by her matter-of-fact demeanor. He knew how much she'd been looking forward to Carla's visit this summer. But he was taking his cues from her; if she wanted to be breezy about it, if she wanted to pretend it was all just fine, he'd go along. He respected her enough to let her talk when she was ready to. *Maybe I could take a few lessons from Nick,* she thought. *Maybe I ought to stop pushing everybody all the damned time, like some fat-assed schoolyard bully. Getting in everybody's business.* Maybe if she stopped doing that, things might go a little better with Shirley. Bell had hurt her sister, wounded her, and Shirley hadn't come home last night. Again.

They parted. The sheriff headed toward his Blazer,

Bell toward the courthouse. Sunlight was drowning the streets in a bright molten glaze, which meant that when Bell's cell rang and she peered at it, she couldn't make out the caller ID. The glare on the screen was too intense.

'Elkins,' she said warily. When she didn't know the identity of a caller, Bell always expected it to be an outraged citizen or pissed-off judge or livid defense lawyer. She girded herself for verbal battle.

'It's Rhonda.'

Relief. 'What's up?'

'Well,' Rhonda said, excitement stirring in her voice, 'I used a few connections here and there. Turns out that as of last week, Tiffany Stark is the proud owner of a brand-new house over in Toller County. Purchase price was a hundred seventy-five thousand dollars.'

Tiffany Stark. Bell was disappointed. She had let herself hope that Rhonda's news was related to the Arnett or Frank murders.

'Go on.'

'So Jed Stark didn't have an insurance policy. No verifiable income of any kind,' Rhonda continued. 'In fact, neither Jed nor Tiffany even had a bank account. He worked strictly for cash – which isn't surprising, given the fact that his work mainly consisted of selling narcotics or threatening people who'd pissed off other people who were selling narcotics. That trailer was a rental and they're five months behind on the rent – or at least they were until today. Tiffany settled up with the landlord. Gave her notice, too. And hired a big moving company out of Charleston to get her stuff over to the new place in Toller County.'

'Where the hell did Tiffany Stark get that kind of money?'

'Mighty interesting, isn't it? Like I said, Jed Stark had no bank account – but as of a month ago, he was named an equity partner in a company known as Rhododendron Associates.'

'Equity partner.' Bell made a noise in the back of her throat that indicated disdain. 'Guy like Jed Stark probably couldn't even spell "equity." And I've never heard of any "Rhododendron Associates" – aside from the fact that it's the state flower of West Virginia.'

'Nobody's heard of it. All I can tell you for sure is that it's got nothing to do with flowers, boss. And everything to do with money. Lots and lots of it. And that's how Miss Tiffany is financing her life change. She got a big payout from that company.'

'Other partners?'

'Well.' With the instinctive flourish of a storyteller, Rhonda lowered her voice dramatically and said, 'According to the articles of incorporation, the CEO of Rhododendron Associates happens to be our mystery man – Sampson J. Voorhees.'

'But how—?'

'Hold on. I know you've got a million questions. I did, too. Like – who is this Voorhees character and what in the world is Rhododendron Associates and where the heck did their money come from?'

Bell had reached the courthouse steps by now. As Rhonda talked, she had continued walking back to her office, noticing neither the heat nor her surroundings. Did a good number of people wave or nod at her, and had she nodded or waved back? Maybe, although Bell couldn't have sworn to it. She'd damn near tripped over a fire hydrant.

'This next little tidbit took me hours and hours to dig up,' Rhonda went on, and then gave a little moan to signify how hard she'd worked. 'I must've called fifty places. No, make that a hundred. And nothing added up. Rhododendron is listed as an investment company, but they don't have any investments. They don't have any clients. They don't do any work at all, seems like. Gotta be some kind of front for the transfer of money. So I had to track back through the information on their original filings, looking for something – anything – that would give me a clue about who they really are and what they really do. And then I found it.'

Bell waited. She was tempted to try to goad Rhonda into speeding up, but given her assistant's personality, felt obliged to resist. To let the story roll along at the pace that Rhonda wanted it to.

'Finally had a brainstorm and called Charlie Dillon,' Rhonda went on. 'Haven't talked to Charlie since law school. He dropped out after our first year. Now he works for the state commerce commission. Lives in Cross Lanes. He and his wife, Barbara Ann, have the cutest little—'

'Rhonda, please.' Bell was too antsy to hold back. 'The company.'

'Okay. Right. Well, Charlie came through, just like I figured he would. He looked long and hard – and he broke about a dozen rules for us, so I think it might be a good idea to put him on our Christmas card list this year – and he went through a lot of records that aren't public and that surely aren't on any digitized databases because they're too darned old. But it worked. Turns out that if you go back and back and back – and if you wind your way through about a dozen shell corporations and another dozen businesses that never did any business and then just put your head down and plow right on past a bunch of false leads and phony trails – you finally stumble across the company that funds Rhododendron Associates one hundred percent. A much, much, *much* older company. And it's private – no public records, no list of officers or employees. Nothing.'

'So that's it.' Bell couldn't keep the dejection out of her voice. 'A dead end.'

'Oh, Belfa.' Rhonda almost never called her boss by her given name. Elation had prompted her to do so, however, and it also caused her to put a chuckle at the end of the two words. 'You know me better'n that!'

'You found out something about the original company?'

'Sure did. I came up with the name of the person who started it – way back in 1957. I'd ask for a drum roll here, but I think you're about ready to skin me alive unless I get to the point, which is what I guess I'd better do.' Rhonda sucked in some air so that she could conclude her story in a single excited breath:

'Our mystery man, the one who's behind Rhododendron Associates – and the payoff to Tiffany Stark – is none other than the former governor of West Virginia. The honorable – and I'm using that term loosely here – Riley Jessup.'

23

She'd spooked herself. That had to be it, right? Yeah. That had to be it. All that talk about how darkness was different in the summer. How it fooled you, made you complacent. Even lazy. Softened you up. All that theorizing in front of Nick Fogelsong. *No dark like summer dark.*

Bell stood beside her Explorer in the driveway. It was well past midnight. She'd not intended to work this late at her office. As always, it just happened. She'd suddenly looked up from an endless stack of paperwork, realized the time, then further realized that she was all alone in the courthouse. The lamp on her desk was the only light in the entire building. To find her way out, she'd had to use the tiny flashlight on her key chain. The corridor lights were switched off at nine each night at the main circuit, to save energy. Sheriff Fogelsong's edict. Once she left the downtown area, she'd not seen another car on the road.

She pulled into the driveway and shut off the engine. The silence was so profound that it startled her. It seemed to have been waiting for her. Worse – it had *plans* for her.

Oh, stop, Bell chastised herself. *Don't be such a girl, okay?*

She stood on the blacktop, while the dome light inside the Explorer gradually expired. This was a moment she usually looked forward to: day's end. Homecoming. Time to shuck off her shoes and – although it wasn't quite so automatic – her woes, too. Tonight, though, she didn't feel relieved. She felt apprehensive. She always left the front porch light on; the bulb must have burned out.

There were no lights on in any other house on Shelton Avenue. Not even in the house belonging to Priscilla Dobbins, across the street and two doors down. Priscilla was seventy-four and sometimes stayed up late to read. Not tonight, apparently. Her three-story Victorian home looked like a big black trunk propped up on one end, tightly secured with straps and bolts and buckles. Was that to keep something outside from getting in – or to keep something inside from getting out?

You're freaking yourself out, Bell thought. *Stop it. Just stop it. Shut the hell up.*

She climbed the steps to the front porch. The house was mired in a darkness made more ominous by the fact that she wasn't expecting it. Hadn't she left a light on in the living room? She was certain that she had. She always did. A portion of her youth had been spent in a trailer in Comer Creek, way out beyond any other houses or trailers, and she knew how drenching that darkness could be. How it provided a handy place for formless things to hide as they whispered past windows, crept around corners.

Well, maybe she hadn't left a light on this time. She couldn't remember. Or maybe she'd left it on and Shirley had come home during the day to pick up a few things – they barely spoke now, they could pass each other in the upstairs hall without a word, and the hell of it was, it didn't even feel strange anymore – and maybe Shirley had turned off the light in the living room. Shirley might not have known how important it was, that beacon – although Shirley, too, had grown up in the trailer on Comer Creek. Wouldn't she have known? She understood darkness as well as Bell did. Better.

So did I leave a freakin' light on in the house or didn't I? She was having trouble finding the house key in her purse. It was so damned dark.

And if she had indeed left a light on, and Shirley hadn't been there and thus hadn't turned it off – but if the light, nonetheless, was turned off now, didn't that mean someone could very well be waiting for her on the other side of this stone wall? Lurking in the darkness just behind the front door? Weapon raised over his head? His eyes would be adjusted to the dark by now, so he need not hesitate, need not guess, need only wait and aim and strike—

Goddammit, Bell told herself. Fear was turning her testy, making her disgusted with herself. *Find the freakin' key and go in and look around. Get it over with.*

She punched the key in the lock. Opened the door. Stepped inside.

Nothing happened. *Of course there's nobody here. Jesus. Grow up, already.* Bell felt like a damned fool. She shoved the door shut behind her. And realized that her hand was shaking.

24

At noon the next day, Bell caught Nick Fogelsong in the act. His first impulse was to fumble for a desk drawer in which to hide the evidence, but to no avail; she'd seen what he was up to. So the sheriff, scowling, miffed at himself for letting her find him this way, gave up. He grunted and flung the object across the top of his desk. It knocked over a chipped red coffee cup filled with pencils and pens. He made no move to pick up the cup or its scattered contents.

'I do believe,' Bell said gravely, 'that this may constitute an impeachable offense. Been nice serving with you.' Then she grinned, unable to keep the joke going. Picked up the book he'd discarded, studied the armor-cocooned knight on the cover. Read the title and the author's name aloud: '*Agincourt*. Bernard Cornwell. Good one?'

He nodded. He was still embarrassed. Reading – especially military history – was Nick Fogelsong's passion, but this was the middle of a workday. No excuse for such lollygagging.

'Well,' she went on, setting the book back down, 'I'll let you slide this once. And I need a favor, anyway, so think of it as quid pro quo.'

He waved her toward the wooden chair that faced

his desk. 'Long as you don't spill the beans about my secret vice, you can have whatever you want.' He pulled out the bottom drawer on the left-hand side of his desk and perched a booted foot there. 'Actually, come to think of it, this is my lunch hour, so I've got nothing to apologize for. Free on a technicality.'

'Hey. Who's the lawyer around here, anyway?'

The office was exceptionally hot. Fogelsong didn't believe in air-conditioning. He'd allow other employees who worked in the courthouse annex to install window units if they so chose, but he also let it be known that he considered it a ridiculous frill. The mountains kept Acker's Gap reasonably cool, he pointed out. *The good Lord surely meant for us to sweat hard,* he'd add. *Little reminder of the effects of hellfire. So we can alter our behavior accordingly.* He was teasing, but with Nick Fogelsong, sometimes it was hard to tell.

Bell rolled up the sleeves of her white blouse. A nod to the humidity, as well as to the fact that she had a serious matter to discuss with him.

Leaning forward in her chair, her earlier levity having vanished, she rapidly filled him in on what Rhonda Lovejoy had discovered about Rhododendron Associates and Riley Jessup. The information had been simmering in Bell's mind since the day before, when only a full slate of afternoon appointments and an evening's worth of paperwork kept her from acting on it right away.

She didn't tell Nick about the absurd little drama she'd enacted on her front porch last night, and never would. He'd worry about her. Think she was slipping. Going soft. There was enough real danger already; threats were common in a small-town prosecutor's office, because a prosecutor had to live alongside the very people whose lives she interrupted with little inconveniences such as jail terms. No sense dwelling on the made-up kind.

'So I'm headed to Charleston in about an hour,' Bell said. 'Want to have a little chat with Riley Jessup.'

The sheriff looked mildly surprised. 'Really.'

'Well, I had a bail hearing scheduled this afternoon on the Fletcher case, but it's been postponed. So I have the time. And it's a nice day for a drive.' She shrugged impatiently. 'Why would a public figure like Jessup be in business with a low-life scumbag like Jed Stark? I figure there's no harm in trying to find out what the connection is.'

Fogelsong gave himself a minute to think before he nodded. 'Okay. So your intention is to go grill our illustrious former governor and see if he's willing to come clean about his private financial dealings.' The sheriff's voice gradually became more serious, shedding its jocular tone. 'You do realize, I hope, that to a man like Riley Jessup – to any politician, for that matter – public image means more than anything else. More, even, than their fortune. They spend years and years building up a picture of themselves in the public eye. Polishing it. Keeping it just the way they want it. No matter what the reality is – and no matter how long it's been since their name was on a ballot – they'll hang on to that pretty picture at all costs. They'll fight like hell to keep themselves looking good for the home folks. Their legacy is everything. Older a politician gets, the more passionate he is to come across like a Lincoln in the history books.' He rubbed the back of his neck. He didn't like sarcasm and tried to keep it out of his tone, but lost the fight. 'And you think Riley Jessup will take a chance on losing all that and answer your questions because – why? Oh, yes. Because you're so all-fired persuasive.'

Bell was stung by his skepticism, but saw his point. Her desire to visit Jessup did sound as if it might be a waste of time. 'I don't think he'll divulge anything in particular, no. Or put his precious public image in any jeopardy. But remember what you taught me? Letting somebody know that you're curious – even if that's all you do – can work wonders sometimes. Can initiate some unforeseen consequences.' It was a twist on the classic Nick Fogelsong truism: You can do as much to put the brakes on bad behavior with a long, slow, level stare – a stare that declares *I'm watching you, mister* – as you can with a cocked gun and an arrest warrant.

He shrugged, reluctant to dwell on the compliment. 'Okay. But you don't need my permission to drive to Charleston. So what's the favor?'

'You know the budget situation around here. Meaning there's nobody to cover the phones in the prosecutor's office while Lee Ann's on vacation. Meaning that if I'm on the road this afternoon, it's a problem.'

'I thought Tina Sheets was helping out.'

'She is.' Tina Sheets worked in the country treasurer's office. 'But only in the mornings,' Bell explained. 'That's the only time they can spare her.'

'Still not following.'

'I was thinking—' She hesitated. Looked down at her lap. This was harder than she'd anticipated. 'Was thinking that maybe I'd ask Mary Sue to come over to my office this afternoon and answer the phone. Just for a few hours.'

She still didn't look at Nick. She couldn't. She didn't

know if the idea would make him angry, if he would lecture her about interfering in his personal life, employing that clipped, cold, exquisitely well-controlled voice he used when his ire was on the rise. Mary Sue Fogelsong hadn't worked since her diagnosis of paranoid schizophrenia. She was effectively medicated now, her symptoms were under control, but she spent too much time sitting at home – or so Bell believed. Mary Sue Fogelsong had once been a third-grade teacher at Acker's Gap Elementary. A good one. She was happiest when she was busy. Now, though, no one asked anything of her – least of all Nick Fogelsong. He thought the best way to protect her was to shield her from the world, and from the world's expectations.

Yet Bell knew what Mary Sue was capable of. She'd seen it. Bell bet her life on it last spring, and she had been proved right.

'Up to you,' Nick said. His voice was neutral. 'Your call.'

Bell stood in front of the square oak desk in the small outer room that connected to her office. This was the desk from which Lee Ann Frickie had run the prosecutor's office for the past forty-seven years, through six different prosecutors. It featured a clean, polished surface with a divided soul: half high-tech, half old-fashioned. A computer monitor and keyboard shared the space with a big black rotary-dial phone.

Bell tapped the top of the clunky-looking receiver.

'It's just like the one that Hick and Rhonda share downstairs. Both of 'em belong in the Smithsonian,' Bell said. 'The phones, I mean, not the assistant prosecutors.' Mary Sue was too focused to react to her joke, so Bell went on: 'I don't think they've updated the phone system in the courthouse since about 1947. And yet we've got Wi-Fi. Go figure.'

Bell needed to be on the road in ten minutes in order to make it to Charleston by 4 P.M., but she was apprehensive about putting any pressure on Mary Sue. So she was trying to sound casual, lighthearted, as if they had all the time in the world. She didn't want to intimidate Mary Sue or fluster her. Didn't want to make her nervous.

To each instruction, Mary Sue nodded grimly, as if Bell were relaying last-minute details about the D-Day landing. She sat behind the desk, back straight, hands clasped on the blotter, watching Bell with unblinking intensity. Mary Sue was a lean woman with short brown hair, hazel eyes, and a wary smile; she had once been pretty, but her illness aged her, putting lines in her face and an unnatural solemnity in her personality. She was trying very, very hard.

When Bell had called her, Mary Sue's response was startled and heartfelt: 'Oh, yes! Yes, I'd love to help. I'll be right there. Oh, my, yes.' And in a way, Bell was glad there wasn't much time to go over things; Mary Sue couldn't fuss or obsess or second-guess herself. Her duty was simple and clear: answer the phone, take messages.

'Because,' Bell explained as she gathered up her purse and her briefcase, 'when people call the prosecutor's office, they don't want a machine. They want a real, live human being at the other end of that line. Even just to leave a message.'

Mary Sue nodded. She had nodded at everything Bell said. At one point she'd even begun to take notes, but Bell put a hand on top of Mary Sue's hand to stop her, murmuring, 'You've got this. You're fine.'

Outside, the heat was fierce. The air felt extra-heavy, clinging to Bell's skin like a layer of Saran Wrap. She looked forward to lowering all four windows once she hit the interstate, letting the breeze cool her down.

She'd just reached the Explorer when she saw him. *Lanny Waller*.

Or as she immediately corrected herself: *Lanny Fucking Waller*. The sonofabitch who'd so far beaten the rap for sexual molestation of three minors because the girls' mother was too chickenshit to let them testify against him – or to testify against him herself. He was ambling down the sidewalk in a dirty red T-shirt printed with a Confederate flag, and baggy plaid canvas shorts, chewing on something sticky, opening his mouth improbably wide with every revolution of his stubble-crusted jaws.

He spotted Bell at roughly the same moment she saw him. Instantly, the chewing stopped. He spread out his mouth to make the biggest, widest, grossest, and most insinuating grin that Bell thought she'd ever witnessed, a grin that showcased a broken row of black and yellow teeth.

Then he gave her a slow-motion, lascivious wink.

Bell felt a tsunami surge of primitive emotion, an emotion that slammed her, overwhelmed her, pushing everything else out of her head. All the fine and enlightening words she knew, all the music and poetry, all the intricate and lovely bits of civilization, were swept away.

I want him dead.

No: It was more than that. Much worse.

Not just dead. I want to kill the bastard myself.

She'd felt this kind of rage before. Walking along Main Street a few weeks after her high school graduation – it was a punishingly hot summer, just like this one – she'd spotted Herb McCluskey. He was first in a long dismal line of foster parents who'd taken her in after her father was killed and her sister sent to prison. Herb McCluskey was a bum. A dirty, conniving bum with whom – along with his equally loathsome wife, Lois – Bell lived for a few months. Finally the social worker was able to get her out of there, and once the paperwork was ready, it happened so fast that the McCluskeys didn't have time to squeal about the loss of the monthly check.

Bell rarely ran into the foster families she'd lived with. Mostly they were the kind of people who didn't stay long in one place, the kind whose lives were as flimsy and fly-by-night as their trailers. But there was Herb McCluskey, big as life, just as ugly as she remembered him. McCluskey didn't say a word to her. Didn't even look at her. Chances were, he'd forgotten all about her. Bell remembered enough for the both of them.

And now, here was Lanny Fucking Waller.

She wanted to lunge at him, she wanted to make a tight fist and take aim at that big fat miserable face, she wanted to—

No.

No, no, no.

Bell recoiled from her own impulse, shocked at the intensity of her desire. She was a prosecutor, for God's sake. An officer of the court. She wasn't an enraged and emotionally disturbed teenager anymore. She believed in the justice system – at least she thought she did. Yet a dirtbag like Waller had set her off so easily, provoking something raw and wild in her. Something vicious and livid and foul, something that seethed in the lowest spot in her soul. Something she worked like hell to keep under wraps.

And the worst part of it was, Waller had seen it. He knew. He'd tricked her into revealing herself. Standing there on the bright sidewalk, goading her with his very presence, he'd figured her out. He'd read her mind from the expression on her face, and what he now knew of her was devastating. She saw the gloating message in his eyes: *Deep down, lady, you and me's exactly the same. Got the same twitch and jump and urge. Being what we are, hating like we do, we're doomed. We're dead already.*

Part Two

25

Lindy distributed the letters across the kitchen table in two rows. With mounting excitement she had moved the stacks of books out of the way, and now she focused on the precious contents of the small tin box. The paper was thin and old and she had to be careful when she handled it, because the letters had been folded over multiple times. When she unfolded each one, the creases designating the folding points were like perforations eager to tear.

She had the night off from the Lester station. But even if she hadn't, she would have stayed right here. Called in sick. Reached her district manager and referred to a stomachache and a headache – a few different kinds of aches, vague and iffy, thrown in there together for good measure, because when a female employee called in sick, they didn't ask any questions, afraid it might involve menstruation, the thing that no man Lindy had ever met wanted to discuss or even to acknowledge – and her district manager would've been fine about it, anyway. Lindy was reliable. She'd called in sick only once, when her father hurt himself. Year and a half ago, it was. Threw himself against the basement wall too hard. Lindy was afraid he'd suffered a concussion and so she stayed with him all night, not letting him fall asleep, waking him up every time his head sank. *Daddy,* she'd said. *Daddy, come on.*

She counted the letters. There were fourteen. Except for the last several, all were handwritten on lined paper with a raggedy edge on the left side, the kind of pages hurriedly torn out of a spiral notebook.

She had hoped they might be love letters. Hoped they'd been written in the time when her parents were courting, when Margaret School-craft and Odell Crabtree were getting to know each other, the shy young woman and the burly coal miner.

But no. She scanned the first few lines of the first few letters and realized they were addressed to her mother from a friend. Lindy had never heard of her, but that wasn't surprising; her mother was not the kind of person who dragged the past into every conversation, like some crusty old fart going on and on about how things were so much better when Truman was in the White House.

Lindy arranged the letters across the table from oldest to newest, left to right. The oldest one was dated July 9, 1972:

Hi, Maggs!!!
This camp is STUPID STUPID STUPID. I mean it. Total crap. Can't believe they made me come here. What's going on there? Can't wait to get home. It's hot as HELL and they make you do this stupid craft stuff. Plus go out in a canoe. Whole place smells like dead fish. God it stinks. I hate my counselor. Some fat-ass bitch named Cynthia. I tried to call her Cindie and she said,

My name is CYNTHIA and she said it like she's a queen or something. Bitch. Hey, gotta go. They're turning out the cabin light.

The letter was signed *Maybelle* in swirling, curving letters that bounced across the page and then linked up below the line, the looping bottom of the *M* attached to the trailing end of the final *e*.

As an adult, Lindy knew, her mother had never been called Maggs or even Maggie; it was always Margaret. But on the rare occasions when her mother told her stories about her childhood, Lindy remembered, the other people in the stories – her sister, her parents, her friends – sometimes called her Maggs.

The name Maybelle made Lindy want to snicker. Sounded like a cow. Or like some little old grandma in a long dress and work boots in a rocking chair up on the front porch, taking potshots at the crows, sneaking slugs out of the moonshine jar. *Maybelle.* Jesus.

Lindy moved on to the next letter. It was dated August 24, 1975:

Maggs,

Gotta go. They're coming real soon and I'm not even packed. I just wanted to say I'm going to miss you and miss this place. I am SO SO mad. I don't WANT to go away to that stupid school. I don't care how great it's supposed to be. You're my best friend and I DO NOT want to leave. They say I can come back at Christmas vacation but I don't trust them. I know what's going on. They want me gone. Last night my father called me a 'g-d troublemaker.' Can you believe that? He acts all holy all the time, but when the front door's closed and nobody's listening, it's all different.

Okay, I really DO have to go now. I wish I was dead. Dead, dead, dead.

Once again the letter was signed *Maybelle*, only this time, the signature was ordinary. No swirls. No curves.

Lindy tried to picture her mother back in the time she'd have received this note. In 1975, her mother would have been . . . right, fourteen years old. Based on pictures of her mother as a teenager, Lindy could imagine her hunched over these letters, sitting cross-legged on the porch swing or stretched out flat on her belly on the floor of the bedroom she shared with her sisters, serious, intent, frowning as she read about her best friend's troubles.

'Daddy?'

Lindy stood up abruptly from the kitchen chair. She'd heard a sound, a faint scuffling. Couldn't tell what it was. Then she heard another sound, and this time it was a familiar one: the stomp of her father's boots on the basement stairs. He was coming up.

She waited, counting the steps in her head. Watched the basement door slowly open.

'Hi, Daddy,' she said to the grizzled gray head that poked out sideways from behind the wood slab. Bloodshot eyes blinked at her, bleary and unresponsive. 'Got the night off tonight,' she added. 'You want something to eat? I can make you some food. No trouble.'

He grunted. Pulled his head behind the door again, like a turtle going back in its shell. The door closed. She counted the steps as the boots clomped back down, the sounds growing marginally fainter. The counting was a habit now. *One . . . two . . . three . . . four . . . five . . .* When she got to fifteen, the steps stopped. He was back home again.

Why had he come up? Did he think she'd left for work – and so now he could go out? Out to do whatever it was he did in the dark? She didn't know, and she found the possibility so troubling that she pushed it out of her thoughts.

Time to return to the letters.

The next batch had been sent at intervals of several months and, at one stretch, more than two years. They were all about this Maybelle person's school days. She hated the new school. Hated the teachers. Hated the other kids. She missed Raythune County, missed her friends, missed her best friend Maggie. She'd thought about killing herself but couldn't figure out how to do it efficiently; she was afraid of messing up. *I don't want to be some kind of vegetable,* Maybelle wrote. *That would be totally TOTALLY gross.*

The eleventh letter was dated February 6, 1992. The handwriting was different now. Little more than a scribble. It wiggled across the page, as if the writer was being called from another room and had to finish up quickly. Or maybe she was just distracted:

Margaret,
   Okay, I hear what you're saying. And no, I'm not mad. Okay? Really. You have a right to your opinion. But you know what? It's my life, okay? My life. Maybe you could remember that, next time you feel like lecturing me. Okay?

The letter was signed *M*. Just *M*. Lindy turned it over and then back again, to see if there was any more to it, but no.

There were two more letters in the same vein – *Don't tell me what to do, it's MY life* – along with a few lines congratulating Margaret on her upcoming marriage. Maybelle made fun of the fiancé's name, asking Margaret if she was going to mind having the nickname 'Crabby,' because that was surely in the cards. Maybelle also made fun of how much Margaret read: *You and that Anne What's-her-face Lindbergh. Jesus. That's all you talk about these days. Her and her books. All that shit about seashells and listening and gifts. BOR-R-R-RING! Who the hell cares about HER, anyway? HE'S the one who's famous!!*

The final note, dated March 19, 1994, apparently was a response to something important that Margaret had written, an offer of some kind:

You're the best friend anybody ever had. I mean it. I'll never, ever forget this. Not as long as I live. I'm in a real bad spot and there's nobody else I can turn to. I know you'll keep my secret. I know it. I also know that I don't deserve a friend like you. I really don't. And I'll make it worth your while. You know I will, right? You can trust me, Maggs, just like I trust you.

Look there. I called you Maggs, just like when we were kids. I miss those days. Everything was simple then. Nothing's simple now. Everything is so goddamned complicated. I don't know what I'd do without your help. I'd be lost. I'd be – well, I can't even think about it.

M.

And that was it. The last letter.

Lindy sat back in her chair. She'd had to strain to read the pages, especially the later ones, the ones with the minuscule, hurried-looking handwriting, and she rubbed her eyes. She couldn't remember when she'd last gotten a personal letter. Everybody used e-mail to communicate now. Or texting. But there was something so warm and extraordinary about handwritten letters. They were *actual,* not virtual. They had shape. Took up space. All e-mails looked the same; they showed up on a computer screen and they left that way, too. Even if you printed them out, they still looked all the same. But each of these letters was distinctive. Lindy wished she had the other side of the correspondence – the notes her mother had written to this Maybelle person – but these were better than nothing. Her mother had touched each one, page by page. And that was enough.

Margaret Crabtree had never mentioned a friend named Maybelle. But it was clear that these letters had meant a great deal to her. She'd put them away in a private place. They were not part of the surge and drift and heave of accumulated stuff with which the house had been blocked and swamped all these years. And maybe her mother, on those rare occasions when she was alone in the house, had reached toward that special spot under the dresser, the one that only she knew about, and drawn out the blue and silver box and read and reread these letters, just as Lindy was doing now. And maybe they made her happy. Lindy hoped so.

She envisioned her mother at nineteen. Her own age. Lindy imagined her mother holding each letter at exactly the same spot Lindy held it, thumb on the margin, sometimes using an index finger to follow a squiggly, hard-to-decipher line as it kinked its way across the fragile page. Lindy wondered if her mother at that age had been filled with the same kind of directionless longing that burned in her, filled with a restlessness that was like a fine powder riding atop every thought and gesture and ambition, like dust from a dandelion gone to seed, the kind of flower that you blow upon with your eyes closed, fist tight around the stem, fiercely dreaming.

26

'They give you any trouble out at the gate?'

They had, but Bell hated to admit it, and so she didn't. She shrugged. 'Not too much,' she replied to Sharon's question.

Truth was, the two bastards in their tight black T-shirts and black jeans had accosted her the moment she rolled up to the front entrance of Riley Jessup's estate, yelling *Freeze!* – clearly, Bell thought, they'd watched too many reruns of *Charlie's Angels* on TV Land – while commanding her to exit her vehicle. She complied. Then they'd advised her to turn around and put her hands on the hood of the Explorer while they patted her down. Aggressively. One of the security men, the larger and younger and uglier one, had deliberately taken his time, grunting and letting his oversized hands linger when they followed the inside seam of her slacks, lingering even longer when they grazed her butt and roved across the front of her blouse. Bell could have protested, could have whirled around and snarled, *You sonofabitch, copping a feel, I'm going to kick you in the balls and see how you like it, you stinking—*

He wasn't worth the aggravation. If she'd made a fuss, she might not get to see Riley Jessup; if she'd complained, then this visit would become a referendum on how his security staff comported itself – not a fact-finding expedition about Jessup and his investments. So she'd waited for them to finish, then waited again while the older guard called up to the house and checked to make sure they were authorized to let her in. Receiving permission, they stepped back. 'Gwan,' the younger man said. He'd punched in a code and then used his palm to slap a metal pad on the side of the big stone pillar. The pillar was the intimidating twin to the one on the other side of the entryway. 'Gwan. Git.' The gate swung open. Bell drove forward, and it closed behind her. Through her open window she could hear the mechanism locking automatically, with a soft *whirrrrr* and then the prolonged and ponderous-sounding *thwwwwunk* of a massive bolt settling heavily in its iron stirrup.

She parked in front of the main house, an overgrown, white-brick edifice with six pillars spaced out evenly across the front, black shutters repeated at each of the myriad windows, and a perky profusion of dormers and turrets. There were five other vehicles parked up and down the wide curving drive, the requisite assortment of beefy-looking black SUVs and a small red sports car as round and shiny as a cinnamon drop. Sharon's car, Bell guessed.

During her approach to the massive double-sided front door and its ostentatious hardware, Bell tried her best to ignore the luscious acreage that sloped gently away from the big house, the grass as smooth and emerald green as a PGA fairway, the treetops swaying in the breeze with a synchronous fluidity that could have been choreographed. Bell had never been here but knew the particulars anyway, thanks to

Rhonda Lovejoy. Rhonda had dropped by Bell's office the previous day to deliver a magazine piece on the place; published a few years ago, the article was a fawning spread filled with exclamation points and copious photographs and quotes that dripped with the pretend-humility of Jessup and his daughter. The estate included the main house and two guest cottages, a tennis court, a horse barn and riding trails, and a swimming pool trimmed in a blue-green ceramic tile that artfully echoed the color of the sky.

Bell had leafed quickly through the slick pages, then sidearmed the thing back toward a marginally startled Rhonda. 'Thanks,' Bell said, sarcasm making something blunt and stubby and notably ungrateful-sounding out of the word. 'Nice to know that Riley Jessup's precious butt is nestled in a soft spot every night.' It wasn't his wealth that Bell resented; it was the fact that his wealth had come on the backs of struggling West Virginians. Hypocrisy was hardwired into his life story. He was, after all, a politician.

Hell, she'd reminded herself. *So am I, come to that.*

Sharon had met Bell at the front door and inquired about her reception at the gate. The governor's daughter was wearing a white blouse, tan capri pants, and white sandals, and as soon as Bell lied to her about the guards' decorum, Sharon smiled. 'Oh, good,' she said. Her shivery little voice was as musical as a wind chime nudged ever so slightly by a minor breeze. This was probably not the same voice, Bell thought, that she'd been using back in Raythune County when the cell phone almost melted from the heat of her tirade. She escorted Bell through a succession of three vast rooms – the walls and essential furnishings of each served as a garish and overbearing celebration of, respectively, the colors green, gold, and scarlet – and into what seemed to have been designated as a sitting room. Sharon asked if she'd like a beverage. Bell declined. Her no overlapped with the unmistakable voice of Riley Jessup, booming across the acreage of the plush beige carpet, followed by the man himself. His walk was a sort of swaying waddle, reminiscent of a child's pull toy that moves as much sideways as it does forward. He situated himself at one end of a gigantic couch, propped up against the padded armrest.

'Your call was mighty welcome,' Jessup declared. 'Not every day I get to entertain a pretty young prosecuting attorney anymore. Not since I left the state-house. These days, I just rattle around this big old place, making more trouble for Sharon here.' He chuckled at his own little joke. He was wearing a lemon yellow suit with a bright white shirt and flowered tie, and white shoes. His hands looked enormous, like bristly gray chunks of a mystery meat that somehow had eluded FDA inspection.

Sharon remained standing. She ignored her father and spoke directly to Bell. 'I'm afraid I have to go now. My son's very ill. He's having an especially bad day.'

'Sorry to hear that,' Bell replied.

Sharon nodded. It was a martyr's nod, serene and self-effacing. As Bell watched, she ascended the wide staircase that dominated the other end of the room, barely touching the twisting cherry handrail as she rose, as lithe and nimble as her father was doughy and tottering. The handrail was polished to a glorious sheen, its rich grain drawn out by the light of the large multifaceted chandelier presiding grandly over the area. Opposite the staircase was a marble fireplace. In the center of the room, four plush white couches had been arranged to form a square. In the middle was a table that featured, along its chamfered edges, a marquetry inlay of leaf-tasseled vines. This was the kind of place, Bell thought, that really should have included a price tag dangling coyly from each item, so that the owners could be absolutely certain that visitors would get the message: *We're rich. And you're not.*

'Don't know what business brings you here today, Mrs Elkins,' Jessup continued, wiggling his backside until it was comfortably situated amid the couch cushions, 'but afore we start, I gotta ask you this: If you got any extra prayers you ain't using, I dearly hope you might fire up one or two for Montgomery. Boy's ailing. Ailing something awful.'

Bell sat down on the couch across from him. She underestimated the softness and pliancy of the cushions, and instantly felt as if she were falling backwards. Had she not caught herself in time, she was fairly certain that she'd have slid into the crease between the bottom and back cushions, arms and legs churning helplessly in the air like a capsized beetle.

'Sorry to hear that,' Bell said. 'I understand that it's a heart problem.'

'Yep.' He closed his eyes and indulged in an aggrieved head-bobble. 'Boy's been sick since the day he was born. Kinda makes you wonder why the Lord would saddle an innocent child with that kind of suffering and let so many worthless sons of bitches just run around without a care in the—' Jessup gave up on the sentence with a sigh. Looked down at his hands. He seemed genuinely stricken at the thought of his grandson's illness. 'Back when I was first starting to comprehend just how bad off the boy was,' the old man said, his voice quiet and searching, 'I had to wonder. Wonder if maybe the Lord was punishing me. I've had a lot of good things in my life, Mrs Elkins. More than I ever coulda dreamed of, truth be told. And so sometimes it seems to me that maybe the man upstairs is saying – saying in that special way He has, the way that nobody can ignore – that it's time to ante up. Time to put things back in balance. What I mean is – maybe Montgomery's paying the price for all that's been given me. And you can understand, I'm sure, just how terrible that makes me feel. Just how it rips me up inside.'

Bell watched him. This wasn't the topic she'd come here to address, but she was fascinated. The governor had the spiel right at his fingertips. Was he sincere? *Damned if I know,* she thought. There was, she reminded herself, only one irrefutable truth about Riley Jessup: He was a politician. First, last, always.

'Now,' Jessup continued, 'what can I do for you, Mrs Elkins?' He had pivoted away from his ruminative slump and perked up, like a plant spotting the watering can. 'Nice as it is to welcome you to my home, I'm thinking you probably didn't drive all the way over here from Raythune County just to say hello.'

'I appreciate that.' Bell decided to plunge right in. 'Governor, I'm confused.'

'Howz that?'

'Well, I have some questions about a company called Rhododendron Associates.' She watched Jessup closely. No reaction. 'I was hoping you could enlighten me.'

'And how might I do that, young lady?' he said, voice as soft and runny as syrup.

'By explaining why a company in which you're heavily involved would have employed a man named

Jed Stark – who had, to say the least, a less than savory reputation. With all due respect, Governor, may I ask you just what the nature of that employment was?'

Jessup didn't seem alarmed or upset at her question. Instead, he looked thoughtful, just as he'd looked when discussing his grandson's ailments. His gaze wandered away from Bell's face, finding a temporary home in the center of the patterned gold draperies that spanned the long wall of floor-to-ceiling windows off to his left. He pressed a cupped palm over each knee. He smacked his lips a few times, as if there was a bad taste in his mouth that wouldn't quite go away. The tip of his tongue lolled too long on his lower lip; it gave him a slightly demented appearance that was, she knew, entirely misleading. He was a bright man – a brilliant one, really, in his own way. You didn't go from squalor to opulence, from Briney Hollow to this place, without a hefty dose of smarts. Yes, luck was involved, too, of course, and drive, and something more than luck and drive – call it a willingness to shift your gaze at the right moment, so as to preserve plausible deniability – but you had to have the native intelligence, the bedrock intellectual capacity, to do elaborate calculations on the fly. Riley Jessup sometimes played the buffoon, Bell thought, because it worked. He embraced the stereotypes of his profession and his region – he was fat, coarse, sloppy, and slow-talking, sipping his bourbon and slipping the bribes in his back pocket – and it did the trick. Even though he'd been out of office for quite a few years now, even though he looked old and harmless, he still radiated a faint red glow of danger, like a decommissioned nuclear power plant.

'Employ lots of folks,' he said. 'You've seen the size

of this place. And I've got some pretty complicated business operations as well. Not sure I know precisely what it is you're referring to, ma'am.' The warmth in his voice had been turned down by about half a notch. 'Maybe you could elaborate just a teensy-weensy bit.'

'I'd like to know why Stark was being paid – and being paid quite well, as it happens – for his services to a company ultimately controlled by you,' she said. 'And why a business card from a New York City attorney was found in his pocket. And why his widow is the recipient of an extremely generous payout from you, apparently in exchange for her promise not to divulge the nature of her husband's activities on your behalf.'

Jessup swung his big head around to face her. A cold steady fire was visible in the slits of his eyes, eyes made squinty by the upward thrust of pressure from his fat cheeks. Bell saw several things going on in those eyes – and none of the things had anything to do with words. Or with fancy drapes.

Jessup moved his lips again, wetly and aggressively. It went on too long to be just a nervous gesture. The smacking sounds conveyed the same sense of slow preparatory menace as would the noise of a knife being sharpened against a stone, rhythmically, ominously, back and forth. Finally he spoke, enunciating each word to within an inch of its life: 'Can't really see as how that's any of your business, ma'am.' His voice had now completely shed the homespun hokeyness that had seemed to append a little curlicue to the end of his sentences.

Now she knew that Jessup had something to hide. She hadn't expected him to tell her anything. She'd just wanted to see how sensitive he was to her questions. Had he chuckled, grinned, and dismissed it, had he shaken his big head and flapped a fat hand in her direction and told a whopper of a tale about how Stark was looking into some land to purchase for him – to build an orphanage, no doubt, or maybe a hospice or an animal shelter, something wondrously noble and shimmeringly selfless and ready-made for the TV cameras – then Bell would have backed off, satisfied that whatever it was, no matter how sneaky and shady, it most likely didn't concern the recent events on her patch of West Virginia.

But he'd reacted. Overreacted, in fact. Revealed himself. Gotten angry. And he'd given her even more reason to keep poking around.

She stood up. Jessup didn't.

'Well, if that's your attitude, Governor,' she said, 'there's no point in continuing this conversation. I may as well head back home. This place is a long, long way from Raythune County. But you already know that, don't you?'

'Hold on.' He still didn't rise. 'I got a question for you, lady.'

She waited.

'My question,' he said, 'is as follows. Why'd you run for public office in the first place? Tell me that.' The good ole boy tone, the one he'd deployed so expertly on that flatbed truck the other day at the hospital, the one that was like honey drizzled on a biscuit, still hadn't returned. His voice was hard. All business.

Bell said nothing. She could see that he didn't really care if she answered or not. This was about him, not her.

'Let me tell you why *I* ran,' Jessup said. 'I ran because

I'd figured out a few things in my life, okay? I finally got it. See, I grew up poor. Dirt poor.' Shook his head, jowls flapping in response like a Greek chorus backing up his point. 'No – we were poorer than dirt. Dirt would've been a step up. Well, it didn't take me too damned long to notice that you gotta have money in this ole world. You can do without a lot of things, but you *gotta* have money. Lots of it. After you get it – and get it howsoever you can – then you can be nice to folks. Sweet. Polite. But without money, all that sweetness is about as useful as a big ole sack of shit.'

He shifted his large bottom on the couch. A bitter frown cut across his face, like a surgical scar slashing an ample belly.

'You gotta rise up, Mrs Elkins.' Sounding canny now. And confident. Setting her straight, giving her the benefit of his wisdom. 'You gotta rise up and up. And that's what I did. I did what the money boys done told me to do – so's I could rise up. You know 'bout the money boys, doncha? Everybody in any kind of public office anywhere knows about the money boys. Always hanging around. Always ready to lend a helping hand, once they can see that you're going places. Well, I used what they give me and I rose up high – higher than anybody from Raythune County ever did or ever will. You know what, though? Them money boys – they don't forget. They come calling one day. And they want what they want. You follow? So – yeah. Yeah. I made some deals. No question. Did some things I ain't rightly proud of. But in the end, if you look at it fair and square, Mrs Elkins, I think you'll see that it all works out. Works out just like it oughta. I helped some folks. Still helping 'em. You were there the other day, right? At the hospital? Sure you were. You have to meet the folks, just like I do. All part of keeping your job, right? Yeah, you were there.' He squinted at her, as if trying to imagine her face in the context of a sweltering parking lot and a rowdy crowd in T-shirts and flip-flops. 'Sure. Musta been. And you heard all about that MRI machine, the one I'm paying for. The one that Raythune County wouldn't have, 'cept for me. And so—'

'Your charitable activities are a credit to you, Governor,' Bell said, interrupting him. 'But I think you did all right for yourself along the way. More than all right, it looks like.' She didn't bother pointing to any of the lush furnishings that surrounded them. She didn't have to.

'God's been good to me,' Jessup said. Piety oozed back into his tone. 'Like I told you earlier, I ain't complaining. Which is why,' he went on, dipping his head with courtly humility, 'I want to make things right. Want to be a positive force in this ole world. Want to leave my mark on this here state before I go off to my heavenly re—'

'Bullshit.'

Jessup flinched as if poked with a stick. Nobody talked to him this way. Anger started to form in his face.

But Bell had heard enough. She was tired of being the one-woman audience for his platitudinous twaddle. 'What I want to know,' she went on, 'is why Jed Stark got a payoff from Rhododendron Associates. That's it.'

Now the anger moved from his face to his fists. He kneaded them fiercely, as if he were cracking walnuts in his palms. 'I thought we could talk,' he said. 'One public servant to another. I thought we had some common ground.'

'Just answer my question and leave the speechifying for another day.'

Jessup stopped grinding his fists and looked her squarely in the eye. 'Go to hell,' he said.

Bell laughed. She'd been on the receiving end of that particular directive on many occasions – it was a standard line flung at prosecutors by disgruntled defendants. Still, she'd never managed to come up with a reply that satisfied her. *You, too* seemed childish. *Meet you halfway* was unimaginative.

So she nodded, as if that settled things between them, and turned and walked away. Headed back through the trio of expansive rooms toward the foyer and the ornate front door waiting at one end of it, acutely conscious with each step of how deeply her heels seemed to sink into the voluptuous carpet. Jessup's life, she reflected, had been just this cushioned for many years now, just this extravagantly padded with money and power and adulation. Whatever he was hiding was similarly swaddled, similarly buried under layers and layers of pretty things. Was it worth the effort to dig it out? She wasn't sure. Sometimes, she knew, when you finished a treasure hunt, the thing you held in your hand at day's end was worth far less than what you'd given up to get it.

Bell was almost to her car when she heard her name.
'Mrs Elkins.'

It was Sharon. She'd emerged from the side of the voluminous house, following the long, shrub-bordered, serpentine curve of the brick lane, trying to get to Bell before she reached the Explorer. A security guard had spotted the governor's daughter and now began his own rapid trek up the driveway from the other direction, but Sharon waved him off.

'I've got this, Leo,' Sharon said.

The guard paused. With close-cropped gray hair and a deep vertical curve on either side of his mouth, he looked older than the other guard by a good three decades, but he was still fit, the tight black shirt stretching across the massive pack of muscle on his chest and shoulders.

'Hell of a security team,' Bell murmured.

'Only what's necessary.' Sharon gestured toward the house. 'You'd be surprised at the trouble we have around here. People trying to break in and steal something. Or just wanting to get at my father to beg him for money. Won't leave us in peace.'

Bell obligingly looked at the house once more. Sharon seemed to want her to, as if the scope and beauty of the place would make an argument more compelling than mere words, answering every question and deflecting every judgment. In a window on the second floor, on the far right-hand side, Bell saw it: a boy's face. The features were fuzzy – he was too distant, the window was too high – but she could make out a fringe of pale brown hair, thin face, jug ears. Was he smiling? Maybe. Had to be Montgomery Henner. From even that fleeting and faraway glimpse, she sensed a kind of quiet yearning in the boy's face, in the way that face was tilted toward the front gate, as if he spent his days dreaming of what it might be like to rove beyond this place, unencumbered by illness and frailty and constant caution. To travel. To have adventures, like any other sixteen-year-old. To see the world – to see, Bell thought, recalling Carla's excitement, places such as London.

To be free.

'You know what?' Sharon said. Her voice implied that Bell had raised some moral objection to all of it, to the house and the grounds, to this blunt and forth-right expression of wealth, even though Bell hadn't spoken. 'My father worked like a dog for every dime he's got.' A hard crust of defensiveness – belligerence, really – had formed around Sharon's voice. 'And he gave up a hell of a lot, too. Sacrificed. Put himself on the line, over and over again.' She recovered herself. Her tone softened. 'Look. I don't know why you needed to speak with my father today, but it's clear that your conversation was cut short. I'm just asking you to remember what he's been through. Which is why he gets a little worked up sometimes. Kind of intense. Even rude.'

'You're wrong,' Bell said mildly. 'Our conversation was over.' She was sure that Sharon had been secretly listening to every word.

'It's changed us, you know? All of us,' Sharon went on, as if Bell hadn't spoken. 'Monty being so sick, I mean.' She bit her bottom lip, then released it. 'I don't know if you have any children, Mrs Elkins, but to have a sick child – it's the worst – I can't describe—' She stopped. When she spoke again, her tone was gentle and confiding; this was one friend talking to another. All defenses down. 'Look, I came out here to level with you. Woman to woman. I caused Daddy a lot of pain when I was younger. Did everything I could to embarrass him. Ran around and made a damned fool of myself. I was a selfish bitch. Drank too much. Screwed every guy in sight. I hated the fact that he was in politics and we all had to be so *good* all the time. So goddamned *holy*. So I went running just as fast as I could in the other direction. I was a slut, okay? No other word for it. Wanted to embarrass him. Wanted him to suffer – and he did. He did. But no matter how bad I was, no matter how much I put Daddy through back then, it's *nothing* compared to what he's dealing with now.' Her chin quivered. 'Watching his grandson get sicker, day by day.'

'I'm very sorry.'

'Just needed to say it. So that you won't judge Daddy too harshly. About – about whatever it is you came to see him for.'

'Understood,' Bell said. Sharon's speech, like portions of her father's, felt prerecorded, maybe even poll-tested. Riley Jessup was a politician – and Sharon was a politician's daughter. Slight variation of the same species.

Sharon backed away a step or two. The security guard moved forward. There was a steady, avuncular protectiveness in his bearing.

'Everything okay?' he asked Sharon.

She nodded. Gave him a brief smile. Then she turned again to Bell. 'I need you to know something else. You called these men a security team. Well, that's not exactly right. Leo here is like family. I mean – yes, he protects us, but he's not just an employee. Leo's been working for my father since – well, how long has it been now, Leo?'

'Forty-six years,' he said. Bell heard the glint of pride in an otherwise bland and stolid voice.

'Leo here knows me,' Sharon said. 'Knows all of us – me, my father, Montgomery. And Whit, of course.' Her husband's name sounded like an afterthought. 'We've added to the staff over the years,' she went on, 'but Leo – and Bob over there, and Rufus and Carl, who're out back – have been with us forever. In fact, Leo was the one who found me and brought me back, all those years ago. When I was running wild. It was

Leo here who talked me into coming home.' She patted his forearm. He had no apparent reaction – no smile, no confirming nod. He didn't look at her. Yet Bell thought she detected a slight quiver in Leo's body when Sharon touched him. A faint, subtle vibration.

Opening the door of the Explorer, Bell let her eyes slide up for another glimpse at the second-floor window, toward the place where she'd seen the boy. He was gone now. The drapes were shut. She could imagine a hand – not the boy's hand, but someone else's, someone charged with keeping him safe – grabbing the fabric and giving it a hard tug, pulling it across the rod, sealing off the inside of the house the way you'd twist on the lid of a jar, securing it, making it airtight.

Bell was three-quarters of the way back to Acker's Gap. She drove very fast and the mountains – steep walls of green rising away from her at a dizzy pitch – flashed by. She relished the freedom and the silence.

It didn't last long. Her cell rang. She slapped the phone against her ear.

'Elkins.'

Heavy breathing. It wasn't an obscene phone call. She knew what it was: the husky aftermath of weeping. A man's weeping. Men cried differently from women; they tried to hold it back, fighting it, walling it off, and the effort ironically made the tears go on that much longer, fortified by having weathered the initial resistance. For a woman, tears came and went like a spring shower. For a man, it was more serious; a bout of weeping was like a tornado, wrecking everything he'd believed about himself and his ability to take a punch.

'Elkins,' she repeated.

The voice was laden with pain and embarrassment: 'Ma'am – I'm sorry, ma'am, sorry to bother you – I oughta call Nick Fogelsong and I know that, but I – I don't want him to – I'm ashamed, I'm—'

Bell let the caller collect himself.

'Ma'am,' he started again. 'This's Wally Frank. My brother Charlie – he was – he was—'

'I know,' she said. She had picked up something else in his voice, the longer he talked. His words were slightly slurred. He'd been drinking. In these parts, grief and whiskey were like best friends in elementary school: You rarely saw one without the other.

'I miss him,' Wally said. 'All the time. He was a strange man, no doubt about that, and lotsa folks thought he was – well, not right in his head – but he was my brother.' A series of wet-sounding coughs. A muffled belch. 'Listen, Mrs Elkins, I can't say this to Nickie – we've known each other too damned long and I'm too ashamed of myself – but I don't know what to do. I just don't know what to do. I just—'

She let his broken-off sentence hang there in space. She thought about the autopsy photos of Charlie Frank. The ghastly wounds. Until Charlie's killer was caught, she'd be getting these kinds of calls. Technically, a prosecutor didn't solve crimes; that was the sheriff's job. But in a small county, the reality was different: She was at the center of the wheel. No way out. She didn't want a way out.

'Thing is,' Wally said, and his voice sounded tinny and faraway now, as if he'd dropped the phone and picked it up again by the wrong end, 'I'm no good for anybody these days. No good at work. No good for my kids. My mother looks at me with them big eyes of hers – and I don't know what the hell to say. Don't know how we're gonna take care of her. Can you – what am I gonna do, Mrs Elkins? What am I gonna do?' She heard a sob and a click.

He'd hung up without waiting for an answer. Which was a good thing, because she didn't have one.

27

'And so I said, "Hey, no! Shut *up*! You'll jinx it!" And Annie said, "Jinx *what*?" And I said, "The whole summer. *Duh*."' Carla took a breath. She'd needed one at least three sentences ago but banged right on, talking in that headlong way she did when she was happy. It was the opposite of how she acted – taciturn, the quiet closed up in her – when she was mad at Bell, or upset at the world. There was no middle ground with Carla Jean Elkins, her mother knew; she was loquacious or mute, a chatterbox or a sphinx.

They'd set up the time for the Skype chat the day before and at 4 P.M., Bell made sure she was seated at her desk in her courthouse office, laptop arranged so that it didn't catch the glare from the window. The image on the computer screen satisfied Bell that Carla was doing fine. Her daughter's eyes were bright, and she was as excited as Bell had ever seen her.

'So weird that it's still light there,' Carla said. She was lying on her stomach on a bed covered with a white chenille bedspread, chin propped in her palm, bare feet waving in the air behind her. Beyond her daughter's toes, Bell could make out a tall leaded window and tidy stacked squares of fuzzy darkness. It was 9 P.M. in London. When she contemplated just how far away Carla really was – across an ocean, for God's sake, even though her presence on the screen made her seem close enough to be hanging out in the next room – Bell felt awe, followed by a wave of immense and overwhelming sadness. She had to swallow hard to keep it out of her voice.

Bell had asked her about Annie Carpenter, the other summer intern in the London office of Strong, Weatherly & Wycombe. That was the firm for which Sam Elkins made obscene amounts of money as a terrifyingly effective lobbyist. *She's okay,* Carla had replied, which was a signal to Bell that the two of them were already close. In Carla's world, 'okay' was synonymous with intensely, unbelievably, eternally fabulous. Annie's only flaw, Carla added, was that she persisted in predicting that this summer would be the very best one of their entire lives – which, as Carla had quickly scolded her, officially constituted a jinx.

'How's the neighborhood where you're living?' Bell asked.

'Oh my God, Mom, it's amazing. I mean, the houses all look like they're right out of *Mary Poppins* or something. So they've got these little fences with little spikes on top and these fancy front doors. Oh, and yesterday we went to King's Cross – the train station where Harry Potter goes to Hogwarts, right? They've got this platform that's like the one he goes through. And the brick wall. Check out my Facebook page – you can see me there. Annie took the picture.'

Bell didn't want to tell Carla that she'd already seen it, that she'd been to her daughter's Facebook page dozens of times in the past few days. She didn't want to seem overprotective, like some crazy stalker mom.

At the words 'Harry Potter,' Bell had felt one of those acute pangs just below her rib cage that always assailed her at the moment her desperation at missing Carla reached a particularly intense pitch. Back when Carla was in middle school, Bell had read the entire Harry Potter series aloud to her, book by book, divvying up the adventures across many bedtimes. Bell could remember how it felt to have Carla nestled in the crook of her arm, while both lay in the big bed in Bell's room, as Bell opened *Harry Potter and the Deathly Hallows* to the spot where they'd left off the night before.

There were times when Bell wasn't sure she could make it to the next moment of her life. It sounded melodramatic, but it was true; she missed Carla so much that she seemed to lose the knack of breathing. The trick of it. She had to remind herself how it was done. And the way it was done, of course, was to stop trying to do it, to let the body go about its business without any interference from conscious thought. She had to settle herself down. *Carla's fine,* Bell told herself. *She's fine and I'll see her again. She's having a great time and that's what's important. Not my neediness. Not my utter desolation because I want her here right now, right beside me.*

'So we'll be doing Stonehenge next weekend,' Carla was saying. She'd gone on talking – babbling, really – oblivious to Bell's distress. Which was precisely how Bell wanted it. Carla didn't need any extra guilt to carry around with her. She already blamed herself for the death of her best friend last fall, a death that wasn't her fault but that came as the result of events she'd set into motion.

'That's great, sweetie,' Bell said, determined to keep

her voice light and cheerful. 'And how about the job itself? I mean, what do you do all day in the office?'

Carla shrugged. Transferred via Skype, the shrug looked like a wavy glitch on the screen.

'So I answer the phone, run errands, get lunch for the senior staff. Stuff like that. But, Mom – it really doesn't matter, because this is *London*. You know?'

'I know.'

'How're things there?' Carla asked. 'How's Aunt Shirley getting along?'

There was a stretch of silence, and so Carla spoke again. 'Mom? Still there? Is the connection still—?'

'Right here.' Bell was trying to figure out how to answer. 'Frankly, it's been kind of rough.'

'What do you mean? Is Shirley okay?'

Her mother had been honest with Carla about some of Shirley's problems; you don't just walk out of prison and back into the world with no residual effects.

'It's not only that,' Bell said. 'We've had some serious crimes this summer. Two murders. An old man and then another man.'

'Yeah.' Carla's voice was serious now. 'Dad told me. Wow, Mom – it sounds bad.'

Damn you, Sam Elkins, Bell thought savagely. *Damn you straight to hell.* She had decided not to tell Carla until now. She didn't want her to worry. Her daughter had been through too much already in her young life – the violence she had witnessed, the emotional cataclysm of the divorce. She had wanted Carla to enjoy her summer.

'So what's the deal?' Carla was asking. 'Are the cases related to each other?'

'We don't know. Nick and his deputies are doing their best, but there's not a lot to go on.'

'I bet everybody's scared to death.' Carla's face was somber now. She wasn't giddy anymore about being in London; she was thinking about Acker's Gap. And Bell silently cursed her ex-husband all over again.

'Listen,' Bell said. She had promised herself she would be casual with Carla, smiling and upbeat. But now that her daughter knew the truth about what was happening here, Bell didn't have to pretend anymore. She didn't have to hide her anxiety. Bell's next words came in a rush. 'I want you to be very careful. All the time. If you're out at night, make sure somebody knows where you're going and who you're with and what time you're supposed to be back. And—'

'Mom. Come on.'

'Okay. Okay. I'll stop. But there are bad things in this world, sweetie. Bad things and bad people. And you've got to be on the lookout for—'

'Hey.' Carla's voice was playful but pointed. 'You said you'd stop, okay?'

'Okay. But just be careful. I mean – really, really careful.'

Carla smiled. Cocked her head. Offered a waggle-fingered wave. 'Love you, too, Mom.'

Bell was still looking at the computer screen, even though there was nothing to see anymore. Carla had disconnected a good three minutes ago. Bell, though, had barely moved in her seat. She wanted to let the conversation with her daughter wash over her, soaking into her bones so that she'd be able to recall it in the days ahead, when the ache of missing Carla – an ache that only intensified or receded, but never went away entirely – grew unbearable.

She was startled by the shrill warble of the office

phone. If Lee Ann were here, Bell could ignore it, knowing her secretary would take care of it; Lee Ann, though, wouldn't be back for another week. Bell let the thing go on for six full rings. The day's business was pressing, and she knew that; still, she gave herself the luxury of a last, restorative thought about her child. Carla was doing well. Carla didn't need her. Carla could take care of herself – which was a kind of double-edged truth, Bell realized, in that it made her both happy and sad.

She reached for the phone. 'Elkins.' With her other hand, Bell slapped shut the lid of her laptop. Time to focus.

'Bundy Barnes here.'

She didn't need the ID. The raspy, crackling, *screw you* tone was a dead giveaway.

'Good afternoon, Mr Barnes.' Bell always tried to be polite, even when – as was definitely the case at present – the person on the other end of the line was a sworn enemy, an eighty-six-year-old county commissioner who had tried repeatedly to have her removed from office by means of electoral recall or legislative fiat. No matter what charges Barnes concocted, his real beef with Bell came down to a simple fact: She was female. And women had no business being prosecutors – or anything, for that matter, other than wives and mothers.

'Ain't nothin' good about it,' he said with a snarl. 'I want to know what you and Nick Fogelsong intend to do about the fact that we've had two murders this summer with no end in sight. Folks're too jumpy to leave their houses at night. We're under siege. And what do I see? I see a prosecutor and a sheriff who spend a whole lot of time doin' a whole lot of nothin.''

'I can assure you, Mr Barnes, that the sheriff and I are—'

'Don't want no fancy promises, Mrs Elkins,' he said, interrupting her doggedly. 'Not from you and not from Nick Fogelsong. We've had enough promises already, dammit. We need action.'

Bell waited. Whatever she said next, and howsoever she said it, she'd be cut off yet again by Barnes; he was notorious for monopolizing conversations, for stomping right in the middle of other people's sentences like a kid racing through a row of fresh mud puddles. He was a crude fool and an unrepentant bully.

But he was also, in this instance, quite right. The violence was unusual and unsettling, and it added another serious and prolonged aggravation to the summer, beyond the heat and the slow-motion deterioration egged on by the sagging economy. Bell could roll her eyes at the sour cantankerousness of Bundy Barnes all she wanted, but the truth was, he had a point.

'We're pursuing several new lines of inquiry, sir,' she said, 'and I really think that soon we'll have—'

'Do your job!' Barnes thundered. The interruption came a little later than Bell had expected. She'd gotten through almost a full sentence before he jumped in.

'Do your job!' he repeated, louder this time, and then she heard the angry crash of his receiver as it was slammed down in the two-pronged slot – Barnes, like a lot of older residents of Raythune County, still relied on a landline and a clunky rotary-dial phone – followed shortly by the bland meditative hum of a dial tone.

Bell returned to her work. She had a two-inch-high stack of transcripts of depositions to review and a warrant to prepare for a burglary case, and so when she heard the door to the outer office open and close, she didn't lift her head; it had to be another busybody, determined to tell her and Nick how to do their jobs.

Well, hell. Take a number.

'Yes?' she said, eyes still on the paperwork that spilled out across her desk.

'Hey.'

The voice went through her like a beam of light running under the surface of a clear stream, leaving a phosphorescent glow in its wake. She looked up. Clay Meckling stood in the threshold between the outer and inner office. The last time she'd seen him, he was mired in a wheelchair, defeated and depressed, with a flat, lost look to his hooded eyes. Now, however, he stood straight and tall again. His face was too thin, but she forgot about that as soon as he smiled. She knew that smile.

'Clay. My God.' She rose and rounded her desk. They embraced, but there was a reserve about him. A formality. She felt it right away and backed off.

'Clay,' she said. 'When did you—'

'Last night. My dad and I drove back from Chicago.'

'How is—?' She didn't know how to ask. How to say, *How is your leg?* It sounded clinical and crass, as if the first thing anybody needed to know about him had to be his disability.

'Everything's fine,' he said. 'Really. Had some top-flight physical and occupational therapists at the Rehab Institute in Chicago. Amazing place. Got fitted with a better prosthetic. Makes all the difference.'

'Glad to hear that, Clay. I'm so happy for you.' Bell wanted to slap herself. Or sew her own mouth shut. *Jesus.* She was coming out with platitudes, with greeting card lines, when what she wanted to do was talk to him. *Really* talk to him – the way they'd talked before, honestly and forthrightly, or lovingly and playfully. The way they'd talked before the events of the horrific morning in the early spring that had resulted in the amputation of his leg. They were lovers, and that had given even their daylight conversations that special frisson rooted in sexual intimacy, an electric thrill born of what you knew about the other person that no one else knew, such as how he expressed himself during moments of intense and enveloping physical rapture. Or how he took his coffee. It was all information, all part of the complex joy of knowing someone right down to the core. Despite the difference in their ages, Bell had felt comfortable with Clay – more comfortable than she had ever felt with any other man. But after the accident, everything changed; it changed not in a single moment, which was rarely how such things occurred, but in an incremental way, as he pulled away from her, refusing her access to his deepest grief and most secret fears.

Or had she been the one to pull away from him? She wasn't sure. And maybe, in the end, it didn't matter, anyway. The point was this: They couldn't recover what they'd had. He clearly didn't want to. And she didn't want to, either.

Did she?

'Bet you've got your hands full these days,' he said. 'My dad's been keeping me up to date. Pretty scary stuff – the murders. Sounds more like Chicago than Acker's Gap.'

She batted away the bad news. 'We can talk about all that later. Come on in and sit down,' she said eagerly. 'I wanted to call – I wanted to – well, I thought

I'd wait to hear from you first, I wasn't sure—' She was flailing, she didn't know what to say or how to be, and her only consolation was the thought that it would get easier in the days and months ahead. Less awkward. She'd see him on the street, at the store, in JP's, and they'd ease into each other's lives again, and one day . . . maybe . . .

She looked at him. He hadn't yet accepted her offer to sit down, so she had to look up; he was that much taller than she was. There was a quiet peace in his gray eyes. And there was something else in those eyes, too: A seriousness. A gravity. She noticed it seconds before he spoke again, which at least gave her some semblance of warning as to what he was about to say, so that she could prepare herself.

'Belfa,' he said. Her given name. Used sparingly, kept for special occasions. Another signal that this wasn't just a casual visit. His cockeyed smile – that was another thing she loved about him, that rascally grin – had faded now.

'Don't really have time to linger,' he went on. 'Just back for a day or so. I've been in contact with the graduate admissions office at MIT and they said I could enroll this fall, just like I planned.' Clay's dream was to study urban design; after the amputation, sunk deep in despondency about his condition, he'd turned down his fellowship. Now, apparently, he'd changed his mind.

'Really?' she said. 'This late? They're letting you—?'

'Yeah. They kept my spot. It might be a little rough at first, but there's a lot of help available. They've got a really good disability services program. Anyway, I need to head up there right away. Get settled. I just wanted to come over and say good-bye.'

'That's great, Clay. It's what you've always wanted.' There she was again, dispensing clichés like after-dinner mints. *Stop it,* Bell told herself. *Just stop it.* But she didn't know what else to say except clichés. At least they filled up space with sound.

'Yeah,' he said. A moment passed, as if he were waiting for something else from her. Did he want to be talked out of it? Asked to stay? She couldn't do that. This was his dream. But she remembered what it had felt like when they kissed, back when they were lovers. The memory almost knocked her over with longing. She had to get hold of herself. Couldn't let him see how much she wanted—

'Well,' he said. He cleared his throat. 'Better get going. Dad's outside in the truck. Gonna hit the mall. Gotta stock up.' He paused. 'I hear Shirley's back.'

'Yes.'

'Good. That's good. I know what that means to you. Working out okay?'

'It'll take time.' Bell was surprised at how casual she sounded now. Just a few seconds ago, she'd been afraid she might topple over from the dizziness of being so close to him. Well, she'd had plenty of practice in the fine art of hiding her feelings.

'Yeah,' he said. 'Bound to.'

Why was this moment so fraught and awkward? Why did she feel the urge to shake him until something real came out – something that wasn't part of a regular, sedate, polite conversation, something that would prove what they'd been to each other, how much they'd shared, the passion they'd known? And why, if that was how she felt about him, hadn't she reached out, kept in contact, told him so over these past few months? Why hadn't she tried? And why wasn't she trying now? Long-distance relationships weren't unheard of. They were difficult, yes, but a lot of people managed to—

'Thanks for stopping by,' Bell said. 'Good luck, Clay.'

He looked at her as if he wanted more. But maybe that was her imagination. Wishful thinking. And she had to protect herself, didn't she? What if she capitulated and told him how she really felt and it turned out that he now regarded their relationship as a mistake? One he was glad to be rid of? He didn't need a damned thing from her. He was going to grad school. He'd wanted that for a long time. And she knew that desire – the itch that tormented you day and night, the one that insisted you try for a life outside these mountains at least once before you died, that called to you. She knew what he was feeling: He was thrilled to escape. Thrilled to be leaving Acker's Gap – and her – behind. It was obvious.

Wasn't it?

'Okay,' he said. His eyes were unreadable now. 'Well, take care of yourself.'

28

Bell had made a promise to Shirley, and so she would go. She cursed the timing; the encounter with Clay an hour ago had left her anxious and frayed. But – well, here she was. For Shirley's sake.

The bar was located just outside the city limits of Alesburg, a town about twenty-five minutes from Acker's Gap. It was small and dark and seedy. The darkness hid some of the seediness, but not all of it. Nothing could hide all of it. There was a dirt-sealed hardwood floor and a low stained ceiling. Four wooden booths were linked up along one wall. A random scatter of round tables and wobbly chairs constituted the rest of the seating. Makeshift stage at one end. At the other, a dark bar with a variety of mismatched stools. Behind the bar was a shelf featuring the liquor selections. The high-end choices – the bottles of Johnnie Walker Red and Grey Goose and anything else that rose above the informal designation 'rotgut' – were furred by dust, so infrequently were they called into service. The people who came into this place, Bell knew, weren't likely to order name-brand liquor. The point was to get drunk as quickly and as cheaply as possible, and for that, the piss-water beer on tap did the trick. Behind the row of bottles was a long cracked mirror that reflected the dimness back on itself, like a perpetual echo of something murky and furtive.

The place was called Crazy Dave's. Familiar to Bell by its reputation. The original owner had indeed been a man named Dave, but he'd died five years ago in an explosion in a dingy basement across town that doubled as a meth lab, and the subsequent series of owners had not bothered to change the name or the sign. If they had, it would have necessarily shifted from Crazy Dave's to Crazy Nelson's to Crazy Billy's to Crazy Suellen's to Crazy Frank's, and the clientele might have been confused. Or maybe not. Looking around, Bell decided that the people who frequented this place surely didn't give a damn about what it was called. Crazy Dave was dead, but Crazy Dave's would live forever.

'Hey, Belfa. Over here.'

Bell turned. Her eyes adjusted to the darkness and she was able to spot Shirley; her sister was near the stage area, holding the handle of a guitar case.

'Hey,' Bell called back.

'You made it.'

'I made it.'

At that moment they seemed to be the only two people in the bar. And no wonder: It was still daylight outside, just after 6 P.M. This place wouldn't get going for another few hours. On her way in, Bell had passed a man she assumed to be the owner, and then a woman she figured was a waitress, but the two were moving constantly in and out of the room, embarked on various obscure errands. Bell couldn't have picked either one out of a lineup, and not just because the bar was so infernally dark. The owner looked like dozens of other middle-aged losers with whom she had to deal routinely in the course of her work: overweight, with a limp that was most likely the result of a motorcycle accident a while back, with a bad comb-over and a sour expression. The waitress, too, was middle-aged, but skinny. *Funny*, Bell thought. *Most of the men in these parts get fatter as they age, but the women get skinnier.*

'Show doesn't start till nine,' Shirley said. 'Band has to get here early, though. To make sure everything's right. Microphones and lighting and whatnot.'

Bell took a few steps across the floor in her direction.

'I told you, Shirley. I can't stay for the show. I just came by because you said—'

'I know. I know.' Shirley's voice was eager. There was a lift in it that Bell hadn't heard before. Or at least not recently. 'Wanted you to meet Bobo. Before he starts working. When he's working, there'll be a bunch of people around him. Fans and whatnot. He'll be here soon.'

Bell took another step toward the stage area. She bumped into a chair, nearly knocking it over. She hadn't seen the chair; the dark wood blended seamlessly into the darkness of this windowless space.

'You okay?' Shirley said.

'Fine.'

'Kinda hard to see in here. Gotta keep it dark for atmosphere. People expect that.'

Bell nodded, then realized Shirley might not have noticed the nod, given the darkness and the distance – two kinds of distance, really – between them, and so she said, 'Yeah. Bet they do.'

The side door opened. A pie-slice of light showed up on the floor, quickly vanishing as soon as the newcomer pulled the door shut behind him.

'Belfa,' Shirley said, 'this here's Bobo Bolland. Bobo, I want you to meet my sister, Belfa Elkins. Everybody calls her Bell, though.'

Bell had fully expected to have a strong negative reaction to the man. He was exploiting her sister, wasn't he? Stringing her along, giving her false hope about making a career out of 'managing' some half-assed bar band that played for drinks and tips? Bell didn't know for sure, but she wondered, as well, if there might be a personal issue here – wondered, that is, if Bobo was screwing her sister in the cruder, more literal sense of the term. Leading her on in that way, too. Pledging a future that didn't exist. Taking advantage of Shirley's vulnerability and neediness. And – most appallingly – her hope.

To Bell's surprise, though, she didn't feel her default hostility when shaking Bolland's hand and taking a quick measure of him. He was tall and lanky, except for his belly, which bumped unstoppably over the top of his belt buckle as if his stomach had recently been pumped full of helium. He had silver hair that he wore long, gathered into a ponytail that neatly bisected his back – Bell glimpsed it when he turned to say hello to Shirley – and his face, a lined and pouchy one domin-ated by a large hooked nose, had a serenity to it, a settled quality that was somehow discernible even in this shadowy place.

'Hey,' he said. 'Good to finally meet you. Shirley talks about you all the time. I was starting to think she was making the whole thing up – this sister of hers, a prosecuting attorney and all.'

'Bobo,' Shirley said, trying to sound admonishing, but Bell could hear the blush in her voice, could sense her pleasure in being teased.

'Oh, I'm real, all right,' Bell said. 'And I wanted to meet you, too. Hear your music.' That wasn't true; Bell was present only because Shirley had insisted. This was a favor to her sister. Nothing more. And while she hadn't had the instantaneous bad reaction to Bolland that she anticipated, neither did she trust him or have any interest in his songs – beyond the fact that he'd managed to ensnare Shirley in his ludicrous, frankly pathetic dreams of show-business glory.

'As I was just telling Shirley,' Bell went on, 'I'm sorry I can't stay for your performance tonight, but I thought I could at least sit in on the sound check.'

'Great.' Bolland took the guitar case from Shirley. His hand was big and stringy, the knuckles sticking up like marbles thrust under the skin. Still looking at Shirley, he spoke again, aiming his words at Bell. 'You probably already know this, but Shirley here's a natural-born manager. She's doubled our bookings in just the past few weeks. Been putting together a YouTube video. And she got me to look into copyrighting my songs. Ain't never done that. Know I should've.'

'Yeah,' Shirley said. 'Folks'll steal them, Bobo. I've been telling you.'

While Bolland tuned his guitar, his bandmates – a bass guitar player named Leroy and a drummer named Calvin, also middle-aged, also tall with skinny legs, and similarly afflicted with bellies that appeared to have been strapped on that morning along with belts, boots, and ball caps – arrived through the side door and began setting up their gear. Shirley checked out the electrical receptacles, angled the amplifiers, used her fingernail to scrape at a small blob of gum on the paneled wall behind the stage. In the meantime, a few customers wandered into the bar. The waitress drifted amid their tables, offering up her round bottom for swipes and smacks and then feigning outrage when they obliged.

'Bell's heard you play before,' Shirley said.

Bolland looked up from the strings he was fiddling with. 'That right?'

'Yeah,' Bell said. 'At Tommy's.'

He winced. 'Real tragedy. Man losing his life like that.'

No more wisdom seemed forthcoming from Bolland, so Bell dragged a chair to the center of the room to await the commencement of their warm-up numbers. She looked around. A nearly-empty bar during the gray indeterminate twilight of late afternoon and early evening was a peculiar thing. Even without windows, you could always tell day from night in a bar. And a bar needed the night. Needed the romance and mystery of the darkness outside, crowding all around the building, matching the darkness inside. Otherwise it was just a wood-paneled box where people congregated to waste their time and their money. She'd never felt the lure of such places, not even in D.C., where the bars were very different – fancier, of course, and more expensive – from an establishment such as Crazy Dave's but which served the same basic human needs: company and diversion. Anything to deflect or delay the painful truths brought on by solitude – namely, that the world's a rigged game, start to finish, and that everyone dies in the end.

'Here goes,' Bolland said. He nodded to Calvin and Leroy, tapped his foot three times and then they started a song. An original. Bell knew because Shirley had been humming it a few days ago, while she folded her laundry, and Bell had said, 'What's that? Sounds pretty,' and Shirley had replied, 'It's one of Bobo's. Told you that you'd like his songs – if I could ever get you to hold still long enough to listen.'

'Train's heading down the track, don't think it's coming back; like the love I had, it makes me sad, that lonesome clickety-clack.' The trite words weren't the part that affected Bell; it was the melody, a haunting one that dipped into its minor chords like a hawk lowering a wing as it soars alongside the face of the mountain, then rights itself and aims for a higher part of the sky.

Bell listened as the song unspooled and damned if she didn't feel a lump forming in her throat. She fought against it. She hated emotional reactions – her own or anybody else's – to anything; emotions caused more trouble in the world than guns and knives. Guns and knives were just accessories after the fact. Emotions were the instigators. Love and hate and greed and lust. Jealousy. Frustration. Despair. Name an emotion, and she could point to a crime it had provoked. To hell with shotguns. Feelings were the real troublemakers.

But she couldn't help herself. Bolland's voice was a sandpapery tenor that featured something fixed and firm at its center, a flinty, hard-earned wisdom, and as that voice sang of train wrecks and tragic love affairs – the latter being really just another kind of train wreck, Bell thought – she had to fight to hold on to her emotional equilibrium. She was wildly annoyed with herself – *Jesus,* she seethed, *this is like Country Music Cliché 101* – even as she admired his talent.

Shirley stood at the edge of the stage area, arms crossed, head tilted, frowning with concentration. She was doing her job. Listening for sound levels, for the right blend of the instruments and of Bolland's voice.

And Bell, as well as she could manage in the swarthy gloom, studied her sister's face. It was different from the face Bell had seen the other night, when Shirley sat slumped at the kitchen table, angry and distraught. To be sure, Shirley's face was still leathery and lined, still worn, but now it was also alert and focused. Engaged.

Bell stood up. She hoped Shirley wouldn't see her slip out. She'd done what she promised to do. She'd met Bolland. Shaken his hand. Heard his music. Given him the benefit of the doubt.

Which was not to say that all doubt was erased. *Not on your freakin' life, mister,* Bell thought, and the incompleteness gnawed at her. The only solid information she had about Bolland at this point, she reminded herself as she drove back toward Acker's Gap, was that, as Shirley had insisted, he was one hell of a musician. Bell still knew nothing about his past – but that, of course, could be easily remedied. Especially by someone who had Rhonda Lovejoy's number on her speed-dial.

29

The voice on the phone was too loud, too fast, too aggressive, and the East Coast accent scraped against his sentences like a rock rubbed relentlessly up and down on a cheese grater.

'You got three minutes, which is more than I ought to give you,' the voice said, although to Bell it sounded like *maw den I otter gev yo.* 'Go.'

She had picked up her cell in a rush, absolutely sure that it would be Carla calling her back. Needing her. It was 10:30 P.M. in Acker's Gap – just a little over six hours since they'd Skyped – and 3:30 A.M. in London, but maybe Carla couldn't sleep. Maybe she was nervous. Upset. Scared. Or maybe she just wanted to talk.

It wasn't Carla. It was, in fact, about as far from Carla as you could go and still remain within the limits of the human species. The man's voice had a macho swagger to it that reminded Bell of every gangster movie she'd ever seen. She half expected to hear a phrase such as 'sleep with da fishes' in his next breath.

She had no earthly idea who the caller was or what the hell he was talking about.

Bell was sitting in her favorite chair in sweats and a T-shirt, an unread book in her lap, an almost-gone

Rolling Rock on the small table beside her. She'd decided to wait up for Shirley, hoping her sister might come home tonight after the gig at Crazy Dave's. Now that things were better between them – weren't they? – it was a reasonable expectation.

'Who's this?' Bell said.

'Sam Voorhees.' The voice was prickly with impatience. 'Now you're down to two minutes and forty-five seconds, lady. Better talk fast.'

Bell sat up straighter in her chair. She could figure out the incidentals – such as why the mysterious Mr Voorhees suddenly had decided to call – later. Right now, she followed his instructions. 'Okay,' she said hurriedly. 'Why was Jed Stark carrying your business card?'

'Who?'

'Jed Stark.' Bell waited. She had the distinct impression that Voorhees wasn't playing a game, that he really had no idea what she was talking about.

'Tell me more,' Voorhees said. 'Like – where the hell am I calling?'

'Acker's Gap, West Virginia.'

He laughed. His laughter sounded like a box of wrenches dropped on a concrete floor. It stopped abruptly. 'God,' he said. Bored and irritated at the same time. 'West Virginia. Okay, yeah. Gotcha. Jed Stark. Lemme look.'

Bell could envision a master file displayed on a glowing laptop screen, through which he did a quick key word search.

'Okay,' Voorhees said. 'Yeah. He was a subcontractor. I hired Stark to do some confidential work for a client of mine.'

'What kind of work?'

'What is it about the word "confidential" that you don't understand?'

'Stark's dead,' Bell countered. 'So what does it matter now?'

'Can't discuss the nature of his assignment. Clock's ticking, lady.'

'So who's the client?'

More silence. Finally Voorhees said, 'You're coming up to your last thirty seconds.'

'It's Riley Jessup, right? The client? Rhododendron Associates is paying your tab.'

'Twenty seconds. Better ask me something I *can* answer.'

'You're based in New York City, right?'

'Yeah.' He grunted. 'Good choice of question. Nice one to end on.'

'If you're in New York – how'd your business card end up in West Virginia? And why did Jed Stark write the name "Odell Crabtree" on it?'

Voorhees grunted again. 'Time's up, lady. I don't talk about my clients and I don't return phone calls from people who *aren't* clients. Except this once. Oh – and next time you talk to Sammy Elkins, you tell him we're all square now, okay? This was the favor. I owed him one and now we're even.'

After his slam-bang hang-up, Bell kept the cell pressed to her ear for another few seconds, contemplating the fact that her ex-husband, that deal-maker extraordinaire, had tried to balance the scale in the only way he knew: calling in a marker. She was bereft about Carla's going to London; she'd made that clear enough with her profane one-word text to Sam. To assuage his guilt, he'd reached out to Voorhees. Induced him to call.

Voorhees had revealed nothing. Except, Bell thought, he actually had.

30

Lindy was thrilled with this new piece of information: Her mother had once had a best friend named Maybelle. A friend so important to her that she'd kept her letters. The letters had been simmering in that box for all the hard years since Margaret Crabtree died, letters locked away, silent and invisible, but still exerting an influence on Lindy's life – because they had mattered so much to her mother.

Lindy's thoughts had kept her company during the overnight shift at the station. That shift was winding down now – it was almost 6 A.M. – and the building's glass walls continued to trend seamlessly from black to gray to the pink of the approaching sunrise. Heat seemed to lurk just behind that sunrise, waiting for its cue to pounce.

What a long, slow night it had been, without Jason to talk to. Or even to ignore, which was another form of communication. Jason had taken the night off; he and his brother had driven their father to Charleston the day before for an appointment with a cardiologist. Jason hadn't been sure he would make it back in time, so he took a personal day. Or night, in this case. The replacement was a woman named Bonnie Skinner. Lindy had no opinion about Bonnie Skinner. There wasn't anything, really, upon which to hang an opinion: Bonnie was medium-sized, with medium brown hair and medium brown eyes and cautious, middle-of-the-road opinions about everything. She usually worked in Drummond, at the Lester station over there.

'How do you guys do the coffee for the morning rush?' Bonnie asked.

'Huh?'

'The coffee.' Bonnie stood by the FILL 'ER up sign, holding aloft an empty carafe to help make her point, its glass sides stained with the distastefully brown residue of Dark Colombian Roast. 'Like, do you all do 'em all at the same time or one at a time? Brewing new pots, I mean. We do 'em all at once, over in Drummond. Dump out what's in there and start fresh.'

Lindy was rearranging the items on the front counter: the cardboard container with the tiny red 5-hour Energy bottles; the tall four-sided plastic stand with sunglasses stacked up in it, their dark lenses smudged with the fingerprints of people who just couldn't keep their hands off them, who had to try on every single freakin' pair while waiting for Lindy to give them their change.

'One at a time,' Lindy replied, but the tone of her voice said something else: *Whatever*.

She missed Jason. The realization surprised her, but it was true. They were a good team. They worked well together, with the natural synchronicity that comes from an accumulation of hours in each other's company. But it wasn't just a work thing, Lindy thought; she was used to Jason, period. Used to his moods and his gestures. She knew by now that when he preened and he bragged, it was to cover up a secret inferiority, and when he acted like he didn't care about anybody else but himself, it was to deflect attention from the fact that he was deeply and habitually empathetic.

In the wide-open prairie of the hours between midnight and 6 A.M., hours that Bonnie Skinner mostly spent sitting on a stool by the cooler, pencil diving at intervals toward a ratty paperback filled with page after page of jumbled-word puzzles, Lindy thought about Jason and the noises he'd make, trying to sound like a rapper. The way he'd move casually toward the front counter whenever a customer came in to pay. Backing her up. Sending a silent message: *There's two of us here. I'm watching you.* Just in case.

'Okay,' Bonnie said.

Lindy looked up. She hadn't realized that her temporary assistant was waiting for her to say something else about the protocol for brewing the morning coffee supply, and that when she didn't, Bonnie just decided to tie off the conversation with the all-purpose 'Okay.'

Finally the day shift personnel arrived. Time for Lindy and Bonnie to go home. They barely said goodbye to each other in the parking lot; it wasn't hostility, just indifference and fatigue. Lindy nodded and Bonnie gave her a weak smile as they split off, each heading to her own vehicle. The sky was already gray and hazy, which meant that the heat, as it intensified throughout the day, would probably hang stubbornly in the mountain valley like a wool blanket tossed over a clothesline.

As she drove home, Lindy thought about how she'd answer Jason when he asked her – and she knew he'd ask right away, eager for a compliment – about how she'd fared without him. Lindy planned to tease him as long as she could, stringing him along: *Oh, man, she was terrific. Pitched right in.*

Better watch it, Jace. Might ask 'em to trade you for her. Permanent, I mean.

Naturally, she would set his mind at ease after a while. Wouldn't keep him in suspense. It was too easy, for one thing. Way too easy. Despite his pretense of sophistication, Jason was pretty gullible. Easy prey for jokes.

Lindy climbed the front porch steps into the house, still thinking about Jason and his face, still amused by the idea of how he'd look when she teased him – the worried frown that would scrunch up his features like a wadded-up paper towel, the perplexity in his eyes while he tried to figure out if she was serious or just yanking his chain.

She was, therefore, preoccupied. And that was why she didn't notice the slight movement of the curtain just before her hand cupped the knob and shoved open the front door. That was why, furthermore, when the vicious blow roared forth from the shadow lurking behind that door, striking the side of her head, she was caught so totally by surprise.

31

'Let me see if I've got it all straight,' Sheriff Fogelsong said. He settled his broad back against the high padded booth, big hands flat on the stainless steel table, musing amid the quiet of JP's in the middle of a weekday afternoon. There was always a lull between the lunch and dinner rush. That made it his and Bell's favorite time to come in and reconnoiter.

'This Jed Stark,' Nick went on, 'was more than just a lowdown troublemaker. He must've been some kind of hillbilly hit man. Voorhees – at the request of Riley Jessup, or so you're theorizing – hired him to do something or other. Stark, being a stupid sack of shit, gets himself killed before he can do a damned thing. And the nature of his employment is so sensitive, so potentially explosive, that his widow gets a nice big windfall to guarantee that she keeps her mouth shut about it.'

'Right.' Bell used her french fry, now heavily ketchup-laden, to point at Fogelsong, the way a teacher might use a piece of chalk to indicate a student who's come up with the correct answer. 'Jed Stark's assignment had to be extremely serious. Only way to explain the money paid to Tiffany Stark. You don't spend that kind of cash to cover up anything less than murder.'

With her first swallow of coffee Bell had realized she hadn't eaten all day, and so quickly ordered fries. Jackie, who'd sent her waitresses home due to a lack of business and now dealt with the occasional customer herself, tried to steer Bell toward the Fruit Medley. No dice. Not even when Jackie used putatively enticing phrases such as 'refreshingly cool' and 'nutritionally advantageous.'

'Jackie,' Bell had patiently responded, 'it may be ninety-five degrees outside, but I've still got a craving for something deep-fried – and really, really bad for me.'

Jackie had let a raised eyebrow serve as her reply. She returned a few minutes later, placing the order of fries in front of Bell with a resigned politeness. 'Salted 'em extra,' Jackie murmured. 'Long as you're indulging, might as well make it count.'

Once they were alone again, Fogelsong returned to his summation of what Bell knew and didn't know. The latter, unfortunately, was well in the lead. 'Okay,' he said. 'So who the hell was Stark supposed to knock off – or whatever it was he was supposed to do? And why?'

'Don't know,' Bell admitted. 'Odell Crabtree's name was on the card in Stark's pocket, but there's no good reason why anybody would want Crabtree dead. He's a sick old man.'

'Agreed,' Fogelsong said. 'All you have to do is wait a little while – and nature'll take care of it for you.'

Bell had procured another fry, but abruptly dropped it back on the plate. 'What did you say?'

'Don't get mad. I was agreeing with you.'

'Not mad. Want you to repeat what you said.'

'Just meant,' he said obligingly, 'that if you really want Odell Crabtree out of the picture, you don't have to go to all the trouble and risk and expense of hiring some skunk like Jed Stark to do it. You can just sit back and wait a spell. Odell's an old man. Had a hell of a hard life. Rumor is, he's half out of his head, anyway. Death'll be a relief. And it's definitely not far off.'

'So what if Odell Crabtree wasn't the target?'

'It was his name on the card.'

'Well, it's his house. The name might've meant the location, not the target. Because he doesn't live there alone.'

'His daughter, Lindy, you mean. Haven't seen her in a long time. Doesn't get out much anymore, except to go to work. Takes care of her father, I hear. Won't accept any help.' Fogelsong frowned. 'Why would somebody go after a nineteen-year-old girl?'

Bell was digging through her wallet for the money to settle her lunch tab.

'Nick,' she declared, 'We've had two homicides already this summer. I'm not real interested right now in the why. I'm interested in telling Lindy to be careful. To keep an eye out.'

Caught in the ardent spotlight of the late-afternoon sun, the house looked just as it had during Bell's previous visit: broken-down, slovenly, engaged in a sort of time-lapse unraveling toward utter ruin. She parked in the driveway behind Lindy's car and waited a moment, taking in the full range and particularity of the dilapidation; it came not solely from neglect, she theorized, but also from natural entropy and from some very daunting odds. Lindy Crabtree surely did the best she could, but the old house and its half-acre lot were more than she could handle on her own.

Bell climbed the crooked front steps. There was no

doorbell, so she knocked on the warped and weather-battered door. No response. She knocked again. She was determined to have another conversation with Lindy – and this time, to be more insistent. Bell was fairly certain that the young woman hadn't been entirely forthcoming with her in their earlier conversation; she didn't blame her for that, because Bell would have reacted the same way herself at that age, in response to a meddlesome stranger who claimed to have her best interests at heart. But the stakes were higher now. Lindy and her father – one or both of them – might very well be in danger. Until her talk with Voorhees, such as it was, Bell was unsure; now, the peril seemed more plausible. Voorhees wasn't the kind of man who wasted his time on trifles.

Bell knocked three more times, waiting a long time between each attempt. Maybe Lindy was asleep. Or reading in the kitchen. There had to be a back door, right? She left the porch and rounded the house, parting the high weeds with both hands and stepping carefully over sharp piles of broken bricks and flung-down lumber.

To her surprise, the back door hung three-quarters-of-the-way open on its rusted red-orange hinges. She hesitated. Before she did anything else, Bell called out, 'Hello?' She'd lived a lot of her life in this region and well understood that – open door or not – you didn't just wander into someone's house without announcing yourself, unless you had a hankering for a bellyful of buckshot.

'Hello?' she said again.

She pushed at the door with two fingers. The resulting creak was the kind that might be produced by a sound effects specialist for a horror movie; it was a stretched-out yelp that rose and fell and rose again, tapering off just as Bell slipped through the slightly widened opening.

Later, she would not be able to recall what the kitchen looked like. The smell would stay with her forever – a knock-you-back combination of spoiled food and galloping mildew and an accumulation of human wastes – but she would not remember the appearance of the sink or the stove, or what color the floor was. She had no recollection of the walls or the curtains in the dingy little room.

Her attention was instantly commandeered by the gigantic old man who sat, hunched and muttering, over the dinette, his clothes little more than rags, a filthy blanket thrown over his shoulders, hands the size of cinder blocks dangling at his sides. His shaggy white head was bent so far forward that his forehead nearly bumped the tabletop. His massive bulk spilled over the edges of the chair; the span of his shoulders had the rough dimensions of a fireplace mantel.

This, she thought, *has to be Odell Crabtree.*

So startled was she by his size – and his very presence – that it took Bell a second or so to note that his thick fingers were webbed with a sticky-looking substance, as if he'd just fought his way through a series of spiderwebs. His voice was a guttural chant. When he paused before taking another rattling, phlegmy breath, she heard moans from another source – *It's coming from the living room,* Bell thought with alarm, *someone's hurt in there, hurt badly* – and then her focus was pulled back to the old man. He was moving now, turning in the chair, his body shaking heavily, still chanting a rhythmic nonsensical chant.

He lifted his huge head and swiveled it slowly, slowly,

in Bell's direction, and the blanket slid off his mammoth shoulders. He raised his hands, too, and held them out to her, palms up, and at that moment Bell realized what the substance was that covered them:. Blood. The old man's hands were smeared with blood. Suddenly Bell was able to understand the chant, could translate his mutterings. *Lindy-hurt-Lindy-Lindy-hurt*, he said as he rocked back and forth in the narrow chair, nearly capsizing it with every clumsy lurch, holding up his hands as if he were asking forgiveness from someone, anyone.

32

Bell had told the story to Nick Fogelsong again and again. Three times now, and they hadn't even finished their initial cups of coffee in the hospital cafeteria. It wasn't that the sheriff doubted her; she told it multiple times for her own benefit, because by repeating exactly what she'd seen, precisely what she'd done, from the moment she found Lindy Crabtree until she arrived at the ER in her own car, having followed the ambulance and nearly matching its headlong speed, Bell hoped to recover more details. To nail down the narrative and make sure she had reported everything. Shock, she knew, could work like a soft clinging fog, obscuring things.

'—and so I finally got hold of myself,' she said, 'and left Odell Crabtree in the kitchen and ran into the living room.' She paused. This part was difficult. 'Lindy was lying behind the front door. Clearly a significant head trauma.' Bell tried to drink from the cardboard coffee cup. She put the cup back down again without accomplishing that. 'Nick, it was terrible. There was a big bloody rock on the floor right next to her. I have to wonder if—'

She paused. She wondered if Lindy would survive. She didn't have to finish the sentence for Fogelsong to know what she was speculating about.

The hospital cafeteria, a square room with a pale green tiled floor, long aluminum tables and chairs, and a row of vending machines for after-hours snacks, was almost empty. A woman and three small children sat at a table near the corner; the kids were eating cardboard cups of orange sherbet with tiny wooden paddles that served as spoons. Whatever had brought this family here tonight – a sick father, a suffering sibling, a declining grandparent – the mother had managed to keep the children happily oblivious. At another table, two women in blue scrubs and heavy white shoes sat across from each other, silently sharing a bag of Chili Cheese Fritos. They were clearly hospital employees, and they looked too exhausted to talk. Every few minutes, the PA system came alive, offering up an announcement that sounded mild and routine – too mild and routine. The nature of the emergency, Bell knew, was slyly embedded inside the mildness, interpretable only by those who knew the code words.

'You called 911,' Nick said. He was guiding Bell back to the story. Back to the events as they unfolded. Trying to steady her. 'They did a good job, Bell. You watched the paramedics work and so you know that. They got her here real quick. She's alive. And that's all we can ask for right now. That's it.'

Bell nodded. Rattled off what the ER doctor had told her. 'Scalp lacerations. Skull fracture. Probably subdural hematoma. If they can reduce the brain swelling, and if she regains consciousness—'

'Got to trust the doctors and nurses,' Nick cut in. 'They know what they're doing.'

With a fingernail, Bell scratched at the side of the cardboard cup. 'Any family members we should notify?'

'Charlie Mathers checked with the HR office at Lester Oil. There's a second cousin up near Morgantown. She's willing to come, but can't get away till morning. Not much family left, I guess. It was really just the girl and her father. Lindy and Odell Crabtree.'

Hearing the old man's name caused Bell to frown. 'So he's in custody?'

'For the time being, yeah. Deputy Harrison handled it. We didn't formally arrest him, but we took him in for questioning. Although from the look of him, that doesn't sound too promising.' Fogelsong finished his coffee with a quick swig. 'Not sure about this, Bell. Not sure about what actually happened out there. You think Odell Crabtree would attack his own daughter?'

'Scene was pretty damned incriminating. Blood all over his hands, mumbling to her about forgiving him.'

'Maybe the old man surprised the real assailant and ran him off,' the sheriff said. 'We've had two murders this summer already. This might be part of the pattern. And it's not out of the question that Odell scared off the attacker. The man's as strong as an ox. Stands to reason – working all those years in the mines. He's old, but I bet he's quite a sight when he's charging at you with a full head of steam, fists up, fire in his eye. Maybe he didn't get an ID on the attacker, but he saved the girl's life. Got the blood on his hands when he was tending to her. And the forgiveness part? The thing he was babbling about? Maybe he felt guilty about not protecting her better.'

'So why didn't he call for help?'

'Not sure he'd be able to, Bell. To figure out what to do. You saw him.'

'Then why wasn't he with her in the living room?

297

He was just sitting there, Nick. Sitting at the kitchen table like he didn't know where the hell he was.'

'Probably didn't. There's some serious mental incapacity going on with the man. No doubt about it. Fades in and out, most likely. That's how it happens sometimes – you've got periods when you're lucid and periods when you're not. He obviously can't handle his own affairs. His daughter's been doing it all. Takes care of everything.' He shook his head. 'Good God. What the hell? Two homicides. This could've made it three.'

'Still might.' Bell's voice was grim. 'Lindy's not out of the woods yet.'

Fogelsong pushed his hat back from his forehead. 'The killer or killers,' he said, 'could've been lying in wait. Maybe they cased the Crabtree place for a few days. Knew when to break in and jump her. She works third shift. Regular schedule. Easy to know her comings and goings.'

Bell looked across the cafeteria at the two hospital employees in the blue scrubs. They were rising now, returning to work; when they scooted their chairs back under the table – first one, then the other – the gestures ignited two short, sharp, overlapping squeals.

'Did Crabtree say anything?' Bell asked.

'Not so far. Doesn't seem to know where he is. Just rocks back and forth and mutters to himself – and then he explodes, throwing himself against the wall and yelling and cursing.' Fogelsong stretched out his right leg and moved his booted foot up and down, then around in a tiny circle, trying to keep the circulation going. He didn't like sitting. Made him antsy. 'Can't get over how strong that old man is. Sick as he is, it took Harrison and a couple of paramedics to get him in the squad car.'

'He's dangerous,' Bell muttered.

'He's a handful. Grant you that. But capable of assaulting his own flesh and blood?'

Her answer came in a flash. 'Hell, Nick. You know as well as I do that anybody's capable of anything.'

33

The call came shortly before 4 A.M. Bell was still awake and sitting in her chair, and answered before the end of the first ring. 'Elkins,' she said. The caller was an ICU nurse; Bell had left her number at the desk, along with a request that she be notified if Lindy Crabtree regained consciousness. 'She's awake,' the woman said. 'I wouldn't have predicted it, but with brain injuries, you just never know. Sometimes it's a three-month coma and permanent impairment – and sometimes, they wake up with nothing but a bad headache, asking for butter pecan ice cream. This girl's young and healthy. I'll say that. Makes a big difference.'

The hospital parking lot was black and empty at this hour, a ghostliness ground in by the fact that a majority of the streetlights ringing the space had been turned off for the night, leaving a lonely few to keep the vigil. Bell had her pick of parking spots. Hard to believe, she thought as she hurried toward the ER entrance – the nurse had instructed her to come in that way, because the main entrance was locked up tight when visiting hours concluded at nine each night – that just a week ago, this same expanse had been bristling with light and people and noise and sweaty chaos, when Riley Jessup came to town.

'Hey,' Bell said.

She'd approached the corner in which Lindy's bed was situated as quietly as she could, not wanting to startle the young woman. The ICU was a long rectangle with separate areas for each patient, like a car-repair shop with bays for individual vehicles. It was a place undergirded by the densely woven hum and rhythmic swish of the workings of complicated monitors.

Lindy was sitting up, sipping a cup of water through a bendy straw. She wore a hospital gown, white cotton printed with a pattern of small blue diamonds, and it was much too large for her, ballooning from her thin neck like a barber's smock on a toddler getting her first haircut. The white sheet that covered her was tucked around her midsection. The wall behind the bed featured a variety of bright screens across which drifted green and yellow horizontal lines, lines that spiked now and again.

The young woman looked at Bell with a blank expression. The wallet-sized bandage on the side of her head had been secured with a circle of gauze that resembled a headband.

'I'm Belfa Elkins. County prosecutor. We met the other day. How're you feeling?'

Lindy's expression didn't change. She set down the cup on the bedside table and peered at her right index finger, to the tip of which was affixed a small white clamp that looked like a plastic clothespin; the clamp, in turn, was attached to a cord and the cord to yet another monitor. In the crook of her other arm, an IV line had been inserted.

The lights were low. The patient beds Bell had passed on her way to Lindy's were bathed in the strange, flickeringly iridescent ambience that defined

ICU units. Even though this area of the hospital lacked windows, somehow you still could tell that it was late at night. *Kind of like Crazy Dave's,* Bell thought. Probably the first and last time that particular comparison would ever be made.

A nurse arrived, black-haired and bustling. It wasn't the nurse who had called her, and Bell was required to explain why she was there; visiting hours were severely restricted in the ICU. The nurse checked Lindy's temperature and blood pressure. 'You're a very lucky young lady,' she said. 'Hope you know that.'

Bell addressed the nurse while she refolded the blood pressure cuff. 'I'm going to have some questions about these injuries. This is a criminal investigation. Where's the nursing supervisor?'

'She'll be right back. Said she had a phone call to make. Something personal.'

The nurse departed. Bell stood uncertainly by Lindy's bed, not sure if she should offer a sympathetic platitude or two before diving in. Bell had often interviewed victims and witnesses in hospital rooms, but usually there were family members here, hovering at the periphery, and they handled the emotional duties, doling out the optimism, so that Bell could focus on the fact-gathering. Lindy, though, was alone.

'Look,' Bell said. She didn't want to bother the other patients and so she spoke softly, as softly as she could without whispering. Whispering attracted more attention than shouting. 'I know you feel like hell right now, and I'd love to let you rest, but I have to find out what happened. No easy way to ask this – so I'm just going to do it.' Her eyes locked on to Lindy's. 'Did your father attack you? Is he the one who did this?'

Lindy's body recoiled. Her small hands fluttered on top of the blanket. She swallowed before she spoke, frowning at the feel of what must've been, Bell thought, a red-raw, severely dry throat. '*Daddy?* No, no, *no*. God, no. He didn't – he *couldn't* – no. No. No.'

'So you remember the attack.'

'Yeah. I mean – well—' Lindy shook her head. That brought another frown, tailing off into a wince. 'Okay, no. But it wasn't him. I'm positive, okay?'

Bell waited. When Lindy was first brought in, the ER doctor had told Bell that most trauma patients don't remember their ordeals; they believe they do, picking up on clues from what other people say must have happened. But their own memories stop well short of the event that caused the injury.

Lindy looked down at the white sheet. She smoothed out a wrinkle. Fingered the hem. 'Okay,' she said. The anger had been replaced by resignation. 'Okay. Fine,' she went on. 'The whole thing's pretty much a blank. I drove home after my shift ended at seven and – and that's it. Nothing past that. I woke up here.' She grew agitated again. 'But it couldn't be Daddy. It *couldn't* be.'

'You don't know that. You don't remember.'

'I'm telling you. *It wasn't him*. It had to be somebody else.'

Another ICU nurse showed up, drawn there by the rising agitation in Lindy's voice. She was a thin-cheeked woman in bulky black glasses who wore her frizzy gray hair in two stubby braids. When she reached up to adjust the dial on a monitor, the ends of her braids twitched against her shoulders.

'Everything okay?' she asked.

'Fine,' Lindy said.

Gray Braids nodded and checked a second monitor, eyeballed the IV drip, then looked sternly at Bell. 'Okay, but let's wind this up,' she said. 'She needs her rest.'

In the silence that ensued until Gray Braids departed, the swishing noise seemed to grow louder and more assertive. It was coming, Bell realized, from a ventilator hooked to the patient in the adjacent bay.

And then they were alone again. 'That nurse was right. You're damned lucky,' Bell declared. 'Had you been hit harder with that rock – or at a slightly different angle – you could very well have been killed. Or suffered an even more serious brain injury. As it is, whoever attacked you must've been in a hurry. They weren't able to do much damage. They hit you once with a glancing blow. Not full force.'

'I know what you're getting at. That somebody hit me who didn't really want to hurt me. Or maybe thought they did – and then couldn't go through with it.' Softer now: 'Like Daddy.' Lindy swallowed and winced, swallowed and winced. 'But it wasn't him. Couldn't be.' The certainty was pure theater; she was plenty scared, a fact that Bell had picked up on the moment she'd stationed herself at Lindy's bedside.

'You're not sure,' Bell said quietly. 'No matter what you say to me, I know that you suspect him, too.'

'No.' Softly, but urgently. 'No. No. *No. No. No.*' Her eyes drilled into Bell's with dark intensity.

'You've wondered for some time,' Bell went on, 'about your father. Wondered if he was capable of something like this. Because there are days when he doesn't even know who you are. And he lashes out at you.'

Bell was guessing. She had no idea if she was correct or not. But she had glimpsed, within Lindy's instant reaction to the idea that Odell Crabtree had attacked her, something more than mere defensiveness. More than daughterly love. Bell had seen something desperate and inchoate in those eyes. Lindy might be horrified at the idea of her father's guilt, but she also was not entirely surprised by it.

'No,' Lindy said firmly. 'No.'

Bell switched tactics. 'Okay, then. Let's say it wasn't your father. Who else, then? Who might've done this? Who'd attack you? And why?'

'Whoever did those other murders, maybe. The ones everybody's talking about.' A thought flared in her mind: 'Where's Daddy? What've you done with him?'

'He's fine. We took him into custody.' Bell cut off Lindy's protest. 'Protocol. It's a temporary hold. He's safe, though. From the look of him, he can't take care of himself. He'll get hot meals and a place to sleep. Until you're out of here, it makes sense. Don't you think?'

Lindy wouldn't look at her. A tacit acknowledgment that Bell was right.

'So,' Bell said. 'How long? How long has your father been like this?'

Lindy's gaze remained stapled to the blanket on her lap. A minute passed. She lifted her face. 'Long enough.'

She coughed. Bell picked up the cup from the bedside table and handed it to her, making sure the straw was angled in the right direction.

'Tell me,' Bell said as soon as Lindy had had her fill and handed the cup back to her, 'what it was like before.'

In the faint glow of the monitors, Lindy's face looked even younger than her years, her skin infinitely malleable, like sculptor's clay minutes before the touch of

the artist's thumb sets the features into place perma-
nently. Lindy's voice was low and lilting, stripped of
the belligerence that had inhabited it during the earlier
part of their conversation.

'My mother was wonderful,' Lindy said. She'd
waited, deciding whether to trust Bell, and then went
forward. 'And Daddy – well, he always had a lot on
his mind. He grew up rough.' She coughed again.
Bell reached for the cup, but Lindy shook her head.
The problem with her throat right now wouldn't be
alleviated by a drink of water. It wouldn't be alleviated by a thousand drinks of water. 'And then my
mother died. Daddy lost his job in the mine and – and
it was all too much for him. He'd already been having
some problems – he was forgetting things, and there
was one day when he got lost while he was driving
home, the same drive he'd been making for fifty years.
He called me in a panic from a stranger's house out
on Coon Path Road. He was scared. Real scared.
He was – he was slipping away. Not just from me. He
was slipping away from everything. From his own
memories. From the world. And he started to get real
mad about it. Frustrated.'

'Violent?'

Lindy waited. 'Yeah,' she said, after the kind of
pause that made her affirmative reply redundant.
'Sometimes he gets violent.' She reached out and put
a hand on Bell's arm. 'But you have to understand.
It's not his fault, okay? Things are just so different
from when Mom was alive. She had a way of calming
him. She used to tell me about how they met and
they fell in love. I didn't know much about that until
right before she died. Daddy, she said, never thought
he'd marry. Didn't expect to find anybody to care

about him that way. But a friend took him to Mom's church one day, and it was like – like she'd been waiting her whole life to meet somebody like Daddy, and he'd been waiting his whole life, too, to meet her, even though he was a lot older. Never thought they'd have kids, but then I came along.' A smile, brief but prideful. 'My mother named me. She loved Anne Morrow Lindbergh – she was always reading and she loved those essays about nature and the seashore and such – but she didn't like the name Anne. Said it was too ordinary. Too common for the likes of me. Because I was going to be special. And so she named me Lindy.'

Tears were spilling out of Lindy's eyes. She had continued talking while the tears came, her voice unaffected by them, as if tears were just something you had to put up with, pass through, like a light rain on the way to your car. Bell didn't rush to comfort her. There was still more Bell needed to know, and comfort could be a muzzle: It closed off revelations.

After a pause to let the sorrow crawl back in its box, Lindy went on. 'But there's still so much I don't know about my parents. And it eats at me. It does. Because that's the only way I can hang on to my mother now – by finding out more about her life.' Lindy's voice acquired a frantic edge. 'It's all I've got. You see that, right? I don't have anything else to remember her by. I found some letters the other day, from an old friend of hers, somebody she'd never talked about – but that's it. And if something happens to my father – if I lose him too—'

Lindy stopped. It was unthinkable, being left with just bits and pieces of her parents' lives. A haphazard, half-finished jigsaw puzzle. A random jumble. She would have no way back to the past, no route she could follow. She'd be marooned in the present. Stranded with no frame for her life, no facts to fill in the picture.

Bell understood. She understood it better than Lindy could ever appreciate; like Lindy, she lost her mother early and had virtually no extended family. There were differences, of course: Bell had hated her father, while Lindy loved Odell Crabtree. And Bell had a sister. But the broad outlines – the quietly terrifying sense of having no context for yourself, of having few close family members left who could tell you where you'd come from or who you really were – matched up.

Another time, another place, Bell might have discussed this with Lindy. Consoled her. Right now, however, there was a crime to investigate.

'I need you to think hard about something,' Bell said. 'I know you don't want to believe your father attacked you. So help me out here. Let's figure it out. If not to rob you – and nothing seemed to be missing, including your billfold and your computer – then why else would somebody assault you?'

'Told you. I don't know.'

'I think maybe you do.'

Seeing Lindy's look of confusion, Bell elaborated. 'I mean that sometimes we know things we don't realize we know. Any friends or coworkers pissed off at you? For something that happened on the job, maybe? Anybody threatening you?'

Lindy snorted. 'More like the opposite.'

'What do you mean?'

'I mean that I've got a ton of people – too damned many – trying to protect me. Giving me advice. Telling me it's not a good idea to work at night. Or to live alone with my dad. Taking care of him. Telling me I should leave Acker's Gap.'

Maybe they're right, Bell wanted to reply, but didn't. No sense in provoking the young woman. Not yet, anyway. 'Okay,' Bell said. 'Let's go over your actions yesterday – up until the moment you were attacked. You work until 7 A.M., right? With an assistant? Same guy every night?'

'Yeah. Not last night, though.'

'Why not?'

'Jason took a personal day. Didn't come in to work. He and his brother had to drive their dad to Charleston.'

'Jason have a last name?'

'Brinkerman.'

'Right.' Bell would find out if Jason Brinkerman really had driven to Charleston – or if that was just a made-up excuse and his absence had been strategic, enabling him to get out to the Crabtree house and lie in wait. He would know what time Lindy returned home from her shift. 'Who covered for him?'

'Bonnie Somebody. Can't remember her last— Wait. It's Skinner.' Lindy made a sound in the back of her throat that indicated how perturbed she was with herself. 'How come I could remember *that* but I can't remember the attack?'

'Just the nature of concussions,' Bell said. 'Mind's a funny thing. Okay, go on. So you drive home. You park. House look odd in any way?'

Lindy gave her a sharp glare. Bell realized that the question could have been intended as a wisecrack, a cheap joke; the Crabtree house was a godforsaken mess. Had been for years. The only oddity would have been if it suddenly appeared presentable: paved driveway, picked-up yard, shiny new roof, gutters that didn't dangle like random severed limbs.

'I mean,' Bell added, 'did you see any evidence that anyone had been there overnight? Tire tracks, cigarette butts, a porch rug moved a little bit, that sort of thing?'

'Nope.'

'Okay.' Bell nodded. 'Listen, you need your sleep. Guess I'd better get out of here before they throw me out.' Lindy's fatigue wasn't her only reason for leaving. She was eager to check on Jason Brinkerman. If the culprit wasn't Odell Crabtree, then Lindy's assistant looked good for the attack.

'I'll come by again later,' Bell said. 'You're doing great. Nurse told me they'll probably be moving you out of ICU in a few hours. Put you in a regular patient room. You take care, okay? And can I bring you anything when I come back? Something to read, maybe?'

A light came into Lindy's eyes. 'You'd have to go to my house,' she said.

'That's okay. Which book? Lots to choose from, as I remember.'

'Not a book. Like I told you, I found some letters the other day that belonged to my mom. I'd like to have them here. Truth is, with nobody in the house – well, I'm kind of worried. If there was a fire—' She looked concerned. 'They can't be replaced.'

'I'll pick them up. Bring them here. Soon as I can.'

Lindy's features were instantly smoothed out by relief. 'Great,' she said. 'They're under the dresser in the bedroom. In a little box. You'll have to move some things around, but you can find it.'

'Okay.'

'One more thing.'

'Hey, don't push your luck,' Bell said, aiming for a jocular tone. 'If you're going to ask for a cheeseburger or something, I'll have to check with the nurses first.'

Lindy's face was serious. 'What do you do if—? How do you—?' She faltered.

Bell waited.

'Look,' Lindy said, 'I don't believe Daddy did this to me. But what if—' Still struggling to find the right words, she plucked nervously at the sheet that covered her. 'What if you find out something about somebody you know – something terrible?' She looked beseechingly at Bell. 'What if you find out something you wish you didn't know? How do you— How do you *live* with it? It's so hard to think that somebody you care about might be capable of – something really, really bad. You know?'

'People are capable of anything, Lindy,' Bell said. She said it solemnly, with no cynicism in her voice. This wasn't a matter of cynicism; it was the deepest, saddest truth she knew.

'Even somebody you love?' Lindy said.

'Especially somebody you love.'

Bell sat in her Explorer in the hospital parking lot. Nick Fogelsong was an early riser. But maybe not *this* early, she told herself, pausing before she touched the digit on her speed-dial that was assigned to his home number. She canceled the call and dropped the cell onto the car seat beside her. In five minutes it would be 6 A.M.; she'd call him at one minute past the hour, and if he sounded sleepy and vaguely pissed off, she'd say, *Hell, Nick. It's after six.*

She'd left Lindy's bedside in the ICU a while ago.

Sunrise was imminent, its mix of red-gold colors simmering behind the mountain. She fired off a text to Rhonda Lovejoy, asking her to dig up some background information on Jason Brinkerman and his family.

Then she unilaterally canceled her earlier plan. She'd call Nick later and check on Odell Crabtree. Right now, she decided, she needed to be on the road. To be in motion. First she'd stop somewhere and get herself a cup of coffee, and then she'd head over to Jason Brinkerman's house to question him. She wanted to do that right away, before he found out from anyone else that Lindy had been attacked. Jason's initial reaction might tell her a great deal.

Thirty seconds later Bell was turning out of the hospital parking lot when a phalanx of black Cadillac Escalades nearly scraped the paint off the driver's-side door of the Explorer. The sleek swarm came up swiftly and silently, like phantom cars spiraling out of the gray morning mist. They were three separate vehicles, but they followed each other so closely, one virtually connected to the next, that they seemed like a single creature, linked and segmented, turning off Rathmell Road and into the large square lot like a continuous string of flexible chrome and stretched-out black.

Bell pulled to the side of the road to watch. There was a military precision to the way the Escalades operated, a vehicular rigor that reminded her of news footage of presidential motorcades. The muscular machines seemed slightly dreamlike, unreal.

She leaned forward in her seat for a better look. The cars didn't pause in the lot but made a smooth synchronous arc directly to the front entrance. The parade stopped with pinpoint abruptness; the second car was lined up perfectly with the wide walk leading to the glass double doors.

Bell squinted. The just-risen sun was in her eyes, its reflection skittering off the massive black flanks of the Escalades. *What the hell—?*

She blinked. Squirmed in her seat, searching for a better angle.

The ID wouldn't have held up in a courtroom, because Bell was too far away and because she saw only the back of a well-coiffed head of cinnamon-colored hair, but she was fairly certain that the woman who emerged from the second Escalade – and who glided into the facility without so much as a glance at her surroundings – was Sharon Henner. And the presence of the extra vehicles surely meant that whatever her mission here might be, the governor's daughter hadn't come alone.

34

Bell sometimes called them the In-Between People. It wasn't an original thought; she'd heard Nick Fogelsong talk about it, about how some families in Acker's Gap resisted easy categorization by economic status. They weren't rich, God knows, but neither were they poor – at least not the kind of poor that spread across the area like a leaf blight, infecting houses instead of plants, and human destinies instead of root systems, and that left a constant swath of parts-scavenged cars, mangy animals, scrawny children with stares as deep as graves and twice as final, and elderly relatives who sat all day long on the front porch until they, too, were subsumed by the ravening misfortune.

The Brinkermans weren't that kind of poor. Not yet, anyway. Bell realized it as soon as she pulled up in front of the house on Bonecutter Road just north of Acker's Gap. Rhonda had called her back with the address. After waiting until 8 A.M. – and finishing off three criminally weak cups of coffee at the Hardee's out on the interstate while she did so – Bell opened her car door and took a long look at the place Jason Brinkerman called home. It was one of a half-dozen houses thrown up along this stretch of road a century or so ago, rote one-story structures with tiny front yards and dirt driveways. The sidewalk stopped after the last house on either end. The Brinkerman place had the small touches that meant somebody at this address still tried, at least a little bit: The mailbox was firmly attached to the creosote-black fence post that served as its pedestal. Hosta had been planted here and there, and measures had been taken to keep kids from trampling the drowsy, big-faced leaves during violent and prolonged chases across the small yard. The grass itself wasn't so lucky.

So they were In-Between People. Not wipeout poor – but late more often than on time with the mortgage payment, and always running thirty days behind. They had jobs, but knew full well that those jobs could – and generally did – go away any minute, on account of a mistake or a misunderstanding or the need to stay home with a sick child. They couldn't let down their guard. Ever.

'Help you?'

The kid's voice intercepted Bell before she'd shut the car door behind her. He looked to be maybe eight years old, with buzz-cut blond hair, beady eyes, enough dirt on his face to darken it by a shade and a half, and a sneer that looked as if it had taken root. He blended so thoroughly with his surroundings that at first she hadn't seen him, standing on the sidewalk in front of the Brinkerman house, bare feet spread wide, fists on his hips, as if he might just take a mind to block her progress.

'Hi,' she said. Played a hunch. 'Looking for Jason. He's your brother, right?'

The kid's lip twitched, and the sneer rose and fell in a high fleshy arch.

'Well,' she went on, 'could you ask him to come out and talk to me? My name is Belfa Elkins. I'm the county prosecutor.'

The kid stared at her. 'The what?'

'Prosecutor. For the county. Somebody does something wrong – I try to make sure they pay for it.'

'My brother done something wrong?'

'Don't know. Won't know until I talk to him.'

With that, the kid's sneer went a little crazy, rabbiting up and down as if it were rigged to his toe with a long string and he'd heard music from afar and decided to tap his foot accordingly. Bell noticed the peeling red skateboard on the sidewalk in front of him. The kid lifted a bare foot and stepped down hard on the edge of the board, flipping it up and into his waiting right hand as if he'd summoned it there with a silent command, like a magic carpet. Everything happened quickly, with a grace so casual and natural and fluid as to mask the fact that it was, indeed, grace. Bell was often astonished at the physical agility of children who grew up in mountain towns – or tough inner-city neighborhoods, come to that. They seemed to have a special relationship with gravity, a secret bargain: Gravity let them have a few good years of leaping and climbing – openly defying it – before it pulled them down for keeps.

The boy thrust the board under his arm, the way a businessman would a portfolio. 'I'll git him,' he said.

Bell waited. It was going to be another hot day; the sun was clear about its intentions, even at this early hour. She remembered days like this when she was a kid. Hot days, when not even the vast shadow of the mountain could cool things down. She and

Shirley never went to a swimming pool – their father would've ridiculed the idea, to cover up his shame that he didn't have the money for them to go – and so Shirley would unkink the shiny green hose and hook it up and spray her with it, and Bell would close her eyes and wiggle all over and squeal for her to stop, although she didn't want her to stop, and somehow Shirley knew that, knew that the squealing and the pleas to cut it out were insincere, and after a while Shirley would conveniently drop the hose and Bell would pick it up and spray Shirley right back, and Shirley, too, would scream and fuss and wave her arms over her head, and they'd both be giggling so hard that they were gasping for breath. They had a wonderful time. A wonderful time, that is, until their father heard the commotion and ripped open the screen door of the trailer and yelled at them: *The fuck you two up to? Gonna whup you both, is what I'm gonna do.*

'Hey.'

Bell realized that another kid, an older one this time, had come out of the house and now spoke to her from the driveway. Bad skin, visible even at a distance. Medium build, with the beginnings of the roly-poly paunch that afflicted even the skinniest kids in these valleys. Black Converse sneakers, oversized denim shorts that hid his kneecaps, and a black T-shirt swallowed up by an unbuttoned red-and-black-checked flannel shirt that hung down his back like a cape.

'You're Jason.'

'Yeah.' Wary but not unfriendly.

'Just want a quick word with you. I'm Belfa Elkins. Prosecutor for Raythune County.'

'I ain't done nothing. Been home all night, lady. You can check with my mom and dad. And my brothers. Most of them are at work right now, but I can give your their num—'

'Relax,' Bell said. 'Wanted to make sure you'd heard about your friend.'

'What friend?'

'Lindy Crabtree.' Bell watched him, ready to take in every nuance of his reaction. 'She was attacked yesterday. In her home.'

Jason looked as if he'd grabbed a live electrical wire. His body shook and then righted itself. He stared at Bell, moving a few quick steps in her direction. Words came in an agitated pack: 'What—? *Jesus,* lady, what the hell happened? Is she okay? Is she—?' Jason swallowed hard. He was breathing through his nose, fast shallow breaths, his mouth a grim line except when he talked. He pulled his hands in and out of the loose pockets of his baggy shorts. 'Was it her dad? He's crazy, you know. I told her and told her to watch out. He's out of his head. If he hurt her – if he—' He took a big breath. 'I swear, lady, if that bastard touched her, I'm gonna – I don't care – I'm gonna make sure he never—' He broke off the sentence. 'Is she okay? Tell me. Please.'

'Yes,' Bell said. 'She's okay. And we don't know who did it.'

Jason looked down at the driveway. By this time, his little brother had come outside on the porch again. The kid cocked a foot between two balusters of porch railing, skateboard still wedged under his arm. Jason suddenly noticed him. 'Get lost, Jimmy,' he snapped. 'Go. Now.'

The kid sneered, yanked out his foot, and went back

inside the house. The screen door closed behind him with a single forlorn smack.

'Can I see her?' Jason said. His voice had a quaver in it.

'Later, maybe. She's in intensive care.'

'But she's okay, right?'

'She's alive.' Bell watched him closely, trying to read his face.

During her first years as a prosecutor, she had depended upon her instincts, certain that she could sense when someone was lying to her; she could, she thought, visualize crime scenes and the participants thereof with an uncanny degree of accuracy. But last spring she'd had a case that destroyed her confidence. She'd been wrong. Wrong about many particulars of the crime, including the identity of the perpetrator. Thus she had no faith anymore in her intuition, her hunches. All she had were the stark and paltry facts.

And so she couldn't tell if Jason's reaction was authentic or trumped up. She didn't know if he was truly aggrieved by Lindy's injury – or just indulging in some quick theatrics to divert Bell's suspicions. Rhonda Lovejoy had already texted Bell a few preliminary details about the Brinkermans and the news wasn't promising: One of Jason's brothers, Levi Brinkerman, was a meth addict awaiting trial on a burglary charge. A sister had been arrested last year for shoplifting at the Dollar Store in Blythesburg. And Jason's father, Dustin Brinkerman, had served five years on an aggravated assault conviction before he was paroled in 2005. Jason's record was clean – so far.

Bell had an idea. A way, perhaps, to rattle the truth

out of him, without the tedious ritual of a formal interrogation after reading him his rights. A sort of prosecutorial shortcut. Doing things by the book would waste too much time.

'Look,' she said. 'I'll be running out to Lindy's house later to get a few things she's asked for. Care to come along? I can pick you up.'

Jason's face betrayed an interest so ravenous that Bell nearly stepped back in the wake of it.

'Yeah. Yeah,' he said. 'Please. Yeah. I'd appreciate that. Anything I can do to help. Really.'

'Okay. Text you when I'm on my way. What's your number?'

Confronted with the scene of the crime, maybe Jason would slip and reveal himself. The blood from Lindy's wound was still visible on the living room floor and would stay there, Bell knew, until the crime-scene techs finished their work. If Jason was guilty, maybe he'd react to the sight of that stain on the old wood. Maybe he'd reveal, with just a slight tremor of a hand or too-rapid eye blink, his culpability when confronted by the gruesome proof that he'd attacked his friend and nearly killed her.

Starting up the Explorer, Bell glanced at the front porch again. Jason had gone back inside the house; his kid brother, the Skateboard King, hadn't come back out. But there was someone else on the porch now: A skinny, squint-eyed, bent-over figure in a wrinkled gray raincoat that was about four sizes too big for him, rubbing his red nose with hard upward strokes of his shaky palm. When he wasn't rubbing, he was taking violent sucks from a cigarette that wobbled in his other hand. *A long hot raincoat in the middle of summer. Jesus,* Bell thought. *Gotta be Levi Brinkerman.* Every meth addict she'd ever encountered was cold all the time. Came with the territory.

Long raincoat. She let the words turn a few times in her mind. She knew she needed to talk to Nick Fogelsong.

35

Shirley was waiting in the living room. Bell didn't see her at first; the shades had not been lifted from the night before, and her sister had arranged herself in a corner of the couch, black jeans and dark flannel shirt blending with the brown fabric like camouflage in a forest.

'Jesus. Nearly scared the hell out of me,' Bell said. She'd charged directly from the front door into the living room, searching for her briefcase. She needed to find some files that Hickey Leonard would require for a sentencing hearing that afternoon. It was Bell's case, but Hick was doing the mop-up work for her. She'd cleared the decks of her day. Needed to find out who had attacked Lindy Crabtree.

'Sorry,' Shirley said.

'My fault. I'm kind of scattered right now.'

'What's going on?'

'Just work.' Moving past the couch, spotting her favorite chair, Bell made an executive decision: Time for a break. Just a short one, but still.

She flopped down in the chair, reveling in the familiarity of its spent springs and stained fabric and broken-down back. She wouldn't trade it for a jewel-studded throne in a palace. She had a million things to do today – but she could take a moment just now. Yes, she could.

This chair had seen her through so many emergencies and disappointments and joys and confusions, so many all-nighters and early mornings and heat-glazed afternoons, that she owed it, she supposed, a little more attention than she'd given it of late. This was the chair, after all, in which she'd been sitting on her first day home from the hospital after giving birth to Carla, when Sam put the impossibly small and impossibly beautiful girl in her arms and said, 'She's got your eyes and your chin, Belfa.' Then Carla had let out a piercing howl, prompting Sam to add, 'And your temper, too.' When this chair was located in the living room of their house on Capitol Hill, it was the place in which Bell sat on the somber day that Sam had explained to her how the divorce settlement would proceed, and the arrangements made – if she approved – for moving her things back to West Virginia. Bell had looked at the list of items and looked at Sam, and then she said, 'The chair's not on here. My chair.' Sam's expression had instantly grown as wistful and wan as Bell had ever known it to be, and he replied, 'Oh, Belfa. Goes without saying.' It did, of course. It was her chair, no question. For one thing, Sam wouldn't have wanted the mildly hideous monstrosity, with its mismatched fabric and torn fringe. For another, she had bought it long before their marriage. She'd found it at a thrift store.

No: It had found her.

Bell eased off her loafers. She rubbed the back of her neck, pinching a hunk of the flesh between her thumb and two fingers and kneading it.

'So?' Shirley said.

Bell looked at her.

'So what did you think of Bobo?' Shirley added.

'Haven't had much time to devote to forming an opinion,' Bell said, sounding – on purpose – slightly testy. 'Somebody else was attacked and we don't know if it's related to the other two or if—'

'Never mind.' Now it was her sister's turn to sound testy. 'But let me know, okay? When you can? I mean, he's important to me.'

'I know that.' Bell closed her eyes and sank back against the lumpy cushion.

'Do you?'

Bell opened her eyes. 'Christ, Shirley – no fights today, okay? No arguments? I've been up half the night with an assault victim and I've got the day from hell ahead of me. We've had two homicides so far this summer and we're not even close to solving them. I won't see Carla for months. And three-quarters of the people I deal with every damned day are losing their jobs or their houses or both. So can I just sit here for one goddamned minute? In peace? Can I? Please?'

Shirley shifted her position on the couch. 'Sure, Belfa,' she said quietly. 'Fine.'

Bell looked across the dim room at her sister's face, which was placid now. Bell was struck by how they'd switched roles – she was the angry one, Shirley the soothing voice of calm.

A minute went by. Another. 'How've you been?' Bell said. She had settled herself down. Let the fury subside. 'You and Bolland, I mean. And the band. The job.'

Shirley nodded. There was, Bell saw, a shine to her. Bell hadn't noticed that shine when she first came in the room; the room was too dark and she was too preoccupied with her own woes. Now it was evident.

She hadn't often seen that kind of radiance in her sister's face. Maybe long ago – she couldn't really remember – but not recently. Life had taken a lot of the shine out of both of them.

Except that maybe it hadn't. Not in Shirley's case. Maybe it had just gone away temporarily.

'What is it?' Bell said, prodding her gently. 'You've got something to say. I can tell.'

In a rush, Shirley declared, 'Me and Bobo. We're gonna move in together. Been wanting to tell you, Belfa. Real bad. But I was afraid – I thought you'd—' She broke off her sentence.

'You thought I'd rip you a new asshole,' Bell said gently, and despite the crudity of her language, her tone was arch, bemused. Not hostile. 'You thought I'd take your head off. Thought I'd tell you that you're making a terrible mistake and that you'll regret it for the rest of your natural life and that he's a no-good bum and you're a goddamned fool for trusting him.'

'Yeah. Something like that.' Shirley laughed, and then Bell laughed, too.

A few seconds passed.

'So,' Bell said.

Shirley looked at her expectantly.

'How's this going to work?' Bell went on. 'You'll have to check in with your parole officer and get permission and then report your new address, right?'

'Right. Doing it step by step. By the book. Swear.'

'Know you will.'

'And Belfa.' Shirley licked her lips. She'd gone a long time without a cigarette, which she knew Bell appreciated; on humid days, the smoke tended to linger in the house, hanging near the ceiling in a smelly yellow mist.

'Yeah?'

'You don't like him much – I'm fully aware – but listen, I can tell you, he's really—'

'No matter, Shirley. None of my business.'

'It is. It's always gonna be your business.' Shirley ducked her head. Her tone had grown earnest, too earnest, and it embarrassed her. 'We're family, Belfa. Plain and simple.'

'Nothing simple about it,' Bell said. She saw Shirley's hand tremble. 'Go ahead and have a cigarette, will you? Making me nervous.'

Shirley laughed. She used two fingers to fish out the crinkly pack from the breast pocket of her shirt.

During the pause in their conversation, Bell thought about the information she'd received on her way home from the Brinkerman house. It came in a text from Rhonda Lovejoy. At Bell's request, Rhonda had done a criminal background check on Harold Bolland. The results were depressing, but not surprising: A DUI in 1989; a felony conviction in 2002 for passing bad checks, for which he'd served eight months in the Toller County Jail; an acquittal on a fraud charge the next year; and a sprinkling of charges such as pot possession and driving with a suspended license, for which he'd been duly punished. It was the usual dirtball litany, a list drearily reflective of the kind of people with whom Bell dealt every day down at the courthouse. Not vicious criminal masterminds – but people who let a little bad luck and a long streak of laziness push them into places and behaviors that, had the ball bounced a slightly different way, they might never have strayed.

She had wanted something different for Shirley. Something better. Something cleaner. She always would. But it was Shirley's life. And Shirley's decision.

'I can't say that I understand, but I'm happy for you,' Bell said. 'I am.' If Bolland hadn't yet revealed his past transgressions to Shirley, he would. He might. Someday. Anyway, his business. Their business.

That hadn't been Bell's initial impulse. When she first asked Rhonda to run down his record, her intention had been to confront her sister with every bad scrap of information she'd dug up on the man, to pass along every single piece of evidence she came across to prove he was a lazy, shiftless loser.

Now it didn't seem to matter. Shirley had the right to make her own mistakes. Lord knows Bell had made plenty.

'Ever think about it?' Shirley said.

'Think about what?'

'How things would've been.' Shirley took a long look at one of her fingernails. 'If Daddy hadn't been a sonofabitch. If Mama had been around.'

'No. I don't. No percentage in it. That kind of speculation, I mean. It is what it is.'

'Yeah. Okay.' Shirley abandoned the fingernail and looked at her sister. 'You know, right? You get why I couldn't let you come around. While I was locked up.'

'Yeah.' She didn't even try to make it sound convincing.

'It's important to me, Belfa. That you understand why I did it. Least I could do was not drag you down. Let you have a shot at a different kind of life. And look. You did great. Real great.' Shirley grinned. 'I mean – *damn,* girl, you went to law school! And now you're a prosecutor. Just look at you.'

'You shut me out.' Bell had promised herself not to talk about this with her sister. It went too deep. She was afraid of the emotions it would ignite in her – emotions that, once aflame, would just keep on burning. But here she was, doing it anyway. Shirley had pushed her into it. 'You decided what you thought was best for me – and that was it. Period. I couldn't do a thing about it. And you know what, Shirley? I missed you. I missed you every single day. Don't think I didn't – just because I made it through. Don't you dare think that.'

Bell's cell went off. The ring tone told her it was Sheriff Fogelsong. She glanced at Shirley. Her sister's expression meant it was all right to take the call, to get back to work. They both needed a break. Both were relieved at the interruption. They'd said what they needed to say to each other. For now.

Nick's voice was cordial. No emergency, then. 'Got a minute, Bell?' he said. 'I think I need to see a familiar face. Somebody who's not accusing me of sitting on my fat ass while a serial killer's out running the roads. If you're available—'

'I'm available.' She understood. He was at the end of his rope. When she was in the same position, he always came through for her. 'Court house?'

'JP's sounds better,' he said.

'On my way.'

36

They settled into a booth. By now it was almost 11:30 A.M., and everything – people, sidewalks, cars, buildings – looked heat-slammed, wilted past any hope of resurrection. The air-conditioning in JP's had a fight on its hands.

The seat of the booth was moist with somebody else's sweat. Bell tried not to think about that as she scooted in. Jackie caught her eye from across the room; Bell nodded, a signal to Jackie that they were just having coffee. Jackie gave her a thumbs-up sign and headed toward the big stainless steel urn. She'd add two glasses of water to their order without being asked.

'You get any sleep?' Fogelsong asked. He removed his hat and used it to fan himself for a second before putting it on the seat beside him. 'You look a little ragged.'

'Well,' she replied, 'it's about two hundred degrees out there, give or take. Nobody's gonna be fresh as a daisy today. Plus, I went to the ICU in the middle of the night to see the Crabtree girl.'

'How's she doing?'

'Better. Once they move her into a regular room, my guess is that she'll be released pretty soon.

Anything turn up to help us catch the bastard who clocked her?'

The sheriff shook his head. Then he lifted his elbows and leaned back; Jackie had arrived with two cups of coffee and two waters, and Fogelsong wanted to make room on the tabletop.

As soon as Jackie had cleared their airspace, Bell spoke. 'Anything new on the Arnett and Frank cases?'

'No. Not a single lead worth a damn.'

'Well, I might have one for you.'

Fogelsong reacted with a surprised twitch of his big head. 'Hell, Belfa, let's hear it. I swear I'm more parched for good news than I am for a drink of water.'

'Levi Brinkerman.'

'Who?'

'He's the brother of one of Lindy's friends. Well, coworker, really.'

'What's the link?'

'Might be a coincidence,' Bell said, 'but remember how your witness mentioned a long coat?'

'Not much to go on.'

'For the moment, let's say it is. I went out to the Brinkerman house this morning to have a chat with Lindy Crabtree's colleague – and got a look at his brother, Levi. Longtime tweaker and certified waste of space. And given to wearing a big heavy raincoat, no matter what the temperature.'

'Worth checking out,' Nick said, nodding. 'I'll send a deputy over there today.'

Bell stirred her coffee with the spoon that Jackie had brought along with their beverages. She always took her coffee black, but there was something satisfying about stirring a cup of coffee. Something that seemed conducive to thinking.

Fogelsong settled himself against the back of the booth. The lunch rush at JP's was just getting under way; Wanda was speeding up her route between the tables and the booths. Jackie was arranging bright pink ground beef patties on the griddle, three rows of four apiece. The door opened and closed every few minutes or so; gusts of hot air came in along with the customers.

'So we've got a man attacked and killed in a driveway,' Bell said. 'And a man knifed to death on the side of the road. And now Lindy Crabtree. Related?'

Nick took a long swallow of his coffee. Let it settle. 'Hard to say. Deputy Harrison spent all day yesterday going over all three crime scenes. She's done it about fifty times already but wanted to try a fifty-first. Found some things.'

'Do tell.'

'Truth is, it's what Harrison *didn't* find that's got me puzzled.'

Bell waited.

'At all three,' he continued, 'there's no evidence of a vehicle coming or going. The assailant had to've come through the woods. Which means the escapes were probably made on foot. Which means they were done by somebody who knows the area. Somebody local. And somebody capable of spontaneous and irrational violence.'

'Somebody like Odell Crabtree.'

Nick shrugged.

'But you're still skeptical,' Bell said. 'Even with the new information.'

'I am.' Fogelsong scratched his left shoulder while he spoke. 'Had a chance to observe Crabtree while he's

331

been in our custody.' He stopped scratching. Looked a little sheepish. 'And it's not just my opinion.'

'What do you mean?'

'Hold on. Got to back up a minute.' His sheepishness hadn't gone away; if anything, Bell noted, it had intensified. 'This involves Mary Sue.' After he said his wife's name, Nick took another drink of his coffee, forcing Bell to wait until he'd finished with it. 'Ever since you had her work for you, she's been coming down to the courthouse.'

'That a problem?'

'Let me finish. Sometime she rides in with me, and sometimes she comes over later, on her own. Goes to different offices. Figures out who's shorthanded. Guess where I found her today? Turns out that Deputy Mathers needed some help at the jail.'

'The jail.'

'Yeah. The jail.' His voice was suffused with a burnished, rough-hewn affection. He had a way of talking about his wife – through her illness, through all the sorrows and all the troubles, he always talked about her the same way, with respect, and with love, and with a mild astonishment that she'd consented to spend her life with him – that touched Bell deeply, although they'd never discussed it. They never would.

'So what was she doing there, Nick?'

'Talking to Odell Crabtree. Just talking to him. Not about anything special. Just keeping him company, you know? So that he didn't get riled up. Sat on a chair in his cell and just chatted with him. Charlie Mathers said she made that old man relax like nobody's business. Crabtree'd been yelling and screaming and throwing himself around, and Mathers was afraid he was going to hurt himself – but Mary

Sue gentled him right quick. They had some real conversations. Sometimes the fog lifts, I guess, and he's his old self again. No telling when it'll happen, but it does. Now and again.' He paused. He'd raised his cup an inch off the table and now he moved it around in a quick little circle, watching the agitation of the liquid inside it. 'Don't know if Crabtree's our assailant or not, or what he's done or not done – we'll be figuring all that out – but it sure as hell makes things a lot easier to have him calm instead of raving.'

'Imagine so.'

'Anyway,' he said, pushing the mug to one side so that he could fold his big hands on the table in front of him, 'for the record, Mary Sue is pretty well convinced that Odell Crabtree couldn't do those things. To begin with, she says, his health is fading fast. And he wouldn't just go out and attack folks like that. Especially not his daughter.'

'That's interesting, Nick. But let me quote a certain sheriff I know: "Opinions aren't evidence. And it's not what we believe that counts. It's what we can prove."'

Fogelsong grinned. 'Sounds like a damned smart fella, that sheriff.'

'He is. Kind of hard to deal with, though. Irascible and headstrong.'

'You don't say.' He waited a second or two after his grin had gone away, to put some distance between the raillery and what he needed to say next. 'Speaking of Mary Sue, I wanted to tell you that I've changed my mind a little bit. I think I've been a little misguided, okay? Holding on too tight. Discouraging her from getting out of the house and trying things. I was just afraid she'd get herself hurt. Afraid she'd fail. I know she's capable of a lot more than what she's doing, but I – I just didn't want to risk it.'

'She *will* fail, Nick. Hell – we all fail. And she'll get hurt. Guaranteed. Can't stop that.' She was thinking about Shirley, but didn't say so. Chances were Nick had figured that out for himself.

He nodded. 'Yeah.' He was finished with the personal topic. 'Anyway, that's where we stand. Don't know a damned thing more than we knew a day ago. More questions than answers.'

'Always the case, seems like.'

'Refill? I can flag Jackie down,' he said.

Bell was already sliding out of the booth. She was thinking about all the office work she had to finish before she'd be free to go back out to the Crabtree house later in the day, to pick up the letters for Lindy. 'Wish I could,' she said, 'Gotta run.'

'Get some rest, willya?'

She eyed him. 'You first.'

By late afternoon a line of lumpy clouds the color of coal dust had barged into the sky over Acker's Gap. Within minutes the rain started up, a heavy, drubbing rain that fell on the dry-packed roads and heat-baked sidewalks with a frantic sizzle, releasing a thick, sour-smelling steam that instantly fogged windows and made the backs of people's necks feel clammy and unpleasant. The rain brought no relief from the heat. It made for a different kind of heat; that was all.

Bell picked up Jason Brinkerman. They drove through the rain toward the Crabtree house. In the dusk of a wet day, the beleaguered old place looked just as bad as it had in full sunlight. Even more sinister, if that was possible. The crooked trees seemed to be crumpling from the weight of their waterlogged foliage. Rain slid off the leaves and the trunks like ointment being hosed off the skin of a prehistoric animal. Bell parked in the driveway behind Lindy's car and turned to Jason.

'We'll just go in for a minute,' she said. 'Lindy wants a few things from the bedroom.' She squinted at the front windshield; it was streaked and grayed by the steady headlong rain. 'Sorry I don't have an umbrella. Hot as it's been lately, I clean forgot that such a thing as rain even existed.'

Jason nodded. He had said very little on the drive over, grunting or nodding in response to Bell's sporadic attempts at conversation. He'd asked her for an update on Lindy's condition and Bell wondered: *Is he asking because he cares about her – or because he fears she might have recovered enough to identify him as her attacker?*

Bell opened the front door of the house. The air inside was muggy and malodorous. She took a step forward, and the bloodstain on the pitted wood seemed to jump right up, a grim tattoo that was much larger than she had remembered. She watched Jason. He glanced at the stain. Quickly turned away. Did his expression indicate anguish or guilt or – as was sometimes the case – a bit of both? Perpetrators could sometimes wail louder than anybody else when in the midst of unmistakable evidence of what they'd done.

'Gather up some of Lindy's books, will you?' Bell said. 'We'll take them to the hospital. I have to get something else. Back in a sec.'

Jason nodded. He moved amid the piles of books

on the living room floor in a sort of daze, picking up one after another, then setting each book back on the stack without really looking at it. The rain was audible on the roof, a dismal irregular rhythm. It sounded as if it might break through the flimsy ceiling any second.

In the crowded bedroom, Bell spotted the dresser that Lindy had told her about. She kneeled down. Reached under. Felt around. The small tin box was exactly where the young woman had said it would be. Bell secured it and stood up. Before rejoining Jason, she opened the lid and scanned a few of the letters, feeling their fragility against her fingertips and marveling at the look of the handwriting, the fierce loops and quick slashes rendered in blue ink that had faded over the years to brown – just as the emotions, too, had surely faded, the way emotions do. Some of them, anyway.

The living room was unoccupied. Had Jason gone into the kitchen?

'Hey,' she called out, moving in that direction, 'let's hit the road, okay? Want to get these things to Lindy as soon as possible.'

He wasn't in the kitchen, either. Bell was baffled. She hadn't heard the back door open. She looked around, her gaze taking in the gray sink jammed with soiled dishes and the one-step-from-the-ragbag curtains and the spindly dinette whose surface was overwhelmed by books. She recalled the last time she'd stood in this kitchen – with Odell Crabtree staring at her – and she shivered.

The thump sounded like a dropped sack of laundry. It came from the basement. Bell was sure of it. *Definitely. The basement.* But why would Jason have gone down there? What was he trying to pull?

She felt a flicker of fear. Just a small, quick spike of panic. She pushed it back down again, refusing to let it get a foothold in her thoughts, but it had made its point. What if he jumped her? She didn't know this kid. Knew nothing about him – except that his brother was a drug addict who might have murdered two people, his father was a convicted felon, and he himself might very well have attacked Lindy Crabtree.

Why the hell am I here? What made me think I'd be able to shock Jason Brinkerman into telling me the truth? Jesus. She didn't have a weapon. This house was a good mile and a half from any other human habitation. Tucked back behind thick woods. Screened off from the main road. *Why did I ever—?*

Another thump. Louder this time.

'Jason?' she said.

No answer.

Could it be Odell Crabtree? Maybe he'd been released and had blundered his way back home. Legally, they were on shaky ground every minute they held the old man; soon they'd have to either charge him or release him, even though his detention was actually a matter of kindness, not jurisprudence. Maybe the sheriff had let him go.

No. Nick would've contacted me. Asked my advice.

But who else would be down there? If it was Jason, then why wasn't he answering her call?

She'd have to check out the basement. No choice. She put the tin box on the table, nudging aside a short stack of books to make a space for it. Then she reached for the battered old two-paneled door, so warped and twisted that she had to yank phenomenally hard on the metal knob to get it to budge. *Sonofabitch,* Bell thought, using all her strength to wrench at the thing, knowing her arm would be sore in the morning – *If I live that long,* she thought ruefully, teasing herself, or maybe not – and then she stepped into darkness.

37

'Jason?' Bell said. She repeated his name on every other tread. 'Jason. You down there?'

Even with the door ajar at the top of the stairs, the basement was frustratingly dim. She fingered the wall for a light switch as she descended, but didn't find one. The cellars in a lot of these old country houses, Bell knew, weren't wired for electricity; the owners sometimes would rig up a light, but usually it was controlled by a string hanging from a bare bulb in the basement itself. Nothing so up-to-date as a wall switch.

'Jason?'

She reached the bottom.

The smell was horrifically foul. Her first instinct was to identify the constituent elements – feces, urine, mold, rancid food – but she stopped, wondering why the hell she would bother to do so. Naming the odors within the dank pervasive stink just made it worse. Better not to know. She felt herself growing dizzy from the rapid head-slaps of the smell. *Don't think about it. Don't think about what you're breathing in.*

Her eyes adjusted partially to the darkness and she could make out the mounds ranged across the floor, mysterious lumps of different sizes. She could also discern what seemed to be a gigantic tree branch lying on its side, spanning the width of the room; myriad smaller branches forked off from the trunk, reaching in all directions like skinny twisted fingers. Peering closer, she saw that some of the black shapes on the floor were boulders, while others were square; they were piled-up boxes and tables.

'Jason?'

She took a step. Her foot skidded briefly on what felt like a thick scattering of gravel. Pushing her foot forward another inch or so, she realized that the cellar floor was coated with small rocks and dirt. The air on her skin felt cool, no more than fifty degrees Fahrenheit. The constant temperature of an underground space – a cavern or a coal mine.

'Mrs Elkins! Look out – he's right behind—!'

The blow came at the same moment she heard Jason's warning, and Bell felt a ferociously sharp pain on the side of her head. She staggered. She'd been hit with a large rock. It knocked her sideways. Swaying and groping for something to grasp, she fought not to pass out. Her right ear felt as if it had been half-severed by the chopping blow. She turned around. She realized that her assailant was getting ready to try again; the breeze rushing past her cheek came from the air displaced by the rock as he raised it once more. Higher this time. She managed to sway to one side, forcing him to recalibrate, and in that quarter-second of reprieve, as the blood from her wound moved down the side of her neck, hot against her clammy skin, she felt a wild surge of strength from an unknown source, and then instantly its origin was clear to her: rage. Rage as pure as flame. *You fucking sonofabitch. You goddamned fucking sonofabitch*. The anger that defined her, that had been a part of her life for as far back as she could remember, hidden behind a polite daily façade of please-and-thank-yous, simmering beneath the pressed clothes and the law degree but always there, reviving itself over and over again in the darkness at each day's end, the ultimate renewable fuel source – flew through her body.

Tucking her chin, she head-butted him in the chest. She had to guess at his approximate whereabouts but rammed him anyway, and she knew she'd guessed right from the resistance she met and from the *Uhhhh* of his expelled breath. She'd knocked the wind out of him. He didn't drop the rock but he was disoriented for another precious second. She heard Jason yelling from a corner of the room – '*Watch out, Mrs Elkins, he's about to—!*' – and she wished like hell that she had a light, any kind of light, to guide her fighting and to enable her to get a glimpse of the man's miserable fucking face, whoever he was, whatever he—

I do.

The tiny flashlight on her key chain.

Shielding her face with an upraised arm, Bell sent her hand plunging into her pocket. She swung the small dot of illumination up, up, up – straight up at the large black rock clutched overhead by a man draped in a long garment, a man determined to crush her skull, and as the light shifted from the rock to his face she saw, to her shock and confusion, a nimbus of frizzy white hair and the twisted-up, livid, hate-filled features of Perry Crum. The postman.

She aimed the light directly in his eyes. That gave her a puncher's chance. He scowled, and in that impossibly short interval she dropped the key chain to free up her hands. She slid to the right and came at him sideways, low and hard, head-butting him again, using her wind-milling arms to gouge at his face. His long coat wasn't a coat at all but some kind of poncho – a rain poncho, slick and thin and plastic – and there flashed across her mind a picture of Perry Crum making his rounds on rainy days, friendly and smiling despite the weather, pale blue poncho sprouting from his wrinkled neck.

He fought her off with the big rock, pummeling her, slamming it repeatedly against her arms and her hands. She ducked and bobbed, protecting her head. She managed to get a fist past the thicket of his blows and without a second's hesitation she slammed it into his nose, sharp and hard, and then she hooked her thumbs into his eyes, jabbing and pulling, and his screams bounced around the small cellar like something being tossed from corner to corner.

Suddenly he was on the ground. Flat on his back, flailing. He'd flung away the rock in order to grab at his eyes and his nose, still screaming, and Bell immediately tackled him. Knees grinding into his chest, she groped in the dark until she found a rock, one she could get her fist around, and then another rock that she could get her other fist around, and then she smashed them down on his face, one after the other, alternating her fists in a rhythmic assault. She could see very little in the blacked-out cellar but in her mind's eye she saw him clearly – yes, clear as day – only it wasn't Perry Crum anymore. The face she saw was Donnie Dolan, her father, the man who had ruined her sister's life and ruined her life, too, the bastard who destroyed them, destroyed any chance they had for happiness, for a normal life, even, and so she would erase him, she would grind his face into ugly pulp and then she would—

'Mrs Elkins. You'll kill him. Please Please stop—'

She stopped. Panting, breathing so hard and so fast that her body rocked and heaved with every raspy inhalation and exhalation; her arms were frozen in mid-arc, the arms that had been descending systematically on the torn face like the urgent swipes of a scythe, back and forth, back and forth. Whose voice? Who had called to her, breaking the spell, restoring her to herself?

It was the kid. Jason Brinkerman.

Her knees slid off the man's chest. Didn't matter anymore. She'd knocked the fight clean out of her opponent. Crum's nose had been relocated to the wrong part of his face and the skin on his cheeks hung in bloody shreds; his whimpers sounded disgustingly weak.

'Mrs Elkins,' Jason said. 'I'm here. Over here.'

She stood up and staggered to the other end of the basement. She retrieved the key chain with its miniature flashlight and used it to find Jason. As she untied him, he told her how he'd gotten there. Perry Crum had been hiding in the kitchen; Crum must have scurried out of the living room when he heard them enter the house. 'Put a hand over my mouth,' Jason said, rubbing his wrists, hoarse and shaky from the adrenaline spikes still pelting his body, 'and dragged me down here. Said he'd kill us both if I tried to holler and warn you.'

She moved back to Crum. Stood over him as he writhed on the cellar floor, squealing and groaning. 'Why?' she said. 'Why, Perry?'

At first he ignored her, cupping his smashed nose in one hand, using the other to scrabble at the loose folds of his poncho. Then he coughed, sputtered, and blurted, 'Only wanted the best. For the girl.' His words were blunted and fogged by snot and tears. 'That's why I done it.'

'Who are you talking about?'

'Lindy.' Crum turned his head, spit out a gob. 'Shit – you broke my damned nose.'

'Sue me,' Bell snapped back. 'Okay, Perry. Don't know what you mean, but if you satisfy my curiosity right here and now, I'll make a note of your cooperation. Might help you at trial. No promises.' She gave him the world's quickest reading of his Miranda rights. 'There you go. This is your shot, Perry. You understand what I just said to you?'

He moaned.

'Can't hear you,' Bell said. She started to swivel away from him and head for the stairs. She resisted the impulse to yelp in pain; every muscle in her body ached in a different way. *Christ,* she thought. *I'm too old for this shit.* She was already planning what she'd say to Nick Fogelsong the minute she saw him, to let him know she was okay: *Hey, Sheriff – thought being a prosecutor was supposed to be a god-damned desk job.*

'Yeah, yeah,' Perry muttered.

'Huh?'

'I said yeah. I heard 'em. My rights'n all.'

'So you're going to tell me what the hell this was all about?'

Crum rubbed the bottom edge of the poncho across his face to mop up the blood, then screamed from the pain the pressure caused him. 'Hurts!' he bellowed. 'Hurts bad.'

Bell wanted to laugh. Why did every tough guy turn into a two-year-old when he got a taste of what he'd been dishing out?

'Let's hear it,' she said.

Haltingly, between gasps of pain, he told her the story. Lindy Crabtree, he said, was special. 'More special'n anybody else in this shit-ass county, tell you that,' Crum muttered. He'd been bringing her books for years now, boxes and boxes filled with books; he knew how smart she was. But she'd never leave. 'Stuck right here in this damned house with a crazy old man,' he went on. 'Working at a gas station. Didn't make a lick of sense. Every time I tried to talk to her, tried to make her see how she's better'n this place, loads and loads better, she'd just smile at me and tell me thanks for bringing the books in the house for her. Like that's all I was. Just a friggin' pack mule. Like nothing I had to say was worth a damn. Like I didn't know what it felt like to give up your whole life for somebody else. Somebody who can't even appreciate what you're giving up.' He spit again, then shivered with a long spasm of wet coughing, groaning each time his body twisted and writhed. 'Had to make her see. Make her see how scary it is out here in the middle of nowhere for a young girl all by herself – just her and that sick old sack of bones, Odell Crabtree.'

'So you attacked her? To get her to listen? *That* was your master plan?'

'Hell no.' Crum's body shuddered. He could be going into shock, Bell saw, and she hoped he'd wind up his tale before passing out. 'Wasn't gonna touch her,' he insisted. 'I went after Charlie Frank. Knew where he walked at night. Everybody knows. But I never meant to hurt him bad. Just scare him, okay? So word'd get out. So Lindy would see why she needed to leave. So she'd see what happens to folks out here on their own. I just got a little carried away, is all. Not my fault

345

Charlie got himself killed. Damn fool fought back. I was just gonna cut him a little bit, but he fought back. So I had to get rough with him. Too rough. Who'd of thought he'd fight back? What's he got to live for? But he fought, all right. I wore the poncho so's there'd be no blood on my clothes.' He coughed and spit. 'Going after Charlie Frank didn't work – so I had to try something else. Had to scare her good 'n' proper. Which is why I waited for her to come home from that shitty little gas station. Waited behind the door. Made sure I didn't really hurt her.'

'Charlie Frank,' Bell said grimly. 'And before that, Freddie Arnett in his driveway.'

'No. No way,' Crum muttered. 'That weren't me. Never touched Freddie.'

'Like anybody'll believe you now.'

'Swear to God.'

She wasn't going to argue with him. 'So why'd you come back here tonight?'

'Gonna dump some stuff.' Crum's voice was failing him now, growing fainter. 'Charlie Frank's boot. To make it look like her daddy done it. So's she'd cut the old goat loose. Put him away somewheres. Where he belongs. Then she'd be free. Free to leave this worthless piece of crap that the rest of us call . . . home . . .'

Crum's voice trailed off and his head fell to one side, chin hanging open, eyes going glassy.

Bell looked at Jason. Swept a hand to indicate the rocks and the boxes and the overturned tables. 'What the hell *is* all this?'

'Best guess? It's a coal mine,' Jason said. 'Or as close to one as Lindy could rig up. Make her daddy feel comfortable. Place he knew best. Place he'd been happy.' He spotted an object on the floor, half hidden beneath a stack of branches, and he picked it up. 'Dang,' Jason said. 'Wish I'd had this a few minutes ago.' It was a wood-handled knife, used to hack at the massive felled tree. Odell Crabtree had tried to keep his path clear as best he could, just as hc'd done in the mine for so many years.

'Let's get the hell out of here,' Bell said. 'I'll call the sheriff. He'll come by with the EMTs and they can deal with this bastard. Now that he's spilled his guts. Here – hand me that rope he used on you. Gotta make sure he doesn't get out.'

Next Bell tackled the cellar stairs. Jason was right behind her. She faltered twice; he steadied her, kept her going.

'Hey,' Jason said. They had reached the top. The kitchen was dark. Not as dark as the cellar, but still dark. 'You were yelling something while you beat the shit out of him.'

'Don't remember.'

'Well, it sounded like you were saying "Daddy" or some—'

She cut him off. 'Said I don't remember.'

They headed for the Explorer, hurrying but watching their step; they stumbled, then righted themselves. The moon's faint light was thwarted even further by a long train of clouds that had stalled out in front of it. Bell groped to find the door handle, missing twice before she secured it.

The rain had slacked off but not stopped. It had the dour, relentless feel of a rain that frankly had no intention of ever stopping, not entirely. Bell switched on the wipers even before she turned on the headlights.

As she backed out of the driveway she took a quick look at herself in the rearview mirror and winced – which made her wince again, this time with cause, because her face was deeply bruised. The cut on the top of her right ear might very well need stitches. Blood was drying in crusty lines along the lacerations on her arms and hands. The skin below one eye was swelling and turning a sickly shade of yellowish purple. She looked like hell. Felt like it, too.

'Sure you're okay to drive?' Jason asked. He asked it gingerly, having seen what a pissed-off Bell Elkins could be like.

'Fine.'

Without either one of them having to name it, both knew where they were going next and why: the Raythune County Medical Center – to find Lindy and relieve her anxiety.

'What's that?' Bell said. She took her eyes off the road for an instant. Jason had something balanced on his lap.

It was the small tin box of letters. 'Grabbed it when we went through the kitchen,' he said. 'You told me it was important to her. We can take care of it until Lindy's ready to go home.' He placed the box in the glove compartment.

Bell didn't waste time with a parking spot. She pulled up in front of the hospital's main entrance. Ditched the Explorer right there.

With Jason at her side, she moved rapidly past the front desk, waving away the receptionist's prissy entreaty: 'May I help you?' Bell wanted to get the news to Lindy as soon as possible. The father she loved had not caused her pain, or caused pain to others.

A few yards beyond the double doors leading to the

ICU, in a brilliantly lighted corridor down which she barreled with a speed that belied the soreness in her legs, Bell nearly collided with a short, worried-looking older woman in a pale blue nurse's smock. The woman wore a name tag with SALLY FUGATE on one line and on the next line, in even bigger letters, this: NURSING SUPERVISOR.

'Excuse me,' Bell said, 'but we're on our way to see—'

'I'm so sorry, Mrs Elkins,' Fugate said, interrupting her in a hushed, professionally sympathetic tone. Her hands were clasped. 'So very, very sorry. I'm afraid I have to inform you that Lindy Crabtree died twenty minutes ago.'

38

'No way.' Jason's voice trembled, but it was emphatic. 'No freakin' way, lady.'

Bell wasn't yet able to speak. She fought against shock, beating it back the way she might beat back a wild animal charging at her. Emotion, she knew, wouldn't do her a damned bit of good right now. The fury that had been so effective during a fistfight in a rock-clogged basement would mean nothing here – it would, in fact, work against her. Power in this realm was measured by the steely elegance of self-control. She needed to get answers. And to get them, she'd have to be calm and systematic with her questions. Not hard and ornery and demanding – which had been her first instinct. Always was.

'Lindy was fine when I left here,' she said carefully. 'What's going on?'

Fugate's voice had a condescending lilt to it, as if she were trying to soothe an unruly toddler. 'These things happen, Mrs Elkins. It's sad, I know, and it's hard to accept, but sometimes, even when the doctors and the nurses have done their very best, nature decides to—'

'No,' Bell snapped, interrupting her. 'No way. She was *fine*. I talked to her. She couldn't have died. It's impossible.' To hell with calm and systematic.

'Unfortunately, it's not.' Fugate closed her eyes and shook her head. She opened them again when the grave theatrical waggle had run its proscribed course.

Bell located her cell. She let her eyes slide over to meet Jason's, and then she sent a quick text to Rhonda Lovejoy.

'I'm afraid,' Fugate said, 'I really do need to ask you to leave now. This is a health care facility and our staff is busy with their professional duties. We appreciate your concern, and we join you in your grief, but we'll take care of contacting any family the girl might have had, and then we'll—'

'What's going on?'

A familiar voice. Bell turned. The question had come from Sharon Henner, who emerged into the corridor from the same door out of which Fugate had appeared moments ago. Sharon wore a bright pink suit and black heels. Had the governor's daughter been here all day? Ever since her mysterious arrival this morning? Behind her were Bradley Portis, the hospital CEO, and the older security guard from Riley Jessup's estate.

'Oh, it's just a very unfortunate circumstance,' Fugate said, looking anxiously at Sharon. 'Regretfully,' she went on, gesturing toward Bell, 'I've had to inform Mrs Elkins here that someone she knew passed away this evening. Rather unexpectedly, I'm afraid. But there are limits to what medical science can do. And as I've been trying to explain, it's important at this point to move past our grief and come to terms with—'

'Bullshit,' Bell declared.

Fugate was startled – her eyes bugged out, as if to demonstrate it – but she quickly recovered her equilibrium. 'I know the deceased was a friend of yours, Mrs Elkins,' she said. Her tone was suffused with gentleness. 'Once you've had a chance to get some closure, I'm sure this unwarranted hostility will dissipate.' She looked more intently at Bell. 'That's a nasty cut on the side of your head. Do you need some medical attention yourself?'

'Lay a finger on me,' Bell said coldly, 'and I'll break your arm. That's a promise.'

'My goodness!' Fugate, hand splayed on her chest, blinked and frowned a pert little frown.

Bell switched her attention to Bradley Portis. She had to look up; he was a very tall man in a very nice suit, his thick hair swept back from a high lined forehead. He had watched her exchange with Fugate – his dark eyes moving back and forth, while his body remained still – with that lofty indifference Bell had observed in other powerful men, that sleek reserve that signaled a staggering load of self-regard. Nothing so small and absurd as the likes of her could faze him. 'Mr Portis,' she said, 'I'm hereby informing you that I'll have a warrant here in half an hour to search your offices for the medical records pertaining to Lindy Crabtree's treatment. There are significant questions about her care in this facility.' She added, with as much authority as she could muster as she fought through a monumental exhaustion, 'Until then, neither you nor your staff will touch a thing – not so much as a Post-it note.'

For a brief interval no one spoke. Bell was acutely aware of the way the two sides had arranged themselves, the opposing forces gathered like a scene in one of Nick Fogelsong's history books recounting pivotal battles from Troy to Normandy to Basra. This might have been a white-tiled corridor with pale green walls and institutional lighting, not a sunstruck rampart seething with soldiers and machines of war, but the line separating the combatants was clear: Portis, Fugate, Sharon, and the security guard on one side. On the other, Bell and Jason.

Jason.

She looked around. No Jason. The kid had a definite flair for disappearing at crucial moments. This time, though, Bell was grateful for it. He had understood her wordless message.

Portis was speaking to her. His voice had the blustery baritone of a man accustomed to being in charge. And there was, in the haughty lift of his chin, a definite edge of contempt, a sense that he really should not have to bother himself with people of her ilk. 'Mrs Elkins,' he said, 'you're overreacting. There's no need for all this grandstanding. I can see that you've been through some kind of physical ordeal – and now you have to somehow process the tragic death of an acquaintance. May I suggest that you sit down and rest for a moment? Mrs Fugate will escort you to a private area and a representative from our grief counseling staff will be happy to—'

'Twenty-nine,' Bell said.

'Pardon me?'

'Twenty-nine minutes. That's the time you have left before the warrant gets here. Give or take. Oh – and just so you can prepare your staff, I want a record of every medication given and every procedure done to Lindy Crabtree from the moment she was brought here. Don't skip anything – not even an aspirin. And I'll be requesting a complete autopsy by an independent medical authority.'

Portis hesitated. He seemed to be making up his mind about whether or not she was bluffing. He changed tactics. 'You know, Mrs Elkins,' he said, voice buttery with condescension, 'this facility has always enjoyed an excellent relationship with local law enforcement authorities. I would think you'd be reluctant to jeopardize that because of a needless dispute over—'

'Brad.' Gently, Sharon interrupted him. Placed a hand on his forearm. Patted it twice. 'Brad, let me.'

She took a step closer to Bell. 'I think I know what you're going through. I've been in the same position. So many times, I've watched my son almost die. He's been so terribly ill over the years – and it just doesn't make any sense.' Her voice was thoughtful. 'The young are supposed to *live*. Supposed to have rich, full lives. It's the *old* who are supposed to die, after a long life. When the young are taken from us, it's the worst. It's tragic and unbearably sad, but it's also – *unnatural,* somehow. It feels as if the entire universe has been turned upside down. As if the young are somehow suffering because of what *we* did. They're not to blame. They can't be. It's us. And so we feel such guilt along with our grief. Isn't that right?'

Bell was weary and sore; she was stunned by the death of Lindy Crabtree. And Sharon's voice was soothing, its emotional logic smooth and impeccable. Maybe she was right. Maybe Lindy's fate only seemed suspicious in the moment because Bell was so distraught over everything else that had happened. Maybe Perry Crum had miscalculated and hit Lindy too hard, just as he'd miscalculated with Charlie Frank.

And maybe she was fighting for nothing. Fighting because – well, because fighting was her default response of late.

Hell. It had been her default response her whole life.

Bell nodded. It felt good – for once – to nod. To agree, instead of being the contrarian. The hard-ass. And Sharon nodded back. *She does understand,* Bell thought. *She really does.*

One question still troubled her. She'd lost the thread of it in the hot maze of the night's confusion but remembered now. 'Why are you here?' Bell asked.

'Drove over early this morning for a conference with Brad and his staff,' Sharon said. 'We're setting up the terms and conditions of my father's gift. The MRI machine.'

Made sense. Bell rubbed her forehead. God, she was tired. Her head throbbed. The muscles in her legs ached every time she moved. Or even thought about moving.

'So we're all okay here?' Portis said.

Bell shrugged. Her way of agreeing. She realized that the one thing she wanted more than anything else in the world right now – even more than a hot bath and a handful of Advils and a beer to wash it all down with, and then about a thousand years of sleep – was a conversation with Nick Fogelsong. She wanted to sit down and talk to him for a long, long time, telling him everything about this night, about Perry Crum's bitter sacrifice for his sister and the crimes it inspired, about Lindy's love for her father – a love that would, it now seemed, be her legacy.

'I'm so glad everything worked out,' Sharon said, in a soft, earnest voice. 'And I hope you find some peace with all of this, Mrs Elkins.'

Bell turned, ready to return to the lobby to track down Jason and then get the hell out of here. She hadn't known Lindy well, but she would mourn her for a long time. She thought about the stacks of books in that disheveled little house, about the hours that Lindy must've spent reading and dreaming. None of it mattered anymore. None of it mattered a damn. Behind her, Bell heard the security man speaking to Sharon: 'Better go. They're ready for us in the room now, Maybelle.'

Bell turned back around. 'What did he call you?'

Sharon smiled a wistful smile. 'Oh, that's my real name. It was my grandmother's. You can blame my father for saddling me with that. Wanted to honor his mother, he always said. Well, I hated that name from the get-go. Easy to see why, right? Legally changed it once I was out of the house. But Leo here has been with the family so long that I'll always be Maybelle to him. Right, Leo?'

Bell had an instant recollection of the letters she'd skimmed, the letters from Margaret Crabtree's childhood friend. The name Maybelle scrawled at the bottom. And as Bell pictured those letters, certain elements began to line up in her mind, fitting together with a crisp snap. *I don't understand all of it,* Bell thought, *but I understand a hell of a lot more than I did just a few seconds ago.* She cursed herself for being so stupid and slow and trusting, for not making the connection faster.

Bell showed no outward reaction. *Not now,* she told herself. *Not here.* She nodded at Sharon's explanation, as if it satisfied her, and continued her progress toward the lobby. She was hoping like hell that her instincts were right and that Jason was a fighter, a rebel, a rule-breaker. Still young enough to defy gravity. And that his disappearance meant he was off doing what she herself should have done, before she'd let herself be sidetracked by weariness and pretty words and phony sympathy: getting to the bottom of Lindy Crabtree's fate.

39

Out in the shadow-webbed, rain-slick parking lot, Bell was relieved to see Rhonda Lovejoy's blue Subaru come to a wobbly, half-hydroplaning halt alongside the Explorer. They conferred briefly, and then moved their vehicles to the side lot, where hospital employees on the night shift routinely parked; their cars would be less conspicuous here.

Rhonda hauled herself out of her Subaru. She frowned at the constant spritzing of the rain, knowing full well what the moisture would do to her buoyant hairstyle, an elaborate structure buttressed with sparkly barrettes.

She took a closer look at Bell's bruised face – by this time the swelling was more pronounced – and her head reared back. 'Oh, my goodness. What in the world—?'

'Forget it. We have to hurry.'

On Bell's way out of the hospital she had found no trace of Jason in the lobby – only the receptionist, still miffed, who gave her a poisonous glare, and a hospital security guard who watched with meticulous care as Bell exited the building.

'Okay,' Rhonda said, dubious but dutiful. She held up a piece of paper, rolled up in a tight scroll like a message recently extricated from a bottle, and then stowed it in her pocket again to shield it from the rain. 'Found the one judge you haven't pissed off lately – Tolliver – and went by his house. He signed the warrant.' She was teasing; Judge Tolliver was fond of Bell. More important, he was fond of justice, and generally tolerant of whatever methods had to be employed in order to seek it. Even the unorthodox ones.

'First things first,' Bell said. 'What kind of shoes are you wearing?'

'Shoes?'

'Yeah. Shoes.' Bell peered at Rhonda's frilly black skirt, then let her gaze drop on down to her feet. She was pleased to see sneakers.

'I was just finishing up my aerobics class over at the Y in Blythesburg when you called,' Rhonda said. 'No time to change. Pulled on a skirt over my tights.'

'Good. Kind of worried you might be wearing those ridiculous high heels of yours. Can't run or climb in 'em.'

'Well.' Rhonda looked hurt, then miffed. 'To each her own.'

'Fine. Come on.'

'Where are we—?'

'Just come on. I'll fill you in while we go.'

Abetted by the rain and the darkness, they slipped across the closely mown grass to the side of the building, pressing themselves flat against the brick, careful to avoid the stubborn blank-eyed stare of the security cameras rigged to each corner of the roof. The grass was wet and slickly treacherous; at one point Bell faltered, and Rhonda grabbed her arm. *Thanks,* Bell mouthed to her; she'd wanted to cry out from the pain of Rhonda's grip on her bruised arm but managed to stifle it. Rhonda tried to ask a question but Bell double-tapped a vertical finger to her own lips, utilizing the universal signal for *Shut up – I'll explain everything later*.

They stopped at a humming quartet of giant square compressors next to the southwest corner of the building. Bell located an unmarked side entrance, a thick metal door with a ventilation panel across the top.

'It's locked, Belfa,' Rhonda whispered, and her tone had a definite *Duh* at the back of it. She was still smarting from the crack about her footgear.

'Of course it is.'

'Then how do you expect us to—?'

The door swung open and Jason's face popped out. He peered around cautiously, after which he used a splayed hand to hold the door open a bit wider, enabling Bell and Rhonda to angle themselves inside.

'Jason texted me right before you got here,' Bell told Rhonda in a low voice, 'and told me which door to go to.' The dimly lit corridor in which they found themselves was the building's power plant; the signs sporting dire warnings about restricted access and high voltage and serious danger were the tipoff.

'But if it's locked, why'd it open from the inside?' Rhonda persisted.

'Fire regulations,' Bell said. 'Can't have doors in public buildings locked from the inside. Gotta give people a way to get out if there's an emergency. Okay, Jason, what'd you find out?'

She looked at him. She realized all at once how young he was, and how high her expectations were for him. Maybe too high. He was still a kid, after all.

Jason's face was greasy from repeated veneers of sweat. His eyes were wide. His big hands dangled and twitched at his sides, as if he wasn't altogether certain what to do with them, and the backward baseball cap was propped even farther back on his head, a scruffy testament to the number of times he'd wiped the bangs off his forehead and nudged the cap back while doing so. His broad, bovine face gave him the look of a tenth-grader blowing off last period to go four-wheeling.

'Not much,' he said. 'Weird shit goin' on, that's all I can say. And I'm telling you – Lindy ain't dead. No freakin' way.'

Before Bell could ask him another question, Rhonda touched her shoulder. 'Hey,' she said. 'I don't mean to get all technical here, but we've just broken into a medical facility after hours. The warrant authorizes a records search, not an illegal entry. Frankly, I'm a little leery of going much further without knowing what's going on. We're not deputy sheriffs. We're prosecutors. And it's not really our job to—'

Bell's expression caused Rhonda to stop talking. She knew that look. It could knock down a steel door if need be. Or at least make a decent dent in it.

'Okay,' Bell said, speaking quickly but forthrightly, her head whipping around, making sure no one else was entering the corridor. 'We don't have much time here, Rhonda, so I'll be brief. The truth? You're right. I don't know what the hell's going on. But something's wrong. Really, really wrong. I left Lindy Crabtree a few hours ago and she was fine. Now they say she's dead. Let me quote our friend Jason here: No freakin' way.' Her voice, she knew, was hoarse and strained. Not commanding. Well, it was what it was. 'Sharon

Henner has to be involved somehow – I don't know how or why, but I know it's so. Listen. Sheriff Fogelsong's on his way. I texted him, too. If I thought this could wait until he gets here, I'd be happy to go sit in the car with the radio on. But it won't. So I can't.' She took a deep breath, having used up a lot of oxygen in the headlong address. 'Rhonda, if you're worried about getting into trouble – and I sure as hell can't guarantee that it *won't* happen – you ought to leave. Just go. Go. I'm pretty nervous about this myself. If it backfires, I'll have a lot of explaining to do – and probably a disciplinary hearing and then a recall vote to face. Okay? So no hard feelings. Really. I'm not talking as your boss right now. Please – take off. Last chance. Door's right back there.'

Rhonda allowed herself a few seconds of contemplation. Then she squared her shoulders and tucked a saucy curl behind her left ear and smoothed down the front and back and sides of her frilly skirt, rumpled from a hasty improvisational scoot along the brick flank of a building.

'Let's go to work,' she said.

They threaded their way carefully along the corridor, not quite certain what they would do or how they would do it, knowing only that it felt good to be in motion, to be doing *something,* to be heading somewhere. Jason was in the lead – he knew the way, having raced through this hall in the other direction just minutes ago to let them in – and then came Bell, then Rhonda. From behind closed doors labeled STAFF ONLY they could hear the heavy vibrations of the medical center's HVAC system, the steady rumble from the workings of the power grid required to keep it all going twenty-four hours a day.

'I'm thinking they stuck her somewhere,' Jason said, in a raspy whisper delivered out of the side of his mouth, 'and we gotta find her.' He gave them a brief rundown of what he'd done after ducking out of the corridor while Bell talked to Sally Fugate. 'Could tell they were giving us the runaround,' he said, 'and figured I could do a hell of a lot more good poking around on my own, trying to figure out what these bastards have done with Lindy.' And so poke he did, he said, moseying across the long halls, their lights turned down to a muted glow because of the late hour. Nobody noticed him. When a guard seemed to take undue interest, Jason said, he found a broom and used it – not with enthusiasm, but lackadaisically. 'That did the trick,' Jason reported, proud of his evasive maneuvers. 'They knew I must be on staff. 'Cause I was a lazy bastard.'

Then he caught a break. He ran into Jimmy Dillon, a friend of his brother Eddie's, who really *was* on the custodial staff, working the overnight shift. Jason showed him a cell phone picture of Lindy, asked for guidance in finding her. Jimmy told him about the hospital morgue.

'Don't tell me,' Bell said, filled with dread, 'that you broke into the mor—'

'No way. Jimmy said I'd never get near the place. But *he* could – just close enough, anyway, to look at the logbook. Came back and told me that Lindy's name ain't there. Like I said, Mrs Elkins – she ain't dead. No way.'

They had reached a crossroads. The HVAC area was behind them; in front of them was a wide corridor leading to the patient rooms in both directions, where the chance of discovery would be substantially increased. 'I asked Jimmy,' Jason added, 'what might be going on. He said, "How the hell should *I* know, bro?" but then he pointed out that she's probably still in the building. Too hard to get somebody out unless you do it in an ambulance, maybe, and there ain't been no squad runs in or out yet tonight.'

His cell made a noise. It sounded, Bell thought, like a sick cricket. She worried about the noise and the attention it might bring, but nothing happened. 'Text,' Jason said. He checked it. A grim smile spread across his pimple-scarred face as he read the long paragraph. 'We're in business. Jimmy's been on the lookout – you can go wherever you want to in this place, long as you've got a mop and a bucket and you keep your head down and your mouth shut – and he says he just saw 'em wheeling her into the surgical wing. Flat on a gurney with an IV in her arm. But still breathing.'

'Surgical wing?' Rhonda said. 'Why would they need to—?'

'Hold on.' Bell had to interrupt her, because the proper response to Jimmy Dillon's information involved a blunt, one-word command and a fierce prayer that it would be followed: 'Run.'

Now she didn't care if they were spotted. There was too little time and too much at stake. Bell took the lead, running as fast as she could through the hallways, pausing only to check the signs.

SURGERY, followed by a long red arrow indicating the proper direction, was the one she was looking for, and when she saw it, she waved back at Rhonda and Jason and they all hurried that way. They passed rows of patient rooms and nurses' stations and an occasional gaggle of empty wheelchairs angled along the walls of the corridor. They passed hospital personnel wearing smocks of white or pale green or light blue, women and men who looked up from their clipboards or their iPads with startled frowns. Bell had been a runner in high school and college, and while she wasn't nearly so fast as she'd been back then, while she wished like hell she was in better shape, she did the best she could. She was faster than Jason, who was half her age but clumsy, and faster than Rhonda. She remembered Lindy's face as the young woman lay in the bed in the ICU ward, a face radiant with belief in her father, and the memory of that face made Bell even more determined to stop a monstrous plan that was, she now believed, the real reason for just about everything that had happened since Jed Stark tumbled to the floor of Tommy's bar, impaled by a Craftsman screwdriver.

'Stop!' Bell cried. 'Stop now!'

She had come swooping around the corner, rapidly scanning the sign on the door – SURGERY PREP – and as she slammed through it and yelled, she knocked over a metal cart on the other side of the door. The tray of instruments made a tinkling racket as it spilled, the contents clattering and pinging against the tiled floor.

Sharon's guard, the man named Leo, charged at Bell, but Sharon immediately grabbed his arm and held him back. 'No— No – leave her alone,' Sharon said. 'They can all stay. Once I explain it, we'll be fine.'

Bell didn't wait to hear what Sharon had to say. Or Bradley Portis, for that matter, who stood nearby. She lunged at the bed to which Lindy was strapped and began pulling at the thick canvas bands around the young woman's wrists. Lindy, awake but apparently sedated, barely reacted to this sudden flurry of events. She looked at Bell uncomprehendingly.

'This,' said Porter, his voice chilly and dismissive, 'is an important medical procedure.' He glared at Sharon. 'These people *cannot* be here.'

'We're not leaving,' Bell declared. 'Shut this down.' She turned. 'Rhonda, I'd like you to document everything in this room. Every name. Every word said. No one comes in or goes out.'

'You can't—' It was Sharon again, her voice strained and anxious. Pleading now. 'I'm begging you. Just let this happen. That's all you have to do. Just stand back and give us some time. The surgeon's on her way. All she knows is that we've got a heart. A perfect heart. We've got a heart, you hear me? We've got one. For my little boy.' She took a short, passionate breath. 'Montgomery's in the next room – they've given him the anesthetic. He's almost ready. It's just a matter of minutes now and we can start. Please. My son. My son – he's dying.' She grabbed Bell's arm. Bell shook her off, but Sharon kept talking, urgently and beseechingly, trying to make Bell look at her: 'Please. Please. For God's sake – *please*. Anything. I'll give you anything.'

Fugate, syringe in hand, was backing slowly toward Lindy's bed, taking advantage of the confusion to administer the lethal dose of morphine. Before she could connect it to the IV line, Fugate's wrist suddenly was snatched up by Jason Brinkerman. He squeezed until she screamed in pain and dropped the syringe. It bounced on the floor and rolled a short distance. 'Hey,' he said. 'What the hell're you up to, lady?'

'Please.' Sharon was still begging, repeating the word *Please* over and over again, more desperate, more hysterical, with each repetition. The tears had made a clownish mess of her makeup; mascara carved crooked

paths down both sides of her face. 'You have to understand,' she said. 'He's too far down on the list. My
little boy is too sick. Twenty patients die every day
waiting for a new heart – do you know that? We can't
wait any more. We're out of time. And money doesn't
matter to those transplant people. *Money doesn't
matter!*' she cried. 'My boy. My beautiful little boy.'

Bell plucked off Sharon's hand for a second time
and turned to Portis. 'You bastard,' she said. There
was disbelief in her voice as well as anger. 'You fucking
bastard. Letting your hospital be used this way. When
I get through with you and your corporation, mister,
you and Nurse Ratched here will wish that you'd
never—'

'Oh, please,' Portis said, interrupting her. He was
angry, too, which surprised Bell. She had expected
denials and evasions and blame-shifting. That's not
what she got.

'Don't bother,' he continued, 'with your self-righteous
indignation. Spare us your noble little speeches. Quick
lesson in economics, lady. The company that runs this
place is required to make a profit. You follow? Four-
fifths of the people who come here for treatment are
old and sick and poor. The only way to keep it going –
the *only* way – is to play ball with the Riley Jessups
of this world. We do what Jessup wants, he gives us
a ton of money, and we buy the equipment so that all
those fucking hillbillies you saw in our parking lot
last week – the crippled old ladies and the coal miners
with black lung who don't have a dime to their names
– can get treatment here.' He folded his arms. Irritated
with the lot of them. 'All I know is that the girl over
there was brought into the hospital yesterday with
brain trauma. The nursing supervisor told me that her

accident was not survivable. Fine. So we do the right thing. We set up for the transplant. Is it strictly by the book? No. But it's for the greater good.

'I don't expect you to understand the advanced moral calculation,' he said, shrugging dismissively as he finished. 'Way above your pay grade, lady. Hell, if you had any brains, you wouldn't be living in Acker's Gap, West Virginia, now, would you?'

Overlapping his last syllable was a howl of pain, a prolonged, pitiful wail that sounded barely human. It was Sharon. She had dropped to her knees and was clawing at the air, sobbing and shrieking. The security guard named Leo reached down and tried to help her up, but she slapped at his hands, and spit at him; she didn't want anything he had to offer. She wanted only one thing: her son's life.

And for a moment – fleeting, but it cut deep – Bell felt sorry for her, felt sorry for this woman who had watched her child grow sicker and weaker day by day, every day of his young life, knowing that the one thing that would save him was just a deal and a few hundred thousand dollars and a scalpel-cut away. Had Bell and Rhonda and Jason arrived ten minutes later, the surgery would have been under way; her boy would have had his new heart, no matter the cost to anyone else. She'd been so close. So close to having her child be well and healthy, her child made whole, her child gifted with a beautiful long life. *So close.*

Bell felt a slight shift in her feelings, the same shift she'd felt when Portis spoke, explaining his actions; she'd never admit it to that arrogant asshole, but his words made a harrowing kind of sense. *It's so damned easy to hate,* Bell thought. *It's a lot harder to figure out just where to direct that hatred.*

She heard a soft intake of breath from Lindy Crabtree. She looked over at the bed. The young woman's eyelids fluttered open; she was struggling to regain full consciousness. And Bell's anger at Sharon and Portis suddenly was revived. She heard Rhonda's voice:

'Lindy, sweetie, let's get you out of here. You ask me, this hospital's got a mighty peculiar idea of how to heal the sick.'

40

The Raythune County Courthouse reared up against the midnight sky. Except for the faint glow in a ground-floor window – on the side in which the jail was located – no lights were on. Thus it was difficult to tell precisely where the courthouse ended and the rest of the world began, so seamlessly did the building's dark contours blend into the blackness of night in the mountains.

It was an hour and a half after events had transpired at the hospital. Inside the old stone building, past the empty corridors and the closed office doors and the locked-up courtrooms, three people – Bell, Sheriff Fogelsong, and Lindy – were heading toward one of the cells. Fogelsong had been blunt with Lindy: Her father was dying.

Rhonda Lovejoy, joined a short while ago by Deputy Harrison, had remained behind at the hospital. After the scene was secured, Rhonda would take Jason home; first she had to wait for the FBI special agent to arrive from Charleston to oversee the arrest of Sharon and Leo. The sweep would include – for their role as co-conspirators – Bradley Portis and Sally Fugate. An agent was already on her way to the estate to pick up Riley Jessup.

The door to the cell was open, and Lindy rushed

inside. Her father lay on his back on the short-legged metal bed, eyes closed, hands stacked on his massive chest. Those hands rode up and down with the staggered rhythm of his labored, irregular breathing.

Bell started to follow her in, but heard a signal from Nick – a brief, meaningful cough – and she stopped. 'Give her some time,' he murmured. Bell nodded, falling back into the short corridor that led to the row of cells. She waited, side by side with the sheriff. And there she filled him in on all that had happened that night, and what prompted it.

Sharon's explanation back at the hospital had been wedged between sobs and wild clawing threats and then desperate whimpers. On her knees, swaying back and forth, the governor's daughter had unraveled before their eyes; like so many of the criminals with whom Bell dealt, Sharon wanted to justify herself. Wanted them to understand. *Everything I did*, Sharon cried, over and over, *I did out of love. Love for my little boy.*

Growing up in Acker's Gap, Margaret and Maybelle were best friends. Lindy was Maybelle's child – the inconvenient by-product of her dissolute youth. By then, Margaret was married to Odell Crabtree, and the couple agreed to take the girl and tell everyone that Lindy was their own. Odell didn't want to do it, didn't want a child to raise, but a hefty payoff from Riley Jessup changed his mind. A few years later Maybelle – now Sharon – settled down in a respectable marriage and had a second child: Montgomery.

When the extent of the boy's health problems became grievously clear, all Sharon could think about was the strong, healthy child she had offloaded on her friend. Sharon didn't want her little girl back; she wanted her little girl's heart. 'Wasn't fair, wasn't fair!' Sharon had screamed at Bell, while Rhonda and Jason helped Lindy rise from the bed, bundling her up in Jason's flannel shirt. Using it as a coat. 'Not fair that my boy suffers like he does,' Sharon went on, incensed by the injustice of it all, 'and that girl's got no problems at all. That girl nobody wanted. A throwaway. A mistake. I had to pay them to take her, you hear me? Margaret would've raised her for nothing, but Odell wanted money. Cash. That's the kind of man he is.'

Only a heart transplant would save Montgomery, Sharon told them, and she'd been forced to learn the grim facts. More than three thousand people in the United States are languishing on a list, waiting for a donor heart. Years might pass before Montgomery's name came up – time he didn't have. 'Those transplant people don't care about our fucking money,' Sharon said, almost choking on her disbelief. 'You can't buy them off. Believe me, I tried.' She hadn't been able to get the girl out of her mind – Lindy, the child she'd abandoned so long ago, back in Acker's Gap. The child who was growing and thriving. And thus Sharon's obsession began: 'The girl. The girl and her perfect heart. That's what Monty needs – her heart. That's what will save my precious boy.'

If the transplant authorities wouldn't take a bribe, maybe Odell Crabtree would. He'd taken one before, when Sharon wanted to dump the newborn; maybe he'd take it again now. He didn't care about the girl. He hadn't cared for her about nineteen years ago, when he'd demanded and received a folded-over wad of cash for his trouble. Odell was a coal miner. A brute. A savage. A symbol of everything that Sharon and her family had left behind when they moved away from Raythune County. Surely he'd like to be rid of the girl – and end up with a nice big payoff for his trouble.

It was Riley Jessup's idea to bring in Sampson J. Voorhees. 'Big-city lawyer,' Sharon said with a sneer, although there was a gleam of admiration in her eyes, too. 'Elephant balls – and able to keep a secret, if the price is right.' From his office in New York, Voorhees tried for months to put the offer before Odell Crabtree, to get the old man on board. But they received no response from Crabtree. The next step: Forget the negotiation. Hire a local to do the dirty work. Get Jed Stark to stir up trouble in Raythune County, attacking a series of random victims. Drive home the point that a killer's on the loose. That way, Stark could murder Lindy – and get the body to the medical center – with little fuss. Nobody would ask questions. She had, after all, no real family. No friends. With her mother gone, there was nobody left to care about Lindy. Nobody to harangue the overworked local authorities to stay focused on the case.

The transplant would be done in Raythune County. Riley Jessup's connections would ensure it. If anybody asked questions later, it wouldn't matter; Montgomery would be alive. They wouldn't take his new heart away from him.

'But that fucking sonofabitch Stark got himself killed in a stupid bar fight,' Sharon said, practically spitting her disgust, 'right after he killed some old coot. Didn't finish the job. Barely started it.' Voorhees arranged for the payoff to Tiffany Stark to keep her quiet about the plan.

At that point, before Bell could go on with her recapitulation of Sharon's confession, Fogelsong spoke. 'So the attack on Charlie Frank was Perry Crum's doing.' The sheriff had propped his backside against the cinder block wall, grateful for the chance to take the pressure off his spine. He looked, Bell thought, about 110 years old. And she figured she looked at least a dozen years older than that. 'It had nothing to do with Riley Jessup,' he added, 'or his daughter or their plot to save the boy.'

'That's right.'

The sheriff frowned. 'So they were chosen at random,' he said. 'Freddie Arnett. Charlie Frank. Murdered by different people for different reasons – but victims of the same bad luck.'

'Yeah,' Bell said. 'Jed Stark came across a defenseless old man working in his driveway in the middle of the night. Perry Crum saw a guy walking along the side of a deserted road.' She let the fact of the unfathomable brutality of coincidence sink in. No way to pretty it up. Or have it make sense. 'For Freddie Arnett and Charlie Frank,' she added, 'it was the wrong place to be. At the wrong time. We were looking for logic. For a pattern. We could've looked forever and never found it – because there isn't one.'

Fogelsong thought about her words. Bell, he knew, was doing the same thing that he was: pondering the malicious miracle of chance in lives that were already twisted into unnatural shapes, by virtue of where those lives were being lived, the burnt and battered ground that constituted the arena for this long pageant of sorrow.

A phone call might have drawn Freddie Arnett back inside his house that night, just before Jed Stark came along, and Stark would've picked somebody else to bludgeon to death. A request from Martha Frank – a glass of water, a readjustment of her pillow – could have delayed Charlie's walk, so that when Perry Crum found himself on Godown Road, Charlie would still have been at home, stroking his mother's head, telling her she was safe, telling her everything was fine, telling her that he would always be right there by her side. And Perry would've moved on. Found somebody else to make his point with.

'Voorhees is untouchable, I guess,' the sheriff said.

'Well, he's been in business a long, long time. Which means he's very good at covering his tracks. I'll try – but I bet we can't lay a glove on him.'

Fogelsong shook his head. Something still troubled him. 'A heart donor's different from a bone marrow donor,' he said. 'People get donor hearts from strangers all the time. Doesn't have to be a family member.' His voice was growing raspy; he'd had quite a night himself, picking up Perry Crum out at the Crabtree house and reviving him and then stuffing the howling, squirming, cursing old man in the Blazer and booking him at the courthouse.

'No,' Bell replied. 'It doesn't.'

'So couldn't Stark have just murdered any young person? Anybody who was roughly the same age and size as Montgomery? Given Jessup's connections around here, they'd get that heart to the boy, anyway.'

'Yes. But Lindy was perfect. Nobody looking out for her. Nobody to ask hard questions about her death. Truth is – Jessup and his daughter really couldn't have done this with anyone else. It was only possible for them if they used Lindy. And not just because of the logistics.' The sheriff looked perplexed, and so Bell groped for a way to explain it. 'You have to understand how Jessup and his daughter justified their plan. How they reconciled it in their own desperate minds.' She paused. 'Everybody's got a story they tell themselves so that they can sleep at night, Nick. So that they're not torn up with guilt and regret every second. And it all comes down to how they looked at Lindy Crabtree. What they saw her as.'

'Which was . . . ?' His sentence trailed off.

Bell swallowed hard before she spoke. 'Spare parts.'

'Daddy,' Lindy said.

The time had come for Bell and the sheriff to join her in the cell. Lindy knelt on the gray concrete floor next to her father's bed. She was still groggy from sedation – during the drive from the hospital to the courthouse she'd frantically rolled down the window and thrown up twice – but she was fighting to keep her mind clear. She knew there was very little time.

Lindy leaned forward. She put her arms around her father's thick torso, or as far around as her arms would go. Odell took one of his puffy gnarled hands and he placed it on top of her head, and he said, in a voice honeycombed with phlegm, 'My girl. My girl.'

Deputy Mathers had called in a doctor earlier that day, and the verdict was swift, definitive: *No need to take him anywhere. Nothing anybody can do.* Odell Crabtree's lungs were long-pummeled and severely scarred and his heart was drowning in its own fluids. His body was beaten down and used up. There wasn't one thing that was killing him; there were many, many things. The shock of finding Lindy unconscious on the living room floor, the confusion of the last few days, seemed to have consumed the final ragged bits of his strength. Yet somehow he had hung on, almost as if he hoped – with whatever reasoning power was left to him – to see Lindy again. And here she was.

Minutes passed with no sound, except for Odell's ponderous, clotted breathing. The intervals between each breath – the spaces between the slow rise and automatic fall of his strapping chest – grew wider. Then wider still. He was running out of breath, which meant he was running out of life.

'Daddy,' Lindy said.

If there was to be any final mercy, Bell thought, let it be this: Let Odell recognize her. Realize she is here. Let the fog in his mind lift for these last few moments.

'Daddy,' Lindy said again, and now she was weeping, her small shoulders bobbing up and down as she embraced the ragged heap that represented what had become of Odell Crabtree, his mortal shape and material being. 'Daddy, you can't die. I don't have anybody else.'

His crusty brown lips moved. His tongue was briefly visible as it touched those lips. He was fighting to speak.

The words were gravelly and slurred with fatigue, but in the exquisite silence of the darkest part of the night, they were comprehensible, if barely so: 'Lied to you, my girl,' Odell said. 'Couldn't tell you that you weren't really our child. You were Maybelle's. Maybelle come to us and said, "I can't keep this baby. I can't. It'll ruin my family. Ruin our name. Be bad for politics. And my daddy'll never give me another dime." And your mama said, "Never you mind. We'll take her. And nobody'll ever know." See, thing is – your mama wanted a child. But I didn't. All I wanted was the money. They paid us to take you, my girl. I'm ashamed to say it, but I took the money.' He had to stop. He was breathing hard, even harder than before. He coughed a terrible wrenching cough that seemed to lift him and shake him and then fling him down again. 'She's not Maybelle these days. Calls herself something different. Her daddy was governor. He's a rich man. Lives in a big house. But you know what? You don't belong to Maybelle no more. You never did. You're my girl. I love you like you were my own child. You *are* my child now. Oh, Lindy, girl.' The coughing fit this time made him gasp and twist.

Another few minutes passed and then he was gone – not dead yet but gone to another place, an in-between place, churning and flailing through the thought-swamp where his memories had sunk once again, stranded like lost ships on the ocean floor – and he blew out a chestful of air and he bellowed, 'Who're you? Who the hell are you?' and he pushed Lindy's head off his chest, angry and confused, and he tried to rise from the narrow bed but fell back again, choking, grasping at the sheets. And then, a few minutes later, he died – for real this time.

In the profound silence that followed, Bell looked around the small cell. Shoved back in a shadowy corner was something she hadn't noticed when they first arrived, something not usually present in a Raythune County jail cell. It was a battered table, big enough for an old man with a wrecked spine to crawl beneath, making a place where he could feel comfortable – or as close to comfortable as he was likely to get, as his mind drifted back to the past: *Ray-boy, you hear me? Hey, Ray. You there? It's Odell. On my way, Ray-boy. I'm coming. Gonna help with that load. On my way.*

Bell didn't know for sure, and wouldn't have a chance to ask until later, but she guessed that the person who'd brought in that table, the person who'd heard the story about what Lindy had rigged up in the basement and who then tried to duplicate it here as best she could, was Mary Sue Fogelsong. Who knew a thing or two about suffering.

The coroner's van came for Odell Crabtree's body. Fetching him was a slow and laborious process; he was a very large man, and there was no easy way for the paramedics to load him into a body bag and swing it onto the gurney and bump the gurney down the courthouse steps in the darkness, a step at a time, and then kick at the collapsible wheels and slide it into the vehicle. Lindy, arms crossed, the tears dried on her face, watched it all; she watched until the coroner's van, the red lights across its backside glittering wetly in the streaming rain, disappeared around the corner.

Now there was nothing more for anyone to do. 'Long night,' Fogelsong muttered to Bell, and she muttered back, 'Longest night in the history of the freakin' world.' The sheriff nodded.

It was just after 4 A.M. when Bell and Lindy left the courthouse to walk to the Explorer. Lindy had agreed to spend some time – at least a week, although Bell was hoping that it might stretch into more – with her second cousin in Morgantown. Jeannie Stump was going to meet them in Charleston, roughly the halfway point, in the morning. Bell would drive Lindy there. Tonight, Lindy would spend the night with Bell. The bed in Carla's room was already made up, Bell told her. She'd been expecting her daughter to come to

Acker's Gap for the summer. That wasn't going to happen. But the bedroom was still ready.

The rain had tapered off to a fine mist. That mist gave the world a gauzy, fretful, half-formed look, as if it were deciding moment by moment which side to embrace – either the dream-spun past, where ghosts walked in their sleep, or the present, a place of clarity and edges, a place where the living staked their claim. Nights like these, with a wet veil cast over everything, Bell felt strangely close to the dead. They had a right to be here, too, murmuring, numinous. That was one of the reasons she stayed in Acker's Gap, perhaps – a reason she would never disclose to anyone, not even Nick. These dead – the ones who had been, in life, bad or good, savage or kind – were her dead. She knew their names. She knew their faces.

After the two of them had climbed in the Explorer and cinched their seat belts, Lindy spoke. 'Thought I might try to get in touch with Montgomery Henner one of these days. I mean – he's my half brother. And that's family, right?'

'Right.'

'I know he doesn't have much time. Unless he gets a donor heart. But no matter how long that turns out to be—' Lindy didn't finish. Instead, she said, 'You know what it's like. Being pretty much alone. Heard your father died when you were just a kid. And your sister—' Once again, she didn't finish the sentence.

'Yeah.'

'Must've been tough.'

Bell let the wipers slap off the wavy accumulation of rain before she pulled away from the curb. Lindy probably knew a few scattered truths about Bell's

childhood, the way a lot of people in Acker's Gap did
– or thought they did.

'We'll talk about it tomorrow. On our way to
Charleston,' Bell said. 'Got lots of time.'

'Complicated, huh?'

'You could say that.'

41

Bell wasn't accustomed to watching sunsets. Usually she was too busy, and sometimes too restless and agitated, to sit and let the live theater of the day's end – the languid wash of orange that spread across the western horizon – play out in front of her. But tonight, that's all she had to do.

A week had passed since the death of Odell Crabtree. Bell sat on a chair on the back stoop of the garage apartment that was now Shirley's home. The ramshackle one-story place with dented aluminum siding was located just outside Blythesburg, on a tan stretch of dirt road that stopped abruptly at the railroad tracks, the way a sentence is brought up short by a period. The road didn't continue on the other side; it simply ended.

Now that things had settled down in the prosecutor's office – Perry Crum had pleaded guilty to homicide and was awaiting sentencing, and the FBI was handling the case against the conspirators – Bell had decided to bring over the last of Shirley's things: two flannel shirts, one red and one blue, that had been in the dryer the day Shirley moved out. And a battery-powered clock radio.

On the drive over to Blythesburg, Bell's cell had

sounded. It was Sheriff Fogelsong. 'Finally had a chance to talk to Jason Brinkerman,' he said. 'Get his account of what happened in that basement.' Bell didn't answer, so he continued. 'Kid told me you were pretty rough on Perry Crum. And paramedics said he looked like he'd been run through a table saw and then finished off in a chipper-shredder. Bastard deserved it – but still. Jason said you were out of control. That you were yelling something. Something that sounded like "Daddy." I told the kid he must've heard you wrong.' He waited. 'Belfa?'

'Nothing to say, Nick.'

'Figured that. Just want to make sure you were still listening.' When she didn't answer, he grunted and went on. 'Look. Your business. Not trying to interfere, Lord knows. But it's a funny thing. Anger's okay in small doses – it keeps people like you and me on the job, it's the reason we push back against all the crap – but it can turn against you, too. Real quick. If you're not careful. If you don't keep an eye out. Manage it properly. You don't want to end up there, Belfa. You don't want to be like some of the people on the other side of the law. Dead inside. Burned up from the inside out – on account of all the anger.'

No reply.

'Okay,' he said. 'I'll leave you be. You don't have to talk about it. Seems like that's how you want it.' Still no response, and so he changed the subject. 'Got some other news. Lanny Waller's dead.'

'What happened?'

'Regina Wills shot him this afternoon. Turned herself in. Used his own shotgun on the bastard. Two slugs – one in the chest, one in the gut. Took him a good hour and a half to bleed out, during which time she sat there and watched.'

Bell remembered the little speech that Riley Jessup had made her listen to that day at his mansion. The speech about rising up. *Different ways to rise up,* Bell thought. Regina had found her own way.

'From what I hear,' the sheriff continued, 'Waller kept on going at those girls, night after night, even while the judge was investigating Missy Wills and her mighty mysterious change of heart. Regina finally snapped.'

'What's the charge?'

'First-degree murder. Lanny'd had the trailer hauled over to Collier County just a week or so ago, so at least it's not our lookout. Amanda Sturm made the arrest.'

'Well, I'll have a chat with Mason Dittmer,' Bell said. She had a good working relationship with the Collier County prosecutor. 'If the evidence supports the facts as you've described them, I think first-degree murder's the wrong charge. Maybe Mason'll be inclined to listen.' Bell tried to find some sliver of regret for Lanny Waller's passing, to be even the tiniest bit sorry that he'd suffered what was surely an agonizingly prolonged death. *Nope,* she realized. *Let him rot in hell.*

And later on there'd be, she hoped, plenty of room in hell left over for Perry Crum and Riley Jessup and Bradley Portis and Sharon Henner. Any pity she might briefly have entertained for Sharon – a woman forced to watch her son fade away before her eyes – had vanished. Any lingering sympathy she felt toward Perry – his long sacrifice for his sister had changed him, and done it so profoundly that he probably didn't even recognize himself anymore – was already gone.

By the time she arrived at Shirley's new home, Bell was ready to talk about something other than the law and its layers. Only two chairs could fit on the stoop; both were the fold-out kind that looked as if a heavy sigh could reduce them to a pile of short aluminum poles and frayed plastic. Bolland had automatically offered the chairs to the women. He settled onto the single concrete step, guitar on his knee.

At first they sat in silence. An amiable silence, not an awkward one. From her vantage point in the chair, Bell could peer down at the top of Bolland's head. His hair looked as if it was thinning by the minute. In no time at all, he'd be totally bald on top. The gray ponytail meandered down his back; it was attached to a few loose strands that looped around his ears. He was an old man. An old man with a young man's dreams. *So this is what you want,* Bell ached to say to Shirley. *This. This life. With this man.* But she didn't say it.

Just before Bolland started his song, a whistle hooted in the distance. Last message from a departing train, a long one that had begun its journey past this spot a while ago, shortly after Bell arrived, its rusty cars packed high and tight with coal. The whistle was a way of saying good-bye. And it worked on Bell like another kind of signal, too, telling her it was time to acknowledge what she knew but had not declared outright to herself. Until now.

Carla wouldn't be coming back to Acker's Gap. Oh, she'd visit for a day or so, now and again. Maybe even stay a week. But she would never live here again. Bell was sure of it. Carla had moved past this place

– the first, no doubt, of many such moves she'd be making, as the landscape of her life expanded, keeping pace with her dreams. Bell had raised her daughter to be independent and headstrong and fearless. There was a price to pay for that. And Bell was paying it.

Bell had once had a good friend who loved the poetry of John Donne, loved the way its grave sagacity and stiff ecclesiastical rhythms were sometimes broken wide open by unruly passion, and Bell recalled a verse that her friend had loved. She could still see it on the page, ancient spellings intact:

> Our two soules threrefore, which are one,
> Though I must goe, endure not yet
> A breach, but an expansion . . .
>
> If they be two, they are two so
> As stiffe twin compasses are two,
> Thy soule the fixt foot, makes no show
> To move, but doth, if th'other doe.

For Carla henceforth, Acker's Gap would be the fixed foot of the compass; she would spin and expand in ever-widening circles, in a profusion of possibilities. Acker's Gap was her past. Not her future.

So I'm listening to Bobo Bolland and thinking about John Donne, Bell thought, chastising herself. *Bit of a stature gap.* Truth was, though, Bolland's music wasn't all that bad. His voice had a kind of wire-brushed melancholy to it, a toughness undermined by the tender recollection of lost loves and old woes. Bell liked his voice. And she sort of liked Bolland himself, another realization that surprised her. He'd had his problems in life, his challenges, and always would; he'd made mistakes. Big ones. *Hell,* Bell thought. *So have I. So has everybody.* And he'd make more mistakes, going forward. No doubt. Maybe even bigger ones.

Point was, he treated Shirley well. That was all that mattered. Or all that ought to.

When she'd arrived a while ago with Shirley's things, Bolland came rushing out of the flung-open screen door and grabbed the bag from her, polite and welcoming. He was nervous around Bell, and he stammered, too obsequious by half, but she could understand that. Assumed it would pass. She knew she could be intimidating. Nobody relaxed around a prosecutor. Foolish, frankly, ever to do so. The whole point of the job was to pass judgment on people.

Now they sat on the little stoop as the day's light died all around them. They didn't turn on the porch light, because they knew it would summon vigorous platoons of flying bugs. The darker the sky turned, the less visible Bolland was, and the more he seemed to morph into pure voice.

He was finishing up an original song. The melody was filled with the lilting misery of minor chords; the lyrics were grim and pessimistic, but pessimistic in that poetic way that could sound almost optimistic because – as Shirley had told Bell just the other day, musing aloud as she wedged her meager supply of clothes in a paper grocery sack – if you can sing about it, you can live through it. 'Bobo taught me that. He's a wise man, Belfa. Really. He is. Give him a chance and you'll see.'

Bell looked over at Shirley. Her sister's eyes were closed and she nodded in time with the music. She wasn't smiling, but she seemed content, satisfied. Not wrought up, at least. Not churned or whirling.

As Bolland moved toward the end of the song, his voice glided upward in an unexpectedly exquisite arc, like a palm sander following the grain of quarter-sawn oak, a wood whose secret is locked away until it is stained and polished and its heart is coaxed out, brought forward for the world to see. Bolland held the final note for a long time. And in that moment, for reasons unfathomable to her, Bell felt the essence of Shirley's life as never before. She felt the yearning and the fear and the frustration – and the beauty, too, the sere and wounded grace – and she felt everything that might have been but wasn't, everything that her sister should have had but now never would: Just one clear day of pure happiness, unstreaked by pain. A single memory that wasn't marbled with loss. Shirley didn't say a word, but Bell felt as if she could hear her speaking, hear her voice falling into harmony with Bolland's last limpid note: *I'm okay now, Belfa. You don't need to look out for me anymore. You can let go.*

And then, too soon, the song was over. The sun was down. And it was, Bell knew, time to go home.

Acknowledgments

Some years ago I met the wise and stalwart wife of a coal miner in McDowell County, West Virginia. She had created a place for her husband under the big kitchen table; because of his many years spent working underground, and injuries to his spine, he was only comfortable in a crouching position. The story has haunted me ever since, and it inspired a key element of this novel.

I am pleased to thank cherished friends Susan Phillips, Elizabeth King, Elaine Phillips, Tom Heinz, Michele Heinz, Tim Bannon, Marja Mills, and Jack Frech.

For their efforts on behalf of my work, I am profoundly grateful to Lisa Gallagher, Kelley Ragland, Hector DeJean, David Baldeosingh Rotstein and Elizabeth Lacks, along with Vicki Mellor and Ben Willis.